Itchy Whispers

by
Nescher Pyscher
edited by
Viriginia Sciarpelletti

Order this book online at www.trafford.com
or email orders@trafford.com

Most Trafford titles are also available at major online book retailers.

Note for Librarians: A cataloguing record for this book is available from Library
and Archives Canada at www.collectionscanada.ca/amicus/index-e.html

Printed in Victoria, BC, Canada.

ISBN: 978-1-4251-1809-9

Library of Congress Control Number:

*Our mission is to efficiently provide the world's finest, most comprehensive book publishing
service, enabling every author to experience success. To find out how to publish your book, your
way, and have it available worldwide, visit us online at www.trafford.com*

Trafford rev. 08/11/09

www.trafford.com

North America & international
toll-free: 1 888 232 4444 (USA & Canada)
phone: 250 383 6864 ♦ fax: 250 383 6804

Christine, this is for you. It's all for you, because it's all about you.

"All storytellers are liars."

Neil Gaiman

ACKNOWLEDGEMENTS

No-one ever reads these, but on the off-chance that some of you might . . .

I'd like to thank the following people. They know why better than I can tell you, and we'll leave it at that. God, 'cause He's God, and He's cool like that, and while it may be a modern culture cliché', I still want to represent my mad love for God. Virginia "Sissy" Sciarpelletti, for being incredibly ninja-tastic and risking serious brain injury in editing every last one of these. Thanks, homie. You freaking rock. Caitlin, for an awesome cover featuring everything I asked for. Lorraine Sautner, for being the friend I needed when I most needed one. The patient and gentle people at Fanstory.com, and Tom Ens in particular. Connie Roberts, nee' Limbaugh, for saving my life and giving me a reason to keep going. You deserved better than you got. John, Mark, Chris . . . well, you know, I love you guys. And finally, Christine, Christine, Christine. Chriiiiiiiistiiiiine. I love you, beautiful. Stars, moons, planets and diamonds shining in the sky.

A Kiss

I didn't know at the time - and really, I still don't - whether I was dreaming or not. It all seemed so very real, real enough to stay with me until now. I share it with you as a warning. You can do with it whatever you want.

It was only later, after I had time to process what happened, that I realized it might not have been either a dream or reality, but something in between - something holy, important and valid, if enormously awful.

Listen:

I woke up because someone sat on my mattress.

You know the feeling. You're sleeping soundly, and some part of your brain – some primal bit in the back that kept us alive when we hid in caves – becomes aware you're no longer alone. It dumps survival hormones into your bloodstream, and you rear up, gasping and looking wildly around.

I could tell by the unique sensation of shifting pressures coming from the area right next to my legs that someone had just sat on my mattress, next to me. They were heavy, whoever they were.

I'm an insomniac, and any little change in my immediate environment usually wakes me up. I live alone; anyone who has keys to my apartment knows I'm pretty jumpy and they need to make their presence known as soon as possible.

My eyes popped open and I rolled over onto my back before I was fully aware of what I was doing.

His face - that gore-covered, hole-ridden orifice, old and diseased, covered in crawling, moving filth - was less than four inches from mine. A maggot, squirming busily from a hole eaten through the top of his left nostril, crawled across the gap and oozed its greasy way down my cheek.

His head was canted on his neck at an impossible forty-five degree angle. It lay on his right shoulder as if resting there. The splintered remains of his spine stuck through the tattered gray meat of his neck. His eyes were the color of a decayed fish's belly and mad. Lost.

The beard he wore was a worm-eaten thing that stuck out at odd angles; patchy, mangy. Cracked and torn lips pulled back from broken, rotten, blackened teeth.

A matted filthy garment that may've once been a fine robe dangled from his shoulders, barely covering his nakedness, like a funerary vestment several hundred years after it should have rotted away.

He sat on my mattress, staring at me unblinkingly. His arms held an enormous bundle in his lap that he kept hidden under his ripped and grimy robes. It had an odd, lumpy, fleshy quality and moved in a slow, humped, wave-like way. Sitting hunched over this bundle, he cradled it close, like a mother protecting an infant, while odd gasping noises of pain, though he didn't seem to breathe, escaped from his lips.

I screamed. There was no help for it. I screamed until I thought my voice would break, scrabbling back away from this ghoul, trying to climb the wall behind me in my haste to get away.

"Traitor," he said, in a voice of broken bone and torn tissue.

It was the very merest whisper, the smallest movement of vocal cords, yet it rode over the top of my screams and shut my mouth at once.

"W-what?"

"Traitor," he repeated, grunting in pain.

And I knew who he was. Just like that, all of a sudden, as you do in a dream or in a sudden flash of insight - no doubt in my mind whatsoever. I looked upon a man I'd never seen, indeed, a man no one alive today had ever seen, and I knew who he was.

On my bed, fouling the air I breathed, grunting ad groaning, staring with his dead, mad eyes sat the greatest traitor of them all. Inches away, dropping filth all over my mattress, Judas Iscariot, betrayer of Jesus Christ, condemned me.

Not even thinking about it, not even considering the impossible nature of this conversation, I reacted to his words in self-righteous anger. No. "Reacted" is too small a word. I "erupted".

"How *dare* you?" I spat. "How dare *you* condemn *me*? You're in no position to sit in judgment over anyone! You sold Jesus out for the price of a slave!"

My fury rose with each passing second. I hissed my anger in vituperative waves of holy wrath.

"You *knew* Jesus! You *ate* with him! Shared his journey on Earth! You probably hugged him and wept with him! You betrayed him with a kiss, you son-of-a-bitch!"

He replied in a low hiss, his head lolling and rolling on his broken neck.

"You know about the slave price, then? Yes. It seems you would, reading Scripture the way you do. But if I sold the Son Of God out, at least I got paid. You don't even go that far. Where I was a whore, you're just a common slut. A tramp. A filthy, rutting beast. At least I was brave enough to do what needed to be done when I committed *my* sin. I didn't whine and cry, beg for mercy and pretend to be repentant. My punishment is eternal and deserved, but *I* accepted *my* guilt. *You* pretend yours doesn't exist, and you continue in it. Where I ended my life as was only proper, you believe you are entitled to live the way you do."

He stared at me with those mad, dead eyes, voice grating and hollow, emotionless and as dead as all eternity.

"W-what?"

Instead of answering, he leaned slowly forward. I was panic-stricken and horror-struck, utterly powerless to move, as he kissed me gently on the mouth -

-logging onto the internet looking for porn stealing money from my parents lying to my friends and family drinking until I passed out feeling self-righteous about people suffering not being compassionate or empathic taking what I wanted or needed and leaving the needy to rot judging others based on their appearance not forgiving running from justice adultery thievery lying murdering my brothers and sisters in my secret heart gluttony lying to God cheating God being disrespectful to what I was given urinating on the gifts of the Spirit and Oh My GOD! **I DESERVE TO BURN IN HELL WHY HAVEN'T I KILLED MYSELF YET PLEASE KILL ME GOD-**

I jerked away, my mind reeling at that brief contact. His lips felt like burned and melted plastic, abrading the skin of mine.

His face hovered near mine. I could smell carrion and death. I could smell the rot of his body seeping out of him. I could smell the sulfurous fires of hell.

"You call yourself a Christian, a servant of God Most High. You've accepted His sacrifice. You did all of these things, and so much more, *after* He saved you. Your crimes are far greater than mine could ever be."

His voice, a thin whisper, cut my heart in half . . .

. . . because he was right.

Judas had only betrayed Jesus to the Pharisees, to the mob mentality that feared change and rejected the spiritual kingdom Jesus ruled over. They wanted a temporal King, someone to save them from Rome.

What was his crime when compared against my continued existence?

Jesus suffered unbearable agonies on the cross. Naked, he bled like a slaughtered hog, lifted several feet off the ground to be jeered at by those He'd tried to save.

Judas kissed me again while tears of guilt ran down my face.

I stood on the hill and watched the men die. They deserved it, the criminals. Taking their time to die, though, weren't they?

"He saved others! Let Him save Himself!" I yelled.

I picked up a stone and threw it at the naked, bleeding man on the cross. It hit him in the face, drawing a pain-filled groan. Blood poured from where my sharp stone had struck, just below His right eye. He lifted His head and looked at me with eyes full of pain. The one I'd nearly gouged out with my stone was rapidly swelling shut. My heart leapt.

A hit!

And a *good* one!

I laughed and spat at Him.

"Come down if you are the Son of God! Come down and I will believe in you-"

I wrenched away. My head struck the wall behind me hard enough to leave a smear of blood. But I only noticed this much later. I was too busy screaming.

"NOOOOOOOOOOOOOO!"

"Yes," Judas croaked. "Yes. Yes. Ten-thousand times, yes."

He pulled the robes away from the bundle in his lap and I struggled not to vomit.

The looping, twisting, torn coils of his guts lay in his lap. Covered in filth and maggots and flies, they reeked of Hell, of damnation, of eternal fires. They were like a separate, living thing, pulsing and moving. He grunted in pain as a spasm swept through the mass.

"My punishment," he said, through tightly gritted teeth. I could feel cold fluid seeping into my sheets. "I deserve it. What do you deserve?"

He reached to the back of his neck and pulled the ripped remains of the rope off his crooked, mangled spine. He laid it in my lap the rope in my lap, and it was warm from the ever-decaying touch of his body.

"Death is the only reward for sin," he said, his lips pulling and tearing like old, rotted leather across those awful teeth.

He stood and the bundle of his guts fell to the floor with a wet slap.

I couldn't take anymore.

"No! Jesus!" I cried, calling on the one I had sinned against to save me from this, to save me from myself.

And I woke. Or came back to myself. Or returned. I'm still not sure which.

There was no rope.

There was no blood.

There was no Judas . . .

. . . except for the one wearing my skin.

Marinda and Stanley

His name is Stanley. Stanley Forbush.

    He's five-two, a hundred ten pounds in his socks. Coke-bottle, wire frame glasses, mousy, brown hair, mousy, brown eyes and a timidity that starts at the base of his spine completes Stanley's resemblance to Nibbler, The Looney Tunes Mouse. Moving through the world in a shy, meekly smiling way, Stanley gives one the impression that he is mimicking furniture: an ottoman, perhaps.

    It would be easy - and erroneous - to assume Stanley suffers from some sort of 'Little Man's' complex. After all, anyone who's been mistaken for a sofa is bound to be the sort of person who takes offense easily and readily. Not so! Not so at all for our man, Stanley!

    Call it meekness, if you like. Stanley preferred to think of it as "pacifistic, non-confrontational conformity". Stanley's the poster boy for the path of least resistance. You may find this hard to believe, sweet reader, but Stanley Forbush, in his thirty-two years in this vale of tears, has never - not once - ever displayed the slightest touch of anger.

    At anything.

    Ever.

    Cool, calm, quiet, timid and meek: that's our Stanley. He's given every skinny geek in the world someone to look down on, every bully someone to pound sand at.

    So as the mental eye of narrative roves ever further and we see Stanley Forbush, thigh deep in brackish swamp water, wrestling, with flashing tooth and wicked nail, an alligator the size of an SUV, we may perhaps be excused our surprise.

    But we'll get to that in a minute. There's back-story to wade through, dear reader.

    The journey to this watershed - figuratively and literally speaking - started for Stanley in high school. More specifically, his senior year. The Prom was just around the corner, and though he had been polite and courteous to each young lady he'd asked, Stanley had yet to find a date. Flipping through his yearbook in later years, Stanley chalked his lack of success with his peers as being voted "Most Likely to Wear Sweater Vests and Become an Accountant."

    Stanley didn't really mind all that much. Dancing was such a sweaty, athletic activity! Then there was the whole process of dressing. A tux was expensive, and he was sure he'd get it on wrong. No, Stanley didn't mind going to the Prom stag - or, for preference, not going at all!

    But there were his parents to consider. Thelma and Bud Forbush. Good, solid, dependable citizens who wanted what was best for their only son, and were determined to pry him from his shell of meek goodnaturedness. Stanley had certain ideas about the Prom, and his parents had others.

    Namely, Stanley was *going* to the Prom, and that was all. Never mind that he couldn't find a date. Never mind that he'd never had a girlfriend. Never mind that he couldn't dance, his feet moved like cannonballs, and most girls laughed at him when he walked by. He was going to the Prom - as a red-blooded American lad his age should! - and that was that.

    Stanley didn't argue. He just nodded his head and said, "Yes, Mother. Yes, Father."

It would be nice, of course, to find some pretty girl with a good smile to dance with - our man Stanley's not *dead*, just meek! - but Stanley knew where he stood, girl-wise. Still . . . someone who smelled nice, someone with grace and class, and a keen appreciation for actuarial tables . . .

Well, a guy could dream, anyway.

For Stanley that someone had a name: Laura Twerflinger. Stanley had a crush on her from the word "Go." Blonde, tall, leggy, and could she fill a sweater? Why, yes. Yes she could, and with "fillage" to spare!

As the captain of the girls cheerleading squad for Stan's high school, she was eagerly sought after by every last one of Stan's classmates. She was currently dating Brock Hulkmeyer, a third generation genetic lottery winner. He had good looks, broad shoulders, and he was the captain of the football team. Not the sharpest tool in the shed, but who cared? His father owned the largest car dealership in town, and he was rich, too. Stanley despised him with a passion that would've surprised Stanley's friends, if he'd had any.

Brock didn't have the slightest idea that Stanley even existed and wouldn't have cared much if he did. So far as Brock was concerned, the Stanleys of the world tended to be classified as "Things that make noise when I hit them". In an honest, forthright fashion, Brock had the uncluttered sort of brain that made him perfect in later life for public office.

As these events are being written, he's up for his seventh term in the United States Senate.

Brock wasn't a bully, really. Nor was he particularly mean in any way, he just wasn't smart enough to realize that not everyone found atomic wedgies to be funny. Stanley, the recipient of more than his fair share of atomics, would've been happy to discuss this at length with Brock. While holding a lead pipe for emphasis.

At any rate, fate brought them together again on the Friday before Prom.

Stanley, after three sleepless nights, had finally mustered the courage to ask Laura out, and waited outside her homeroom anxiously. He was desperately hoping that the fluid he felt collecting in his palms and other crevices wasn't dripping in puddles around him. The bell rang. Laura walked out of her homeroom wearing a knee-length poodle skirt, a cashmere sweater the perfect green of sea grass, bobby socks, and saddle shoes. She wore her hair loose, and Stanley could swear he saw angels playing in it.

Stepping boldly in front of her he loudly asked, "Laura, will you go to Prom with me?"

Well, that's not strictly true. He did step boldly out in front of her, and he did speak to her. The actual transcript of their conversation is as follows:

Stanley - "Lau . . . Lau . . . Laura . . . You, umm . . . .Will you . . . uh . . . " He paused here to wipe his palms excitedly down the legs of his corduroys. Then he dropped his books with a clatter, failing to notice the look of absolute horror on Laura's face as he bent to pick them up.

Laura - "What?!"

Stanley, after taking a deep breath, and swallowing hugely, finishes his question while on his hands and knees, directing it to the hem of Laura's skirt.

"Willyougotothepromwithme?"

The silence from above him was painful. He dared not look up at Laura, and he thought he heard a noise like a sob.

Then a dreaded and all too familiar voice boomed out from behind him.

"Huh-huhh. A cockroach. Let me help you stand up, cockroach."

Stanley sighed the resigned sigh of the meekly born. Brock's furry, seal-clubbing hands rooted around in the waistband of his pants for the third time today. Hulk found what he was looking for, and with a one-armed heave, pulled Stanley off the floor by his underwear. This was normal, what made it mortifying was the rain of giggles coming from Laura.

"Oh, Brock. You're soooooo silly!" she squealed delightedly.

Stanley sighed again, pulled his undies from their unmentionable crevice, and moved off to class. Brock's voice, as he walked away, taunted him with its usual pithiness.

"Huh-huhh, Cockroach. I am funny, aren't I, Laura?"

~~~~~~~

Marinda Gluefenflegel was a German exchange student at Stanley's school.

She was, politely, a "robust" woman. She had victoriously blonde hair mounted on an ever jovial face the size and shape of a large pumpkin. She had blazing cherry cheeks, with an ever present smile, large, glacially blue eyes, and a body like a Sherman tank. She stood 5'11, and topped the scales at two-hundred, seventy-five pounds, easily. Her claim to fame back home was a talent with the glockenspiel that bordered on genius.

She played Chuck Berry's, "Johnny B Goode" at the Talent Show to raucous applause from the students, and muted laughter from the faculty. She was a woman who didn't let her size define her, and had a smile that could swallow your soul. She was enormously likeable, enormously well-liked, and generally fun to be around. She had a heart like a roasted marshmallow, and she couldn't stand being unhappy, or seeing other people that way.

She was brave, she was noble, and she knew what she wanted out of life, and how to get it. And she had her eye on our hero, Stan.

Marinda was eighteen and of a mind to get married. America suited her just fine, and marrying a nice American boy would enable her to stay here. So she started looking around for likely candidates. She'd witnessed Stan's humiliation at the hands of Brock, more than once, and this latest time seemed like a little bit more than the poor soul should be asked to bear. She watched him walk, slump-shouldered toward his class, and a tear the size of a dime ran down the skin of her perfect face. Reaching a sudden decision, she moved in like an overfed buzzard.

"Excooose me, please. You are Shtanley?"

Jolted from his reverie, Stanley had to fight from rocketing himself back from the smiling, moon-like face looming over him. "Ye-ye-Yes. I'm Stanley. You're Marinda, right?"

"Yah! I am Marinda! I haf no date to Prom, either. Ve maybe go together, yah?"

Stanley bravely swallowed a few times and fought to get air into his lungs and across his vocal cords. Marinda was quite attractive in a "big girl" sort of way, and he liked the way she smelled ever so subtly of cinnamon. Her smile was pretty, too. But being Stanley, he wasn't used to Marinda's directness, and he felt like a deer in the headlights of a train.

Frankly, she terrified him.

"We-we-well, act-act-actually I . . . "

"Das ist gut! Ja! You vill pick me up at sefen, ja? Bring lots of chocolate! Maybe you get lucky!"

Giggling delightedly, Marinda trundled off to class, leaving Stanley gasping like a freshly caught fish behind her.

Prom was a delight for Stanley. Sure, his date was the largest human being there, and she looked something like an oversized wedding confection in her Prom dress. But she also "playfully" held Brock's head in the punchbowl for a minute or so when Hulkmeyer made a "cockroach in a suit" comment.

When Brock emerged, spitting bits of sherbet and passion fruit seed, he'd tried to start a fight with Stanley as a sop to his male ego. Marinda proceeded to whomp his furry, oversized ass all over the gym, shouting imprecations at him in German and English.

"Shweinhund! Shizakopf! Ja! You are a ninny-compoop and I vill shave you and mount you on my vall! Ja! How dare you touch my Shtanley! I vill new-ter you and mail you home to your momma!"

For Stanley, seeing Brock gasping for breath with Marinda's arms locked around his neck and head was quite possibly vindication for his entire life up to that point. He didn't even mind being thrown helplessly and bonelessly around when he and Marinda danced. She giggled the entire time, and while "graceful" wasn't an apt description for their dancing, they were having more fun than was strictly decent.

The faculty, choosing to do what was "right" as opposed to what was "proper", turned a blind eye when Marinda rubbed her body against Stan's and kissed him with lip-smacking fervor. They rigged the election and crowned them King and Queen, too.

As Principal Skinbottom later said, "If a guy like Stanley and a girl like Marinda can't benefit from abuse of authority and election rigging, than what the hell are we doing being teachers? The little guy's gotta win every once in a while, right?"

Afterwards, in the back seat of his father's 1951 Buick Roadmaster, Marinda made a man out of Stanley.

"Take me, Shtanley. Take me like a Viking Varrior!"

Stanley swallowed and confessed that he had never even kissed a girl, much less "Ta-ta-taken one." He could feel himself blushing furiously and desperately hoped he wasn't embarrassing himself too much.

Smiling like an overfed jack-o-lantern, Marinda rumblingly whispered, "That is okay. I vill show you."

And she promptly did exactly that. The earth moved, the sky imploded and Stanley, meek, timid, little Stanley was ushered into the deeper mysteries of manhood with an enthusiasm that left him bruised and battered for a month.

Stanley's Dad had to replace his shocks and springs.

And that's how it started. Marinda led her campaign against Stanley with a forthrightness and tenacity that Patton would've admired. The poor guy had no chance. Not that he minded. Stanley found himself falling deeply in love with Marinda, despite their differences, and asked her to marry him a week before graduation on bended knee. Marinda swept him up into her arms, weeping bilingual ally, smothered him with tears and kisses, and only broke two of his ribs hugging him.

Marinda knew she had to consolidate her position quickly. Her visa ran out a month after she graduated, and she needed to be married before that. She bulldozed Stanley into a small ceremony, and three days after graduation, they were married. Stanley looked like he'd been beaten over the head with a happy stick, and Marinda kept breaking into half-happy, half-sobbing German song.

Stanley got a good job at his Dad's firm and went to work just long enough to tell his new boss he was going on his honeymoon. His boss, a friend of the family handed him five-hundred bucks.

"Take good care of her, boy. She's a keeper."

Stanley's parents were delighted with Marinda. And while it's true that anybody who married their boy Stan would've delighted them, Marinda was just a hoot. They paid for the entire she-bang, set them up in a snug little bungalow a block from the ocean, and even sent the two of them to Florida to honeymoon.

Driving along I-75 in southeast Florida, Stanley looked over at his smiling, profusely sweating bride, and felt a sudden surge of manly affection towards her. "Marinda, if . . . if . . . I could give you anything you wanted, what would you like?"

Now, believe it or not, Marinda had never had a man ask her that. It was true she had an agenda with Stan, but she did love him all the way down to his cute, argyle socks, too. He was a fine man, and he treated her like a princess. Tears sprang to her eyes and she looked over at her "leetle knockenvurst" and her great big heart swelled with love.

"Oh, Shtanley. There ist nein . . . no . . . there is nothing I vant, Shtanley. Being married to you, that is all."

Stanley's jaw firmed, for the first time in his life, and a manliness he'd only felt when Marinda was screaming his name swelled his chest.

"Nope. Won't hear of it. You answer me. If I could get you anything you wanted - anything at all! - what would it be?"

Marinda wasn't the kind of girl who went in for expensive gifts. For Marinda, sweet, big-hearted Marinda, it was all about the effort behind the gift. Stanley, being one of "those" kinds of guys, showered her with useless friff-fraff constantly. She had more jewelry than she'd ever wear, more perfume than she'd ever use, and she had flowers all over their one-bedroom house. She "oohed!" and "ahhed!" appropriately, but it wasn't something she *needed*.

But she was the kind of girl who wanted to keep her man happy. Marinda looked at him, saw that glint in his eye and saw the set of his jaw. Hiding a smile behind her hand, she turned full on to her new husband, and smilingly said, "Vell, Shtanley, since you asked, there is somesing I haf alvays vanted.'

Stanley, his jaw as hard as steel, kept his eyes on the road.

"You just name it, beautiful. I'll do whatever I can to get it for you."

Marinda sighed. It was one of those deep-seated desires, a secret wish she'd never told anyone. But here they were, driving to a romantic hideaway to honeymoon, and her heart was bursting with love for this eager little man.

"Shtanley," she whispered, her voice a low purr, "I haf alvays wanted a pair of alligator shoooes."

Laughing, Stanley replied, "That's all? Just a pair of alligator shoes? You can have anything, anything at all!"

"That's all I haf efer really vanted, Shtanley. Efer since I vas a leetle girl, I haf alvays vanted a pair of alligator shoooes."

"Then that's what you'll get. If my lady wants a pair of alligator shoes, my lady will *get* a pair of alligator shoes, dammit!" Feeling a hot surge of rugged manliness running through him, Stanley resolved to stop at the very next shoe store he saw . . . and that's when he saw the alligator.

It was sunning itself at the side of the interstate next to a wooded area. It was on the other side of the interstate from Stanley, but even at forty-five miles an hour, and across eight lanes of traffic, Stanley could see it was a big one. Slamming suddenly on his brakes, he whipped his father's Buick across the four lanes of traffic on this side of the road, ignoring the frantic honking of his fellow motorists. He bumped across the meridian, and directly across the four lanes of oncoming traffic on the far side, with Marinda screeching mightily the entire way.

He came to a halt at the side of the road some ten feet away from the alligator. Grabbing his new wife around the waist, he planted a huge kiss on her tear streaked face, and said, "I will return with your shoes, or not at all!" and leapt out of the car.

Up close, Stanley could see the 'gator was nearly twenty feet long, and looked to weigh a good five-hundred pounds or so. It was also hissing, and oddly, talking to Stanley in Brock Hulkmeyer's voice.

"Huh-huhh. You wife wants a pair of shoes, huh? Well, come get 'em, cockroach."

With a high-pitched scream of rage Stanley leapt to do battle. But before he even landed, the 'gator whipped around and fled into the forest.

"Oh, no you don't!" Stanley screamed at it, and followed.

The 'gator was fast. No doubt about that, but Stanley was feeding off adrenaline at this point, and he could just see the 'gator's tail tip ahead of him. It led a terrific chase. Breaking through bramble screens, being ripped and gored by thorns the size of spears, eaten by bugs the size of helicopters, nothing daunted Stanley. For about an hour, the 'gator fled, and Stanley followed. Finally, the 'gator slipped into a bog, with Stanley leaping on top of it.

An epic battle of claw, tooth, bony fist, and wire-rimmed glasses ensued. The 'gator snapped, rolled, and bit. Stanley slapped, punched, and hit. Back and forth, back and forth. The water ran red with the blood of the combatants, and time itself stood still for just a moment to witness the carnage being wrought by these two titanic gladiators. Mud and water sprayed everywhere and the noise was cacophonous.

Stanley screamed like a banshee, and the 'gator was hissing, coughing, and barking. Stanley finally managed to wrap his arms all the way around the tiring gator's neck, and with one mighty heave, snapped it through. The mighty 'gator shuddered violently, and then stilled as death took it.

Panting, and gasping, finally feeling the pain of his many bloody wounds through the tattered remains of his once fine suit, he heard a crashing in the woods, and his beloved calling, "Shtanley? Shtanley! Vere are yoooooooou?!"

With a victorious grin, Stanley placed his hands under the 'gator's stomach and heaved it over on its back.

Marinda would never forget the sight that greeted her. Her poor bloody, muddy, bruised and panting Stanley, standing over the floating body of a modern day dinosaur with a stunned look on his face. The vegetation in either direction for a hundred yards was mangled, bloody, and mud spattered.

In a frightened timid voice, Marinda asked, "Shtanley? Vat is it? Vat is the matter?"

Looking disconsolately at his bride, Stanley whispered brokenly, "I'm sorry, Marinda. I'm so sorry."

"But Shtanley, vy? Are you alright? You look hurt! Let me help you!"

Stanley held a bleeding hand up, warding off his beautiful bride. With tears of failure and pain running down his face, he choked back a sob.

In a whisper no louder than the breeze in the tree tops, he said, "I'm sorry, Marinda. I'm really sorry. I tried, I really did, but this alligator's not *wearing* any shoes!"

And with that, Marinda's self-control broke, and she leapt into the swamp to cradle her brave Viking Warrior against her awesome bosom.

You Ever Have One of Those Days?

You ever have one of those days?

You know what I'm talking about. I'm sure I'm not the *only* unlucky slob to stumble into a perfect set of awful circumstances.

It started out likely enough. I had the place picked as a pigeon hole months ago. Tottery king, over-burdened treasury, gullible townsfolk, etcetera, etcetera, etcetera. It was *custom-made* for a guy like me! It couldn't go wrong, right?

Wrong.

But listen. Here's how it went down.

You ride into town, waiting for the sun to hit *just* the right spot so it'll catch your armor with those necessary dramatic glints. It's all about appearances at this point. You don't even need to be very good looking or strong, just dramatic. Give people an image they'll remember and that's what they'll think about long after you've absconded with the princess' virginity, the crown jewels and the king's favorite charger.

You swagger, making sure your squire is following along behind at the proper distance, and you wait until you've got the right audience.

Anybody will do. These yokels can't tell Lancelot from Guinevere, nine times out of ten. All they see is the armor and the sword.

Once somebody is watching, you stroll up to the Sword in the Stone.

I can't tell you how many of these I've seen in the last five years. Any place with more than ten people living in the rough equivalent of a street has their own version. I've seen the Axe in the Melon, the Mace in the Well, the Sword in the Silo and more variants than I can count.

And it's all too easy. See, there's always some long-bearded jerk that smells like burnt salt-peter and partially-digested-bat-parts who's itching to overthrow the king for some reason. Maybe he got passed over for "Commander-Of-Examining-Chicken-Guts" or something. Maybe the king listened to the *other* long-bearded jerk about something. Whatever it was, it stuck a bee up the guy's nose. So he gets some overfed local boy to stick a weapon of some kind into a convenient repository, and he starts bellowing about the *real* king being the one who can pull the sword from the privy without getting his feet sticky, or whatever.

There's always a trick, too. See, the average peasant doesn't spend a lot of time thinking about angles and leverage. He thinks about "yanking on it until it squeals, baas, or dies." He looks at a sword buried to the hilt in twenty-five pounds of concrete, and he thinks that if he yanks hard enough, long enough, he'll get to be the king and swan around in shmancy robes, giving orders to other peasants.

A simple creature, your average peasant.

They most definitely don't think about twisting the sword ten degrees to the left, and pulling it out at an oblique angle. So the long-bearded-jerk gets mileage out of the attempts, and the king looks like a shlub for not being the *real* king.

I figured the trick out a long time ago. It's easy. All you have to do is find the long-bearded jerk.

Sometimes all it takes is listening to them bawl about their grievances. Sometimes you need to get them drunk. Or laid. And yes, sometimes you need to do a little arm-twisting. But the *initial* trick, at least, is finding the long-bearded jerk.

The town had one, and he was pissed at the king for a whole list of reasons. I actually had to slap the guy around for a little while before he gave it up. But I got the trick to pulling this version of Merlin's greatest con.

You walk up to the – in this case it was an Arrow In A Wheelbarrow Wheel. Something funny to do with circuitous thinking and alliteration, I think – and you pause. You put a hand on your heart and you look heavenward.

This part is important. You want the yokels thinking about your connection to divinity and your humility all at once.

Image, remember.

So you take a minute, and then you twist the stupid arrow a half turn to the right and pull the knot holding it to the wheel free with your other hand while your squire makes appropriate "oohing" and "aahing" noises.

And then it's done.

And you get taken to the castle and the elderly king is so grateful to see you, he throws a banquet in your honor – and that puts you off your stroke for a minute, but you rally magnificently and drink with the best of them.

So it's the next day, and you get up, and you fall over from all the ale you quaffed last night. Your head feels exactly like Humpty-Dumpty's must've when the King's Men gave him that sad, frowning, head-shake.

"Hey, Humpty. We . . . we, uh. We got some bad news, dude."

You know, that whole, "Awww, crap!" feeling.

It takes some time, but slowly you start to remember what last night was all about.

It seems the king has a dragon problem. And you're the stupid shmuck who wandered into town, pulling weapons out of things, declaring yourself the promised savior.

Your mouth tastes like an obese gnome that'd been eating moat-carp for a month used it for a toilet at some point, and you just know that somehow, somewhere there's a bunch of long-bearded jerks you pissed off, nursing various injuries, passing along crystal-ball pictures of you yakking into the Queen's Punch Bowl.

And they're laughing about the way you're going to taste to the dragon. Gleefully.

As if all that weren't bad enough, you've got one of those gluey messages sticking to your face. And what do they make that glue out of, anyway? All I know is that it smells vaguely of boiled horse.

When you unroll it, it reads;

To: Prinze Charming

From: Loyal sqire

Re: My too weaks notise.

Dear Sur,

I regrret to inforem yu that I wil no longer be able to be yur sqire. I haf ben affered a posishun by the Blak Night of Wilderberry, and he doesunt drink nearly as much as yu do, nor does he try to steel my date."

Sinsearlee,

   Sqire Bobbin

P.S. Don't ferget, yu promised the king yu'd take care of his draggin problim today. Glad I am not going with yu.

   Well, they don't call you "Charming" for nothing. And you briefly consider finding Squire Bobbin and explaining a few things about the Black Knight of Wilderberry's idea of a fun Friday night with the "boys", but you figure he'll discover that for himself soon enough.

   Probably shortly after Wilderberry tells him to do his underwear laundry. While wearing it.

   So.

   What do you do to start improving this kind of a day?

   Well, for starters you get up - hoping that when the body lying next to you finally emerges from her stupor (You don't know her name, but a good assumption would place her as Squire Bobbin's amour), it isn't some kind of a troll (given Squire Bobbin's usual predilections), and it isn't hungry - and you try to find something to drink.

   Quick.

   Anything'll do, just so long as it's got a high alcohol content and you can get it down your gullet before your stomach knows you're awake. Otherwise you're going to have a really bad day. It's called "Hair of the dog that bit you," and it's a sure fire cure for a monster hangover.

   Of course, this problem can be badly compounded when you're blindly reaching for bottles around the bed without looking at labels. In your state it's hard enough to read anything anyway, but you may want to make the effort to pull the tattered shreds of your consciousness together long enough to read labels.

   Naturally, this is all moot if you've already drained the bottle labeled "Draggin A Tracter," - in Squire Bobbin's less than perfect patois - as you've just done.

   Give it a minute.

   It'll come to you.

   Right!

   There you are!

   Cured your hangover right away, didn't it? Do you suppose it was the actual dragon piss, or the sudden realization that you're going to be biologically informing every male dragon within a hundred leagues that you're fertile and ready to mate?

   So.

   Now that you're completely awake, and the spicy, somewhat . . . musky taste of pure, concentrated dragon urine has burned the inside of your eyeballs out, you begin to worry just a bit.

   Meanwhile, your latest conquest snores alarmingly and contentedly in bed. She's got an awful lot of teeth, doesn't she?

   Yeah. *That* kind of a day.

~~~~~~~

Well, you've got a choice here. Knowing that whatever you do for the rest of the day you're going to be attracting dragons kinda puts a bit of an impetus in your step. As in - "Wow. I've gotta find a place to hide! And in a great, horkin' hurry, too!"

So.

You can run, and pretend that you were operating under a long-bearded jerk's geas. It *has* worked a whole bunch of times before, after all. Look at that sod Lancelot! He couldn't put his hose on without falling under one. 'Course, having the brains of a lobotomized, pickled hedgehog probably doesn't help any.

Orrrrrr, you can do what you set out to do, albeit unknowingly, for the king. You know, that guy with the loyal legions of heavily armed and armored soldiers backing him? The guy whose wife's punch bowl you've already befouled? The guy who's probably already sent a squad of Infantry to come "collect" you?

So it's a fiery, toothy, dragon that's going to be sexually aroused by you! So what!

~~~~~~~

You get dressed. You put on your armor. You put on your scabbard, and nothing fits right, and you realize that you haven't the faintest idea what you're doing without Squire Bobbin there to help you. And it's while you're clanking around, cursing vehemenently, that Squire Bobbin's toothy, heifer-ish date wakes.

Remember that lady you got introduced to after the king and the queen? The "only daughter of His Majesty, Princess blah, blah, blah"?

Remember her?

Yeah, her. The one that looks an awful lot like the chick in bed over there. That whole "beloved-only-daughter-of-an over-protective-father" kind of thing is now clanging away alarmingly in your head. Suddenly, a quick dip in the moat followed by a bracing run to the nearest border doesn't sound all that implausible, and you're perfectly confident that if you don't survive the fall, it'll still be better than anything Princess Blah, blah, blah's old man can cook up.

You wonder - somewhere in the darker, less crowded spaces in your head, those places left not squirming in abject terror - if she's smiling at you in that special way for a specific reason or a general one. This is only a brief sort of consideration though, because your mind is shrieking holy bloody panic at you.

And all of a sudden, you haven't got any choice at all.

And for a brief, glorious moment you wonder what it'd be like to be a peasant. Something totally safe, utterly boring, and without all the "thrills" your life seems to have. Something like a beet farmer. Where the most dangerous beast you'll *ever* have to face would be a rabid, rampaging tuber. And not, say, a legion of pissed off long-bearded jerks, a strong and not-at-all-tottery king with legions of soldiers, a smiley-faced princess and a hungry dragon.

Yeah.

And there's a parade to see you off, and the king pulls you aside, and with a high, crazy light in his eyes, he tells you it'd probably be a good idea to either kill or be killed by those dragons, 'cause otherwise he's going to have you drawn and quartered in the public square.

"And then I'm going to feed the pieces to the carp in my moat," he assures you with that same half-crazy smile.

Guy must really have been upset about the punch bowl, huh?

~ ~ ~ ~ ~ ~

So you go tramping into the woods, all brave-like, which lasts until the last peasant has fallen from sight, and you then immediately start sneaking around. After all, a dragon can kill a body!

And it's while you're sneaking around that you find the temple. Before you can run in the other direction as fast as your feet will carry you - preparatory to returning with a squadron of brow-beaten-beaten-freshly-broken-armed-long-bearded-jerks to reduce the place to a smoking heap of gelatinous slag - the three male dragons emerge.

Not one dragon, mind you. *Three.*

They've got strangely reptilian, befuddled looks on their faces like "Why does that human meat snack smell exactly like a horny chick?"

There's nothing crankier than a love-besotted, confused dragon, and you raise your sword to the attack . . . . just as you remember that you left your sword at the castle with Bobbin for cleaning, and all you've got is a ceremonial thing made of tin, little better than paper. Your scabbard might as well be empty.

Ever have one of *THOSE* kind of days?

A Necessary Lesson

My parents are strange and wonderful people. When they met, they both lived in a Jesus-freak, dope-smoking, hippie commune. Four years later, my Dad joined the Army, and it's been a total adventure of absolute incongruities ever since.

They raised four very strange little people who grew up to be four even stranger big people: namely me, my two brothers and my sister.

This story is something of a tribute to them. It's two parts visualization exercise, two parts true story, and three parts a naked (but loving) "Neerner-neeeener-neee-eeener!" at my parents for being such rampant non-conformists.

I love them dearly and it is with affection and respect that I dedicate this to them.

Hopefully they'll put the bong down long enough to read it.

~~~~~~~

My eyes open and I'm staring at the wall. A sliding glance toward the alarm clock on the other side of the room tells me I'm awake three hours before my alarm was set to go off.

The dark surrounds me like a warm blanket. I can feel the cat sleeping at the end of the bed. The sound of the radio playing in the other room and the noise of the fan eventually pulls me back into reality. My speeding heart gradually slows.

The dream, again: a variation on a tiresome theme, almost life-long. It's like a memory I can't quite coalesce into conscious observation; something I'm repressing. When I was younger the dream featured automobile-related threats. Whether it was a dump truck closing in from a long way away or cowering in a VW Bus while the Frankenstein Monster stomped towards me (that one featured the Muppet Grover. He said not to be scared, but he didn't do anything helpful, either.) There's always a car featured in the dream somewhere, somehow. I've never understood it.

Since joining the world of adults the theme of the dream has changed just a bit. In my adult dreams, I'm almost always driving - something I take a great deal of pleasure in - small, fast cars, built low to the ground. Sometimes an impression of space and luxury surrounds, other times it's little more than a roll cage and a steering wheel - a go-cart arrangement. Small differences exist in every dream, but they always fade in response to the forward impetus of the overall theme: I'm driving and I'm about to have a horrifying accident.

One I've had several times features the 'Schwinn Effect'. I'm rolling along, and hit the brakes hard enough to lift the back end of the car off the road. I'm rocked forward in my seat as though I'm riding a bicycle headfirst into a wall. The feel of the forward movement makes me sick with fear and phantom pain. It happens over and over and over in the course of one night's dreaming and I wake unrested and cranky, sometimes with sore muscles.

Tonight's was only a bit different. I lay on my side, sifting through the fading fragments. I had to think about it for a bit, putting together the thin scenes I could remember. (I often think about the way we receive messages: whether from God, ourselves, or the universe in general, messages come at us from everywhere.) We try to tell ourselves things that are important in dreams. We try to make ourselves heard and all too often we make that nearly impossible. I think maybe, for once, I managed to hear myself.

In this evening's dream, the car I'm driving is starting to spin and I am going fast enough for this to be a very serious problem. The car is spinning like a top. I am missing the other cars on the road by the barest of inches. There's a high-pitched noise generated by my passage. My hands lock on the steering wheel and a traitorous, self-destructive part of myself gives in. I watch, removed, as I take no action to save myself. I sit, terrified, my hands on the wheel, and allow things to happen. I begin to call on Jesus almost at once, the familiar fear and dread crawling over me.

The fear builds, and I scream to Jesus to save me. Then, like sunlight, awareness breaks. I watch, still removed and outside of myself, as a slowly panning inner camera draws my mind's eye from my terrified face, fixed in a fear-grin-rictus, to my hands - still locked on the wheel and pulling it sharply in the direction of the spin - to my feet.

My right foot is firmly pressing the gas pedal down.

I stay in bed for a long moment, trying to go back to sleep. I don't sleep well most nights and waking up some three hours before I have to is inconvenient, to say the least. I say a small prayer, in the belief that waking up like this is God's way of telling you someone needs you to intercede for them, and lie still on my mattress, trying to find the inner peace necessary to waft back down the river of sleep.

It's no good.

I'm awake.

I sigh, stumble out of bed and walk into the bathroom, flicking the light on as I pass. I blearily peer at myself in the small mirror over the sink. My reflection stares back, emanating resentment at me. My eyes are dull and tired, and my hair has formed a sleepy crow's nest. Without wanting to I can see the face hiding behind mine in my reflection. His hair's much longer, he's skinnier, and his face, though dirty, doesn't seem to reflect as many years of compromise as mine now seems to. His eyes, below the silent, wordless anger, betrayal, and hurt, radiate with the spiritual ambition to change the world and everything in it.

He's not me. I don't think he's ever really been me. Or, no . . . I've got that backwards. *I* was never really intended to be me. I was supposed to be something far leaner and meaner, sharper and harder. I was supposed to be an axe; a knife; a sword. Instead, I'm a spoon.

His lips - with the prerequisite titanium studs - move soundlessly, but I don't need to hear him to know what he's saying.

'You've forgotten. You've sold out.'

He's far skinnier than me. Angular. And he's so angry - so passionate about change and making the world a better place. He's militant and liberal; furious and impassioned; and he's ready, willing and able to storm the gates whenever the call for revolution comes. I can't remember, now, why he was always so angry, so ready to commit violence in the name of the people.

Sometimes I wonder where he went, and when, exactly, he left. I know he was there in high school, and disappeared before I hit my mid-twenties. It's easy, when you decide it's time to grow up and put away childish things, to forget who you were and where you came from, isn't it?

Another crime to lay at my feet. A man's got to eat, though, so I don't spend too much time regretting his untimely death.

Deli, the short-haired brindle princess who lives in my house and eats my food, prances around my ankles, grunting and meowing, doing her level best to let me know she wants to be fed - just in case I forgot this is 'treat time'.

I walk into the kitchen, fetch her two treats, and move into the living room, despite her protests.

I sit, picking up the book I left propped on the arm of my 'fat-boy-chair'. I read a few pages, letting the radio behind me tinkle quietly to itself on the bookshelf while I try to relax enough to fall back asleep. The glorified electric typewriter on my desk sits like a gloating toad and I can almost hear it muttering.

'Not gonna write anything tonight, huh? Just as well. You suck. Probably shouldn't have quit rolling barrels or delivering furniture. Not much else a dumb gorilla like you would be any good at.'

I flip another page, ignoring it. It's right. I *do* need to write - had intended on getting up early every day to do so. But I don't want to give it the pleasure of knowing that.

The voice of the electric 'under-toad' on my desk croaks again. *'Will you blinkin' credit it? Now he thinks he can ignore me! Well!'*

I continue to do precisely that. Deli, injured and offended, jumps in my lap and purrs like a

constipated chainsaw.

A third voice, neither silent ghost or gloating-typewriter-undertoad whispers at me, and it's not going to be ignored. It's like a biting flea in a warm, moist, unreachable crevice of flesh. It flicks around on the surface of my brain, whispering, digging, scratching and calling, and I give in after only a few minutes.

The chair is waiting, whispering and calling.

It's not a very nice chair: a thin, reclining thing with a feeble footrest; the kind of piece you'd expect to see in a modern bachelor's home in the 1950's. Covered in a burgundy, shag-like material, it itches something fierce when I sit.

Just a bit used, the condition of the chair isn't all that bad for something rescued from the trash. At the moment, it's wedged in between my bed and the bedroom wall, with about three feet of space separating them. There are three boards, old shelving material, wedged between the chair and the wall.

I turn off all the lights and move back into the bedroom, where the soft whiff of the fan mingles with the voice of the chair, beckoning me. I pull on a pair of socks, and smile, thinking, 'It's *cold* in the void!'

I move the radio from its place on my bookshelf, and plug it in the socket closest to my mattress, turning it to face the chair. I pull out the new CD my best friend loaned me - some heavy piece of bluesy-rock - and put it in the radio, turning up the volume to the preset level I've determined is 'just enough'. I don't want to disturb my neighbor any more than necessary, and I have to believe he wonders about the rhythmic knocking noises coming from next door.

I sit in the chair, wedge my legs against the mattress, put my arms on the arm rests and let my fingers find the indentations I've already worn there. I press play, close my eyes and begin to rock.

You've seen it before, I'm sure. It's a simple forward and back movement; you rock forward, you rock back, sitting in a perfectly stationary chair. It's a telling characteristic of autistic individuals, and people with certain kinds of mental illnesses.

I've been doing it my entire life - rocking and pushing my consciousness into an inner sanctuary.

It originally began as an expression of my enjoyment of music. I'd rock in time with the beat, listening to whatever happened to be playing.

'Put on music, watch Nescher bobble.'

As I got older, I learned it's a fabulous way to meditate. You almost achieve a state of auto-hypnosis. Your immediate awareness fades out. You lose touch with the present and drift through skies of your own making. It's like a drug. You can completely lose yourself in the rhythm, the sweat and the music.

I've done some reading on the matter. Many religions the world over use a very similar technique to achieve an 'ecstatic' state (voodoo practitioners use drums and dance, to give an example). For myself, I've noticed a sensation of 'opening', as though I'm flowing into a larger space than the one behind my eyes. I feel like I'm lightly surfing along the soap-bubble-thin membrane of some enormous sphere.

It's very hard to explain without resorting to spiritual, quasi-mystical language, but the basic feeling is I'm a seed opening and rising towards a sunlit sky.

I enjoy rocking. Other than the exercise, and really crunching out to some seriously killer music, it gives me an opportunity to do the 'filing'.

The theory runs a little like this: your head, like anything else dealing with input and output, occasionally fills up. It gets clogged, plugged and stoppered with the constant barrage of crap coming at you on a daily basis. Thoughts, hopes, dreams, ambitions and desires contribute to the general mess, and every so often you need to clean the drains. Take a bit of time, sweat a whole bunch, and move your way through your own head, cleaning house. I don't know if that's really the way things are, but I know I sure feel better afterwards.

The music starts and washes over me. I envisage myself as being a silvery, naked, nearly perfect lance of human-shaped light.

I swim through the dense cobwebs of my head as lightstorms flick on and off behind my eyes. When I was younger, I used to think the display going on behind my closed eyes when I rocked were the skies of another universe, one that existed just beyond the horizon of the seen and known. I'm older now, with some letters in the air above my head, and *intellectually* I know the colors, the bright spirals and the swirling clouds of light I'm watching are probably the result of my brain crashing against the front and back of my skull.

In response to all this learnin', I've taught myself to 'rock' my head instead of 'banging' it. I let my skull 'surf' on my neck with a gentle forward and back movement. It's probably better for me, but I do miss the vibrant 'laser-light' displays of my youth.

The music's pretty good. Good hooks, licks and rhythm, but I'm not getting there. I still feel dense, hard, tight - like I'm firmly anchored to myself. The music's okay and I'm working up a bit of a sweat, but experience has taught me that there are further depths to plumb if I want to.

I do.

I *always* do.

I stop the CD player, taking the CD out. I put in a CD that always manages to somehow appeal to that part of my brain that responds almost immediately to rhythms and beats. I like to think of my response to it as being something like a reptile finding a warm place in the sun. The music from this CD goes directly to my hind brain and fires off all the right kinds of responses.

I turn the lights off. Some things are just better in the dark.

I close my eyes, turn the music up, and rock.

It's like a sonic assault. All at once, the music starts. Primal guitar licks, and a driving, booming, ear-bleeding drum rhythm.

Awwwww, yeah. This'll do. This'll do *juuuuuuust* fine!

The hairs on my arms and the back of my neck stand up, and a wave of hot adrenaline rushes through me. My knuckles start to itch.

Awwwww, yeah, baby.

A younger, leaner, harder me, a me that looked out at me from the mirror a few minutes ago, starts yelling inside my head for a mosh pit.

There never seems to be a mosh pit around when you need one, does there?

My skin moves against the fabric of the chair.

I sweat.

My breathing slows to a cadence I've trained myself over the years with, taking on an automatic, almost hibernative nature. My throat closes and becomes dry. My head lowers to my chest and my hair dances around my face.

I rock, finding the beat, and let the music swirl into my needy places. It wraps its way around my head, fully cocooning me, and I start to drift.

The lights and colors behind my eyes splash and swirl in time to the music. I lance myself upward into them, arms wrapped around me. I'm clothed only with the music, and I move in time with it and the dream of possibility behind my closed eyes.

The anchors of reality fall away, and I shoot away into innerspace.

I'm rather proud of this sanctum. I'm not entirely sure where it is. A scientist would tell you it's all imaginary, existing only within the walls of my skull. I'm not sure I agree, but it isn't all that important.

Description. Yes. You've never been here, so you don't know what it looks like.

Basically, I'm an arrowed lance of silvery light floating within a nebulous void, swirled with lights, sounds and colors. It's a bit like a nursery for stars.

The colors and swirls embrace me. I lose where I end and the music begins. I float on the surface of mind, riding a wave of righteous-music-driven-anger, and drift where the current takes me.

Above, below, and all around are polychromatic, opaque spheres. Some shine like the sun on a perfect spring day. Others are dark, with frightening depths. Still others have a color that makes me think of skin that's been dead for a very long time.

I drift forward, with the music playing all around, and slide effortlessly through the skin of the nearest sphere.

The room is dark and nearly empty. A crib, with a baby – perhaps six months old – wrapped in a handmade blanket and sleeping peacefully on its back, next to a cat purring contentedly, takes up the center of the room. A painting hangs on one wall.

The cat - a long-haired black female, named, for reasons only certain drug-addled names will ever know, 'Creamapara' - and the painting, I recognize. The baby, I don't.

Beautifully regal in the sphinx-like way of all cats, she sleeps, nose buried, in the warm hollow formed between the baby's head and the head of the crib.

Her contented purring fills the chill, waiting silence of the room. She wakes for just a moment and looks up in the bored, disinterested way of a truly happy, comfortable cat when I glide in.

Peering at me for a moment with sleepy eyes, she seems to shrug. Lowering her head, she goes back to sleep, her purring never missing a beat.

A dirty, badly used, hand-me-down thing of rusty struts and clattering wood, the crib looks like a Victorian torture device. A bare, musty mattress - how I remember the smell! - sits within, and if it weren't for the warm, pastel-colored blanket wrapped around the baby, there'd be nothing protecting him from the cold but the cat.

The young stranger who stared back at me from my bathroom mirror walks out of the wall the painting hangs on. He's got his belligerent glare in place before he's even fully through.

I shouldn't be surprised. After all, anywhere I can go, he can go. It's a *shared* universe.

He says nothing. To each other, we are both deaf and mute: nothing can be said across this personal universe, nothing can cleave the distance of time and space we've put between us. But we know each other of old. Body language and gesture says more between the two of us, than words ever could.

A black t-shirt with an enormous red, anarchy symbol on it hangs from his bony shoulders. It looks like blood. Dirty, torn jeans cover his lanky shanks. 'Poverty-chic,' I think, meanly, on seeing them.

A pair of beaten, beleaguered, outsized, hand-me-down-from-five-generations-distant combat boots makes enormous clown's shoes of his feet, and blood drips from his knuckles in a steady stream. It slowly disappears from view before hitting the floor. A neat trick, that. Mine ache in a muted sort of empathy.

Thick beige calluses, an inch thick, cover his fingertips. He spends far more time in the chair than I do.

Writing covers his arms from wrists to elbows. It is his attempt at tattooing. He uses an ink pen, a marker, lipstick; whatever comes to hand. It's an everyday thing. Songs, poems, lyrics, bits of doggerel; he doesn't care. Whatever occurs to him ends up on his arms.

Today, the left arm has a badly scrawled song by his favorite band. I don't need to see it to read it. The words are a part of my mental landscape, and I mouth the first few words to myself while looking around the room.

"It's never been easy to be who I am,
I can only do the very best I can."

He looks at me in disbelief, as if I have no right to remember. He thrusts his right arm at me, and the writing here is clear. Another song. One we wrote together so many years ago. This one I sing in a quiet voice.

"A cold, dark night; a bitter, biting wind,
a man walks the streets alone, covered by his sins.
Tears many years unshed silently fall,
He falls to his knees, broken as he desperately calls . . . "

No, it isn't very good, but it was written with a passion you can only really get to when you're still young.

The last three words have nearly been carved into his skin, with the force of his feeling.

'*NEVER GIVE IN*' has been scrawled, with considerable force, in red ink across his left wrist.

I remember that one. He wrote it over and over for a month, re-inking it every day. The skin grew irritated and inflamed. He got an infection that required antibiotics. I remember him hoping it would scar.

This was all long before he started stealing his father's razorblades - before he started reflecting the outward pain of his nearly impossible environment.

I look at him and briefly wonder at the miracle of me. How did I ever survive to be who and what I am? How did I ever manage to live into adulthood? I wonder what he thinks of *my* tattoos. A small part of me hopes he approves.

I nod teeth and fists clenched. Oh, yes. I remember.

He keeps reaching up to his face to disentangle the chains and piercings there. I grin and he glowers in response. He crosses his arms over his chest, and his dog-chain bracelet twinkles in the uncertain light.

The facial piercings are, of course, de rigueur, but nobody told him how annoying they are. Twisting and tangling, getting cold and infected, the metal he pierces his face with is a cross he bears, a perpetual sacrifice to the god 'cool'.

We stand, facing each other, over the Amontillado-ian crib and look around the room, curious. There isn't much to see if you're looking the wrong

way.

There is no door in the doorway of the room. It looks like the hole left by a missing tooth (Door wood, especially *old* door wood, makes great firewood. Dry and quite dense, it burns with a smoky, woody odor that mixes quite well with the musky smell of pot).

I remember that. I remember them being so poor that burning the inside doors in their little pot-bellied stove was just one of the many economies they practiced. Someone would collect old newspapers, cardboard boxes, twigs, even: anything that would burn.

A beaded curtain covers the hole where the door *should* be. Some of the beads look like lovingly polished stones, giving the overall effect a handmade look.

Loud, rough voices, raised in warm, muted conversation come from beyond the beaded doorway. It sounds as if they are arguing about Exodus.

"Moses, man, Moses was . . . was . . . well, he was, just a *man*, man. Like, ready to be used by God, man."

Rumbles of affable agreement and the voices fade as if conversation has lulled.

A millipede - easily a foot long - crawls busily along one wall, tracking its way to the ceiling. It looks like something that would've been happy in a swamp with dinosaurs. It finds a crack and disappears inside the wall with a whispery slithering noise that sounds like a snake over sand.

I suppress a shiver.

The painting on the wall behind my youthful companion is also part of my mental landscape. It shows an ephemeral angel, trump raised to the heavens, standing atop a knife-edge mountain peak, while a star supernovas behind it. Sullen colors - angry purples and blues - dominate. They are the colors of a final judgment.

Written at the bottom of the painting are the words 'Many are called, few are chosen' in a contrasting, brilliant white. It is a phenomenal thing. The hand that rendered this painting had a profound understanding of depth, light and shadow. I can almost feel a cold, angry wind blowing out from the wall. When I was a child, I used to stare at it and wonder who took the picture. Where did they stand with the camera so the angel wouldn't see them?

My friend looks over. Then he looks back at me.

31

The meaning in his eyes is clear. "Many *are* called . . .

" . . . have *you* been chosen?"

I don't need this from him. Not here, not now. I shake my head in annoyance and turn away. I've become what I had to become so I could eat. Passion is for young men; practicality is for the adults they grow into.

A pungent odor - redolent of incense, pot, fried food, cat urine, sex, booze, baby poop, lamp oil, and burning wood (probably an old dense, door) - permeates the thin, dingy, peeling walls of this room. I'm not smelling it, of course. I'm *remembering* it.

The baby sleeps through it all - a small, dirty critter, utterly naked, save for the blanket and a cloth diaper that has been washed many, many times. The diaper itself is faded, and while I can't really tell what material it's made of in the dark of the room, I have a sneaking suspicion it is buckskin.

The diaper is held on by one rusty, large safety pin at the left waist.

It would be quite easy to simply catalog this household as being monstrously neglectful and abusive. It would be easy to ignore some of the smaller clues, and simply call these people 'poor white trash'.

They'd say they *are* poor, but only in a material sense. Yes, the baby is a little skinnier than he should be, and dirty, but he also almost seems to shine with good health. Yes, the mattress is bare, but the blanket is warm and made of all the colors of the rainbow. The making of it required the skills of a weaver: a gift of love.

Poor, yes, but their priorities are exactly where they should be. My young companion glances at everything, and then looks at me. He indicates our surroundings with a smug sneer on his face and outspread arms.

For no reason I can adequately explain, I feel hot, guilty tears rise to my eyes. I stare down at the baby to avoid the judgment in my friend's gaze. The baby remains utterly undisturbed by the cat, or the voices raised in rough laughter from the other side of the doorway.

A quiet moment falls in the other room. I feel a brief tension, like the hardening, all at once, of a vital artery.

The walls of the room, though making no visible movement to my mind's eyes, seem to contract. I feel like a dying moth in the hands of an incautious, over-eager child. My companion looks, arms still crossed over his chest in a hostile way. Whatever is happening is happening only to me. He remains unaffected. I am being squeezed by the forces around us. My breath comes in hot gasps, and my heart thunders in my chest.

Something is trying very hard to tell me something.

"Alright! I'm listening!" I manage to gasp out. A voice, like oily smoke, pours out of the other room. The walls around me contract brutally a final time, and then snap back.

And as if I needed this final clue, music I've been listening to for as long as I've been alive follows that voice with a reedy, scratchy, ill-played guitar.

"I'm walking down this beat-up track. I've got dusty tears in my eyes, and I'm trying to read a letter from my lonely home."

The baby opens his eyes. A blue gaze swivels around the room for a moment, taking in the darkness. The cat, sensing the baby has awakened, stretches out her neck and purringly sniffs his nose. The baby screws his face up and gives a quiet sneeze. This bothers the cat not at all, and Creamapara settles down to an extended bathing session, doing what it can to improve the condition of the baby's hygiene.

The baby follows this movement, and reaches out one tiny hand. The cat rubs its jaw along the hand, and the baby giggles.

The music continues to play in the other room. I can hear fingers trying to snap to the rhythm, and whispered comments coming from the listeners.

"Yeah."

"Groovy."

"Sing it, mama."

Creamapara loses interest in the baby's hand, having gotten it as clean as possibly with cat spit, and goes to work on the top of the baby's head. The baby stares interestedly at the ceiling. For a long moment, he does nothing. He seems to be listening to the music, despite his young age. Then he rolls over on his stomach. Lifting his head, he listens some more. I watch, grinning, along with my silent companion, as the baby begins to bang its face against the mattress of the crib, driving it into the wall.

"Alright!" I shout, and bang my head in response. My companion grins too, and starts to mosh with himself.

From the other room there is a sound like a box of wire hangers being dropped, and the guitar stops playing. I hear the sound of strings being scraped roughly across a cement floor.

'That's where that dent came from!' flashes across my mind - a thought perfectly articulated and shared between me and my companion.

The baby, lost in his world of four-four time, and metronomic beats, continues to bang his face against the mattress.

A voice asks, "Hey, man. Do you hear that?"

Another voice, torpid and heavy, replies, "It sounds like it's comin' from the kid's room, man."

Bare, running feet slap across the concrete floor. I grin from ear to ear, as a young, skinny, long-haired thing walks into the room, an enormous bong with a toad body in its hands, and concern on its face. I know who this is, having seen pictures proudly displayed to my girlfriends over the years, but it still takes me a long moment to decide that 'it' is a man.

He is gloriously dressed in his 'anti-establishment' paraphernalia. A psychedelic, hand-knitted-yarn, knee length serape-thing covers his shoulders. I can see his belly button peeking out underneath it, and the skinny stack of his ribs.

His dirty, ripped jeans probably qualify for EPA Superfund status. They are covered in patches that seem to do double duty as advertisement, and make up the majority of the material: peace signs, smiling, wise, non-descript, big-eyed creatures, crucifixes, and a large, idealized patch I strongly suspect is supposed to be Gandalf.

He smells an awful lot like the bottom of a well-used hookah. The black curly hair on his head stands out like an enthusiastic tumbleweed.

A rough, hand-carved, wooden crucifix, easily a foot long, tied with bootlaces at the intersection, hangs from a leather thong around his neck and swings freely at the level of his navel.

My companion jumps up and down and points at the man. A beatific grin covers his face, and I realize my friend is seeing something that maybe *he'd* forgotten and had come to remember. It is a comforting thought.

We all change. We all grow. We all mutate into versions of ourselves that we could never anticipate. Sometimes we change for the better, sometimes, however briefly, we change for the worse.

Bruises cover my friend's arms and shoulders; his thighs and his back. They are up high, under the covering of his tattered t-shirts; always someplace out of sight. I realize why he's here. He's come to see where it all started before it all went wrong.

I can look back and give him *some* perspective. There would be pain, and tears, and blackest recrimination, but eventually, after climbing the mountain until your fingernails bled . . . eventually there would be forgiveness and reconciliation.

He has years yet, and my eyes fill with sympathy for his remembered pain.

The man peers over the edge of the crib, scratching gustily at his scalp as if to dislodge invaders. A moment later he's joined by a short, skinny, brown-haired woman wearing what looks like a beige cape. She's missing most of one arm and smiling vapidly. (She smells a bit more bong-like than the male figure.) A high, slightly wild light shines in her eyes, and my grin fades a little at seeing it. My companion stops jumping up and down, and his grin dies a bit as well.

We both remember the abject failure of our protector. Forgiveness will come eventually, we hope.

We can see what would later put her in the nursing home dancing around in the back of her eyes; giggling and glinting.

The man puts his arms around the woman and in a heavily slurred voice, asks, "Dana, what is the kid doin', man? Is Nescher alright?"

The woman smiles and pats his cheek condescendingly. Her voice is heavily slurred as well. "I told you, Dale!" she says, grinning widely, "He loves the music!"

"Oh, wow! Far out, man! You guys! Come check this out!"

Other people crowd into the room: long-haired, dirty cast-offs and cast-aways of a society they've rejected or been rejected by. Some look like heavily amphetamined bikers. Others look like vagrants. One fine young specimen wears a clerical collar and smokes a joint eight inches long.

They all share the same look: a light that has been lit within and shines, uninhibited, from their eyes. Stupid, helpless tears pour down my face. They are not my blood, but they *are* my family, the roots I grew from.

My friend throws his head back and laughs joyously. He hasn't learned yet how to cry in joy. He's still a teenager, and I don't learn that for several years yet. It is the first noise he's made that I've heard.

The people crowded around the crib watch the baby for a moment, grinning and laughing like stupid, stoned loons. I don't recognize most of them, but there's my godfather, Frank Romano, bearded and in his Road Rat regalia. He smells like his Harley, and the taint of Vietnam still stains his eyes. There's Bob, and his wife – or maybe they're not married yet. I'm not sure of chronology – Debbie. I can't begin to list what I owe them; I can't begin to repay them for what they will do for me and my family later in my life.

Others, less important and more. My heart hurts with the love I feel for them at this moment.

The baby in the crib, who's belatedly realized he has an audience, stops banging his face against the mattress, and looks at the stoned, smiling faces surrounding him with wide blue eyes.

Creamapara meows inquisitively. She'd been interrupted from a nap *and* a bath! There's a round of spontaneous, bellowing laughter.

"That's my kid, man!" shouts my father, and he picks me up, carelessly dropping the bong. He kisses me on the lips, getting hair, chicken grease, bong water, and his own tears all over me. He carries me in his arms, accompanied by back slaps, and raucous, good-natured laughter, back into the other room. After a moment, the guitar starts playing again. It's a different song, and sung twice as loud, by all.

"Innnnnnnnnnnnnnn the eeeeeeeeeeeeveniiiiiiiiiiiiiiiiin' . . . "

My father's voice comes from the other room. I can hear the joyous tears in his voice as he shouts, "That's my son! That's my Eagle!"

And that's enough for the two of us. We've come so far, but this is where we both began. We can lie to each other, and deny each other as much as we like, but neither one of us can deny the skinny, ratty little thing in the crib, being adored by his stoned mother and father and the rest of their commune.

My younger self looks at me from across our crib, and nods knowingly. His face, free as of yet of the beard I will eventually wear, breaks into a smile. His mouth works silently, but I can see what he's saying, his lips are mine, after all.

And try not to forget it this time!

We share a nod of mutual understanding, and he walks out of the memory sphere, back into his life.

I wipe my face and whisper, "I won't, Nescher. I won't." I stand there for a long time, listening, crying and remembering.

After a while, my alarm goes off back in the real world. It's time for me to return, to get up and get ready for work. I sigh and the bubble 'pops'. I resurface, turn the CD player off, and stand.

I wipe the tears from my face and walk back into the bathroom.

I turn the water on in the shower, look into the mirror, and with a grin, bellow, "And who're *you* tellin' not to forget, you skinny little punk?!"

At the edge of hearing, there is a warm gust of all too familiar laughter.

Ways To Annoy Your Lover

"*Do you love me?*"
       "This again?"
*"Yes. This *again.*"*
"So if I answer this question we can move on with our lives, stop circling around this over and over again, and just be happy?"
"That kinda depends on your answer, there, skippy."
"No need to be snappish."
"Just playing with the cards in my hand sweetie."
"Whatever."
    . . .

    . . .
"Well?"
"Well, what?"
"I swear I'm going to have to kill you in self-defense . . . "
"What?!"
"Answer the question!"
"What question?!"
*"Do you **love** me!"*
"Oh. Right. Never got around to actually answering you, did I?"
"Counting to ten here . . . "
"Alright, alright. I guess you've suffered enough. Yes. Yes I do."
"Why?"
"Ohhhhhh, no. No, no, no, no, NO! That's not part of the deal! You asked me if I love you and I told you I did. You don't get to tack on a "Why?" That's a whooooole 'nother set of arguments-"
"Suck it up. Answer the question."
"I just did!"
*"Not *that* question! The other one!"*
"What other question? I swear, you're driving me bananas!"
"Why. Do. You. Love. Me. Answer. Answer me now!"
"What do you mean, "Why?" Why does there have to *be* a "why"? I just do."
"Well, why do you love me? I mean, there's got to be a reason, right?"
"Why do I feel like there's no right answer to this question?"
"Hey, fine. If you feel that way, forget I said anything . . . ."
"Now, hold on a minute. Don't get mad. What I meant was it felt like a loaded question. No matter what answer I give, every chamber's got a bullet in it designed to spray my brains across the carpet. If I say, "I love you because you're beautiful," you'd come back with *"Oh. So all you care about is physical beauty, huh? Typical."*

"If I say, "I love you because you're intelligent," you'll say *"So I'm a repulsive toad, huh? Love me because of my "great personality", huh? Tell your friends I'm a great cook who makes all my own clothes, do ya'?"*

"And if, God forbid, I choose not to answer at all, you go looking for excuses as to why. I can't win!"

"Look. It's a simple question. Why. Do. You. Love. Me. Answer it, don't answer it. I'm just trying to talk to you."

"Yeah. I believe that. I can predict the future! Watch!"

"Now don't start this . . .."

"No! Seriously! I see me . . . it's several hours from now . . . I've chosen not to answer, and the bedroom door is locked . . . I'm sleeping on the floor . . . my nose is bleeding . . . ."

"Do you want *to sleep on the floor?"*

"Nope."

"Then quit teasing me and answer the question."

"You're not going to be dissuaded by my attempts at being witty, then?"

"Nope. Answer the question."

"You want to know."

"Yes."

"Do you *really* want to know?"

"Yes."

"Really?"

"Yes!"

"Really, really?"

"I'm going to hurt you . . . ."

"Okay. Sorry. Well, if you really, really want to know . . . ."

"Yeeeessss . . . ."

"I don't know."

" . . . "

"Weren't expecting that answer, I take it."

" . . . "

"Look. You asked, okay? It's not like I can sit here and analyze why I love you. I can give you trite and pedantic reasons that'll make you feel good, but that wouldn't be honest. I can tell you all the things you want to hear, or I can blow smoke up your behind until your ears glow. But to be perfectly honest, I don't know why I love you. Why does anybody love anybody? Do we even know what love is?"

"Whatever it is, it's all that's keeping me from pulling your arms off . . . ."

"I can sense that, believe me."

"Okay, smart guy. Well, I know why I love you."

"Do you?"

"Yep."

"That's awesome!"

" . . . "

" . . . "

"You're not going to ask me why, are you?"

"I was hoping you'd make that realization, yes."

"Don't you want to know? Don't you care?"

"Nope."

"You don't."

"Nope."

"You can see the rage building, right? Now, I'm going to ask why, and there'd better be a good answer."

"I don't care . . . "

"Yes?"

"Because it's enough for me that you love me."

*"Oh, come **on**!"*

"I'm serious! I'm just grateful that you love me. If I spend too much time trying to figure it out, I'd be looming over you menacingly all the time."

"Was that a thinly concealed jab?"

"Was it obvious? I was kinda worried it might just be a little obvious."

"You're lucky I love you."

"Well, all kidding aside, yes. Yes I am."

"Okay, that was pretty darn smooth, right there."

"Thanks! I'm a smooth kind of guy!"

"Don't be smug. It's not becoming."

"Sorry."

" . . . "

" . . . "

"You really do love me, then?"

"I really do love you. Now, then, and whenever."

"Okay. That's all better, then."

"I thought it might be."

"I love you. But you're a huge dork. You know that, right?"

"Yeah, well, you love me. What's that say about *you*?"

The End

Vae Victus

The crimson and silver banner of our king flowed from the herald's horse with the wind of our passage.

We rode ten-thousand-thousands strong, the thunder our hooves shaking the very roots of the world. I put my head back and laughed, imagining poor Atlas wincing at each blasting impact and cursing us in his old, dead tongue.

From my place in the vanguard, I could see for miles. The horizon stretched before us, an unbroken line of rolling plain, perfect for the charge.

I opened my mouth and tasted the wind. The smell of blood was strong and high, like a fine wine. Our armor glinted in the sun like tears. It shone and bedazzled the eye. Our swords and spears, our shields were enough to deafen a man.

Surely! Surely to ride, to fight, to die, is the noblest ambition of man!

I laughed again, imagining the spilling blood of the foeman. How like deepest drops of warm, ruby wine it would be! How like most precious gold it would run and melt and spill, collecting in small hollows and pools on the field of battle.

I longed to feel the pierce of my sword, the thrust of my spear.

I longed for the anguishing cries of the foeman.

I longed to hear the fearful shriek of the defeated, the beaten.

We rode until the sun crested the horizon and then stopped for a meal and the watering of our mounts. They too thirsted for battle, but it would do no good to ride them so hard in our flight toward it.

"I am afraid," said the one riding nearest me. He was a thin man, and I could not see his face very well. It appeared, in the flickering light of our shared fire, almost to be a skull.

"Afraid? Of what? Our enemies will be scattered like dust before us. We will fall on them like the locust, like the eclipse. We will kill, maim, ravage and destroy!" I said this with a fierce grin on my face. The pull of the coming battle was strong within me. The clarion call of the war pipes, the beating of the battle drum, the rough banter of my fellow warriors, it all stirred my blood.

"Nevertheless, I am afraid. The shamans read ill omens-"

"Pah! Shamans! Stirrers of chicken guts and drinkers of their own urine! Who cares what such maggot spawn as they see in the twisted stews they call augury? Who cares what omens and ill fates they read in the tangled ordure of their breakfasts? No, my friend. Give me a sharp sword and an enemy to swing it at, and I will defy death himself!" My face glowed with battle-joy, and my companion, he who should be my stout shield mate, my dearest brother-in-arms, stepped back in alarm.

His eyes glowed with flames for a moment. How strange that I should not know his name, should not be able to see his face.

"Speak not so! The gods of battle and strife hear such boasts, and live to break the sword of the mouth that speaks it! So say the priests-"

"And a pox on your scurvy priests as well! Woman who wear skirts, hiding behind foul smokes and fumes! What care I for their dull and unblooded mutterings?"

I drew my sword, my blood riding high and singing. I strode to a nearby hill from whence I could see the far horizon.

"Hear me, oh Death, oh gods of battle! I defy you! I lift my hands toward you and I spit my pride into your eyes! I am unconquered and my sword shall never break, come what will!"

My shouts rolled back at me. I lifted a hand to my ear and pointed it at the blue, untroubled sky, as if waiting for a response.

"I do not hear you, fickle fates!"

From my back, my battle-mates - lords and strong lions all - my fellow riders roared their approbation and love in resounding peals of laughter.

I turned to the fearful one, a smile on my face, the shine of battle joy in my eyes. "And that, my brother, is how a warrior faces death! His sword in hand, stout companions at his back, and the foemen in front!" I shouted, lifting my hands above my head to yet more roars and laughter.

He waited until the others had drifted away to find their mouthful of water and food. "You do not fear the sharpened blade? You do not fear the spear in the back, the bite of arrow in the lung?" he asked, eyes still wide and trembling.

"Fear? Nay! I never fear! I welcome bony, clacking Death with open arms, like an eager lover! Let that yellowed, ivory hand reach for my heart if it can! I will draw my sword and strike it off at the wrist, my curse on my lips, and a laugh rolling from me like sweet waters."

He was so fearful, this trembling, shrinking woman!

"Show me the foeman, my brother! And I will teach you what you should fear!"

"Nevertheless. It is not good to defy Death so. It is said he hears such words and comes to find the lips that speak them," he said, almost whispering now, eyes hidden in the shadows covering his strange, thin face.

I laughed again, shaking my head. His fears were his own and nothing to do with me.

We rode for a day, a night and another day, and below us was the camp of the foeman. They covered the hills like ants, befouling the air with their pestilential fires and the filth of their droppings. Sweet battle music played within my soul, and I longed to hear the charge of the King's trump.

"You still do not fear?" My strange companion, his face bony angles and sharp planes, looked at me with eyes of wonder set deep in his bony skull.

"Hear me, my brother. For the third and final time. I defy Death in all its forms, and I will never fear!"

I did not hear his answer, for at that moment, the trump signaling the charge sounded. I drew my sword, reveling in the ringing of my blood within my ears.

"Stay close to me, shrinking mouse. I will protect you!" I roared and slapped him on the shoulder to give him some of my courage. I felt bone beneath my hand and nothing more. But the foeman was before us, and I paid it little mind.

We rode into battle and glorious was the fray that day.

Men died, still clutching their killers by the throat. The wounded fell and bled where they lay, felling others in their turn from their place on the dying floor. The blood ran in streams and pooled, making the ground underfoot treacherous.

I wept with joy, loving the foeman. And why not? He was brave, as was I. He was strong, as was I. He feared not death, and we were, in that brief eternal instant, brothers - kin of spirit and strong heart.

They beat at me with their swords; they clashed at me with their axes. I felt the calciferous kiss of Death, and I pulled him to me in eager dance.

I bled, I wept, I laughed and I rejoiced.

Here, I am alive! Here, on Death's dance floor, I truly live!

We beat the foeman back and back, and I took my share of blood until my sword was notched and its edge looked like a saw. My hilt grew slippery with blood and I drank it down like fine wine in my thirst.

Glorious!

Glorious!

And then, when victory seemed within our grasp, my sword broke under my hand, and I felt the cold bite of a blade slide into my chest, piercing a lung and nicking the wall of my heart.

My brother, the poor trembling mouse, stood beside me, his sword in my side like an accusation.

His face was a skull. How had I not noticed it before? How had I not noticed the black, bottomless pits that were his eyes? It was so clear to me now.

"And are you afraid now, noble warrior? Now that Death slides his sword into you, do you still defy him?" His voice sounded like the closing of a king's tomb. His sword felt like the end of the world.

I looked into that face and the cold light of eternity shone back from the empty sockets of a skull.

I opened my mouth to laugh, to spit my final defiance in his face, but my voice was lost in the rush of blood . . . .

To Hunt the Great White Bear

The wind blew: low and cold. Snow crossed old Lemo's face in an age-old dance. He smiled wearily as he felt its glass-like scratchings.

Old Man Winter would be cruel this year.

Lemo pulled back inside. The sun was up as high as it got at this time of year, and it was proper to begin the hunt when the sun rose.

He looked to the fur-wrapped bundle that was his grandson. Mio smiled brightly at his grandfather and said nothing as he had been instructed. The Old Ways may be dying here in the land of the People, but Mio waited for his grandfather to speak, and that was proper. It brought hope to Lemo's weary heart.

"You must be quiet, Mio. We hunt the Great White Bear this day. He hears and he smells far, far better than we do. Do you understand me?"

"Yes, grandfather."

"Then come. Today you become a man." Gathering up only an ice-axe and his special satchel, Lemo left the warm and cozy igloo the men of his tribe made when they hunted.

He cast about, looking for scat. It didn't take long. The Great White Bear liked this section of ice. The wind blew unimpeded across the glass-like surface, cooling his hot, heavy skin under its layer of insulating fur.

Even through the special Otter-fur coats and leggings they wore, the cold was an all- pervasive thing. Many of the men of the People had adopted the new materials of the outlanders. "Why wear Otter-fur when we can wear Nomex?" They asked.

Lemo was saddened by this. Like so much, the ways of the Old Ones were being lost, not through the encroachment of the White Demons so much, but through a general apathy. He sighed and looked again into the bright, eager eyes of his grandson. Mio would at least have a taste of what it meant to be a man of the People. He would drink hunt-blood spilled the old way, and preserve the traditions of the People in his mind, hopefully to pass them on to his children.

After some searching, Lemo found an airhole in the ice: a large opening by which the Great White Bear came through the ice to swim and catch seals and fish. He beckoned Mio over and showed it to him, as well as the enormous paw prints leading to and from the icehole.

"See? The Great Bear comes here often. We will catch a large one here, Mio!"

Mio was silent, buy Lemo could see he carried questions in his eyes.

"What is it, Mio? What are you curious about?"

"Grandfather, how are we going to catch the Great White Bear? You have no rifle, no harpoon. You carry only a skinning knife!"

Lemo smiled a knowing smile, and laid a gnarled finger against the side of his nose. "We will catch one the Old way, Mio. You will see. For now, we wait."

Finding a likely hummock in plain view of the icehole, Lemo hunkered down behind it, keeping only his eyes above. He showed Mio how to cover himself with the heavier snow so as to block most of his scent and stay insulated from the wind. Then they waited.

After some time, a large polar bear trundled down to the icehole and splashed in. Lemo waited a moment, until he was sure the bear wasn't coming back, and then he opened his satchel.

He took out what he found inside, and motioning Mio to stay put, he moved to the icehole. Mio watched, wonderstruck, as Lemo moved around the icehole, putting something tiny on the ground every few inches around the ice, all the way around the icehold. He came back, carefully erasing his trail, and bringing his goods with him.

Lemo looked at his grandson and saw the questions were back.

Lemo showed Mio the items he had taken to the icehole. A can opener and an empty can of peas. Mio looked at the icehole, and yes, the small items did look like peas.

Lemo smiled when Mio turned confused eyes back toward him. "My grandfather showed me this, Mio. It never fails."

"But how will peas catch a Great White Bear?" Mio asked, momentarily forgetting the rules of the hunt.

"The bear will come out of the hole, all the way, trundling across the ice with his kill."

"Yes, grandfather," Mio said, respectfully, as he had been taught.

"He will smell the peas, however, and he will come back to the hole. The Great White Bear cannot resist the smell of peas."

"Yes, grandfather, but . . ."

Lemo smiled, holding a hand up. "As I said, Mio, The Great White Bear cannot resist the smell of peas. So when The Great White Bear comes back to the hole to take a pea, we rush up and kick him in the icehole."

Mio nodded in understanding, and they waited for the bear to return, the wind blowing away the questions, the answers and all confusions.

The Queen of Sheba

She cups my face in her hands and stares down at me with her dark, dark eyes. Her lips - so full, so wet - are inches from mine. The heat of her breath is making my skin tingle.

Her breasts, round and full, are heaving in a way that tells me I've done my job correctly.

She sits atop me, taking charge of our intimacy in a way that brooks no argument.

I love making love to her.

She likes to take her time, to enjoy herself. She approaches sex like it's a buffet instead of a meal with one course. There's seduction, teasing, foreplay, and finally, the great consummation itself.

Don't hear me complaining at all, do you?

She's lowering herself onto me, her movements slow, languid. Her body is telling me she'd be perfectly happy to do this all night long.

I'm only too glad to let her.

The skin moving slowly beneath my hands is the color of burnt chocolate. I gently cup her left breast in my hands and suckle sweetly on her nipple. It tastes like the coconut oil she uses to keep her skin soft and moist. She cradles my head in her hands, pulling me up toward her. This pushes me ever so slightly inside her, and she makes a contented noise.

"Dark am I, yet lovely," she says in my ear before kissing the top of my head and rocking her hips forward.

She pushes me away from her and arches her back above me, slowly riding her way down until I've reached all the way inside her. She looks down at me, her lips quirking into the smile I've come to love. There is sweat forming on her upper lip and on her brow, and I raise myself just enough to taste it.

This pushes me deep inside her, and she gives a quiet, involuntary gasp of pleasure.

I smile up at her and pull her down into my embrace.

~~~~~~~

We met at school. She was studying anthropology, and I was muddling my way through a post-doctorate. For whatever reason, I'd seen fit to get my degrees in Folklore, with a specialization in Biblical applications.

I was going to starve to death, but I'd be happy about it, anyway.

The college had a Student's Night at one of the local bars, and feeling the need to drink some cheap booze and mingle with others of my social set, I went. She was sitting at the bar with a group of her friends, and the first time I laid eyes on her, I was absolutely smitten. It took me twenty minutes to work up the nerve to approach her, and then hr friends wouldn't leave. Eventually, serendipity interceded, and a seat to her left opened up. Without thinking about it, I sat down next to her.

"Hi. Would you mind if I joined you?"

She looked me over coolly, giving nothing away. Her eyes, though uninterested, were gorgeous, and I found myself writing silly poems about them in my head.

"Free country. You can sit wherever you want."

"Thanks! . . . Hey . . . Uhh . . . Shit. Look, I'm uhh . . . ."

I fell apart and nearly spilled my drink. I didn't actually start hyperventilating, but my hands were shaking pretty hard and I could feel sweat running down my back. She sighed and rolled her eyes up.

"White boy, whatever it is, I ain't interested."

I nodded and rose from my stool, disappointed but unsurprised. I'd heard the stories about black and white dating; how many black girls turned white guys down as a matter of course, and vice versa. "Yeah. Well, to be honest, I kinda thought that might be the case. I'm sorry if I bothered you. I'll find someplace else to sit. You have a nice night, okay?"

I could feel her eyes on me as I walked away, making my way through the crowd. The music was up pretty high, so I'm still not sure how I heard her.

"Hey!"

She was standing near her stool, smiling at me. I walked back, not sure what to make of this.

"Yeah?"

"You're just gonna give up like that? You aren't gonna try to run some moves on me or something? You ain't even got some snappy one-liners? Damn, boy! You could of made some kind of an effort!"

There was no mistaking it. She was smiling from ear to ear. I wasn't sure if she was making fun of me or not, but I didn't sense any malice in her voice or eyes.

"One-liners?"

Not the best rejoinder, I know. But she had me off-balance and reeling.

"Yeah! One-liners! You know, 'Girl. You look so fine, you make my eyes sweat! But you know what? I can't see so good. Whyn'tchu take that dress off, let me get a closer look?"

"That's pretty good!"

"You like that? I had a brother drop that one on me the other night. It made me laugh so hard I spilled my drink."

Now I was smiling. I'm not suave or sophisticated with the ladies. I tend to use the "Bull Ahead" approach: "I like you. Wanna date?"

"Boy. That'd be useful here, huh? Well, I ain't got none of those. Sorry. I can burp the alphabet while doing a goofy dance I learned when I was a kid. Would that work?"

She snorted a laugh.

"Are you making fun of me, white boy?"

The "white boy" was a challenge, and I recognized it. It was the second time tonight she'd used it. She was testing my mettle, so I thought I'd rise to the bait.

"No more than you are of me, black girl."

She tried to go all flat-eyed and mean, but she was smiling a little too much to pull it off. I made use of the moment to bull on ahead.

"Can I buy you a drink?"

"You know what? I think you can. I like your style."

~~~~~~

She was so dichotomous. She was the most articulate, literate and well-spoken person I'd ever met, but when she wanted to make me laugh, or she was making a point about black-white differences, or she just wanted to yell at me for something, her voice took on what she referred to as an "ebonic" quality.

It made me smile. When she stared dropping "bruthas", consonants, and elongating her vowels, I had to bite my lip to keep from laughing. She grew up in Connecticut, for crying out loud.

She asked me about it once, and I tried to explain it to her.

"I know what you're about, white boy. You're all about getting with a sister because you know we start fires in bed."

"Yeah. I've heard that. I always kinda assumed it was a stereotype, though. Kinda like white comedians making jokes about black guys' penises."

"So that's not what you're after. That's what you're trying to tell me?"

"I could care less. You're the woman I love. You make me smile, you make me laugh, you make me think, you make me crazy. You make me come, beautiful, just by being you."

"And me being black as the ace of spades don't mean nothing at all? You sure you don't just have a world-class case of jungle fever?"

"What'd I just say, woman?"

Her eyes widened and she put a hand on her hip. I smiled, knowing what was coming.

"Awwww, no. You tryin' to get hard with me, honky? I'll snatch you up like yo' momma should've!"

I snorted a laugh. "You're sooo strict, momma."

"Shut up, white boy."

She smiled at me and my world melted again.

~~~~~~

I remember what we were talking about, and I remember him saying it, but I don't remember anything much after that until she had her arms around me and I realized I was hitting her.

We'd gone to a local diner. Just thrown on some clothes for decency's sake, a pair of ball caps, and left.

We sat at a booth, next to each other, holding hands and talking. The sultry, nectarous, aroma of our lovemaking clung to us. I kept leaning over her and breathing it in. I bit her bottom lip and the nape of her neck, and tickled and pinched where the tickling and pinching was good.

"I love you."

"I love you, too, beautiful."

"No, I mean it. I really love you. I love the way you just . . . I don't know, 'be you,' I guess. It's not . . . it's not . . . Hell. I don't know. I guess I never really thought about it before, but if somebody'd asked me about loving a white person . . . "

I interrupted her. "It's not important. It's just- Listen. The color of your skin is about as important to me as the color of my hair is to you."

"You know, I still think you'd look good with some cornrows."

"Look here, girly. You make me listen to R. Kelly sing when I'd rather have live ants poured into my ears. We'll talk about the cornrows when I see you headbangin' to som-"

"Well lookit the nigger an' her sweet little-boy nigger-lover."

I wish I could tell you that the person who'd said this was some greasy, hairy, smelly, inbred redneck stereotype. I wish I could tell you I answered reasonably and logically. I wish I could tell you anything other than what I have to.

My head whipped around. A man was standing there. His skin was white. His hair was short, blonde, and cut close to the skin. He wore a black t-shirt with nothing on it. His blue jeans were clean. His sneakers were new.

He looked to be in his early twenties, and his eyes were dull and twisted with a hate he didn't understand.

"What did you just say?"

My girl laid a placating hand on my arm. "No. Please. Don't . . . "

"Better listen to your little nigger-cunt there, you dirty race-traitor-nigger-lover. Time is comin' when all her kind are gonna be wiped-"

I jumped up and hit him and the fight was on.

~~~~~~~

"But don't you understand, boy? He won. Not you!"

"What are you talking about? I kicked that jerk's butt!"

"Oh, yeah. You kicked his butt, bookworm. He's gonna have those scratches for weeks. What'd that accomplish, white boy? Huh?"

"Did you not hear what he called you?"

"Yeah. I heard it. I've been hearing it my whole life from people who don't know any better. And you know what, white boy? It's just a word! Where is "Nigger-land"? Huh? Where do niggers come from? What language do they speak? Huh? I mean, I've been staring at maps for hours trying to find Niggerania on a map, and I couldn't find it anywhere."

"Come on. You know-"

"No. That's just it, sweet-heart. I don't know. I get mad at that poor white boy, he has power over me. You understand? That poor, uninformed racist, spreading his hate and his bile all over the place, he has power over me, a sister of grace and poise. You understand?"

"Nope. Not even a little bit."

"How many black people you think he's called that? You remember the way he was grinning and leering? You know why? That silly boy, he's been calling us black folks that for a while now. He does it because some black folks get angry, and that makes him feel good. Smart, rich, articulate black people, the white boy calls him a name and they start fighting down at his level. It's what he wants! Don't you get it? He wants to see them pounding away at him in the dirt. He wants to see them get their clothes all torn and get dirt on their faces. He wants to enslave us again! People like that, they think black people are little more than apes. When you piss one off, it starts hooting. What you did by hitting him was set his cause forward that much further."

"So I should've just let him say those things to you? Is that what you're saying?"

"It's a free country! Anybody can say any dumbass thing they want to! That's the definition of Free Speech! What's it to you? What do you care if that ol' boy says dumb stuff? Huh?"

She was shouting at me, but her eyes were soft and sad, full of a disappointment I didn't understand.

I was cleaning my knuckles as best I was able. Near as I can figure, I'd managed to tear them open on his belt-buckle. They stung like fire and oozed blood all over. The fight hadn't been much of anything. I'm an academic, not a cage fighter. I've never been in anything more serious than a pushing match in seventh grade. I jumped up and hit him as hard as I could, and then kinda flailed at him as we went down. It probably looked a bit like two chickens slapping at each other. Not one of my prouder moments.

The diner's waitresses and cooks kicked us all out and shouted from behind locked doors that they were calling the cops. We got in our car and went home.

She pulled me away from the sink and put her hands on my shoulders. She looked me in the eyes, and I was surprised to see a smile.

"Think about his life for a minute, baby. He's never benefited from the noble grace of a sister. He's never had a proud, strong, wise, black prince of a brother in his life to give him a righteous beatdown when he's acting a fool. He's never had a Momma love him and lift his name to Jesus in front of all the neighbors. Baby, if anything, you should feel sorry for the empty, hollow, shallow life he must lead. Any interactions he's had with black people have been colored by his hate. He's never had a meal with us, never been to a dance with us, never held one of us close in the dark of the night. His heart is empty, baby-boy. I mean, a life without some soul in it?"

I grinned ruefully at her at that, and said, sheepishly, "I'd rather be dead, myself."

"Yeah, well, you ain't all that dumb . . . "

"Why, thank you."

" . .. for a stupid-ass cracker."

"Yeah, yeah. Remind me not to ever defend your honor, ever again."

"Learn to fight, first."

She gave me one of her hot, slow, heavy kisses, and, with a smile of open invitation, walked into the bedroom. I grinned, bandaged my knuckles, and followed.

The Fist of Hand

Well now. Here we are. Like it? All nice and cozy?

No?

Yeah, well, it's going to get worse, I'm afraid. A lot worse.

It used to belong to my Dad. He was a real nut for old-school cars. I used to think that he'd buy 'em just because they were big and old.

I imagine you've got a great view of all the work he put into the underbody: all those reinforcing struts and heavy brackets. Must weigh a good couple of tons.

Now what you're feeling there is a special recipe of mine. Yeah. It'll make pretty short work of your clothes and the first few layers of skin. The next few hours are going to be pretty awful for you. It's slow acting stuff and it's bound to be just as painful as all get out the entire time. Interestingly, you can buy all of the ingredients in a grocery store. I call it "bathtub napalm". I love this country. Did you know you can buy half-gallon containers of battery acid in larger hardware stores? It's true! And that stuff you're swimming in, I bought all of that at a grocery store. It's basically just a stew of different over-the-counter cleaning products mixed into a diesel fuel base. If I lit a cigarette, they'd hear the explosion from about a half mile away. It's amazing what you can find on the internet, isn't it?

It works like this: the rope hawsers on your wrists and ankles keep you nicely suspended over a hole I dug a few days ago. I put one of those big troughs you can buy for watering cattle and stuff in the bottom of the hole, and filled it with my special sauce.

Now you'll notice that I've got you suspended over this hole and underneath the engine block of my dad's old baby.

Big, isn't it?

Well, learn to appreciate it, because the ropes will gradually stretch and sag under the weight of the engine block, pushing you into the trough. You can stay alive pretty much indefinitely, assuming it doesn't rain, the sides of the hole don't shift, and you're able to hold muscular tension. Of course, if you do manage to somehow survive the next few days, you're going to be horribly scarred, disfigured and in an obscene amount of pain.

So isn't that nice? I've given you an out.

Listen; let me ask you something. Did you know anything at all about your father-in-law? No? Well, consider this to be a graphic illustration of how beneficial hindsight can sometimes be.

See, your father-in-law has what's known in my line of work as "connections". He knows people, that know people, who can get things - and I mean most anything at all - done. In your case, he asked around until he got a name.

Mine.

Well, no, Hand isn't my real name. It's a title. But it's what I answer to, and there isn't anyone alive who knows better. I ought to know. I'm pretty thorough.

He met me, gave me a lot of money, told me what he wanted, and well, here we are.

It's times like this, with the sound of birds chirping somewhere nearby, the wind blowing fresh and clean from the rising sun, the smell of bathtub chemicals and the panic-stricken shouts of perfect human terror in the air, that I find focus in remembering my very first time.

You're just one of many, dude. One of a very long list.

Does that bother you? Seems to me like it shouldn't matter one way or the other, but whatever. Some people are really weird that way, like they're sleeping with a prostitute or something.

"Ohhhh. Don't *you* kill me. Get somebody else!"

Like we've got cooties or something.

Anyway.

So.

We've got some time to kill here. You a fan of sports?

No?

What about politics? You want to talk about politics?

No?

Okay. Well, maybe I could tell you a story.

Yeah. A story. I'd like to tell you a story.

You don't mind, do you? I mean, it's not like you're going anywhere, right?

No, don't move. That'll just hurt. Look. We're going to be here for a long time. You might as well relax and let it happen. Fighting is just going to rob you of your dignity and nobody's going to hear the screaming. I mean, we're in the *sticks* here.

What?

Why?

Well, I can tell you, but it I don't know that it'll make any difference one way or the other. Are you sure you want to know? It might actually make things that much worse. I mean, don't believe the movies, dude. There's no last minute rescue thing gonna happen here and this is going to be pretty bad all the way around.

You sure?

Well, alright. It was like this.

I was actually having a very nice lunch of steamed clams and shrimp toast at this little hole-in-the-wall place I go to when I'm in town. Mimosas to die for! And they do this thing with coconut milk and rum that'd make your whole face go numb. It's run by this little Korean couple: an old woman and her husband, or brother, or whatever the hell he is. They kind of look a little alike, but I understand couples who've been married for a long time sometimes do.

So, whatever. I'm in there, chowing down on the fusion-cuisine-thing, when this crawling lick-spittle walks right up to my table.

You know, if you're going to do that, it's going to be really hard for me to tell this story. Just bite the inside of your cheek or something! I don't want to have to gag you! You gonna be quiet? I could easily reach in there and cut your tongue out. It wouldn't be all that hard.

Alright. Keep it shut.

Anyway. This bag of maggots walks up to the table.

What?

Well, yeah, he's nothing to me. An insignificant annoyance. But he's a *paying* insignificant annoyance, and you're the job. If I started doing the job the wrong way, I'd never hear the end of it.

What?

Nope. Can't do that. And you're wasting your time asking.

No, I don't care how much money you offer me. It's the principle of the thing. Besides. At this point you'll say pretty much anything in the hope that I'll stop. In fact, if I wanted to I could make you say anything at all! I can twist this hawser here, like so, and tell you if you sing three verses of 'Little Teapot' I'll untwist it.

No, no, no!

Shrieking it at the top of your lungs, as fast as you can spit it, isn't what I had in mind at all! I'm a serious connoisseur of music! Take a deep breath and sing it in four-four time.

Come on! You know the words! I'm sure you sang them often enough in your little boudoir, you sick bastard. "I'm a liiiiiitle teaPOT!"

That's okay. I can wait.

That's a little better. Two more verses.

You're getting there! One more time!

There! Now I'll untwist it! See? That wasn't so hard, now was it?

Where was I?

Okay, okay. Stop shrieking!

What?

Well, yeah, maybe. I mean, *all* people are insignificant bugs, but you men are just that much worse. What do you call that? Miso . . . meeee-soooo . . . miso, meso-something. Misogyny, but dudes, not chicks. Don't get me wrong. I hate chicks, too. In fact, I hate people in general, but weak people just make me sick and weak men make the rage within me just boil up all over in a sad flood. This dude incarnated all of that in a pathetic little, comb-over, horse-haired suit. He looked like eighteen pounds of used cat-litter in a five pound bag. But you'd know that, wouldn't you? He's your father-in-law.

Look, just pipe down, okay? You had to know this was coming eventually.

So anyway, this fly-bait walks up to me and asks me if he can join me at my table. He's got a briefcase that I assume is full of money.

You have no idea how much that pisses me off. I mean, here I am trying to have a nice, quiet lunch, and this weakling comes looking to hire me for something he should be taking care of himself.

If it was me, and it was one of my kids you'd been messing with, I'd've just knee-capped you and dragged you down to the tide-line one night. I know this little tidal pool an hour's drive from City Hall. With all that rich, salty blood draining down your legs, and all the thrashing and screaming you'd've been doing after I dragged you, naked, across a mile of open beach, you'd be shark-bait in no time.

Sink or swim, baby.

But, tragically, most people just don't have my well-defined sense of perfect self-interest. I should be grateful, I guess. I'd have to work for a living if they did.

So he sits down and he starts telling me his tale of woe. His lovely daughter has married herself a pedophile - that's you, dirt bag - and instead of doing what any good father would do, two large caliber bullets to the back of the head - he's come to me with a pile of money and a set of instructions.

Now me, I'm all like "Your dumb broad of a daughter married the creepo, and he was no doubt a pedophile before he married her. Why are you getting all bent out of shape and pretending like your daughter is this vision of innocence?"

See? I stuck up for you. It takes two to tango, and all that.

But he got all self-righteous and indignant, and he's telling me all those sob-stories about his innocent wife and the crimes being perpetuated against her.

It's not polite to yawn, I know, but what are you going to do, right?

He told me all about you, big boy. He told me about the studio you've got in your basement and he told me about the glory holes. He started crying when he got to the part about his grandkids.

I mean, don't get me wrong. I hate the whole human race, but it takes real talent to make me pay attention to a tale of woe. You can take that to hell with you as you go, homie. I'm impressed by your absolute devotion to debauchery. It takes a real cockroach to prey on his own freaking kids like that.

So anyway, he's telling me all about you, how sick and depraved you are, and I find my sense of personal outrage waking. Funnily enough, at *him*, not you. You're a sick bastard, no question, but he's almost as bad. He's too weak to protect his own family. If it weren't for the fact that nobody's paid me for it, he'd probably be under there with you. Hell, it'd almost be a public service. A little chlorine in the gene pool, retroactive birth control.

I learn what I can about you through his nearly incoherent, dissociative, sobbing ramblings and then I interrupt him with a number.

It's about style, see? You can't just go "Oh, okay, Leonard. I'll do that for this much money and you have a good day!" No. You gotta give 'em good value for their money. Me, I like to go all steely-eyed, lean into, like, a falling shaft of sunlight, and quote my price in a single word. It's drama, and it's showmanship and it's smart business. More often than not, they crap their pants and agree to whatever price I quote.

You should be flattered. The price I quoted your dear old dad was five times what I normally charge for this kind of thing. His eyes nearly bugged out and I could see him wanting to protest. I nearly ganked him right then and there, dude. I really did. A freebie, just for me. Here he was, all sobbing and bent out of shape about your crimes, and when he finds somebody who's strong enough to do what he's not, he quibbles about the price.

Douchebag.

I fix my eyes on him and I watch as his face crumples. He paid, son. He paid, and through the nose, because he hates you more than anything, that's true. But he also paid because he's too afraid of me not to.

He tried to get his dignity back after that, wiping at his eyes, and trying to look at me all hard.

"I agree to your demands, but I want him to suffer," he says, like he's in charge.

I just nod. I've already dismissed this meek, jowly, Armani-encapsulated little whore.

"That's what I do," I say, all hard and cold. It was like something right out of a movie.

He leaves the briefcase and I finish my lunch. I pay the bill and I go looking for you.

Didn't take me long to find you, did it?

You done down there yet?

No?

Okay, guess I'll ramble on some more. It's not often I get a captive audience like this. You like stories?

I do. I *love* stories. Wanna hear one?

No?

Too bad. It ain't like you've got a choice. You're the one dissolving in bathtub chemicals, not me. Seems to me you'd want to be a little nicer to me. But whatever.

Wanna know what my inspiration is?

I'll take your silence as a tacit agreement. See, it's like this: most people are insignificant bugs. Sounds sick, doesn't it? It's true though. Most people deserve to be turned into cat food and buried in a landfill. The few interesting ones usually want something of you that's well beyond what you're willing to offer.

Needless to say, I'm not much of a people person. You talk to me; you should probably consider yourself pretty amazing if you walk away with all your body parts.

I don't like people.

I prefer to work alone.

Now, before you get glassy-eyed and full of dramatic ideas, it's not because I'm some sort of 'lone-wolf-vixen'. I've worked with others before, even been a part of a team. There's no classically romanticized reason for my preferring solitude. With a partner you have to split the profits and if there's one thing I *do* like, it's money.

I find my solitude suits me. It gives me time to know myself, to strip away the layers of concealing make-up and identify exactly who and what I am. I move around a lot, too. I don't know that many people would enjoy moving around the globe a couple of times a decade.

My general rule of thumb is 'three years in one place at a time'. Three years is enough time to set up shop, touch base with all the most prominent players likely to be interested in my services, establish a bit of a rep, and still avoid being fingered by the more attentive police organizations. I'm very careful about not having an M.O., but all it takes is one mistake and one police investigator paying attention to something other than the finger up his nose.

It's not an easy way to live for the undisciplined. You've got to cut away all the unnecessary fat of life and live spare, sparse and hard. For instance: like horses? Like watching horses run? Well, if you want to pursue my line of work, you can't go to a racetrack more than once a year, and never more than twice in a decade. If I lived in Louisville Kentucky, I could go see the Derby once in ten years.

Once.

Imagine that.

'Why is that, Hand?'

Well, if you start establishing a pattern of behavior, eventually somebody somewhere is going to notice it and you'll become a liability. Nobody wants to hire the young lady with the great, big target on her forehead and the t-shirt that says, 'Hey pigs! Here I am! Come arrest me!'

You've got to learn to strip away the romance, too. In this line of work I bump into an awful lot of people who think that being a contract killer is some sort of an excuse to walk around in dark glasses and a glower, with weapons strapped all over your body. I try not to giggle when I see that, but I can't help but think 'Mullethead with a pair of nunchucks' every time.

Look, black leather pants and a pair of evil sunglasses don't make you a killer. Having your arm up to the elbow in somebody's guts and not gagging makes you a killer.

I was watching this show a couple of months ago. I was in Dallas, Texas, doing a job for an oil company, and I'd set up shop inside a dingy motel on the uglier side of town. I was eating some take-out and flipping through the channels on the TV, trying to find something that'd be remotely interesting.

I came across one of those real-life journalism shows, where they interview some horrible scab about something unspeakable. Like, nympho cannibals, or something. This show featured a guy who'd killed some people. You could tell he liked that; the attention of the moment. He was basking in the adulation and fear of the interviewer and he was milking it for all it was worth. I almost choked, I was laughing so hard. Guy killed three or four people in as messy a fashion as I've ever seen, used a big knife, got caught, and now he's a 'mad-dog killer'?

Please.

Guy's a retard who deserves to be horse-whipped. I volunteer for the honors.

Killing somebody doesn't require any real skill or finesse or anything. If you've ever killed a bug, you can kill a person. It's simply a matter of over-riding your head's reluctance to follow the commands your body wants to anyway. What requires skill and a bit of luck is getting close to the loser in question, doing the job, and then getting away with it. This moron got caught because he wanted everybody to know how very dangerous he is.

What a tool.

There's nothing glamorous about this job. If you think there is, you're in the wrong line of work. There's nothing pretty about slitting a screaming mark up the middle like a fish and letting him watch his intestines splash the ground. There's nothing glamorous about having sex with a fifty-year-old, fat man who smells like pigeon droppings so you can get close to a mark who's a friend of his. There's nothing fun about pulling a bullet out of your left forearm, with a pair of boiled tweezers, because going to the hospital is out of the question.

You're a whore.

You contract out your body for a specified amount of time to accomplish a very specific goal. Sure, they pay you a lot more than the average hooker makes, but you're still a whore.

It helps to be clear-eyed about who and what you are.

'So why are you the best, Hand?'

I'm the best because I do whatever it takes to do whatever you want me to. My rates are whatever the hell I feel like charging you. People who want the best pay without saying a word, and they know they've paid for a job already done. I never ever walk away from a job that's undone. I take a ten percent 'meeting fee', up front, without hearing the job's details. I take half before the job for expenses and I collect the rest when it's done. The decision to proceed with the job is solely mine. The right of rejection is mine as well. Either way, I keep the ten percent, and no one will ever hear about our meeting. People who look for people like me appreciate that sort of discretion more than anything else I do. I've never disappointed a customer yet.

My work comes in three categories: embarrassing people, hurting people, and killing people.

Embarrassing people is for the lord-high-mucketty-mucks of the world. Suppose you're running for public office, and you've got an untouchable opponent. He/she doesn't smoke, doesn't drink, doesn't gamble, goes to church three times a week, kisses babies, pets puppies and is faithful to his wife and children. Well, that's where I come in. For a steep fee, I'll guarantee your opponent's downfall within a specified period of time. You either agree to pay, or I walk.

I did this once for an election in Greece. A young man badly wanted to be a mayor but his opponent was likable, squeaky clean, handsome and attended church regularly. He wasn't gonna be beat. So this douchebag gets ahold of me. I took his money, hired some actors, and a week later, a photo-shop-altered photograph of the douche bag's opponent, enjoying the dubious pleasures of an S&M orgy with four girls under the age of fifteen and five boys even younger, were being sold around town in every newspaper. I understand those photos made three trips around the world. It cost me three hundred bucks to hire the actors. Fifteen minutes with a scanner and a good color printer later, I was done.

The douche bag won his election, I was paid handsomely, and everybody walked away happy, except for the opponent, I guess.

Hurting people's even easier. You tell me who you want hurt, then you tell me how, and I go do it. I've broken bones, I've altered features, I've set fire to hair, I've tossed acid, I've removed digits, whatever. Who, when, where, and how: that's all I need. If you'd like me to say something to the victim, that'll cost extra.

I tend to charge more for these kinds of jobs because they can get ugly. People don't like being hurt - I know I don't like it - and a combative mark is a hard-to-service mark.

I remember one job where a minor drug lord in Venezuela was convinced his mistress was stepping out on him. He wanted her to hurt for hurting him, so he contacted me. The mistress had this glorious mane of dark hair, like the fall of a raven's wing. It was thick, lustrous and it fell to the backs of her legs, this foaming, delightful wash of glorious hair. She was famous for it. Did interviews and made commercials and everything.

"I want that belo' bald! You take her someplace an' you make her bald as a feesh! All of her hair!"

"All of it?" I asked

"All of it!"

I took her in a mall she frequented. Just stuck a pistol in her ribs and walked her out to a van. I tied her hands and feet together, flipped her over on her stomach, and stuffed a gag down her throat. I cut all of her clothes off. Then I went to work.

I clipped the hair down to the skin, shaved it with a straight razor, and then used a bottle of barbacide on her freshly shaved pate, making sure I rubbed it in really well.

I did the same thing to her eyebrows, eyelashes and all of her body hair. Her eyes ran tears and she shook with barely controlled sobs. She looked like a bit of raw chicken liver when I was done, all pink and processed.

When she was as bald as a fish, I cut her bonds, held the gun on her and tossed an attention-getting outfit at her: a loud Hawaiian shirt and pair of orange shorts. I told her to get dressed. When she was done, I drove the van to a downtown intersection and made her get out.

Then I drove away.

Her hair never did grow back.

Last I heard, the drug lord had married his little fish and had four kids. Some people like skin, I guess. Go figure.

So. Where was I?

I gotta tell ya', this story telling is thirsty work! I could kill a Red Bull!

Where?

Oh. Right. Killing people. Well, to kill people you gotta find work. And finding work can be a problem. It's not like you can just go to the newspapers and advertise. You have to make contacts, and you make contacts by doing 'freebie' jobs.

My method was to find a local bar and ask around about getting some weed. Eventually a name pops up. I buy a baggie, do a few tokes with the dealer, then ask him if he knows anybody who needs some work done. Sometimes you hafta go all the way up the ladder before you get to somebody with decision-making power, but eventually somebody'll be hiring. You do a few jobs to establish your street cred, and our name gets around. You might be there for a little while, doing smaller jobs, but the program usually pays off. Careful and concise, that's my motto.

When you establish your willingness and ability to the right people, eventually the money comes in. Until then you've either got to find a job, or live off macaroni and cheese in a trailer someplace. It can take a very long time. It took me three years.

Others prefer having a 'broker' or a 'handler'. I've worked with one in the past, but I've since found them to be unnecessary. Once you get to the point where you can afford my services, you've gone well beyond the means of a simple assassin. My name is known in all the best and highest circles at this point. I basically just need to show up and let the heavy hitters know I'm in town. It isn't hard, either. Cap somebody in the news; maybe break a leg of a local bully, whatever.

I'm the very best, after all.

Besides, I don't want or need a pimp.

My first and only 'handler' was a guy named Jackson. I never asked if that was a first or last name, and I never really cared. We'd met through an associate of mine. There was this twenty-year-old-Valley-Girl-blonde I knew, who called herself 'Hula'. We met when I was doing a job. This little retard walked up to me, in a public place, her head tilted to the side, and her eyes emptily vacuous, and asked me if I was Hand.

At the time I was on extended contract for a local crime family. I did the dirty things that required an anonymous touch, yet sent an unmistakable message. I fit the bill quite nicely, but I was starting to feel the urge to move on. The work was nice and steady, working for mafiosos always is, but staying in one place, holding down a nine-to-five job for one person has never really appealed to me.

I was at a McDonald's, of all places, watching my mark, and thinking about moving early. Maybe someplace warm for a while.

The mark was an easy one. The guy had a thing for McDonald's quarter-pounder that bordered on religious devotion. All I had to do was follow him to McDonald's when his munchie urge hit. He'd been dipping his fingers into family funds, and the boss wanted them removed. It was to be a 'graphic, public demonstration'.

I was sitting in a booth, my duffle, with over-sized wire-cutters at hand, and was just waiting for my mark to sit down and eat his quarter-pounder. A quick wrist lock, a snip, and I'd be done.

Hula, the silly thing, was eating a Big Mac in a booth on the other side of the restaurant. When she saw me, she did a double-take, stared at me for a few minutes, and then walked right up to me and asked me if I was Hand.

I looked at her, wondering if I was going to have to kill her here and now, in front of all these potential witnesses, when she'd laughed and handed me a card.

It had been her business card: home phone number, cell phone number, and the name 'Jackson'.

The rest, as they say, is history.

Jackson had been a great handler, up until he decided he wanted to move our relationship into a personal level.

He got me some really good gigs. Jackson knew movers and shakers and they always want something ugly done by a professional. He took a nominal ten-percent off the top of every job, and he never went anywhere with my money. If it were in me to be grateful, I'd be grateful to Jackson. He helped to make me the name I am today.

He was quite a looker, too. His skin was the dull dark of burned ebony and he had an infectious grin. I won't say whether I succumbed to that grin or not, that's none of your business. If I did, you can be assured it I enjoyed it immensely.

He dressed well and carried himself with a dignity that never-the-less allowed him to laugh as loud and as hard as anyone I've ever known. I admired the way he moved. His every action was like a dance, moving fluidly from one position to another.

He had a vast breadth of conversation and interests that spread from wine to music to Greek philosophy. Yes, Jackson was very easy to like. I'd probably still be working with him if it weren't for his one mistake. What is it about men that make them believe that they can have you just for the asking?

He'd called me late one night and told me he had something he needed to discuss with me. I knew he wouldn't just ring me for a Booty Call, so I went over to his place. I knocked on the door and he was standing there in a bath robe. There were candles lit all over his apartment and I could smell something delicious cooking on the stove. He smiled that infectious grin at me, and told me he wanted to 'discuss our future together'.

I left him face down and bleeding in the linguini.

The wine had been pretty good, though.

You whine a lot for such a big guy, you know that? Seems to me you should spend a little less effort begging for your life, and a little more effort pulling those ropes tight. But, hey, what do I know, right? I'm not the one being pushed into a pool full of chemicals. Maybe you know something I don't under there. Whatever.

You want more of this story?

Too bad. I feel like talking.

Being a woman in this line of work is tough. There seems to be some sort of expectation that you're either a 'dangerous black widow', a crazed nymphomaniac, or some sort of silent, deadly, exotically-beautiful, but horribly-damaged flower. Like, "I just want someone to save me from myself!" I blame James Bond and Anne Rice. I'm not any of those, though I've played them to get what I want.

No, I made a choice to live this way a long time ago. There's nothing romantic about it. Nothing that can be labeled as 'lonely' or 'noble' or any of that other crap.

It's simple. I take money from people to hurt or kill other people. It's a job and I'm the very best at it. That's it. You don't get this 'Mission: Impossible' thing happening, and it's not like I'm being chased through the streets of Paris by shadowy Worldwide Conspiracy groups. It's a job like any other.

No, I'm not beautiful, I'm not exotic, and I'm not some sort of slinky, pajamed ninja.

I'm a whore that kills people.

I was in Europe this year. I've found life in the Americas to be a little too confining. Americans in general are reacting like a bruised membrane: seal off the point of injury and close all borders. Makes things a little hairy in my line of work. The South Americans are just as bad. They're being pressured by their bigger, louder neighbors to the north, and it's all just a little too much for little, old me.

I've been there before, of course. I had a pretty good time in the late nineties. Stayed in a nice little flat overlooking the Thames. This was my first European cycle this decade, and it's almost like a vacation.

I like Europe. There's a certain air of 'laissez faire' that seems to lie over the entire continent. In Asia, or America, there's this 'Go-Go-GO!' thing happening. 'Got to make my millions, got to be a success. Got to have a bigger pool in my McMansion's back yard.'

I walk down a street in, saaay, I don't know, Berlin, and I'll see Germans sitting at sidewalk cafes, drinking a coffee or reading a paper. Paris, same thing. Europeans know how to stop and reprioritize. Americans have never figured that out and Asians - specifically the Japanese - actually have a word for 'dying while on the job due to overwork'.

Despite this, Europeans, as a people, seem to need my services more than any other nationality I've run into. I know. That's not very PC, is it? Kind of lumping a whole race of people together, aren't I? Well, you know what you can do if you don't like it. It's not like I'm hiding.

There's something about the Franco/Gallic mindset that just cries out for someone like me. I'm not sure if it's the tendency toward neatness, or if it's a romantic inclination to vendetta, or what, but I make loads of money in Europe. I've been approached by financial conglomerates, religious groups, and governments. I've done jobs for royalty and local crime families. I've left a string of bodies buried all over this continent, like a rope of macabre beads.

No, I'm not going to give you any names. Don't ask again. I could tell you, but is knowing worth a double-tap between the eyes? Well, in your case it'd probably come as a relief . . . but, whatever. I'm still not telling you. Professional standards and all that.

Sometimes you just can't help it. You know it's unprofessional, you know it might get you caught, you know you might end up getting labeled as soft, and you go do it anyway.

A job goes off in such a way as to resemble a work of art. It's graceful, it's beautiful and it's perfect. You could just walk away and let the art of the moment speak for itself, but sometimes you have to see the final results, the loose and untidy ends resolved, come what may.

I was in Chicago for the week and I was contacted about making a hit on a local businessman named Arnold "Sticks" Stickler. He ran heavy numbers in the auto salvage industry and he was beginning to crowd less-reputable business interests in the same area.

Translation – "Sticks" Stickler, a rags-to-riches success story, half crippled from childhood polio; vigorous and active at the age of seventy-nine, was pushing into mob-controlled territory and they didn't like it.

"Bust a cap in 'im," was the terse, succinct instructions I received, along with a bulging briefcase – my initial ten percent.

These boys don't play nice. They either do the work themselves or they contact someone like me if things are a bit . . . 'sensitive' . . . I guess.

I figured it'd be an in and out kind of job. Sticks was an affable guy, well-liked by the community, and not into security in a big way. If I was lucky I could do the scouting in a day or two, make the hit by the end of the week.

Arnold operated out of an uptown office, a new place, with wood and brass and all the trimmings so necessary for the up-and-coming, high-powered, rich executive looking to impress his golfing buddies. He owned three floors in the seventy-nine floor plaza. Security was of the mickey-mouse-variety. 'Hand 'em a badge, make sure they sign in, wish 'em 'good morning', and go back to your coffee and donuts'.

It's amazing what some people will accept for the illusion of security.

I spent twenty bucks downtown, making copies of the architect's blueprints, specifically focusing on the air conditioning system.

Seems like it'd be pretty Hollywood, but many buildings really do provide major access to their central-air ducts in the bathrooms on every floor. Central air ducts provide access to most every office on the floor. For those of you not paying close attention: access to the air ducts equals access to every office.

There's a "We won't disturb the employees if we need to fix something," school of thought at work here, and it's a joy to see.

This doesn't mean I was gonna be climbing through an air duct. I just needed to know how they were laid out so I could fool a guy who worked in the building: the security guard. Sometimes - not often, but every once in a while - you get a guy who wants to eventually be a cop. He's keen and he pays attention. Little details count. Knowing where you're supposed to be going when you play a role is important. Dressing up isn't enough. Knowing a thing or two about the person you're pretending to be is vital.

I came in through the front door, duffle-bag in hand. I had on a pair of work coveralls that proudly displayed the logo of a local HVAC company, with matching ball cap. I had my hair pulled through the hole on the back of the hat and I looked for all the world like nothing more than a college student who's trying to pick up a bit of extra cash over the summer.

The 'disguise' was a nice bit of work on my part. Twenty minutes of sex with a lonely janitor and I had my pick of uniforms. Sure, I could've just ganked him and taken what I wanted, but people notice dead bodies. You wear him out with sex, leave him sleeping on a desk, and you can prowl around unimpeded without worrying about a thing. Plus, the janitor could tell anybody he wanted to about the 'hot sex he had with a hot college student' over the weekend, and nobody'd ever believe him. It's a layer of cover, and you can never have too much.

Hollywood gives you the impression that you have to use all kinds of disguises and secret 'ninja' techniques to enter a building with the idea of killing someone. You can, I guess, but that makes for a lot of unnecessary work on your part. For myself, I like to use the 'act like you own the place' method. It works, nine times out of ten, because people refuse to believe that anyone will buck the norm in any significant way. It's why people like Tom Green and Andy Dick have careers. People notice freaks.

The security guard barely looked up from his racing magazine as I walked in. His eyes went directly to the logo and his brain just shut down.

"You new?" he asked, as I signed in with an indecipherable scrawl.

"Yep. First day," I said, affecting the bored, work-a-day drawl of a common laborer.

"Anything serious?"

"Nah. They just want me to crawl around in the ducts for a bit, testing common pollen counts."

I was proud of that little detail. It sounded plausible, and this nine-dollar-an-hour-jerk wouldn't know any better anyway.

"Yeah. I used to do HVAC (he pronounced it Aitch-Vee-Ay-Sea. I nearly choked.) myself. We were always getting called out to these rich people's houses for the very same thing," he said, while his mind continued to sleep and his hands filled out a visitor's badge.

"Bread and butter, man. Gotta do what ya' gotta do, right?" I said.

"Ain't that the truth." He handed me the visitor's badge and sent me on my way with a "Good luck with the creepy-crawlies in there."

I walked in, did what I was being paid to do, and walked out. Scout, hit and clean up took less than forty-five minutes. I even spent a minute gabbing with the security guard about the elevated "common pollen counts" on my way out the front door.

There was just one teeny little detail, and that's why I'm here tonight, on top of the building directly across the street from the police station, with a directional mic, guffawing my guts out. I wish I'd brought a tape recorder. Hell, even a video camera. Bertrand was squirming and this was too funny to be believed!

~~~~~~~

"Just tell us what you saw, Bertrand," said the one cop to me. I figured he was doing the 'good cop' part of this. He was smiling and his eyes were kind. The 'bad cop' half was off in the corner scowling at me, his arms crossed. I could feel a bead of sweat trickle down my spine.

I don't mind telling you; I was scared.

I'm not sure why they were treating *me* like this. I mean, it's not like I killed the old bastard. Sure, everybody knew the mob was gunning for him, and it was just a matter or time. Stickler should've kept out of their area of control. Everybody knew it! But no, I had to be in the wrong place at the wrong time and no the cops were trying to pin his death on me! I didn't even *know* the guy all that well!

"But . . . but, I keep telling you officer! I didn't *see* anything! I was-"

"You know, I've heard just about enough from this mug," said the growly voice from the corner.

I looked over at him. He was scowling, clenching and unclenching his fists. He stood up from his casual lean in the corner at rushed at me with a noise that must've come straight from the inside of a predator. He put his sweaty, greasy, coffee-stained face right up next to mine, and breathed out at me through tightly clenched teeth. I nearly gagged on the smell.

"Now you listen to me, you oily, little creep. I'm this close to taking you apart with my bare hands. We've got *you* in the private latrine. We've got *your* fingerprints on the body, and we've got umpteen witnesses claiming they saw you rushing out of Mr. Stickler's office in a panic. Now I've been nice and polite up 'till now, but if you don't stop treating me like a mushroom, I'm gonna start really getting angry."

"T-t-treating you like a mushroom?"

"Yeah. You've never heard that expression before, Burrrrr-trand?"

He drug the "brr" out for nearly twenty seconds. I watched spit form on his teeth as he did it. I was so scared; I felt some spotting in my underwear.

"N-n-no, Officer. I never have."

"It means you're keeping me in the dark and feeding me bullsh-"

"I think you've made your point, Farley," the good cop interrupted.

He turned toward me with a smile that was like the sun rising.

"Bertrand, we really want to help you here, but this whole thing doesn't make any sense. Go over it with us one more time. Maybe we can figure something out."

I swallowed and nodded my head. I took a deep breath, wiped the sweat from my face, and tried to make sense of it.

"I'm not sure what I was thinking. I believe it might have been one of those 'good idea at the time' moments. Last night I went out to a local wing place and had a couple pitchers of beer and a few platters of wings with some of my boys. It was a good time. We caught up, flirted with the waitresses and watched Delarenzo get the living hell kicked out of him by Hoyter on the bar's big screen.

"I stayed out way too late, and when I woke up this morning, I felt the ominous rumblings of gastric rebellion. I was half-tempted to call off sick, but I took a personal day a week ago to go golfing.

"I'd be the first to admit I'm overly-ambitious, but I *do* like my job. I think I'm finally getting noticed by some of the big boys down at my office, and I'd really like to parlay that into a vice president's office.

"Assuming I still have a job, that is.

"I went on into work this morning, despite having a digestive tract full of partially chewed chicken and gallons of beer. I kept having hot farts, and I'm pretty sure I managed to soak my underwear, but I was really doing okay, all things considered. Then, right around lunch time, my guts rebelled; all at once and with no denial.

"I leapt out of my cubicle and ran down the hall, tightly holding the back of my pants. I could feel hot fingers of . . . well, never mind.

"The first bathroom I came to was the executives' restroom. It has a door that opens directly into Stickler's office. The bathroom has semi-private cubicles, with walls that extend to the floor and the ceiling. They're really swanky. I rushed into the first one I came to, locked the door behind me, dropped trou, and let loose.

"It was like Niagara, man.

"I sat there, for ten minutes, groaning and sweating, while my insides tried to twist themselves into a knot. I heard the door to the restroom open and somebody came in, opened the stall next to mine, and evidently got on with whatever business they had.

"I remember thinking, 'Awwww, man! That's just what I need! Some executive hearing me . . . and *smelling* me!'"

"I began to wave my hand around, hoping to dissipate some of the odors. That's when I started to hear the noises from next door. I remember being a little intrigued, thinking it might be somebody *really* senior, and I could learn something damaging. You never know what might come in handy during evaluation time. If I could hear what sounded like . . . I don't know, like, a colostomy bag or something, something really embarrassing . . . well, you just never know."

"At first there were just the common sounds of somebody getting partially undressed in order to go to the bathroom. I heard the soft rustle of cloth; the 'tink' as the seat was lowered, and a gentle grunt as the body followed. I quit listening at that point as I wasn't sure there was anything I really wanted to hear after that."

"Then there were some clinks and clunks; a gentle 'tunk' or two; and a soft 'whump'."

"Like I say, I'm not sure what I was thinking. I might've just been relieved that the senior executives in my company have to evacuate their bowels too. Whatever it was, something prompted me to open my mouth."

"'Dang, man! What have you got over there?'"

"For a long time there was no response, and I was beginning to regret opening my mouth. What if the exec recognized me? Then, I swear, this *woman's* voice answered me! I have perfect recall of every word! I swear I do! Her voice was soft and I almost had to strain to hear her, but this is what she said, word for word: "A knife, soft copper wire, a 9mm Glock - semi-auto with fitted twenty-five round magazine. I've got hollow point, low velocity rounds in it at the moment. The high velocity stuff's nice, and it's enormously dramatic, of course, but I like to see the spalling of a low-velocity round, myself. Nothing beats digging a hole in someone's face with a low-velocity, 9mm round. Wouldn't you agree?'"

"She stopped talking for a minute, like she was waiting for me to respond. Then she went on."

"'Anyway. I've also got a custom silencer I had made in Italy by this absolute, perfectly darling genius of a man named Italio, if you can believe it. I'm probably going to have to either marry Italio or kill him. I haven't quite decided which yet. I've got a small pry tool, just in case, don't you know, and a nicely chilled can of Red Bull. How about you?'"

"I didn't say anything. Just then my insides twisted violently and a stream of hot feces squirted out of my already well-abused butt hole. There was a silence in the cubicle next to mine. Then she said, 'Sounds like a toilet-full to me.'"

"Then, I swear, I heard something that sounded like the action of a pistol, and the door opened. I couldn't help it. My guts just emptied on me."

"'Do you think you could flush? People are trying to work in here!' she said, from directly outside my door."

"I flushed. I heard Stickler's door open. I heard five seconds of muted conversation in the office, and then I heard a soft 'whutt, whutt, whutt.' Just like that, all close together. Stickler's door opened again and somebody went back into the cubicle next to mine. I heard the same sounds, all over again."

"'You need more fiber, buddy,' she said."

"I heard the bathroom door open again, and that was it."

"The whole thing couldn't have taken more than five minutes, all told. I sat there for probably another fifteen minutes, my sphincter as small as a raisin. I was as scared as I've ever been in my life. When I couldn't stand it any longer, I jumped up, pulled my pants on, and ran out of the bathroom. All I can say is, I must've been confused, or something. I guess instead of the main door to the bathroom, I ran into Sticker's office. I tripped over something, and there he was, lying on his back, an enormous hole in the center of his forehead. Everything above the bridge of his nose was just . . . gone. There was blood everywhere. My clothes were covered in it. Stickler's walking sticks lay underneath him, and he was twisted around, like he'd done a full spin before he fell over."

"I remember thinking 'Huh. Low-velocity rounds really do work well for that kind of thing.' Then my sphincter loosened again, and that's when I called you guys."

I stopped talking and looked up at the cops. They were both looking back at me with looks of disbelief on their faces.

"That's how it happened! I swear! I didn't get any kind of a look at her, but I remember her voice! I can ID her for you guys!"

"And that's what you expect us to believe is it? I'll tell you what I think, Bertrand. I think you did Stickler yourself, and you're too much of a chickensh-"

"Farley, that's probably enough. I think we got what we need here. Bertrand, you're under arrest for-"

~~~~~~~

I turned the mic off. I'd heard enough. I wiped the tears from my face and tried to recapture a bit of girlish dignity.

It's not often that you get to laugh in this job and it's not often that karma, fate, or whatever it is lines up just right to flush a prick like Bertrand. He never got a look at me, and I affected a vacuous, girly-girl voice when I was talking to him, so IDing me will never be any kind of an option. In and out, right through the front door, in one day. I could spend a few days here relaxing. The pay for this job was great, but the bonus of Bertrand was even better.

Paris.

City Of Lights.

Place Where People Need Killing.

I'd been commissioned by a cadre - an environmental, guerilla group that will remain nameless - to kill a corporate stooge of some kind. I have to sit and listen, as this guy in a dirty parka, with a beard that reaches to his navel, lectures me about the 'evils of oil development'. His teeth are spit-shiny, and his eyes are empty, wild and vacant. I immediately dub him 'Dirty Parka'.

Dirty Parka wants me to understand why it's so very important that I kill this guy.

"He's an OPEC subcommittee member. His hands are covered in blood! The spirits of the children he's murdered in underdeveloped countries . . . ."

And he goes on like that, for forty-five minutes. He tells me about gas flaring, oil-production-pollution runoff, and all kinds of other things I could care less about.

The guerilla group offers me a nicely obscene package of money and small, portable goods to plink this subcommittee member. They want proof, though, and they hand me a cute, battery-operated saw to get it.

"His death must be a graphic, visual example to all others who follow his path!" Dirty Parka says, flecking me in the face with his passionate spit.

The mark lives the good life in a quaint, Parisian neighborhood. He's purchased a building and tricked it out with all the latest high-tech security gear. He's got PIR sensors. He's got bulked-out, heavily-armed-security-guards in Armani suits with high powered automatic weapons bulging their jackets. They know Do-Jew-Ji-Jutso and ILL-Ki-Won-Ton, number three. They can flip and twist and kick and "Hi-ya!" with the best of 'em. The Armani Squad has trained attack dogs on site with very blood-thirsty appetites. The mark has food tasters, bullet/shrapnel-proof glass installed at what had to be a very nice price: seven, eight digits, if I'm still up on my Gall's Equipment Lists.

And none of it means anything. Every security system, no matter how advanced, has a hole. An attentive person - like me - can take easy advantage of it.

And yes, you've gotta worry about law enforcement, and their CSIs, and their forensic ninjas and DNA, and all that other crap. But let me tell you a little secret. DNA works from a basic human profile. Yes, it fits a specific fingerprint, and eventually you'll end up as an anonymous fingerprint in databases all over the world, but if you don't go around doing dumb things like smoking cigarettes and dropping butts everywhere or urinating on your freshly processed mark, it isn't all that big of a deal. You can always get caught. Always. But if you take some basic precautions, the risk is pretty minimal. Don't believe everything you see on TV.

So here are the basics on killing someone for money:

Get commission.

Who, what, where, how, for how much. That's all I need to know. Once we finalize that, I go to work. Once you're in, you never do anything for free, ever, no matter what. Always get something in return: drugs, gold coins, human commodity, get something you can port and sell quickly if you're not actually getting a suitcase full of cash. You have a set price. Make them pay it. This is not a charity, it's a business.

For this Paris job, it broke down like this:

Who - the mark.

What - Kill him, take a trophy as proof.

Where - it doesn't matter to the group, but he lives in Paris.

How - "We leave that to you." I do LOOOOOVE to hear that.

For How Much - A nicely sizable sum in cash and a couple thousand dollars in what looks to me like unprocessed, laboratory-grade cocaine. Probably "liberated" from some animal-testing facility. Gotta love environmental wackos.

For this mark, starting the scout work is a simple matter of signing a six-month lease on an apartment close by.

'Why, Hand?'

Security holes. CCTV is a nice feature. So are armed, attentive guards with drooly dogs on leashes. But every screen has a hole. I'm looking for regular visitors. I sit in my window, or at a near-by cafe, and I watch the mark gets at his house. Who's an employee? Who's a girlfriend? Who's a mistress? Who's a wife? Who's a family member?

Once I establish a traffic pattern, I move to Phase two - Entry.

B. Entry. (Otherwise known as penetration.)

This is the part they make movies about. Sean Connery stars opposite Catherine Zeta-Jones. It's not at all glamorous, most of the time, but nobody every really asked me, either.

In the movies, an assassin faced with this sort of security rig would put on a ninja's outfit, do all sorts of contortionary, high-wire acrobatics, and accessing of high-voltage power sources. There'd be sleeping gas, throwing knives, snipers shooting out lights, explosions, top-secret, experimental gases, and all kinds of things like that.

I can throw a knife. I'm pretty good at it. Nine times out of ten, I can actually hit my target. But I don't know anyone who can kill someone with a throwing knife by throwing it. You're much more likely to hit them with the handle, or not hard enough, or any one of ten-million, zillion, grillion other mistakes most people make with throwing knives. It's a well-marketed conceit. 'Learn to kill! Throw a knife!'

I know this guy who got capped because he hit an armed guard with a throwing knife. He hit him dead square in the back of the head . . . broadside. The guard whipped around, rubbing the back of his head, mad enough to spit teeth. He emptied a clip into the knife-throwing-hero.

I do carry them, of course. They're useful sometimes, mostly as a deterrent. Three feet of steel sticking out of ya' will usually slow you down, and nobody likes to bleed.

No. My entries are dull, meticulous things that I create for each and every mark. No throwing knives (usually), no sleeping gas, and no accessing of high-voltage power sources. I think my way in, by carefully finding all the corners, seeing outside the box.

It takes me a month, but I have my traffic pattern.

My mark employs a chef. The chef is one of these pretty-boy types, who likes working for someone 'dangerous'. It makes the chef feel all important and dangerous in turn. He drives a fancy, red, sports car; a little Italian number with exciting curves and an engine like a rocket. He dresses in silk shirts, and he wears a well-crafted toupee.

The name he gives out is "Phaeton, but call me 'Tony', for shorter."

He fakes a bad Italian accent, wears horrible sunglasses and lots of bad gold jewelry, speaks pidgin Italian, fluent French and horrible English. He frequents Parisian nightclubs where the girls are cheap, free and easy, and he throws money around like it's glitter at Carnivale.

Perfect.

I walked into the club and felt the heavy weight of male stares.

It's funny what you can do with a little red dress.

I'm not much to look at. I'm fit, of course, lean and muscular, but I'm short, and my natural hair color is an uninteresting black. My eyes are the color of warm mud. My skin is nicely unblemished, with a few cute freckles sprinkled here and there, and my breasts are on the smallish side. When I'm not at work, I wear loose-fitting clothes to obscure my body's profile. My skin has an olive tinge to it. Most guys would say I'm 'cute' at best, and leave it at that. I rarely get a second look, being dismissed as some sort of adolescent. I'm utterly unremarkable, in any way, in most places on the planet. It helps me be the very best at what I do.

But put fifteen pounds of makeup on, do your hair up with kinky little stick things, get a red dress and some stretchy, padded, elastic undergarments, and all of a sudden, I'm Pamela Anderson.

Men. If you put it in a tight enough package and slap enough sex on it, a man will burn his house down - with his weeping wife and children inside - to get at it.

I walk up to the bar, swishing for all I'm worth, and look for Tony. The music is loud, the club is hot, there's smoke in the air.

Tony's holding court at the bar, surrounded by a grunting herd of groupies and man-whores. I sip my drink and make very direct eye-contact with him. I call it my 'Come on over if you're brave enough,' stare.

It works. It always works.

"Hello, my sweet. Come here often, do you?"

"No. I don't. Don't call me, 'My Sweet', unless you're gonna be sweet."

A round of sycophantic laughter from the groupies and the man-sluts.

"Ooo-la-LA! A feisty one, boys!"

This erudite statement is followed by a round of sycophantic laughter from the groupies and the man-sluts.

"I'd make your head explode, little boy. Are you going to offer to buy me a drink and take me to a table, or do you need your boyfriends here to tell you how to seduce a woman?"

Tony smiles weakly. He doesn't like being led. I need to rein it in a little, salve and stroke his ego. So I give him my very best 'I want it as bad as you do' stare. His smile widens and I know I've got him. He leads me to a table, an intimate little corner, and he's leaning all over me. I let him, even though he smells like leeks and olive oil.

"So what is your name, my sweet? Hah? What should you want your big daddy Tony to call you?"

"Why bother with names, Tony? I just want to fuck."

Twenty minutes later, Tony is sweating and groaning atop me and whispering badly pronounced idiocies in three different languages.

He really sucks, but entry made.

Choose a technique.

You can't just run the mark over in a big vehicle and drive off, hoping nobody saw. You've got to do it quietly, cleanly and the way the contract wants it done. I have very specific instructions, so I have to go in close and personal.

I date Tony for a few weeks. Actually, it's not so much dating, as it's 'Let's get naked and hump like drunken monkeys.'

Some of us would be a little concerned about that. Prudish types, I guess. I mean, you don't have to lie down and spread your legs. Guys don't care, just as long as it involves their little tallywhackers somehow. Put your hand down their pants and their brains stop. They might be wanting something particular, but if you give them anything at all, that's good enough. You give it to 'em often enough and they quit asking questions, quit worrying about who you are or where you come from. Sometimes they maybe get a little grabby, so you've gotta keep it in between the green and the red zone. Don't push the needle too far or you end up having to pop a gasket.

Whatever.

Tony spends his time bragging about his virility and the complexities of his job. The virility is questionable at best. I'm not one of those girls who worries about size, but Tony could stand to be a little more . . . convex. He kinda makes me think of the last green bean at the bottom of the can.

"I tell you, my sweet, the man is a nightmare!' No shellfish, Tony. I'm allergic to shellfish, Tony. Don't cook me shellfish, Tony.' Every day he tells me, and every day I smile, and I nod, and I say, through gritted teeth, I say, 'No. No shellfish for the boss'. I swear, someday I cook him the shellfish, just to make his throat swell and he shuts up!"

Catch that?

"You know, Tony, I'd love to see where you work. Maybe meet your boss. Is he single?"

"Single? HA! The man is married, with three children! But what's in it for Tony, hah? Why should Tony introduce you to him, hah?"

"I dunno, Tony. Maybe you introduce me; I get you a pay raise. You know, a little sweet for the boss from a grateful employee. Besides. I like to keep my guy happy."

And I give him a slow, seductive smile. The creep grins back at me while I light a cigarette.

"Yes! The boss would like you very much, my sweet. He'd soon be grateful to Tony, wouldn't he?"

And that's the other thing about guys. If it isn't related to their little trouser hose it goes to their appetite somehow. Food, beer, money, whatever; every guy's got an appetite that needs to be satisfied. Tony's is money, and the "respect" he gets from his man-twats as a result of his money. Money and their penises. I swear. It's like Pavlov's dogs. It's almost too easy.

I do my hair up in pins when I meet the boss. Kinky little sticky things. One of the sticks is actually a hollow drinking straw Tony left lying around one night. We'll get back to that, though. The whole thing gives my hair an exotic, oriental look. Tony told me his boss has a thing for Oriental women.

I take a small, flirty handbag with me. It holds my cute little saw just right.

All those fancy, high-tech security gadgets and armed guards, with their machine guns and their trained attack dogs, smile and wave us in through the front gate. They've seen me around often enough, at all times of the night and day. No need to do a search of the sweet little thing in Tony's car. That's Tony! He works here! He's one of us!

"Hello, Tony! Come to bring us all a little treat, 'eh?"

"You wouldn't know what to do with her, Bernardo!"

I spread my slow, seductive, man-eating smile around. There's a chorus of guttural, male laughter, and Tony drives us in.

Fifteen minutes later, the mark has got me to himself in a bedroom with a locked door. I know the door is locked. I locked it.

I languorously remove my hairpins, watching his eyes as my hair, carefully treated, cascades in a dark waterfall. Took me forty-five minutes of careful conditioning, curling, gelling and spritzing to get my hair to do that five second display.

It works. His mouth opens and his eyes glaze.

I play with the hollow drinking straw for a slow, seductive moment, licking both ends in a 'porn-star' way. I work it like it's a pickle and the juice just keeps running. The hard part is keeping a straight face.

I put the pin to my lips.

Well, I'm sure you get the idea. I give him a very racy show, my eyes closed to half-lidded slits. It looks like the only thing in the world I want to be doing right now is this; like I'm in boiling ecstasy, licking and sucking on my hairpin.

It takes me all of two seconds to line my shot up.

Blowguns are a little tricky. You have to be pretty close and you have to take a lot of different variables into account. They're touchy at best, and the ammo can't be bigger than the straw. A pin, a needle, maybe even the end of an insulin syringe you bought at the drug store down the street for twelve cents.

They only really work if some kind of a virulent toxin is immediately introduced into the system. You're not going to hit an artery, so you have to work with a contact toxin. Luckily for me, the mark is as allergic to shellfish as vampires are to tanning.

My little oyster-juice-shrimp-body soaked needle hits the mark under his left eye. The thing has been soaking in a plastic container in my refrigerator for a couple of weeks. I change the juice every other day to keep the juice pretty fresh. I imagine it must feel like getting hit in the face with a needle lined pillow.

Tupperware container in the fridge. Can't beat it for 'top-secret-experimental-neurotoxin-container'.

The licking? That's to dissolve the salt plugs I capped the drinking straw with.

I like salt.

Funny thing, allergies. Some people are so allergic, they experience symptoms immediately. Every occurrence of exposure makes the next one even worse. Evidently my mark was more allergic than even he knew. He's gone the exact color of a ripe mango, and he's breaking out in hives the size of half dollars. He's still twitching, but his throat has closed off. His airway's blocked.

I stand near the door, hands at my sides, watching him die. All the thrashing noise he makes for the next three minutes or so are neatly covered by my 'ecstatic moans' of pleasure. Four minutes and thirty seconds later, he's stone dead and perfectly still.

I pull the cute little saw knife out of my handbag along with a pair of disposable gloves and a large, closable freezer bag. The only part of his body I'm actually going to touch I'm taking with me, but you can't be too careful. I pull the needle out from under his left eye; wipe a careful finger across the injection site to remove any of my spit, and go to work.

I don't know why some people feel the need to take trophies. I'm not a trophy girl myself. I have no problem collecting one from a mark, but it's not something I need to validate me, either. And why people insist on tallywhackers as trophies more than anything else, I'll never know.

The saw's a powerful little tool. It makes short work of the guy's pants and underpants. There's some shrinkage due to his dying, but he's still pretty engorged due to my sexy-dance, too. I try to minimize the blood by cutting quickly. Takes three minutes.

I take a shower to remove the blood, still wearing my disposable gloves. I fill the tub, and, using one of the enormous towels in the cabinet, I carefully drench every surface I touched. Yes. I did keep track. It's one of those details you just have to - and wipe them down in a swirling, circular fashion.

In and out, almost soundless and undetectable, because I came in under their screens, in under an hour and a half, with my carefully filled handbag.

The guards don't so much as wink in my direction as I walk out with part of their boss.

There isn't a whisper in the news for a solid month. Then there's a small, back-page item about a 'probable-fish-chewed-body' being found along the coast.

Security people, especially highly-paid, Armani-suited, Wee-Joo-Di-Jay-Jutsu-knowing highly-paid Security people usually don't let their failures get talked about. Somebody waltzed into a compound under their control and took their primary out. It's an embarrassment, but more importantly, it represents the loss of stockholder money.

My guess is that somebody dumped the body, cleaned the room from top to bottom, and then called the police with a story about him being gone. You never know, with security people. They can be as ruthless as we are, without the scruples.

I disappear, of course. Tony is nicely set up to take the fall for everything. After all, security let him and 'an unknown individual' into the compound.

Tony's body is the next one found. His death is as a result of a 'fall' down a flight of five stairs. My guess is that they had to toss him four or five times.

I meet with Dirty Parka, give him his grisly trophy, and collect the rest of my fee. My plan is to spend a few weeks on the beach. I've got some money to burn, after all.

What the hell, right? It beats working for a living.

~~~~~~~

Misandry!

That's what that doggone word is! I hate that, don't you? When you can't think of a word?

What?

Just adding some more of this stuff. It tends to stick to your skin and I end up not having a full hole.

You're doing really good, I have to say. So far you've managed to keep your screaming to a minimum. Makes talking less of a chore when you don't have the yell above shrieks.

What?

We've already talked about that. You don't have enough money. I've already got your wallet, your PIN, your ATM card. There's nothing else you can offer me.

What? Look, if you're going to sob like that you need to not talk.

Oh. Really. Worth that much, huh? Where is it?

Nooooo . . . you tell me where it is, then I'll decide whether or not to pull you out of there.

82

Uh-huh. Never heard that one before. No, no. I think I'll let you stay down there and digest a little more.

Well, yeah, I *could*, but you're going to die anyway, and it's nice to have an audience, even if you're captive.

So to speak.

A captive audience.

You get it?

Hey! That's funny stuff and I'm just giving it away here!

Yeah, well, some people have no appreciation for genius.

Anyway. Wanna hear another story?

Now, now. There's no need for bad language. You can't stop me from telling it, and I feel like talking.

I'll tell you a story about my very first time. People like you are always asking people like me about our first times. It's like, losing our virginity, or something. This torrid tale of how we 'fell from grace'. And you can listen, and make appropriate 'Mmm' and 'Uh-huh' noises, and I'll let you go back to dying horribly.

My first time was the catalyst for all the other times.

It's funny. I've never told anyone this. Telling you won't exactly matter, but it still feels like confession somehow.

Well, whatever.

You ever hear about those people who've lost their sense of smell? These folks, they have no sense of taste, either, so they put really heavy spices on their food to compensate. I don't understand it myself, but the thinking seems to be that if you put, like, I don't know, a habanera pepper in your mac and cheese, or whatever, the heat of the pepper will provide at least some texture to the food, some return of sensation, some freaking feeling to the meal.

Now listen. This is important and deep stuff.

See, these people have lost an important part of their lives. They've lost sensation, connection, all that kind of thing that says 'We are human. We are alive.' At the point when I first started this, that's what my life had become: a pursuit of feeling, connecting, trying to be . . . well, human, I guess. I was doing everything I could to pull the flat lack of sensation off my mac and cheese of reality, and it wasn't doing me a bit of good. Don't get me wrong. I had a great life. Supportive parents, a good education, all the bells and whistles of an upper middle class upbringing. I was set for life, man.

But I couldn't feel, you know? It was like the whole world was outside this blue, buzzing, electric haze; like one of those Star Trek force fields. It surrounded just me and I couldn't touch anything outside it.

Sorry. Got lost in thought in for a minute.

Where was I? Oh yeah.

It was his tone that decided it. I don't even remember what we were arguing about. Some silly something I wanted, or something, I'm sure. I was pretty shallow back then. But I remember being amazed at his tone, his casual disregard for my wants, my needs, my feelings!

I mean, how dare he even raise his voice to me! And when I confronted him about it, all he said was 'You heard me.' No apology, no remorse. And that was that. That's when I decided. I don't remember being mad, actually, just perfectly decisive.

I grabbed his wrist with both hands. At first he probably thought I was being conciliatory. He didn't resist me at all. It was really very easy. I gave him a strong, off-pulling tug and I wrenched his arm around behind his back, yanking his hand well above his shoulder-blades. Then I wrapped my free arm around his throat. I let go of his wrist and wrapped my arm around his head. Then I kicked the back of his left knee.

He crumpled, gasping for breath, and I rode him down, moving my arm to the back of his head and lifting his skull with the pressure of my forearm. He hit the floor on his face, with my leading weight on top.

The snap of his nose breaking and entering his brain was like an electric shock through me. It cut right through that blue ozone that kept me from the world and bathed me in gloriously ionic sensation.

I could feel!

My whole life spread out before me in that perfect instant. I could see what I needed to do and who I needed to be. It was all so wonderfully, gloriously simple!

He thrashed for only a moment, dying far quicker than I thought possible. I kissed him on the ear, thanking him for this last, final gift. It's not every girl has a father who dies for them.

I went to go find my mother, giggling at the irony of using self-defense lessons Dad'd paid for, as 'protection from those hooligans at that college of yours' to get my life off on a grand, glorious start.

Mom was even easier, and the sensations that raced across my skin as I broke her open like a melon are beyond description.

I gotta tell ya', it feels really good to be able to tell someone about this!

From that day to this, I remember my purpose, my focus, by remembering my first time.

So here we are, several years later.

Your pops told me where to find you, I slipped you a little something interesting in those gin and tonics you were swilling, and we drove out here in your car. Even your friends just assumed you were getting lucky with an enthusiastic bimbo you'd managed to pick up.

And that's it. That's who I am, that's what I do, and that's why.

Now, if you'll excuse me, I've got some dinner to go get. I'll be back sometime tomorrow morning.

If you want some free advice, I'd sink into the hole as soon as the rope gets slack enough. The last guy I brought out here took three days to die. I know because I sat here, watching him the whole time. He screamed himself hoarse well before the napalm had finished.

Just a thought.

So, how we doin'?

Want some coffee?

Well, no, but I can pour it over your face.

How's that?

Too hot? What? Get outta here! It's barely steaming!

Lemme see. Yep. Hair's about gone, clothes dissolved, it's only a matter of time now, hot stuff.

Oh, wow. Must be some serious shrinkage going on, huh? You must be dang near retracted all the way back in.

Well, looks like we got just enough time for one more story. By the time I get done, you probably will be too.

So let me tell you about Teshuga. And I swear, if you make a single comment about Uma Thurman or those Kill Bill movies, I'll do something horrible to you.

What?

Probably take a blowtorch to your tallywhacker. How's that grab ya', pee wee?

Anyway. Her name was Teshuga.

It was one of the very first things she said to me. She went on from there to make a speech about Yin and Yang, hot and cold, woman and male, heat and damp, and all the many reasons she was better than me. I didn't listen to most of it, I'm afraid. I tend to zone out when people ramble on. I do remember our initial introduction, though.

She lived in a battered house boat on the river, claiming that's where the local 'daimyo' had chased her. She needed a student, and hinted at being the sole possessor of 'hidden lore'.

I didn't care. She was cheap. When you're first starting out, you take what you can get. And it's funny what you can get. If you need to learn how to be a sniper, you go find one who works for the police, throw some money around, maybe some booty, and you get what you want. Explosives? Same thing. People are perfectly willing to tell you everything they know about their jobs if you're the least bit attentive. If all else fails, use a Google search. I can't tell you how many times the internet has come through for me.

I was in Okinawa. Never mind why. I'd gone over there for a job, and ended up staying on. I spent a couple of months learning basic, conversational Japanese before taking on my hit. I could converse, after a fashion, with most of the people on Okinawa. It wasn't perfect, and there were more dialects than I could've imagined, but I wasn't pointing and grunting, either.

Okinawa's one of those places that doesn't really belong in the twentieth century, I think. There's all this rare esoteric knowledge lying around; dojos to every conceivable martial art on every corner.

Okinawa's kind of a "source". If you want to learn a martial art - unsullied by western thought and practice - you go to Okinawa. It's as simple as that. If you're really lucky, patient and willing to spend money like water, you probably won't get beat up too much for asking, and might be able to limp to your plane.

I saw a lot of Okinawa that summer before lucking on to Shihan Teshuga.

I was standing outside of a dojo, bent at the waist, gasping for breath and desperately hoping the smiling little man in front of me wouldn't hit me again. My ears had been ringing for nearly a minute, and I was pretty sure I'd soiled myself.

"You think you are ready for me to teach you? You are not ready for me to look at you, much less teach you."

"Pl . . . plea . . . please, Sensei. I want to learn."

"I cannot teach you. If you must learn, find Shihan Teshuga. She can teach you. More importantly, she is willing to teach you."

Catch that?

Yeah. That's kind of a typical attitude toward uppity, western women in some parts of the world.

The name 'Shihan' basically means 'Teacher of Teachers'. The word implies that you've been teaching - at the top of the heap - your martial art for at least twenty years. 'Teshuga' supposedly means 'Little Flower'.

I asked around, got laughed at, spat on, and thrown around quite a bit. One guy picked me up - with his thumbs! - under my chin, and asked me if I was ready to die. At that moment, I was. It hurt pretty good to be suspended like that on a pair of horny little thumbs.

He was pretty impressed when I grunted out "Can you show me how to do that?"

It took the better part of a month before I finally tracked her down. She didn't look like a teacher of any kind when I found her. She looked like a drunken old bag lady, puddled all over a bar stool.

"Excuse me-"

A hand shot out and wrapped around my mouth. I could feel my upper jaw creaking under the pressure of those steely fingers.

"What do you want?'

Her voice was like the bottom of a whiskey bottle.

I mumbled something. Her fingers tasted like eel.

"What? Speak up!"

Eventually I was able to get a coherent sentence out, and the whole time those fingers, smaller than a monkey's paw, were squeezing the bones in my face.

She sat up and looked me over.

"You wish to learn Teshuga-Jitsu?"

"I do."

"Very well. My name is Teshuga. You will call me "Shihan Teshuga". You are here to learn. There is nothing you have that I am interested in, and you can not pay me for what I teach you here. Therefore, you will serve me until such time as our instruction is done."

And that was it. I walked her home, put her to bed, and began my sojourn in hell.

You could tell it was really important to her; this putting me in my place. I mean, I'm a western woman, after all, and she's eastern. She's got ancestors and speaks three different languages, and can blow holes through cinder-block walls with her feet. I'm reasonably certain of who my father is, I want to learn how to blow holes through people, and the only language I speak is money; which, incidentally, she still took, the filthy little crook.

The next day she rolled out of bed, perfunctorily washed up, and had a small breakfast.

"You. Student. Show me what you know."

I'd taken a couple of different martial arts. I was good at it. No, I'm not as strong as a strong man, but as a woman, I'm better balanced. My gravity is spread cleaner, and I can move with more dexterity than any man could ever dream of moving. It's funny; only the very best male dancers, gymnasts, and martial artists, have the same balance and dexterity as the average woman.

I took a swing at her. She knocked me down.

I kicked at her. She caught my foot, threw me over her shoulder and planted a knee in the back of my neck.

I attempted a grapple. She did something to my wrist that felt like it was breaking in four different places, threw me on my stomach - again - and slapped me in the back of the head hard enough to show me pretty stars.

"Hmm. I see," she said, allowing me to stand. "Not much. Well. You will get better.'

"When will that be?" I grunted. I was cocky. I admit it.

She smiled mirthlessly and pulled something from the filthy folds of her gi. She held it in her open palm up to my eyes.

It was a carved jade dragon, about three inches long. There were perfectly faceted rubies for the eyes, each the size of a small pea. The claws and teeth were done in gold. The detail was amazing. I could see every hair. It had a tremendous weight of age and it immediately awoke my possessor's lust.

I like pretty things. What can I say?

"You westerners are fond of tests. Everything is a test, a contest, a new colored belt!" She waved her hands in the air in a ridiculous fashion at "colored belt".

"So be it. If I teach a westerner, I will use western ways. When you are ready you will take the dragon from my hand-"

Yeah.

I snatched at it. Couldn't help myself.

But her hand was already moving, and she hit me dead center of my forehead with a horny little fist.

I saw more pretty stars. I may have puked just a little.

"You are not ready," she needlessly said.

I stood up, brushed myself down and nodded.

"There will be a daily workout. You are slow and fat, and as a woman, you are weak."

I was young, she smelled like freshly-cooked eels, and her misogyny was getting on my nerves.

I nodded, maintaining eye contact, and she didn't like that either.

"You will not look into my eyes. You are a woman-"

"Bite me," I said, smiling winsomely at her.

She hit me across the mouth so hard my pants fell down. I didn't even see her move. I landed on the floor again; swallowing what I suspected was a tooth.

Rocky start, I know. Still, you had to wonder if she'd take that sort of superior tone with a man . . . .

The kick is a simple maneuver that can get complicated when you have a pelvis.

Over here they teach you to take it nice and slow; find your center, cock the rifle - your leg - and then fire it into the opponent with whatever force you can muster. I've taken a couple of classes, so I thought I had some idea.

Teshuga, however, had never taken those classes, so she had no appreciation for my subtle kick dynamics.

"You are not performing that kick correctly. Your body is not centered. You are throwing your foot at the opponent, not kicking him. Again."

I wiped the sweat from my eyes with one hand. I'd already managed to kick a hole in the practice dummy. This was after several hours of effort, and I was proud of my little hole.

"Shihan," I said, lowering my eyes demurely. I'd learned respect for the bugger in the months we'd been practicing. She'd beaten it into me with those bony, calloused little fists of hers. I put my hands in the sleeves of my gi and stared at the floor. "With respect; what difference does it make how I perform the kick if the end result is the same?"

I indicated the foot-sized hole in the rattan dummy as I said this, hoping she'd get the point. It was a respectable hole, the size and shape of my foot, right where the dummy's stomach would be.

"What difference? What difference? The difference is night and day!" She glowered at me.

She stood in front of the dummy herself, knocking me out of the way with a brusque shove.

"Here!" She looked at me in her gimly-eyed way, her feet shoulder-width apart, about six feet from the dummy.

The dummy hung there, towering over both of us. Dummies do that. This one was roughly seven feet tall. The rushes it was made of were hand-harvested, by me, before the sun rose every morning. Teshuga required me to pull the rushes up by their roots and then strip them, all without the use of any tools but my hands.

The rushes in our dummy were covered in a tarp-like apron of thick, old leather. That apron could've been used, and probably was at one point, as building material. It was the toughest cloth I'd ever seen. Bullets would bounce off that leather apron. Superman couldn't tear that leather apron. A meteor, streaming down from the heavens- . . . well, you get the idea.

The entire affair was tightly bound with good rope. It weighed close to three-hundred pounds, and pulling it off the floor every day - a rope slung over a beam, and then hoisted by main strength - was part of my basic daily duties.

Teshuga was pretty small: four feet tall or so, with wispy grey hair and a dirty gi. I never knew her age, but I put it up there in the late-seventies. Her yellow skin looked like dirty horsehide under the flickering fluorescent bulbs in the dojo. Her teeth were perfectly white, perfectly even, and they didn't fit in her mouth correctly. She tended to spit when she spoke, and her teeth clattered and clacked in her mouth, sometimes falling out. She'd clench her teeth, and pull them back in with her jaw and neck muscles. It was a disgusting display of ill-fitting dentures at their very worst.

Her eyes looked like yellowing-ivory billiard balls.

She hated Chinese people with a passion that bordered on religion, and she really, really, really didn't like western women.

"Poisonous tarts!" she would shout, at least once a day, and then glower at me.

She was, in short, the perfect stereotype of a Hostile Martial Arts instructor - Mr. Miagi - or Ms, I guess - without any of the charming qualities.

She slowly lifted her left knee until it was up to her waist.

"Here!"

Without trembling or shaking or correcting her balance in any way, she then extended her leg until her left foot was pointing at the dummy like a yellow, dirty-gi-clad dart.

"Here!"

In one continuous movement, she put her left foot down and then launched herself, from where she stood, into the practice dummy. Her dirty feet made no sound as she made a six foot horizontal leap, and a four foot vertical one.

The noise as this eighty-pound goblin hit the three-hundred pound dummy was deafening. Teshuga managed to blow a hole through the dummy, right below the head. The whole thing tore loose of its harness and fell down to the cruddy tatami with a crash. Teshuga landed atop - and partially inside it - with a nimble little twist.

"Night and day," she said, glowering at me. "We are finished today. You will go and prepare my dinner, then you will clean this mess up."

I bowed my head.

Every day was the same: pull rushes from the river's edge, enough to fill a fifty-pound barrel. I carried the barrel back to the dojo, a distance of about a hundred yards, on my back. I rebuilt and hoisted the dummy off the floor. Then I prepared breakfast for the two of us, after buying it at the local market. Teshuga insisted on fresh ingredients for every meal.

This all happened well before the sun rose.

Then we exercised. Running, jumping, push-up, sit-ups, several hours of repetitive exercises of all kinds. Teshuga paced the dojo while I sweated and groaned and bled, wheedling and droning on about the weaknesses of western women, her hatred of Chinese people, and the intrinsic superiority of all things Japanese.

We had lunch at noon - after I went to the local market and bought it, brought it home and prepared it - and then we practiced on the dummy until Teshuga said it was time to stop. I then got to wash her dishes, do her laundry and generally keep things nice and tidy while she went off to watch soap operas at the bar down the street.

I was tired every day and every day I woke up more determined to follow my path.

I had nothing else, after all, and Teshuga would either make me strong or kill me. Would it surprise you to learn that at this point I didn't care either way?

Time went on.

I grew strong and able, quick and resilient, hard and solid.

She tested me once a month with the dragon, and once a month I hit the floor like a bag of rocks. She'd hold the dragon over my head while I lie there bleeding, or nursing a sore head, or recovering from whatever attack pattern she'd taken this month. She'd dangle the dragon just in front of my eyes, taunting me with it.

"You want this, don't you? I can see the lust for it in your eyes. It is a rare and beautiful treasure, is it not? A thing of holy beauty. Perhaps carved by an emperor. It has been in my family for generations beyond counting. Its worth is incalculable."

She'd lovingly stroke the dragon, making love to it with her eyes. She always put the dragon back in her ratty little gi at that point and smiled down at me.

"You can have it when you take it from me."

Teshuga's art was a cobbled together force of action that neatly combined grappling with fiercely speedy kicks and punches. Her philosophy was, "A woman cannot match a man, blow for blow, strength for strength. So a woman must take the strengths she already has to beat the man."

Kicks were devastating, delivered from a pelvis that was designed to bend in opposed directions along it own axis. I still can't kick as hard as Teshuga could. I don't think anyone can. But I can kick a sizable hole in your ribs, anyway.

Punches were fast, powerful distractions to set you up for a painful, bone-breaking grapple, or a head-over-heels throw.

"Do not hit. Punch! You cannot hit as hard as a man can! But you can punch him hard enough to make him step back! Then throw! Kick! Grapple! Hurt him and make him bleed!"

She was a master of the female body; an artist of form and function, and her like will never be replicated.

Three years I took her abuse. Three long years of bruises, falls and scrapes. Three years of blood and broken skin.

Then it happened, and I was free.

We were sparring, at full speed.

Well, I call it sparring, but she was hitting me, and I was desperately trying to avoid being hit. Sparring is more of a give and take activity, usually.

She'd taken it upon herself to teach me the use of the escrima - weighted sticks, about three-feet long, and four inches wide. When they crashed against an offending limb, you almost felt like a bone had been knocked loose. They were dangerous weapons in the hand of a master, and none were better than Teshuga.

"Escrima. A pipe, a branch, any length of something solid becomes a weapon. Learn it!"

And then she'd bring them thing down on the side of my head and I'd see pretty little stars for a while.

She was thrashing me soundly, for the fourteenth time today. Blood was running down my hands, slicking my escrima up and my face was swollen in half a dozen places. Suddenly, she just stopped. She stood there, not even breathing hard, while I panted and sweat and bled. Her hands slowly fell to her sides, and her face took on an oddly blank look.

"Shihan?"

She looked at me, but her eyes were vacant. She stared at me for a long moment, saying nothing, then abruptly sat down.

I dropped my escrima in confusion, wondering if this was some sort of new technique. A small trickle of blood began to drip from her left nostril. With a trembling, shaking hand, she wiped it away, and looked at me in fear and confusion.

"Am . . . am . . . I . . . ." Her voice was thick and clotted. Her hands were shaking and her nose was beginning to drip blood.

"Shihan?" I said again, a beautiful suspicion beginning to work through me.

She swallowed, and struggling over every syllable, said, "I . . . need . . . an . . . ambulance."

I looked at her in astonishment for a moment. In three years she'd never complained about anything but me. Heat, cold, fatigue, pain, wet, dry, drunk, sober: she was utterly indifferent to them all. This admission of need nearly made me stagger.

My slow smile was answer enough, I think. Her eyes grew very wide, one pupils slowly dilating.

"Really? And why would that be?"

She looked up at me. The fear in her eyes was like a fine wine. There was a dreadful knowledge of the future floating around back there behind those dying pupils. She knew it as well as I did and yet she still tried to stave it off, to stave me and my rightful revenge off.

She wasn't the first, but she was probably the one I enjoyed the most.

She reached a shaking hand into her wretched gi and pulled the dragon out. She tried to smile at me, but by this point one side of her face was sagging and the effect was hideous. Her dentures were sliding as well. She held the dragon out to me, smiling that horrible smile, her eyes bleeding hope and running tears.

I looked down at the dragon, seeing how beautiful it really was in this most perfect of all moments. Its worth had just increased ten-fold. For the cost of a phone call, I could be set up for life.

I took the dragon from her hand. Ohhhh, to feel that moment forever! The solid weight of all that exquisite gold and gem-work - finally, finally! - sitting in the palm of my hand. It weighed as much as the world and was five, ten, a million times more precious.

I ran a loving fingernail over each scale, caressed the gems and squeezed it in my hands to feel the sharp points gently pressing against my skin.

The whole time Teshuga looked up at me in way that suggested "You'll help me now, right?"

I wiped a happy tear from my face. It was too much to believe!

With one finger, I poked her in the forehead hard enough to knock her flat on her back. She made a glotty sobbing noise before collapsing like a scarecrow.

I squatted down on my hams next to her, still gently squeezing the dragon. She was shivering all over, and her eyes were running naked tears.

"Looks like you're having a stroke, old girl," I said, conversationally. I dipped a finger in the blood running from her nose. It was pooling in her mouth and slowly choking her as her ability to swallow diminished. I drew an idle swirl on her left cheek, leaving a strange icon in her blood there.

"Crummy way to die, I'd think; a stroke. I mean, personally, I'd rather die with three feet of metal in my liver, or a nice, quick, clean, bullet to the back of the head, but hey. What are ya' gonna do, right?" I said it with a chummy little wave of my hand.

We sat there for what seemed a very long time.

When I judged she was finally and truly dying, I held the dragon in front of her eyes. She was no longer trembling. Her breaths were coming in labored, choking gasps as she tried to clear the steady trickle of blood from her airway with muscles that were no longer responding to her will.

I held the dragon in between two hands that were now as strong as steel cables. Her eyes seemed to weep tears that begged for her life and for me to stop what I was about to do.

I can't tell you how much I enjoyed denying both.

With a surge of strength, and a nearly sexual growl, I broke the dragon, her prized possession, into two pieces.

She globbered something unintelligible at me, her head shaking weakly back and forth in denial. I nodded and patted her head.

"I know, I know. But I'm only a woman, and a western tart at that," I said, smiling gently.

I put the pieces down. Then slowly, gently, and lovingly trod them flat.

"I guess I'm ready, Teshuga."

I dusted my hands off over her, watching her weep, bleed and slowly - oh, so slowly - die, enjoying it immensely. I walked to the front door. She made a final bleating noise of hate and rage from her place on the floor.

I turned the light off, leaving her there, in the dark, and walked out.

And that's my life. I'm good at what I do, and I have no intention of stopping anytime soon.

Sure, every once in a while I'll think about settling down, meeting somebody I don't want to kill after five minutes, maybe watching TV, eating dinner and going to, like, clothes stores for sales, or whatever. You know: normal chick stuff in a normal chick world.

And I'll try - hard! - to imagine myself having a nine-to-five job and never again experiencing the exquisite pleasure of bones breaking under my hands, and I'll put those fantasies away for a while.

Well? What do you think?

Heeelllllloooo? Anybody awake under there?

Oh.

You're dead.

Well, alrighty then.

The Edge of the Ice

He sat down in the booth across from me, uninvited, pushing his walking stick - cum - cane before him. He made little shuffling noises and grunts of effort as he scooted across the hard plastic seat into the shelf formed by my little window.

Yes, okay. I was annoyed. I was enjoying the solitude, the sunshine and a cup of coffee before going home. It had been one of those 'Lemme piss down the back of your neck! You smile, now, bo'!' kind of days, and I was tired. I didn't particularly feel like having a conversation with anyone, much less a stranger.

I lowered the paper I was aimlessly scanning and considered the invader. He was a hirsute gentleman, with sun-bleached hair, beard and skin. He looked weathered; the sun had leeched him dry, wrung him out, and left him without any juice.

His eyes were closed, he seemed to be napping. He wore the faded remains of a field jacket; a bandanna that I suspected had started life as a t-shirt, and an indefinable air of confused dignity.

He also smelled like incontinent cat, badly cooked feet, and ripe bologna.

"Help you?" I asked, in what I hoped was a 'closed-body-language' way.

"I've forgotten my name," he said, in a whisper. Even his voice was thinned of color, but it had a light Nordic tang to it, like a slice of lime in a pitcher of ice water. It sounded like the recording of a clipped, staccato breeze. His breath wafted over me, and I was surprised by a cold wash of mint. He didn't really seem to be talking to me, it was as if he were talking, and I happened to be there.

I sighed, inwardly. 'I just wanted a friggin' cup of coffee!' I thought at him.

He remained deaf to my astral hostility, and seemed for all the world to be content to wait until I responded. I wasn't sure I was going to until I did.

"Wow, dude. That sucks. Bet it makes cashing a check a real chore, huh?"

My flippancy was wasted. He sat, his closed eyes not gazing at me, waiting.

I sighed, outwardly this time, and set my paper and cup of coffee aside. I reached my hand out and told him my name. "And you are . . . ?"

He tilted his head to one side, as if he were watching the play of sun on the window through his closed eyes, or listening to music only he could hear. He smiled, then, his face breaking into leathery, salty creases. It was a beautiful smile for all of that.

"I don't know. I've forgotten my name. I thought I mentioned that."

I shook my head and withdrew my hand.

"A wise woman once told me to protect my name," he said in that same voice. "She said 'You fold your name under a corner of your heart, like a maid ties coins in her kerchief, or a whore hides her precious things from prying, stealing eyes. It'll protect your name. You understand? The hard muscle of your heart, it'll protect your name from tarnish, from the blows the world will land on it.'"

His head drooped then and his smile faded, "But I didn't listen, and now I've forgotten my name."

I sat back in my plastic seat, wondering why this sort of thing always seems to happen to me. No one else in the restaurant was paying us the least bit of attention. It was as if we had been excised and placed outside the sphere of humanity.

I thought an unkind name at them. And then I considered simply breaking for it, when my table mate spoke again.

"Sinter Klaus comes close, I think, but I have no blackamoor companion."

"What?" I said, my voice finally expressing my exasperation.

He sat, silent, gazing at the insides of his eyelids.

"What did you say?" I asked, "Santa Claus? You think you're Santa Claus?"

"Him, too, I suppose. I give them what they want, you see, and he does the same thing. Maybe we're the same person? I'm him when he's not me?"

"That's so amazingly Zen, I'm stunned," I replied, my mouth making noises that hadn't been cleared by my head, but I'd figured this guy out. "Listen. I don't have much money, but you've really got to get off the junk, okay? It'll end up destroying your li-"

"I touch them, you see." He rode right over the top of me as if I weren't there. "It doesn't matter how, really. A touch to the hand, a brush on the face. I touch them, one person or animal per day, and ask them what it is they want."

"Sounds very Goodkind-ish," I replied. "Sword of Truth. Mother Confessor, all that. Are you a fan?"

Again, he seemed to talk at me.

"And they tell me. The answers rarely surprise me. This one wants his wife to love him when he really means 'worship him'. That one wants to be rich and famous. Men want to be rugged and handsome; women want to be thin and pretty. Taller, shorter, fatter, skinnier, I've heard every petty hunger imaginable."

He paused again and then, with unflinching accuracy, plucked my coffee from its saucer and drained it dry, without spilling a drop.

My mouth fell open. Yes, it was a neat trick to do that with closed eyes, but I was more shocked at his audacity. He gave a great sigh of satisfaction while I gaped at him, and he continued speaking as if stealing a man's coffee were something he did as a matter of course.

"I touched a woman yesterday. A beautiful young thing. I was sitting on the bench in the park, and she walked by, her head down, her face sad. I reached out, gently took her wrist, and asked, 'What do you want, child?'"

"And they just tell you, do they? Just stop what they're doing and come out all over with their desires?"

"Yes."

I was so surprised he had answered; I didn't have the time to ask him something else.

"Oh yes. They have to. They tell me what they most desire, what lives at the very bottom of their heart and defines them, drives them, motivates them. and I give it to them. I have all the time I need to give them what they most want. It's part of the magic, you see."

"Magic," I said, derision and naked unbelief coloring my tone.

"We stand there, or sit, or even lie, waiting, as they tell me exactly what they want. It happens instantly to the outside world; one second I'm touching you, the next I'm not. She stood there, her face full of an inexpressible longing, and I asked her again, 'What do you want, child?' She had everything, you see. Money, power, an important husband, all the things that make some people happy, and she wasn't. And I love to make people happy when I can."

He sat silent for so long, I had time to remember that he was an invader. "So then what happened? What did she say?"

Instead of answering my question, he wiped a hand through his beard. He combed his fingers through it for a moment, and I could feel the weight of his thoughts.

When he did speak, he ignored my question completely. His voice was stronger, though, more confident. It was as if he were gaining strength through the telling of the story.

"The desires that are easiest to fill are an animal's. People believe that animals are simple. And they believe this as if it makes them superior, somehow. 'I am human, I am better than a simple animal, as I desire more.' That's silly. An animal knows exactly what it wants, and knows exactly how it wants it. An animal does not lie, prevaricate, justify or try to hide its motivations. Some animals want to play throw-ball. Some want to play chew-tug. This one wants a belly rub, that one wants a back scratch. They are beautiful in their desires. They are pure and simple and honest and almost holy."

He paused then, and ran his fingers through his beard again. I had almost decided to prompt him when he spoke again.

"I once gave a junkyard dog in New Jersey its heart's desire."

He stopped again and reached for the menu lying against the napkin dispenser. He opened it and slowly lowered his head, his eyes still closed, as he seemed to look it over. I waited. While still looking at the menu through closed eyes, he went on.

"And I gave her her heart's desire. This massive, drooling, biting engine of canine death wanted just one thing in life. It was the only thing she truly wanted, a perfectly formed picture inside her head that made her heart beat faster, would fulfill her entire life, and make her happy."

"What was it?"

"Grass-stained feet," he whispered. "She wanted to feel something beneath her feet other than concrete. So I gave it to her."

He went back to the menu, running his closed-eyes-gaze over it slowly, deliberately.

"And the young woman?" I asked it with a thinly concealed impatience. He smiled again, and looked back at the window.

"I held her wrist, and I felt her life pump beneath my fingers. Her face broke into a sob, and she replied, 'I want sunshine.' That took me aback, that did. And I said, 'But why, child? You have sunshine. It's a beautiful day,' and she interrupted me. 'I want sunshine for sadness. He loves me, but he loves me as a favored pet, a beloved play thing. I want the pleasure and the pain of love for itself.'"

He stopped again. His face falling out of that slow, syrupy smile.

"So I gave it to her. I gave her exactly what she wanted, and I watched as she cried, and I took what was due me for my gift, and she went her way, and I went mine."

"Wait a minute. What do you mean, 'took what was due'?"

"It used to be a glass of whiskey and a bit of fish. Then there were cookies and milk. Now I take what I can, like a whore. I take for my gifts. Only on top, that's true, but I take. She had seventy-five dollars in her purse that she was going to spend on a track suit. I took it, and she went her way."

"You robbed her?"

He turned his face away from the menu and faced me again.

"If you like."

I shook my head.

97

"I touched a boy yesterday. I put my hand on the back of his head, and I asked, 'What do you want, child?' and his answer was immediate."

He opened his eyes, and I saw they were the color of old, old ice, ice that's been around for thousands of years. I looked into those eyes and shivered.

"And he said to me, 'I want to die.' This child of nine years old looked me in the eyes and told me his heart's desire. 'I want to die.'"

He fell silent, his eyes slowly closing.

"But why?" I asked.

"He said to me, 'I want to die so that I can go to Heaven without worrying about screwing up anymore. I don't want to worry about life anymore. I just want the fear and the doubt to end.'"

His voice lowered even further, and each word came out as though it hurt him.

"This poor child, innocent in every way, was asking to be sent to Heaven as an innocent. He was so worried about hell and the things he'd been told about growing up that he wanted to die before life could touch him.

"Can you imagine being that scared of living?"

I shook my head. I couldn't even begin to understand.

"So I did that thing. I gave him what he most wanted. I wrapped my hands around his throat and I broke his neck with a twist of my wrists. It took so little effort that the boy was dead before he knew it. I emptied his pockets and went my way."

I sat back in my seat, shaking my head. Part of me wanted to laugh at the 'silly old man jerking my chain', and part of me wanted to run out of the restaurant, screaming.

A hand lifted from the table, as if it had a mind of its own, and slowly reached toward me.

The noise of the restaurant faded away. The light streaming into the window muted. The sounds of the street beyond a single thickness of glass faded out. It was just me, him, and that hairy, liver-spotted, emaciated, leathery and terrifying hand.

I sat further back in my seat. In that instant, he ceased being a harmless crazy, or a battered old junkie. He was my every fear incarnated in a shambling, mumbling, smelly package.

He sat across from me, his eyes closed, his gnarled hand reached toward me. He radiated an air of absoluteness. In a way I have never been able to understand since, I knew - knew! - that if I took his hand, he'd give me my one true heart's desire.

And that petrified me.

What do you want? What do you really want? Deep down inside, under all your petty, human needs and desires, what actually makes your mouth go dry and your palms sweat?

Is it money?

Sex?

What?

Can you answer me?

I couldn't.

I couldn't face the knowing of what that would end up being. Did I secretly want to be dead? Did I secretly want to be miserable? Who ever really knows themselves?

I watched him, terrified that his lips would start to move, and 'What do you want, child?' would emerge from them.

And I'd have to tell him, wouldn't I? I'd have to tell him what it was I most want, and I couldn't face that.

So I shrank back in my seat, shivering and sweating, holding my body as far away from that hand as I could.

We sat there for the longest moment, my heart thundering in my ears. His hand did not shake, nor did it move; it pointed at me like a gun.

And then, he slowly withdrew his hand and sat back.

I let loose a breath I didn't realize I had been holding.

"As you wish," he whispered, and the sounds of the world crashed in on us. I looked around in confusion for a moment, and a waitress walked up and refilled my coffee cup.

He sat there, silent. And remained so as I finished my coffee and then finished another. I didn't want him to speak. I was afraid that if he did, I would be told something horrible.

But he remained silent. He said nothing as I stood up, walked to the cashier and paid my check. He didn't respond when I came back to the table for my jacket. And he remained silent as I left a tip.

I walked away, trying not to run.

I wish I could tell you that the next time I visited that restaurant, a waitress came to me and said, "Oh yeah. That's 'Crazy Benny'. He tells that story to everybody that comes in here."

Or 'What crazy old guy?' And we all mug, simultaneously, at the now empty table.

But he was still there when I walked out of the restaurant, staring at nothing, and no one said a word to me about him.

I went home that night, and wondered, as I have every single day since.

Sir Robere and Bill of William

*F*or me, the goal is, and always has been, storytelling.

    There is a world of difference between writers and storytellers.

    Writers can be enormously gifted with their wordsmithing. They can craft analogy and metaphor in such a way as to build a glittering castle of words, made of spun-sugar and glass. They are artists with the written word and well deserving of respect. Writers are an elite group of people who will often find that they can change the world, given a large enough readership. If a writer is lucky enough to be published, that's often enough for them. Seeing their work in print is all the reward they need. Although I'm told the money's nice, too.

    A storyteller, on the other hand, is bit of a vampire. A storyteller is anyone who can make you stop and give them your undivided attention when they tell you a story.

    A homeless man, sitting on a bench, reeking of his own bodily wastes, can be a storyteller without peer. A four-year-old-boy, one who doesn't even speak your language, can be a storyteller with gesture and body language. It's all about conveyance; trapping your mind and refusing to let it go until the story's told. Good or bad, right or wrong, storytellers must have an audience. If one person listens to their story, that is enough - but someone has to hear it.

    I spend a lot of time thinking about my storytelling.

    It seems that many of my characters are in transit somehow. It's like they're in one place, just waiting for a ride to their next destination, or moving from one point to another, or leaving one place after a short time. They almost never seem to stay, build families and communities, run for public office, etc.

    I'm afraid that many of my characters are tramps and rogues - shiftless, literary hoboes who would be thrown out of finer establishments for forgetting shoes.

    I'm not entirely sure what this says about me, though I have my suspicions.

    This piece was inspired by a Berke Breathed cartoon from the early eighties. It turns the aforementioned tendency of mine on its ear.

    Enjoy.

~~~~~~

For the last hour, the only thing I'd been hearing was the wind toying with the leaves around me. It was a playful sound, albeit a solitary one. Hearing the burble of water ahead sent a frisson of delight through me. I'm still enough of a little boy to enjoy splashing and frolicking in a creek.

I'd decided to get started at first light this morning. I'd torn down, eaten breakfast, and rucked out, all within an hour of waking up. There's just something about being in the woods that makes the passing of idle day seem almost blasphemous.

The sun still struggled to burn the ground-fog off. Heavy light lanced through the trees, throwing sharp spears of gauzy, fog-laced shadows everywhere. The scent of pine, earth, and water was heavy on the morning breeze and birdsong surrounded me.

I followed the noise of the creek and came upon it a short while later. It was as pretty as a picture.

Framed by a small glade of ash trees on the far bank, the ground gradually sloped down to the water's edge. This created a natural 'ramp' of sorts that put me at water level with no difficulty. It was almost like stepping into a wading pool at some fancy hotel.

I splashed some of the water on my hands, face and neck. It was deliciously cold and wonderfully refreshing.

Tasting the water, I found it to be as sweet as could be. It is still possible to find sources of perfectly clear, clean and pure water in some places - untouched and unpoisoned by the hand of man. I filled my canteen and drank until I was sloshing.

The water rolled and chuckled over stones in the creek's bed, and it was pleasant to simply sit and listen for a few moments. I found a large flat rock nearby, and after dumping my ruck, I sat, positioned my knife to be at hand – I was in the deep woods, after all, and you could never be too careful - and relaxed into the magic of the place.

Time passed with slow indolence, and I could feel the mana working on my tired spirit. The noise of the water was gently soothing, and stray breezes would occasionally brush against my face with gentle, teasing fingers. I sipped from my canteen from time to time, more to taste the water than from any thirst I had. I'd just taken another drink, rinsing the water around in my mouth, when I first heard the bell-like jingle that could only be a horse's harness.

Listen; you don't grow up in Kentucky and not know what a horse's harness sounds like!

It was an odd moment; hard to describe. One minute I was enjoying the peaceful solitude of the picturesque creek. The next, I looked across the water, and there he stood: Sir Whosawhatsit in full regalia, looking over at me superciliously.

He hadn't been there a moment before. I know he wasn't. I know what it feels like when you're in the woods and something else is in there with you. You can feel their eyes on the back of your neck. It's impossible *not* to know. Besides, I'd like to credit myself with having heard *this* horse-jockey approach!

The tricky light threw dense shadows, but I could see him easily enough. Despite what had to be a crushing heat, he wore metal-head-to-foot armor and held a lance easily twelve feet long.

There was nothing funny or playful about that lance. The head of it would poke a hole in you bigger than a bowling ball. That lance would pin you forever to a concrete wall.

He sat his horse like he was a part of it. The horse stood seven feet tall at the shoulder. Sir Whosawhatsit's head rose five feet above that. Four to five feet wide, he resembled, in more ways than one, a golf-tee.

The sun kept glinting off his metal breastplate. The horse whickered at me in greeting, a friendly sort of noise.

In my panicked "Oh, God. I'm gonna die! Sir Whatshisbeard's gonna stick a lance into me!" mental state, I felt a stab of pity for the poor horse. The man was almost as big as it was!

The scent of sweat, metal, and tired horse wafted across the distance then, several long seconds after man and horse appeared. You pay attention to smells in the forest. Little things let you know who's about. The stink rolling around inside my head should really have been there several minutes ago, giving me lots of time to prepare for this meeting.

Like I said: the whole scene was *strange.*

My mouth, still full of water, ballooned my cheeks like a fish's, and my hand tightened around my knife in a death grip that sent stabbing aches into my shoulder. I'm not really sure what I thought I could accomplish with my little hunting knife. Maybe it was simply an in-bred survival reflex of some kind.

I swallowed and let my knife go, all without looking away from this exotic neighbor. He saw me regarding him, and lifted the visor of his helm in a way you *know* he had to have practiced in front of a mirror for a week. He tugged at his forelock - yes, it was spit-curled, just as you'd imagine it to be - in greeting.

"Ho. Well met!"

His voice, this cultured, melodious bass-thing, came from somewhere down around his armored kneecaps. And you know he had an accent, right? One of those really good accents that you can only get when you've got royalty for great-great-grand-whatevers, and butlers and castles and all that kind of jazz.

For no reason I can give you, I had this sudden mental picture of certain older Disney movies.

Now, I was raised right. I've got good manners. When a man says something in greeting to you, you respond - simple as that. Even if he's getting ready to stick a twelve-foot-long lance in you, you respond.

Yes, I was a little freaked out, and kept wanting to grab my knife, but I responded in as polite a manner as I felt I could manage.

"Hey."

He dismounted in as graceful a way as you could imagine, laid his lance reverently against a nearby tree, and knelt at his edge of the water.

"Oh, Lord; I thank thee, for this, thy most gracious bounty," he prayed, in a sincere, humble way, his head bowed, eyes closed. It was the kind of prayer you could imagine somebody like King David making just before cutting beheading somebody in a righteous display of fury and indignation.

He looked when he finished.

"Hast drank thy fill, then, sirrah?"

I gave off an inarticulate grunt in response. Not one of my better moments, I'm afraid.

"Whut?"

He pointed at the creek. Patiently, he repeated what he had said, carefully mouthing each syllable.

"Have you drank your fill of yon water?"

"Oh. Yeah, man. Go ahead. Help yourself."

He took off a pair of black leather gauntlets that clanked like a pocketful of loose change, and laid them carefully in the sweet grass at the verge. He washed his hands in a thorough, thoughtful way, humming some ditty beneath his breath.

Next, he removed his helm – as big as a witch's cauldron - and washed his face and neck. He drank a few handfuls of water just upstream from his horse – who wasn't waiting to be invited, and did its level best to lower the water level of that poor creek – and then he filled a large leather bota.

I've seen botas before. My parents had a hippie version, no doubt filled with some kind of hippie-love-potion - a manufactured piece of crap that smelled like badly cured horsehide and resembled a leather box with a pouring mouth on it.

His bota looked like it had been made from most of the carefully tanned hide of a large sheep. The *entire* carefully tanned hide of a large sheep. With silvered filigree and an ivory mouthpiece, it looked like it could hold twenty gallons of water. This bota was the great-grand-daddy of all botas everywhere, a gorgeous piece of perfectly common equipment, and he treated it in the same way you or I would a screwdriver.

His horse, backed away from the creek's edge, and lowered its head in a muted jingle of harness, tack, and barding. It began to quietly eat the grass from the verge, apparently deciding the humans could work things out for themselves.

The man stood after his bota was full. A certain determination firmed the noble features of his face. It almost looked like he'd decided something for himself, and was relieved to have finally reached the conclusion. He grabbed his lance and planted the butt-end in the ground. It wasn't a menacing gesture, but I didn't realize that then. I gave off a frightened little squeak and scampered back a bit.

He pretended not to notice – or maybe he *didn't* notice. Guy was seriously noble, and maybe the shortcomings of others were something of a blind spot. At any rate, he extended his right hand, palm up, toward me.

You've seen the gesture before. It's the common, primate 'I'm not holding a weapon, and I'm not going to brain you, so relax,' gesture, familiar to all of us humans everywhere.

"Wouldst know whom I share yon water-course with."

I gave another one of my half-language grunts.

"Whurr?"

"Your name, sirrah. Wouldst know your name."

He spoke slowly, his voice rising in volume, articulating every syllable.

I lifted my own hand in a nervous wave. Yes, I was quite freaked out at this point. Wouldn't you be?

"Oh. Yeah. Um, my name's Bill. Bill Bailey."

"Bill! Wouldst be short for William, then?"

"What? Oh! Umm . . . yeah. Yeah, I think so. My parents named me for some rich old uncle, or something. I don't really know. I just kind of go by Bill."

"Bill of William. A fine name. Your namesake was a conqueror and a mighty warrior who strode the earth with grim mien and fierce tramp. A fine name, indeed."

"Uhh . . . yeah. Okay. I guess. Sooo . . . who're you?"

He smiled, and that smile would've broken your heart. I swear it would've. I'm not gay or anything, but for a minute there . . . well, never mind.

Lifting his right hand solemnly to his heart, he clanked the lance with his left against the solid metal of his breastplate so that his arms were momentarily crossed. It was almost as if he were just waiting for me to ask, the gesture so beautiful and dignified. I've tried mimicking it myself, but I always end up looking stupid.

"Sir Robere Dunnamore, of Conley; lately of lands hereabouts. Tell me, squire. Wouldst know the way to fair Eire?"

My head heard what he said, and it tried, desperately, under the tide of survival hormones that it pumped into my bloodstream, to keep up with current events. I'm not the fastest salmon in the river, though, and it wasn't doing a very good job. When he asked me this question, my brain gave up and started singing folk songs at me in a husky woman's voice:

"How many roads to fair Avalon? All of them, and none."

I wanted to help Sir Robear Donomore of Conley. I really did. But . . . I mean . . . I'm . . .

Well, *you* know.

I shook my head. "Naw, man. Sorry. I sure don't. You got a cell phone? A laptop? You could go online, or maybe call an auto club for directions."

Yeah. That's exactly what I said. Pathetic, isn't it?

He took it in this really dignified, knightly stride. Almost seemed not to mind at all.

"Ah, well. No matter. Come! We've a fine day ahead of us! Though the journey be long, we shall wile the time away in story and song! Two stout companions for the road! What, ho?"

Okay.

Now, stop for just a second.

This guy's as big as a grizzly bear. He's got a lance as long as a telephone pole and looks like he eats guys like me for an appetizer. Hell, the thing he carries water in is bigger than I am! His horse is bigger than my first apartment!

What would *you* say to such an invitation?

I wasn't at all dignified, I'm afraid. My mouth started working like a vomiting bird's, opening and closing.

"I . . . I . . . I . . . can't, man. I'm . . . I've got this meeting . . . my vacation's over as of tonight, and . . . laundry . . . . people will be looking for me . . . . work . . . ."

Lame, wasn't it? But I swear to you that's *exactly* what I said. There may have been a few more "uhhs" and "umms" in there, but I don't think I want to remember those. Preserve a *little* dignity, you know?

His face slammed shut like the closing of a tomb. The light and animation just bled from him. I was utterly, utterly dismissed.

"Suit yourself, squire."

He vaulted effortlessly into the saddle, somehow still holding onto his lance, with a ringing jingle of metal. He turned his horse and rode away without another word.

He disappeared into the dusty sunshine, and I listened until the small, bell-like tinkling of his equipment died away.

It stopped after a surprisingly short time - like something had been turned off, or unplugged.

Like a door had been shut forever.

"Sir Robeer?"

No answer.

"Sir Robeare!"

Still no answer.

"SIR ROBARE!"

Nothing.

Something inside me realized it had lost an opportunity of immense value, and I panicked. I called his name, over and over, even going so far as to shout it in a bad imitation of his courtly accent.

No response came to my calls. I didn't really think there would be.

I waded through the creek. Casting about, I saw a single hoof print deeply embedded in the moss right about where his horse had been. Though I searched up and down the creek for a good long while, there was no other sign he'd ever been there.

None.

And the whole time, my brain sung it at me, letting me know exactly what I'd just allowed to leave my life.

"How many roads to fair Avalon? All of them and just one. You just let it ride away, nimrod."

Schrodinger's Cat

This will probably come as a surprise (except to those that know me well), but I really am a pretty smart guy.

I'm enormously well read, and I have an interest in many diverse subjects ranging from ancient history to cryptozoology. I read voraciously and continually. I have since I was old enough to hold a book, it seems.

*An area I take a special interest in is astrophysics. While I hardly understand MOST of the math involved, astrophysics is an area where space, time, and everything in between can get downright . . . mystical. Things can exist as both particles and rays, stuff spontaneously teleports, things exist and then don't exist, and then **RE-exist**, and it gets even odder the further you go.*

I'm really only interested in numbers when they're weird.

Pythagoras once said that "All is number." The Jews have developed an entire theosophical system devoted to a similar precept. Numbers can be quite strange at times . . . almost magical.

That, at least in part, is the inspiration for this story. That, and a locked door.

Enjoy.

I've been fired.

I knew it was coming; after all, I hit Chester in the face with an axe. Granted, it was the blunt end, but still . . . .

I don't know if he's going to press charges or not. I'm not really worried about that. I'm more concerned they're going to decide I'm insane and put me away somewhere.

That might not be so bad; I just wish *somebody could understand me!*

I know what I saw.

I know what I experienced.

No one else may ever understand, but I will know.

I will remember . . . ..

~~~~~~~

I started working for Ajax Amalgamated a little over a year ago. A buddy of mine had gotten on, and he turned me on to them. "They need a maintenance specialist, dude. That's right up your alley."

So I applied. I sat through an interview or two, and a week later I was Ajax Amalgamated's newest maintenance guy. I was really surprised at how easy it was to get on. There were literally no barriers, and like, no wait time at all. I had half-expected to be rejected due to a lack of experience. I even mentioned it to my interviewer, but he just smiled, and asked me some more questions.

It was frighteningly easy.

The job was easy, too. Aside from the occasional work order, I just had to ensure that the water kept running, the AC was on when it was hot, and the heat when it was cold.

Piece o' cake, right?

Right.

So I get there the first day, right? I figured there'd be some sort of orientation, so I showed up a little early. The maintenance supervisor shows up and without so much as a handshake, he starts dragging me around the building.

The maintenance supervisor was this great, big, corn-fed white boy named Chester Dole. He had a crew cut and his hair was fire engine red. He had an unfortunate predilection for red coveralls, so he looked like a big, red brick. (When he got mad, his face turned the same color as his hair.) He stood at about six eight, and looked to weigh three-eighty, easy. He had this really sincere smile, and his teeth were just as white as all get out. He didn't smoke, he didn't drink coffee, and he had a constant pocketful of those red and white swirly mints on him every day. He carried a cloud of mint fragrance around with him.

Chester spoke with a sort of staccato, drill-sergeant delivery. You could easily picture him bellowing his lungs out over the top of some anxious, sweaty recruit. He never actually raised his voice, and he never used curse words, but he somehow gave off this impression of 'intensity.'

Chester was a hard kind of guy to define, but 'anal-retentive-to-the-absolute-max ' comes close. He was a guy who wanted it all done his way, and if you weren't doing it his way, then you were doing it wrong. Period.

(We actually got a long quite well until I hit him in the mouth with a fire axe. Oops.)

So Chester's dragging me all over the building, sucking and slurping away on those mints, okay? He shows me the boiler room, he shows me the air exchangers, he shows me the fire suppression systems, and he shows me the janitorial closets. Nothing out of the ordinary, right? We're on the third floor and I'm trying to memorize the layout of the building in my head when we walk past this door. Chester, he breezes right past it without even mentioning it, which is really odd since he's been going out of his way to describe everything else.

There was nothing really remarkable about the door. It was a standard, wooden door, much like all the others in the building. It was the only feature of an otherwise featureless hallway, and it was painted the same color as the walls surrounding it. It had a brass doorknob with no keyhole.

I stopped and looked at the door; Chester kept right on going, talking as if I were still next to him.

Wanting to be the best at my job that I could be I interrupted him and called, "Hey boss. What's this?" I tried the handle, but it was locked.

Chester turned around, saw me, looked *directly* at the door (That's important. He looked directly at the door. I mean **right** at it.) and said, "What's what?"

I pointed at the door and jiggled the handle again for emphasis. "This door, boss. What's in here? A closet?"

I tried the handle a final time, and then looked at Chester. There was this strange, relaxed slackness to his face- like he was asleep or stoned or something. He was looking at the door and his mouth was hanging open and his eyes were totally unfocused. He looked at the door - not saying anything, and with that strange, idiot look on his face - for a long, slow count of thirty. I . . . sensed something then. I still don't know what it was, but I could feel it there in that hallway.

I was just about to reach out and shake Chester, when life rushed back into his face and eyes. He kinda shook himself a little, blinked a few times, and then turned around and went back to telling me all about the vending machines down the hallway as though the last two minutes had never happened.

It was the strangest thing I had ever seen in my life.

I caught back up to Chester, and kept my mouth shut. I thought that maybe he was one of those people who suffered from 'gray-outs.' (I was new, okay? I didn't want to rock the boat by asking my new boss, "Hey. Holy crap! That was weird, man! What's that all about?")

~~~~~~~

A week went by. I was fitting in nicely, learning the ropes and the faces at Ajax. The people were warm and friendly and I felt right at home.

It was a really good job and I'm going to miss it.

Towards the end of that first week, I found myself standing in front of that door again. I had been cleaning the carpets on three, and in the very normal process of ensuring I got all the carpets, I found myself in that hallway, in front of the door. Perfectly plausible explanation, right?

Right.

I turned off my carpet cleaner and looked at the door. I had this strange, sudden feeling that I was being regarded by the door in turn. It was the oddest feeling in the world. I felt like I was being . . . weighed somehow. Like, my various worths and faults were being catalogued on some sort of cosmic scale, like a, "if my sins weren't as light as a feather, I was going to be eaten," kind of thing.

I looked at the door.

It was a door. Wood, industrial gray, brass handle, floor to ceiling fitting. Normal hinge arrangement, no lock, no keyhole.

I reached out and tried the handle.

No dice. It was still locked, most likely from the inside.

The handle was colder than it had any real right to be. It felt like it had been sitting in an ice chest for a few minutes, and it was very, very gently vibrating.

I had a ring of keys, but this door had no lock. I walked around to where I judged the other side of the door to be, but it was just a blank, featureless wall. I knocked, and the wall seemed pretty solid.

I walked back to the door, reached into my pocket and withdrew my pocketknife. I unfolded it and slid it in-between the latch of the door and the jamb. I was just feeling the latch start to give when Chester crackled over the radio. A pipe had burst on the first floor, and it was flooding office space. I was needed down there right now.

Without a second thought, I raced downstairs to deal with the pipe. It wasn't until much later that I thought about the timing of that event.

That night I had a dream.

I dreamed I was at work, in uniform and everything. I was standing in front of that same door. I knew - like you do in dreams - that it was going to open. Part of me desperately wanted to nail it shut, and bury it so that it'd never, *ever* be able to open. Part of me was rejoicing, 'cause I'd finally be able to see what lay inside. As I stood there, in an agony of indecision, the door slowly and soundlessly swung open . . . .

. . . and I jerked awake, sitting bolt upright in bed. My heart was jack hammering away, my head hurt, and I was sweating. There was no immediate cause for it, near as I could tell, except the dream. I was sitting there, sweating, trying to figure it out, when a fierce nausea began to build within my lower stomach. I sprinted to the toilet, my hand over my mouth.

I threw up for a really long time. When I finally stopped retching, my lips were flecked with blood.

~~~~~~~

I took a long weekend and came back to work the next week. I felt tired, drained, all week. I managed to slog through, though, and by the end of that week, I was feeling much better.

Then I got a work order for the third floor.

Somebody had decided the third floor hallway needed painting. I decided to go see Chester about a color and tried not to think about the closet. Chester told me that Ajax only wanted industrial gray, and there was plenty of that on hand.

I nodded, and then nonchalantly asked Chester if Ajax wanted me to paint the door, too. He looked at me for a minute and then asked, "What door?"

See a pattern, yet?

Long story short, Chester told me I was crazy. The only door on three was the door off the elevator lobby and the stairwell door at the end of the hall running off the elevator lobby. Three didn't have a janitor closet or a bathroom. It was a large, open office space. Rather than argue with him, I nodded and said, "Okay, boss. But hey, give me a hand with the paint, will ya? I don't want to have to make multiple trips."

He nodded, and we slogged the buckets of paint up to three. I deliberately set a bucket in front of the door. It seemed to be radiating a certain smugness. Like, "I know what you're up to, and it won't work."

Casually, I called out to Chester, who was hauling buckets off the elevator and onto the floor. "Hey, boss. Come tell me if this color's okay. I don't want to screw up or anything."

Chester came down the hallway, the floor thudding gently under his gargantuan feet. I held the bucket of paint directly in front of the door. Chester looked at the bucket, and I watched as his eyes skipped over the door and landed on the wall. He even took the bucket from me, and held it against the wall next to the door. I noticed that he was very carefully *not* touching the door.

"That'd be fine," he said, and smiled at me. "Have fun." He then tromped off down the hallway.

I put the bucket of industrial gray paint down. I looked at that smug, self-satisfied door.

I tried the handle again, and pulled with all my might.

Locked.

I faced the door directly, and said as loud as I could, "You haven't won yet!"

The smugness was becoming suffocating.

I went back down to the paint locker and rummaged around a bit. When I went back to three, I had four buckets of paint under my arm. I painted the walls of the third floor exactly as the client wanted them. For the door, I did something a little special.

That night I dreamed again.

I was back in front of the door and it opened. This bright, white, pure light was pouring out from the door. It grew and grew in intensity, and I could hear this noise like music pouring out from the door as well. It grew in resonance with the light.

Does that make sense? It was like, as the light got brighter, the music got louder.

I couldn't see, and the music was starting to vibrate in my head . . .

114

. . . I woke up, and threw up all over myself. My nose bled for twenty minutes and I could feel something trying to give in my stomach.

I didn't go back to sleep that night at all.

~~~~~~~

The next morning I left for work early. I took my Polaroid camera in to work with me and went directly to the door. I was half-afraid that my paint job would have changed over night. Like, some cosmic guardian would come and paint over my lovely masterpiece. But no, it was exactly as I had left it.

I had divided the door into four quadrants, and had painted each of the four quadrants a bright, eye-catching color, and then polka-dotted the quadrant with a different color. I used "Parking-lot yellow, Industrial Hazard Red, Child's Room Blue," and my *piece de resistance* "Mother's room pink."

The door looked like it had an exotic form of measles.

I took several photos of the door and tucked them safely away. I turned towards the door, and under my breath, I said, "If you can beat this . . . ."

Chester came in to work to see four photos of a brightly painted door on his desk. He looked at each of them in turn, and said, "Fine job. Looks like you got the grey on just right."

He smiled, laid the pictures down and asked if I wanted to go to breakfast.

I could almost hear a high, somehow wordless, "Na, na, na, na-nahhhhh!"

~~~~~~~

I found myself standing in front of that door every day that week. And I tried to break in more times than I could count, and every time I was allllllllmmmmmoooost in something happened to prevent me. There was always a plausible explanation. A leak, a re-wiring job, cooling problems, bad telephone connections, it was always something perfectly reasonable and easily explained.

I knew better. The door was mocking me!

~~~~~~~

Time went on. I'd watch the people on three. They never acknowledged the door in any way either. They'd walk right past it, avoid looking at it, and even go out of their way to avoid touching it.

I went so far as to dig up old blueprints to the Ajax building, but found the originals had been burned in a fire a short time after the building was built. A new set had been commissioned, and I found, without surprise, that the third floor 'mystery door' wasn't on them.

~~~~~~~

More time passed, and I tried to put it out of my mind. It never worked. Eventually the door started mocking me directly. I was up on three, working near the door, breathing in all that self-assured smugness every single day. There was always something that needed doing on three and nobody seemed to notice. If there were as many incidents of mechanical or electrical failure in a building anywhere else, the building would probably have been torn down. I fixed things that I had fixed the day previous. I replaced things that somehow aged overnight. I put things back together that had been welded, and I pulled things apart that had been fused. No one ever said anything about it. If I were a less scrupulously honest person, I could've made a fortune, just charging time to fixing crap that broke on the third floor.

I tried to push the door out of my mind, but it was like not thinking about the white elephant. It was like this itch I had once on a date.

There was this really gorgeous girl I was carrying a torch for, and after months of trying she finally agreed to let me take her to dinner. I took her to this really nice place, *The Gilded Truffle*, I think. One of those places where they set the food on fire and stuff.

I put on all my very best charm and got all spiffy and everything. We're sitting down, having a great time, when I get this itch inside the very top of my left nostril. From the very deepest bowels of hell this itch attacks me. I mean, it itches so bad that my eyes start to water! A simple nose rubbing wasn't going to do the trick, it needed a finger.

So I'm sitting there, my eyes watering, and a feeling like a maggot burrowing into my sinuses. I know that if I reach up to rub my nose, I won't be able to stop myself. I can almost hear this whining-grinding noise coming from the inside of my nostril.

Finally, I can't stand it anymore and I jam the first finger of my left hand to the third knuckle into my nose and scratch for like, thirty seconds.

She never went out with me again.

The door was like that.

Every so often I'd hear a noise coming from the door when I was up there. One night I put my ear against the door, and I heard the sounds of gears, with like, I don't know, like, scaly skin, or something.

Another night I swore I heard a steady heartbeat.

A third night I heard a cat. It scratched the inside bottom of the door, and 'meowed' once, plaintively.

~~~~~~~

Last night I dreamed about the door again. I was standing in front of the door, same as always, and the door opened, same as always. The light and the music started, but this time I could see. I was just beginning to make out shapes, and to understand . . .

. . . when I woke up, and repeated the whole, 'sweaty-puke-all-over-myself-and-bleed-from-three-different-orifices' thing. It's a lovely way to start your morning. It really is.

~~~~~~~

I didn't bother with a shower this morning. I smelled like vomit and blood, and I didn't care. I went to work in my pajamas, an hour and a half late. There was a stack of work orders for the third floor on my desk. I ignored them and went to the fire locker. I pulled the emergency axe off its hooks. It was really more of a sledge-hammer with a sharp edge, a heavy piece of metal and wood. I smiled and hefted it onto a shoulder.

Chester chose then to walk in. "Where you been, boy? You're late."

I stood and looked at him, not answering. He walked towards me, a concerned look on his face, his hands spreading as if to block my progress. The door was using its bodyguard to stop me. That couldn't be allowed.

"You okay?"

I shook my head and looked down at the floor. "Chester, I'm really, really sorry about this and I hope you forgive me."

I lowered the sledge and hit him in the face with the blunt end. I hadn't put any real force behind it; just enough to knock him down, and hopefully, out. He collapsed like a popped balloon, taking his desk with him, and lay there groaning.

I sprinted out of the office.

"I'm coming for ya', door!"

~~~~~~

I raced to the third floor, knocking Ajax personnel down left and right. I stood -heaving and sweating, in a miasmic cloud of my own funk - in front of a blank, industrial-grey, standard fitting, wooden door. I didn't even notice that the grey paint covering my masterpiece was still wet.

I tried the handle.

Locked.

I put my ear against the door, and I could hear it all: ancient machinery, still humming along, doing its job in a quiet, forgotten, corner.

My nose itched.

I could hear the sound of water dripping into deep pools, from rusted pipes.

Something was crawling around on the inside of my nose and I wiped at it.

Deep underground, something with a slow, steady heartbeat and dry, scaly skin, moved with a bumping thump, seeking a more comfortable position to sleep millennia away. It was an ageless, echoing sound.

My fingers were wet, and something was coming out of my nose. My ears started to itch, so I rubbed them.

Stars sung a high, wordless symphony of music that could never be replicated, never be described, only endured.

I considered my fingers briefly. They had blood on then

A rushing cataract of water, like every waterfall on Earth, all at once, filled the space behind the door.

My pajama top was wet, and I could smell copper. I tasted iron. For some reason, my upper lip was wet.

A lonely, hungry cat scratched the inside, bottom of the door.

I absentmindedly wiped my face, flung the blood away, and spat on my hands, each in turn.

It only took me a minute or so to knock the door to pieces in my frenzy.

And there it was.

Hanging in the black, thick, cloth-like texture inside the door was a fervently burning, swirling wheel. There were white-hot dots, clustered all together that looked like powdered cream in coffee. The dots gave off an intense heat and light, and I thought they looked like stars. There was a beautiful music streaming from the inside of the closet, and I realized it was the continuing sound of "***Let there be . . . !***" echoing through all of space/time, possibility and probability.

Fractal-like, my vision was drawn in closer. I felt the waves of heat washing over me and I beheld the magnificence of the wheel. I looked closer, and I realized the clusters weren't stars or rather, they were, but not as I supposed. The tiny clusters, spinning and burning there, were galaxies. All of them.

For one glorious moment I was allowed to see it all. The spinning, fervently burning wheel was slowly revolving there in that vast black, echoing, space that was somehow the same size as a standard janitor's closet. The micro within the macro, vice versa, turned around and reversed. I felt tears streaming down my face, mixing with the bloody mess covering my chin. I experienced the glorious epiphany of all of creation - All of it! Every bloody micron of space, time, and everything in between, all of it, all at once, was poured out of the closet in a glorious, painful, relentless display of radiant brilliance- in one timeless moment.

Then, like sunlight on dew, it slowly burned away. I was looking at an empty closet. There was a cobweb in one corner, some dust-bunnies on the floor, and a lone, feeble sunray was shining through a barred, dirty glass window.

I screamed as loud as I could. I had been robbed! Denied! I charged into the closet, feeling sick, weary, and desperately sad. I threw my hands around, searching for contact with something, anything!

But whatever had happened, whatever I had seen, was now gone. Done. Finished.

I fell to my knees, sobbing and coughing.

I felt rough hands on my shoulders, threw up for the last time, and passed out.

~~~~~~~

I woke up here in the hospital. The doctor told me I lost a lot of blood, and I probably had a stroke. He's running some tests now, but since I can't move part of my face, and I'm having difficulty talking, I can assume he's probably right.

Chester came by and shook my hand. He said that he wasn't mad, that I was probably just exhibiting "pre-symptoms of the stroke. Doc says you're gonna be fine, though. "

His lips were puffy, but it didn't look as though I had knocked any teeth out. I was glad for that. I tried to explain, but my words were all mush.

He sat with me for a while, and then said he'd have to let me go. He actually seemed to feel bad about it. After an enormous struggle, I managed to lift my right hand and give him a passable handshake. He smiled, patted my shoulder, and left.

The nurse came in an hour or so ago and put something in my IV. She explained that it would help me sleep.

I've been fighting it, but I know I'll drop off eventually. I kinda wonder what my dreams will be like, now. I'm hoping they'll be boring.

But if somebody doesn't shut up that damn cat . . . .

Rorshach Test

The wind-driven sand hissed and swirled ominously around the toppled pieces of limestone, skitting across the freshly revealed walk.

Even though the hour was early, on Christmas Eve no less, the sun had risen, and the air was rapidly taking on the quality of the inside of a kiln. The three archeologists barely noticed. Licking dry and cracked lips, they excitedly surveyed the building that a year's worth of hard labor by thirty locals had finally revealed. Standing some three-hundred feet tall, fifty feet wide, and fifty feet long in its trench, was a large limestone building. As far as could be ascertained it was one large, solid block of limestone, with a single door - twenty feet tall - of gold. The door had no hinges and the three archeologists believed it was more of a seal than a door; much like the stone rolled in front of Biblical tombs.

Carbon dating already performed on sample pieces of the limestone put the building's erection before the building of the Sphinx. There was nothing remotely like it anywhere in the world. There were no seams, no quarry marks, no evidence of stone cutting; nothing that would indicate this was a man-made structure, were it not for its perfectly squared sides, its alignment to true north, and its surface covered in strange, petroglyph-like writing.

Between the three of them, the archeologists had eighty years of academia under their belts. There were fourteen doctorates floating in the air above their heads, seven masters' degrees and more languages than could be conveniently counted. Esteem Egyptologists, the three of them, and yet that hadn't the slightest idea what, exactly, they had uncovered.

The writing was completely unfamiliar and according to the youngest archeologist - thirty-five, easily excitable, with a tendency to study what the other two thought of as "Fringe Archeology" - predated even Sumerian texts.

"We may finally have found proof of the existence of Atlantis!" he shouted excitedly. The two older gentlemen sighed and exchanged knowing glances.

The door was covered in a repeating glyph. The glyph depicted a tallish man with a crocodilian-like-head holding a human head in one hand and a large sword in the other. It was repeated over and over. One of the locals - a superstitious, tightly-wound bunch if ever there had been one - had already run screaming into the dawn upon seeing this glyph revealed.

The three archeologists, sensing their remaining work force was getting antsy, quickly set them to work levering the twenty-foot tall door out of the way. It took quite a lot of effort, as the door was revealed to be one solid piece of gold, weighing several hundred-thousand pounds. Levers broke, ropes snapped and pulleys groaned. More than one man twisted muscles and bones were strained. Eventually, however, the door was laid gently on the sand. Intending, later, to study it in full, the three archeologists entered the cool depths of the building.

Proceeding down the stone throat-like hallway thus revealed, they noticed the walls inside were covered with the very same glyph repeated over and over. Walls, floor, ceiling, there wasn't a single inch of stone that wasn't thus covered with the crocodile-headed figure holding a sword and a human head. Excitement building (After all, only a king could afford such exquisite stone work!) the three threw scientific procedure to the winds and ran down the hallway, excitedly laughing the whole way.

The hallway ended in a large room. Their flashlights revealed the gleam of gold, and they stopped in unison with a dramatic intake of breath. The room was full of ancient grave goods, each a key to unlocking bits of history and ancient wisdom, each a treasure sufficient to dry the mouth. Each piece would've satisfied any archeologist's lust for discovery for some time. These pieces were ignored, however, in favor of what stood against one wall: an enormous sarcophagus. It stood eleven feet tall, gleaming with he mellow, warm tones of well-worked gold.

A tomb. An unplumbed, pristine, Egyptian tomb predating the Pyramids! The actual temporal, material worth was astounding. The archeological worth of this find was priceless. With a collective shout of "Whoop!" the three set to work with a will.

They ignored the grave goods and set to work on the sarcophagus itself. It was done in the classic "nesting doll" fashion of other sarcophagi found throughout history - each layer covering a layer of further wealth and beauty.

It too was covered in the repeating glyph: a tall character with a crocodilian head holding a severed human head and a large sword. The surface of the sarcophagus was covered in this repeating glyph. Over and over and over. On the surface, under the surface, on the surface revealed, under that surface, over and over and over. Each new layer, carefully peeled from the sarcophagus, revealed this same glyph and nothing else.

Finally, the inner coffin was revealed. It resembled a tall character with a crocodilian head. Interestingly it resembled the glyph almost exactly. Its arms were crossed in the typical Egyptian manner, but instead of a lotus and a flail its golden hands held a severed human head and a large sword. Smothering their growing unease under a layer of cool professionalism, the three archeologists prepared for the final assault. Taking a deep breath, the three pried it open, revealing the mummy inside.

Afterwards, they could never quite agree on the order of things, nor what happened, precisely. The two eldest were closest, but the youngest had the best view, as he was doing most of the actual work. What is clear is that the three archeologists awoke some time later, lying on their faces.

The sarcophagus - along with everything else the room had contained - was gone.

~~~~~~~

The three went their separate ways. They had compared notes, and as they were unable to explain what happened, or indeed to come to any sort of consensus, they did what most scientists do with the completely inexplicable: they ignored it. They agreed, to a man, to never reveal that they room had been full, and the three of them overcome by . . . something.

The two eldest went on the talk circuit and capitalized enormously on their find. The door of solid gold had remained, as had the building itself. These two finds were more than enough to grant the three tenure in any school in the world, and an easy, care-free retirement, should they wish it. The archeological world's imagination was fired, and expeditions were sent to their find to comb over every square inch.

It was compared to King Tut's tomb, or even finding a parallel to Stonehenge in Egypt.

Riding a wave of spiritualistic New-Age modernism, the eldest archeologist was doing very well for himself. He wrote several books capitalizing on the gullible, and built a large mansion for himself in among the horse farms of Lexington, Kentucky.

Christmas Eve, five years after the plundering of what came to be known as "The tomb of Pharaoh X", the eldest archeologist threw a small party. He invited several of his colleagues from the university to attend. Relaxing in his new pool room with several of his guests, he started to tell the story of discovering the tomb. It was often asked about, and the eldest archeologist never got tired of telling the story, always putting himself in the very best light.

He had just reached the point when the three of them entered the darkness of the stone throat after carefully removing the gold door when the inner-coffin of the sarcophagus burst through the ceiling of the pool room, landing on the pool table, collapsing it, and killing three of the archeologist's guest. Screams rang through the room, darkened by dust, and the eclipsing of the inner-coffin.

The screams were silenced by the sound of the inner-coffin opening with slow creaking, and a horrible moan. A mummy, masked in an enormous crocodile-head, lurched its way free of the inner-coffin, lashing fiercely out with its enormous arms at any unlucky enough to be standing too close. With a horrible crunching noise, the mummy opened wide its masked mouth and closed it on the archeologist's head. Continuing to chew, it dragged the still-flailing body into the ebony depths of the inner-coffin. With an audible "pop", and a fading scream, the inner-coffin disappeared.

〰〰〰〰

The second archeologist had managed the unthinkable. Leveraging his tremendous wealth and fame, he talked himself on to the President's staff. His specific role was "Scientific Advisor to the President". His job was mostly honorary.

Five years after the massacre at the eldest archeologist's home, the second archeologist was giving the President a briefing regarding the nature of sand in the Oval office. The President was doing his level best to keep his eyes open. The archeologist's voice was soothing, the day was a warm one, and the temperature was at that perfect degree when sleep in most agreeable.

All this silence was shattered when the inner-coffin ripped through the windows behind the President's desk. The crocodile-headed mummy burst free of the inner-coffin, and knocked the President out of the way with a high-pitched scream of inarticulate rage. It latched onto the archeologist's head with one filthy, grimy, bandaged-wrapped hand. Ignoring the bullets thudding into it by the frantically firing Secret Service agents, the crocodile-headed mummy opened wide its masked, fanged maw and buried its teeth in the archeologist's throat. With a ripping, sawing motion, it completely severed the head, and grabbing the rest of the body, dragged the motionless, blood spouting remains into the inky darkness of the inner-coffin. With an audible "pop" and a lingering smell of copper, the inner-coffin disappeared.

〰〰〰〰

By this time the third archeologist was frantic. He had been paying very close attention to the events surrounding the death of his colleagues and he realized that he was undoubtedly next.

He spent everything he had accumulated in the years following the events in Egypt to buy the top three floors of a high-rise building in downtown Louisville, Kentucky. He outfitted it with a state-of-the-art security system, including tungsten panic doors, a motion sensitive CCTV system, and a crack, armed security staff. He spared no expense, including the installation of a high-speed, personal elevator system that only opened on his three floors and the ground floor. One button, keyed to his thumbprint, would drop the elevator at a speed dangerously close to terminal velocity, to the ground floor. It had a special braking system, and the inside of the elevator was deeply padded. This insured any passenger would arrive alive, if badly bruised and shaken.

Five years to the day of the last killing, Christmas Eve, the youngest archeologist was sitting in his living room, with a loaded, twelve point seven millimeter anti-aircraft gun - on a tripod - pointed at the door opposite him. He'd picked it up from a gunrunner with connections in the Chinese military. It had cost him a pretty penny, but he was confident that with the twenty-thousand depleted uranium rounds at his disposal he'd have little or no trouble stopping the inner-coffin and its deranged occupant. He watched the clock tick its way to midnight with feverish eyes.

At the stroke of midnight, he heard, above the gently chiming sounds of his clock, and through three steel-reinforced floors, the sounds of his security staff firing at something below him.

The sounds of awful death floated faintly up from the floors below. Blood-curdling screams of pain and gruesome horror, combined with a chilling, creaking, chewing sound filled the air.

It was here!

He pulled the safety off on his weapon, fitted it to his shoulder, and pointed the enormous barrel at the door.

Let it come, then. Death waited for it here!

The sounds below were horrifically awe-inspiring. The archeologist could hear his security staff screaming like pigs. An occasional burst of high caliber gunfire was followed by sporadic screaming.

Finally a heavy waiting silence reigned. The archeologist hit the panic doors, and with a booming thud, the thirteen inch, tungsten doors that waited at every entrance to his suite, slammed shut. Behind doors - graded to survive a direct strike from a nuclear weapon - the archeologist waited. Sweating, he watched the cameras on the security monitor next to him. All he could see were the bent and twisted remains of his security staff, smoke, and blood sprayed everywhere. It looked as though someone had turned on a high-pressure hose and covered the walls in thick, bloody paint.

Silence.

Heavy, waiting silence.

Five minutes of it.

Ten minutes of it.

Fifteen minutes of perfect, waiting silence.

The archeologist sweated and squirmed, his hands slicking up the stock of his enormous machine gun.

There was a single creak from the door opposite him: the noise of a dying mouse's final song . . .

And then . . .

BOOM.

He watched, as the door directly in front of him - made of the highest possible grade of the hardest metal metallurgical science could make - bowed outward by three inches.

BOOM.

Another three inches, every so slightly to the left of the first bulge.

BOOM.

Three more inches of bulge at the site of the first bulge, and the metal was showing signs of breakage!

The booming noises sped up.

BOOM...BOOM...BOOM. BOOM, BOOM...BOOM, BOOM, BOOM...BOOM, BOOM, BOOM...BOOM, BOOM, BOOM...BOOMBOOMBOOMBOOM.

With a final tearing noise and the screech of much-abused metal, the coffin knocked the door down and stood, bits of torn flesh and blood covering it like gaudy party-streamers, in front of the archeologist. It slowly began to open. With a scream of defiance an animal from the primordial ooze would recognize, the archeologist opened fire.

"DIE YOU SON-OF-A-BITCH!"

The juddering staccato of the heavy caliber weapon covered all thought. With a ripping, screaming whine, the bullets thudded home. Knocking the coffin down and causing it to dance, skip, hop, and roll. The archeologist emptied all twenty-thousand rounds into the coffin, and only stopped when the weapon dry fired for a full minute.

Gasping and choking on the smoke, the archeologist waited. After a moment, the sprinkler system turned on, bathing the cordite and sulfur from the sobbing archeologist. With his ears ringing, the archeologist watched and waited.

He began to moan as the coffin stood, unharmed, from the corner it was lying in, and began, again to slowly open. The archeologist, turned, ran to his high-speed elevator, and with a gasping sob, jammed the call button. He could hear growling noises from behind him and leapt into the elevator when the doors opened. With a scream of fury, the coffin threw itself at the elevator doors just in time to see the archeologist jam the high-speed drop button.

The archeologist curled into a fetal ball on the floor of the elevator and wept. From above he could hear the scream of twisting metal. With a descending whistling noise, the coffin threw itself down the shaft and landed inside the elevator just as the archeologist threw himself out. Not paying the least attention, the archeologist ran across the street into a twenty-four hour drug store, the coffin directly behind him. Crashing through the glass of the drug store's picture window, the coffin landed with a booming thud on the floor and knocked several shelves down. It began, again, to open, slowly revealing that darkness from beyond the skies of hell.

In a blind panic, the archeologist picked things up off the floor and threw them at the coffin. He picked up a large box of tampons, and fighting through the debris the coffin had created, threw it at the steadily advancing coffin, slowly opening coffin. It had no discernible effect, of course.

The archeologist cried. He sobbed. He crawled on hands and knees while the occupants of the drug store looked on in stunned disbelief. He threw broken glass at the coffin, he threw nail clippers at the coffin, he threw a huge box of diapers at the coffin. Nothing stopped it, or even slowed it down.

The coffin backed the weeping, retching archeologist into a corner. The archeologist watched in horror as the crocodile-headed mummy was fully revealed, its snarling lips pulled back in anticipation of the bloody feast to ensue; the empty eye sockets, that nevertheless glowed with a dull, red, evil light. The archeologist saw the bloody remains of his colleagues in the black, void-like space behind the mummy. Their eyes dead, the bodies chewed and mangled, they nevertheless lifted broken, destroyed hands toward him and beckoned.

Feeling frantically on the floor next to him with his groping fingers, the archeologist found an enormous bottle of industrial strength cough medicine. Hurling it at the coffin with all his might and preparing to give up the ghost, the archeologist watched as the cough medicine burst all over the coffin, spraying thick, red, syrupy cough medicine everywhere. The cough medicine dripped into the soulless darkness waiting for the archeologist, and . . .

. . . (waaaaaaaaaaaiiiiiiiiiiiiiiiiiittttttttt for iiiiiiiiiiiiiiiit)

STOPPED THE COUGHIN'!

Phone Call

The phone rings.

Without any conscious effort on my part, without even really being aware of it, I psychically tense. It's as if I'm standing - chained to the post, with my hands over my head - waiting for the whip to fall. It feels like I'm trying to clench my brain or harden the soft walls of my heart.

It's a dysfunctional response to a phone ringing, and I'm sure I could make some therapist's next book, but there you are.

I'm not expecting a call from anyone. I never do. The people I talk to regularly know I'm not a phone person. They call, say what's going on, and then hang up. My friends know I'd much rather have a conversation with them in person, and so they almost never call. It's an understanding that works for us.

If the phone is ringing this late in the afternoon, it means someone wants something from me. It always portends someone else's need. Whether it's 'You owe us money. When are we going to get it?'

Or –

'Nescher. I need you to come up here and type for me. No, I can't pay you, and I know you don't want to wander into the sick, diseased, mire-like minds of sexual predators for four hours, but my secretary's dog is sick and she called off. Please come help me.'

He's paying the secretary, or rather, the *office* is paying the secretary, and she's making more than I am, and all she's doing is sitting at home with her dog. Knowing my father, the reason he can't pay me is because he's paying the secretary's sick day out of his own pocket. He gets mad when I insist on gas money. I think he believes I should feel entitled to come help him do his job. I really do.

Or –

'Can I please speak to Mr. Nescker Psyker? Mr. Psysher, this is the Beautiful Little Children With Horribly Disfiguring Diseases Foundation. How are you today, Mr. Psicker? Mr. Pisker, I wonder if I could ask you to contribute a little bit of money to our noble cause? Five dollars? No, I'm sorry to have wasted your time today, Mr. Pisher, but our minimum donations start at thirty-five dollars.'

I don't say anything to this person about asking people - who don't have it - for money, and then setting 'donational minimum guidelines'. That seems to run counter to the entire idea of charity to my eyes. He disconnects - without *saying* as much, but making me *feel* - as though I'm disfiguring these beautiful little children all on my own with my selfish, selfish refusal to part with my hard-earned thirty-five dollars. It's not because I don't *have* thirty-five dollars, mind you. It's because I'm a tightfisted miser who hates children and is going to hell.

There's always somebody on the other end who wants or needs something. I almost never get 'Hi, Nescher. How are you?' phone calls. It'd bother me a lot more if I were more telephonically active, but I *do* appreciate those rare calls inquiring about *my* well being.

As a result of all this personal animosity for the world in general, I keep my phone unplugged much of the time, letting my answering machine pick up in my stead. I know it's an avoidance tactic, but, unhealthy or not, it works for me, and you can't argue with that. It keeps me from becoming a complete misanthrope, so that can't be completely bad, can it?

I'm whining, but bear with me. I *do* have a point.

I lumber over to the phone, putting my book down, and answer it.

"H'lo?"

"Hello. Nescher?"

My heart falls within me and I can feel my throat locking up. It's something like swallowing a sob. Love, like an older dog gnawing at the softly rotting remains of a favorite chew toy, rolls over in my heart and whimpers within me. It's ancient, powerful, primal love and it rocks me back a step. I hear that voice and something from the very beginning of time grabs me by the neck and shakes me with a growl.

The voice is flat, devoid of emotion or conversational commitment. There's a tone in her voice that I can hear without even looking for it. It's not an 'It's so nice to hear your voice!' tone. It's more of an 'I didn't have anything better to do at the moment, so I thought I'd call you.' tone.

It hurts.

I wonder, sometimes, if she remembers what I look like. The last time I saw her she was loaded to the gills on so many different drugs, she was hard-pressed to remember *her* name, much less mine. She kept nodding off as I talked to her, passing out mid-sentence.

That hurt, too, but I tried to gut it out.

I wonder, sometimes, why she bothers to call me at all. After all, she made her decisions, and part of that whole 'I've got to find out who I am' process sure looked like - and *felt* like - writing me off.

I'm not sure why I expected any different. She'd written me off almost as long as I've known her. I can be practical about it, chalking her failures up to her lifelong mental illness, but your heart won't listen to intellectual platitudes, will it? The rips and tears aren't soothed by "She tried, dude. Her brain was just melted."

I can see her face in my mind's eye, holding the phone: it's dull, emotionless, like looking into a reflection made of ice, trying to find something other than cold, frozen bits. Her face, her gaze, her affect are flat, with eyes like boiled, dead eggs looking back at me from a haze of pharmaceutically-induced nirvana.

I'm sure she's quite happy, in her damaged, dysfunctional way. I can go for months without hearing from her, and nothing ever changes.

Confessing this to you feels like truth, so here it is: I hate myself for feeling this way. I hate myself for wanting to pretend I've got pressing business in order to put the phone down.

But I hate myself most of all for continuing with the conversation as if everything's fine, as if I'm not hurting already, as if I don't carry within me far too many years of resentment and pain. I hate myself for responding to her with badly strained reserves of love and a light, happy tone in my voice while I swallow everything I'm really feeling.

"Hi, Mom."

One Perspective

"*W*hat are you doing?"

"What, now? Right this very moment? This sparkling, scintillating second dazzling us with its whimsy and flights of ne'er to be returned?"

"*Cripes. I ask a simple question, I get the return of Bloody Alameda the Lopsided. No. Not THIS second, THAT one: the one scuttling by on crippled-*"

"I do wish you wouldn't extinguish my flame before I've lit the merest candle."

"*Fires are no good to us and ours. You should know that by now. You get the shivers, you start to think, 'A bit of heat would go down a treat,' and you try to find some; next thing you know they're wrapping you in a shroud and it's all for nothing, Betty. 'Sides, flames reflecting in all your eyes? You'd be flame-blind for more months than you've legs.*"

"I speak in metaphor, dear sir."

"*Why, I had a mate, got too close to one of them wood-burning stoves, you know, and they had to wrap him three, four times. The smell was enough to put you off your dinner, it was . . .*"

"Or even glittering analogy, so bold, so bright, so beautiful."

"*. . . and if there's one thing a chap can't stand it's . . . whotafor?*"

"What?"

"*What?*"

"You said something?"

"*I did. I said 'Whotafor?'*"

"Metaphor."

"*Well, where'd you meet him, then and does he have a sister? Hur. Hur. Hur.*"

"You're winding me up now, aren't you?"

"*Naturally. It's the curse of the lesser gifted. Least ways, that's how YOU lot think. Here now. Are you going to help with this, or not? What are you doing, by the by?*"

"If you must know, I'm dreaming."

"*Dreaming.*"

"Yes. Dreaming."

"*Well, that'd explain why I'm doing all the work, then. You're dreaming.*"

"I'm dreaming. Yes. That is correct."

"*Oh, come now!*"

"No! I'm serious! I really am dreaming! Such light and fanciful constructs of air and spirit-"

"*Right. Pull the other one. It's got bells on.*"

"What? I can't dream? I can't yearn to reach above my low station to touch the webs spun among the stars? I can't listen for the winds that hiss among those celestial strands? I can't long to caress the globular forms of planets and nesting galaxies?"

"*You can. Certainly you can, but do it too much and you'll starve to death. Oi, now. Give us a hand with this.*"

"Ah, but I dine on such heavier stuff! And at once such lighter! For me, to sup at Angel's Wing is a much finer dish than any fat bit of-"

"Is that so? I don't suppose you'll mind if I nip into your pantry then? See if I can't find myself a wee bit of something to eat? 'S'hard work, me doing all the pulling and tugging and you, sitting there, getting your head lost in the fog and dew."

"Here now! You stay right out of my pantry! That's mine, that is! And you've no right to it!"

"O-Ho! So who's being all practical now, then? 'Dream all you like, Guildenstern, but touch not the barley and the mead', is it? A time of 'celestial angel's feast', indeed. What a lot of gut wash."

"I am wounded, sir! Wounded to the quick! You've cut my heart straight from my bloody breast, you have!"

"You're a right diva, you are."

"Tell me, then, oh noble critic, what do you dream of?"

"Me?"

"You. Yes, you. Who else would I be speaking to?"

"Alright, alright. No need to get all twisted. A chap likes to have his p's and q's minded, is all."

"Aren't going to answer then?"

"Says who? 'Course I am! I'm just about to."

"I await with bated breath."

"Hrrmph."

" . . . "

"I . . . "

" . . . yeeeeees . . . ?"

"I dream of stars."

"What?"

"You heard me. Stars. I dream of stars."

"No!"

"Yep."

"You?"

"Me."

"But that's fantastic! To think, all these time we've been mates and I never knew! Why, you've the soul and spirit of a poet as much as I do! You're as much the longing artist I am! Wait 'till I tell the boys-"

"Now hang on a minute. Let me clarify your thinking a bit before you get all excited and over-heated. It's true I dream of stars, but not in the way YOU think, with your 'gossamer delights bedecked by whosit kisses'. Nah. I'm of a far more practical mind, myself. I dream of 'em same as any honest chap."

"Oh dear. Are you saying . . . ?"

"S'right. Proud of it, I am, too."

"Heavens save me the fate of the dead soul!"

"Dead nothing! Think on it for just a minute-"

"Weren't it you, not five minutes ago, telling me that our kind should stay away from fires? 'Fires are no good to us and ours', you said. 'Make you turn all crinkly and smell bad. Make you get wrapped in an over-'"

"Here now! I didn't say any such thing, and even if I did, I certainly didn't sound like THAT!"

"You most certainly did, dear sir! And what do you mean by 'THAT'?"

"'That' what?"

"Never mind."

"Well, I was only going to say, I certainly didn't sound like I had a blowfly shoved up my nose when I said what it was I didn't say."

"Lovely. Your gift of description is only exceeded by your gift for exaggeration. I regret this conversation ever took place and I wish to purge myself of its merest memory."

"You started it - and anyway, if I hadn't come over, you'd never have finished this, and you'd come crawling to my place, looking for a handout. I'm only doing you a favor here, keeping your feet firmly pointed toward the ground."

"That's true. And I thank you for it. You are a friend beyond compare. But please, can you not tell me, setting aside the factor of fire for the nonce, that you dream of stars in a context other than your gut?"

"Nope. Think about it for a second. Big as those things must be to hang in the sky the way they do, and never fall out of it - you catch one of those things in your web; you'd eat for a decade. Now shut up and hunker down. Here comes a couple of cockroaches."

One Night Way Out West

"What do you mean, "We're lost?"" Olaf asked in his thickly-accented voice, looming dangerously over his smaller companion Zhing. His face was darkly flushed with anger, and his fists were clenching and unclenching with barely suppressed rage.

"Are you having trouble again? Do you need to go to your happy place? I think I can rustle up a sheep's skull form somewhere." Zhing said, unconcerned at the man-mountain rising vastly above him, "I know your people have only got 'north' down, really, as that's where the cold comes from. I was hoping for more from *you* though. Are you really not familiar with the other three cardinal directions, or is your brain just frozen?"

"Was that yet *another* 'Stupid-Cracker-McWhitey' joke?" Olaf retorted, his voice lowering ominously.

"I ask you," Zhing replied, his voice still unconcerned. "You're surrounded by reindeer eleven months out of the year. You eat meat as an appetizer, a meal and dessert. You've killed every single animal we've come within fifty yards of and eaten ninety percent of its still-twitching carcass. If you could get a tooth or a finger into the crevice, you ate it. And here we are, on our way to the single most important event in all of history, bar-none, and you just *have* to stop, losing us the map in the process, and why, I ask you? To get some bloody *beef jerky* from a bloody convenience store!"

"Gee. I'm *so* sorry. I guess I was just tired of Rover-cutlets-over-rice-with-unidentifiable-vegetables!" Olaf snapped, his temper dangerously close to the breaking point.

"Fellas!" Ahmed said in his quiet, disarming and dignified way, putting his not inconsiderable bulk in-between Olaf and Zhing at the same time. "Can we stop arguing? We have a certain dignity to maintain, certain comportment. Do you want history to record we had flushed, sweaty faces and torn robes? Can we really expect to be taken seriously if we're all disheveled?"

"So the 'brutha's' worried about his 'dignity', huh?" Retorted Olaf, while still eyeing Zhing belligerently, "Ahmed, I can appreciate that you're trying to be the best of us, and I'm sure you're working your way toward some sort of 'shining empires in the south of Africa' speech, but save it this time, okay? It's just wasted air. Let me fill you in on something that may not have occurred to you as of yet. There's not going to *be* any meeting since 'Dingy Zhingy' here got us lost!"

"*You* lost the map!" Zhing retorted, jabbing Olaf ineffectually in the chest with one finger and demonstrating a bit of temper for the first time in the conversation

"It was covered in unreadable squiggly writing, anyway! How you people get *anything* done with that 'epileptic chicken scratching' you call writing, I'll never know!" Olaf shouted back

"Unngah! Me hit rock with hammer! Call it 'rune'!" Zhing said, cannily imitating Olaf's voice, "Yeah, it's 'rune-d' all right. And that poor rock never did anything to you!" he finished, an evil smile crossing his face.

"Listen here, you runty little Asian. I've pulled squirming things out of my beard bigger than you!" Olaf said, pushing Ahmed out of the way, and reaching for his hammer at the same time.

"That's it! Olaf, it's *go* time!" Zhing screamed, falling into an attack stance.

"Oh? Oh? Gonna go 'Crouching-Monkey Hidden Badger' on me? Bring it, you wizened bit of bear poop!" Olaf bellowed, finally getting his hammer free from his belt.

"GWAAAAAAAAAGGGGHHHH!" Zhing threw himself at Olaf, his arms and legs spinning and flailing, while Olaf held his hammer in a way a professional ball-player would recognize and admire.

"Fellas, please!" Ahmed said, still trying to remind his friends of their forgotten dignity.

Just then the sky lit up, splashing all three of the struggling men with a brilliant, blinding display of multi-colored light. There was a sound; a sound 'as of a rushing, mighty wind', and the three were washed with a sweet, warm breeze that was there and gone in an instant. Olaf dropped his hammer and caught Zhing one-handed, gently setting him on his feet on the ground. The three men stared at the sky, utterly dumbfounded.

When Olaf Thundersson did break the silence, his voice was amused, and a smile was on his face.

"*That's* convenient."

"Isn't it? I just gotta say . . . He sure makes an entrance with **style**," Zhing Lou replied, admiringly.

"The three wisest minds on the planet, a prophet, a seer and a magician without peer and we couldn't predict *that*?" Ahmed-Sun-Drinker said, shaking his head and smiling.

Olaf clapped Zhing companionably on the shoulder, knocking him to one knee. "I'm sorry about that, Zhing. Pressures of travel, travel-rage, you know. I'm tired, I'm cranky, I'm getting old, and I'd really like to sleep in a bed without my legs hanging off the end. You know how it is," he said, his voice subdued and his face abashed.

Zhing smiled up at Olaf and said, "No harm done, my large friend. I can certainly appreciate what squeezing your enormous frame into a small bed must be like. I too, have been quite distressed for some time now. No decent bathing facilities and I haven't had a cup of good tea in so long I've forgotten the taste. I apologize for being a bloody stupid git."

Olaf turned to Ahmed. "Ahmed, listen-"

Ahmed smiled and raised a hand. "No need, Cracker-McWhitey. If friends can't lash out at each other in a moment of anger and stress, than what good are they? Besides, it's not your fault you were born the wrong color."

Olaf through his head back and laughed so loud the sky shook.

The three of them shared a tired, embarrassed smile and embraced warmly.

Their fight of a moment before forgotten, their normal amiability restored, the Three Wise Men turned their caravan towards the new star shining down upon them and followed it east.

One Night on Adam's Square

"*Darling, you simply MUST try some of this canapé! It is to die for!*"

I look at the small bit she is offering me. It's caviar within a small, glazed pastry puff. There's warm steam rising from it in a fragrant cloud.

The candlelight reflects soft, glimmering, warm light around the room, throwing scintillating daggers of radiance everywhere. I can see warmth spreading from her cheeks.

The Duchess leans towards me in anticipation of our first kiss. After my long and laborsome perusal, I welcome it with a semi-feral smile . . . .

There's an itch along my right side.

I reach in under the layers of clothing and scratch. The scent of my body arises from my clothes, and I nearly gag.

I can feel something moving inside my clothes: something small and hoppy with teeth. I scratch and scratch, and soon feel warm blood under my nails.

I sigh and pull my hand free. I don't think about infection from the filth under my nails, or the way this'll have every cat and dog within three blocks

sniffing around me. Just another one of those wonderful 'fringe benefits.'

It's a nice night, at least . . . .

She's screaming at me. Calling me names, telling me I'm a loser, a bum, a reprobate.

I've never known how to respond to her abuse. I've never been able to stand up to her, never been able to look her in the eye.

I move away and that's when she hits me. With all the force in her meaty arms, she hits me across the back of the head. I fall, land on my face. My nose breaks and I can feel blood pooling under me.

A black, billowing rage rises within me. For the very first time there's something other than disgust on her face when she looks my way.

I've only ever wanted to see love or affection, or even a gentle exasperation, but after this, I'll settle for the fear . . . .

I don't want to go there. Not tonight. Please, just one night without going there. That's all I ask.

I wing a prayer towards a sky gone to brass.

What the hell, right?

If He's listening at all, if ANYBODY'S listening at all, maybe they'll hear this one.

I wipe at my nose ineffectually. I've had a cold for three weeks now, and I can feel something heavy shift within my chest.

Great.

Pneumonia, probably. I shift on the bench. The lady sitting a few benches over crinkles her nose at me. I want to stand up and shout at her, "Hey. What SHOULD I smell like, huh? You think I like it any better than you do?"

Instead I eat my sandwich in silence - ignoring some of the less identifiable, crunchier bits - and try not to notice the blood that flecks my lips every time I cough. I've eaten worse . . . .

A tricky bit of my sandwich hits the back of my throat, and I cough like my lungs are breaking for the fifty-yard line. The lady looks over at me and there's something in her eyes that's almost feral.

I'm trying not to disturb your lunch, lady.

Buck looks over at me and says, "I don't think we're going to make it this time, Bunky!"

I shake my head while I wrestle with the controls. We took a direct hit from their plasma torpedoes, and I know we're going down. The planet's surface is looming large and forbidding in the view screen. I grimly smile at Buck, and reply, "Never say never, Mr. Rogers!"

He laughs wildly with me, and we enter the atmosphere. The ship begins to bounce and rock and we're still wrestling with the controls. Smoke begins to fill the cabin, and I start coughing, laughing and crying all at once. I may be seconds from death, but I'll go out with a bang, by all that's holy . . . .

It was the coughing.

I wipe more blood from my lips and beard and look around me. He walked by a second ago, his keys 'chinking' gently on his belt. I heard him from three blocks away.

I was here yesterday, too. I wondered if he'd stop and talk to me. Half of me hoped he would, half of me hoped he wouldn't.

At least he hasn't chased me off. You get some real jerks sometimes, and then you get some good ones. I figure he's either too new to be a jerk yet, or maybe he's one of the rare good ones.

I hope it's the latter. This is a really nice, quiet spot.

Before he walked off around the dock, he ostentatiously reached into his pocket and pulled out a handful of change. He dropped it on the cement about

twenty feet away, making sure it made noise.

I have no idea why he did that. Does he think I need his charity? Is he too good to walk up to me and offer me money, maybe have to stop and chat for a minute? I'm a human being for God's sake, not some sort of unwanted discard!

I resist the money for a long time. I'll go get it, eventually. I know I will. But I take pleasure in letting it lie there for now.

I'm so tired . . . .

I've been digging through this same trash can for a month now. There's sometimes some really good stuff on the bottom. You have to root a little, but it's worth the effort. Today there was a half-eaten peanut butter and jelly sandwich, most of a soda, and a cold cheeseburger.

I snacked on the food and kept rooting. I felt good about my chances today, and I'm glad I stopped again tonight.

Down towards the very bottom of the can there was a half-read newspaper. I took it and one of those scratcher lottery tickets fell out of it. It looked like the guy who bought the paper bought one of those tickets at the same time, and then forgot about it. It wasn't scratched off, beat up or anything! It looked brand new! I figured this might be my lucky night, so I sat down, and scratched it.

It was a winner.

A big winner.

I won three-hundred-thousand dollars.

I sat back, blinking at it, wondering if this could possibly be real. I realized I was having trouble seeing. My vision was all blurry, and I wiped at my eyes. I was amazed to feel tears running unchecked down my face, into my beard.

I felt this warm, smearing pain building in my chest. It feels kinda like a sob, or a laugh. I haven't done either in a long, long time. I closed my eyes, and surrendered to the tears, the pain, and the happiness . . . .

~~~~~~~

"Sixty-five to base."

"Go ahead, sixty-five."

"Yeah. I'm out here on Adam's Square. Looks like we've got a DOA."

"Ten-four, sixty-five. I'll send an ambulance out."

"Ahh, yeah. Base, don't bother. He's been dead for a while, and he's pretty ripe. Stiff, even. Look, just call Metro PD. Sixty-five, standing by."

"Ten-four, sixty-five. Base clear at oh five forty-eight."

"Sixty-five, out."

On the Surface of the Eyeball

The air, whistling around my head, is whipping my hair into my face and eyes. It makes seeing things problematic, at best, and I can't hear a thing over the freight train whine of the wind in my ears.

But those brief glimpses of what I can see . . . .

It's funny what goes through your mind at a moment like this. You start wondering if maybe you've made a mistake of some kind, if maybe this wasn't a good idea.

But those are doubts and regrets and I don't want to deal with right now. I want to think positive, uplifting, edificational thoughts.

I want to accomplish this with verve and style.

I want to make everyone who sees it smile.

It's tempting to say that this is a life-defining moment. But in order to do that, I believe you have to see life as being a line: a sequential series of events with cause, effect, beginning, middle and end. Days follow days; weeks follow weeks, month and years, all in their properly ordered, perfectly reasonable sequence. You're born. You go to college. You build a career, as . . . I don't know, a space-shuttle-pilot, or whatever. If you're lucky, you fall in love, get married and have fifty-leventy kids. If you're not, you get married to whatever chick will have you and have kids anyway, but maybe you don't like them as much. Either way, you get old.

You die.

People, in the way of people everywhere, forget.

So I'm bucking that trend. I'm taking a different route down to the bottom, baby, and nobody'll *ever* forget me!

I read this thing once in a book. This poet was talking about like, all these brave and noble American Indian warriors. How they like, strode across the plains like 'conquering kings without crowns'. Guy went on to call them like, gods and sorcerers and I don't know, all kinds of noble junk. He said they were worshipped while they were alive and forgotten when they were dead.

This dude said that they were all-important when they were running around, like, taking scalps, or whatever, and nobody alive now could tell you their names or where they were buried.

Lemme see if I can remember at least part of it:

"and I lift my hand to point to Shelly's Ozymandias as a final testimony against them.

"'Look on my works, ye mighty,' and tremble, tremble, tremble. .. "

Yeah.

Like that.

You get all tricked out. You're pimpin' it, all on top of the heap, up where the air is thin. You know? Top of the food chain. And all of a sudden, nobody knows who you are anymore, 'cause maybe your chute didn't open in time, or you're grinding a sick rat tail and the board comes down wrong, you face-plant into the street, and paint your brains down the middle of the road.

How boring.

How dull.

How utterly without meaning.

But you've got a safety chute, a life-line, a spare. If you choose not to look at life like that, you can avoid the fate of the unremunerated, forgotten gods of yesterday.

I don't see life as a line. I see it as more of a loosely-connected stream of events; sometimes chunky, sometimes not so much. You remember the chunky or important events. The not-so-important-thin-broth events lay in the twisty meat of your mind, waiting to be played like one of those cheesy slide shows the secretaries down at the Court House have playing on their computers: little toddlers all decked out in like, vegetable costumes, and nobody's ever got bad teeth.

And you gotta watch the show. That stuff stays in mental RAM until it's needed, until it's necessary.

Like now, for instance, when you're whipping toward Mater Firma Terra at fifty-six-some-odd-meters per second, with a big ol' stoner's grin on your face and the last conversation you had with that stupid skank running through your brain.

"Where were you?"

"What do you mean?"

"I mean, where were you at? I've been trying to call you all day!"

"Yeah, my bad. I was out skating. I pulled this sick trick off a loading dock. I managed to get about thirteen feet of air. It was tight! I broke my own vertical record on that one. Think I might've cracked my board, though. I wish you had been there to see-"

"I went to the Doctor yesterday. The tube came out blue."

"What?"

"Pregnant."

"What? How?"

"The condom broke. That's how."

"What?"

"You heard me. The condom broke. I didn't want to carry your baby so I went to my Doctor."

"What?"

"Will you listen to me? I'm trying to tell you something important here."

"I'm trying to wrap my head around the idea of me being a Daddy. Give me a minute. I'm happy about this!"

"That's what I'm trying to tell you. You're not a Daddy. I went to my Doctor and he gave me a prescription. I lost a day of work, and I expect you to make up the difference."

"What are you talking about?"

"You know, I'm not sure what it was I ever saw in you. You've got to be the densest guy on earth. Listen: I got pregnant. I went to the Doctor. He gave me a prescription. I took it. I had massive cramps and I couldn't go to work. I must've been on the toilet all day long."

"You flushed my baby down the toilet?"

"What do you mean your baby . . . ."

We fought about it, but she was right. It was her body, and I'm not so sure I was up for the responsibility of being a Daddy. I'm not sure why she even told me. It would've been so easy for her to just keep it to herself. I think that it was meant to be a barb of some kind. I inconvenienced her, so she hurt me.

At least, that's what I think she was thinking. Who knows what goes on in their minds, though?

It would've been nice. It would've been, I don't know, polite, I guess, to have been at least *asked* for my thinking, my input. Still, she had a career, and who'm I to ask her to toss that away after one night of margaritas and casual sex with a thirty-year-old-skate-punk she picked up downtown at a bar?

Still, it would've been nice.

Wish I could remember her name.

~~~~~~~

See?

Right there. That vista. You see how the earth kinda curves away at the far horizon? I mean, you can't even see this kind of thing BASE jumping.

I climbed an antenna once, couple of months ago. It was reported as being seven, eight hundred feet tall. I couldn't see much from the top. Ground fog, smog - all that crap, caught up in the air - made it impossible to see much. I sat up there, clinging to a thin sheath of metal that vibrated, thrummed and hummed as the wind blew it, watching the sun peek over the horizon. It was rocking like a boat on the ocean. It was too awesome for words, man, and I hated to have to surrender to gravity.

Wish I could fall back on something poetic here. I mean, it was like the sunlight was all pouring across the land. You know? Like it was chasing the darkness back, making the sky glow all pink and rose and gold.

I watched the sun come up and then I jumped off.

Managed to swirl in within two feet of my target too. I was stoked.

Wish I had brought my IPOD up here.

'Course, I don't think I could hear anything over all this wind, either. Yeah, well, Mice and Men, right? 'Sides. A view like this should really be uncluttered by extemporaneous sensations. I'm all trying to embed this on the surface of my memory.

The sun is just right. The feeling of the cold, chapping my lips, my nose, my face, is like frozen silver, somehow.

I need to write a poem about this, I think. But before I can even start, I'm thinking about that stupid hooker again, and the things we talked about before I took her home. Some song by Joni Mitchell was on the jukebox and she was half-singing along, her eyes closed.

"What do you think about as you sing that?"

"I think about a river, a frozen one, and how cool it'd be to ice-skate on a frozen river."

"Oh?"

"Yeah. 'Cause with a lake, all you've got is a circle. And no matter how big a circle is, it's still a circle. But with a river, you could just go . . . and keep going."

"I think I'd enjoy watching you skate down a frozen river."

Yeah.

Good stuff. Good stuff.

~~~~~~~

See the way the moon is reflected on the side of that building? See that big, white, dead eye in that building's glass? Wait. Let me get a quick shot of that.

Yeah.

That's good stuff right there. Supposed to be really magical when a full moon and the sun are in the sky at the same time. Like, time between times when anything is possible. The borders - night and day, life and death, heat and cold - are thin then, and just about anything is possible.

Yeah.

I read this thing once, about how like, back in the day, they believed that the last thing a person saw was like, etched on the surface of their eyeballs, and that like, if a person had been murdered, they could reveal the murderer. Kinda makes me wonder if like, way back in the day they had techniques for viewing those images.

Ever since I read that, I wanted to capture some truly killer image. To make it like, this grand, rolling vista that was forever lasered across the surface of my mind.

I thought about it for a really long time. This was after I started doing BASE jumps. I started waiting longer and longer to pull the rip cord. You know? Like, I was tempting fate, God, the Universe, or whatever, to make my death be a spectacular splatter.

It never happened. Something inside me rose up in protest, and I pulled the cord out of an in-bred sense of self-preservation. It really used to piss me off.

I think I got it beat, though. Late last night I snuck into a high-rise downtown. It didn't take much. I just waited until the security guy made his rounds. Some of those buildings, they've only got one guy on duty.

I snuck in, rode an elevator to the top floor, and found an access hatch in a stairwell. I had my wire cutters with me, and twenty minutes later, I was on the roof.

The highest building downtown is close to 1500 feet tall. There's no abutments or adjoins. It's a straight, 1500 foot drop to the pavement from the roof. A glorious freefall, all the way down.

I climbed out to the edge, looked around, and waited for the sun to rise. I took off all my tools, my wallet, anything that might get in the way. Then I took off all my clothes. I looked around, watching the sun's light bleed into the surrounding night.

Once it had drained the dark far enough for me to see, I jumped.

I can see the grains and cracks in the sidewalk beneath me. It's time.

I spin over, looking toward the sunrise

Yeah.

That's gonna be perf-

Lit from Without

The Outside opened the world, giving noisy, labored birth to it, once again. The world responded as it always did, with groans of hate and pain that went unheard by The Outside - who cared nothing for the world or its people. The Outside existed only as a force of "TAKE" to the world. It ate the world as it pleased, took what it wanted and left the world as suddenly as it came.

And so it was, and so it will always be. But The Outside is blind, deaf and dumb, and the people of the world are not. This is their experience, their song, their pain.

~~~~~~~

Light.

Pure, steady, white and clean.

With the light came a slow susurration of sound and form. Memory, slower in coming, beaded and coalesced in the larger droplets needed for full return, like watching water run down a glass pane.

He stood, muzzily wiping his eyes and blearily scratching his naked body. He'd been asleep, and had no memory of who, or what, or where. He stood alone, on a mist-covered emptiness, and waited.

He'd been asleep, but the time had come for him to awaken.

The mist - lit by that pure, steady, and yet diffuse light - slowly receded. He watched, not understanding, or even being aware, as others began to be revealed. They were all alike, in their cold, unknowing nakedness, and looked blankly at one other.

That was when the First Words were spoken, in rolling thunders, by The Outside. The First Words buffeted the remaining mists and sent them spiraling into crazy curlicues of light and color. Memory returned with a rush, and though he'd been driven to his knees by the First Words, he still heard them rolling off into the distance.

"HE'D NEVER ASKED FOR MUCH FROM LIFE. A WIFE, A JOB, A PLACE TO LIVE. HE WAS A SIMPLE MAN WITH SIMPLE NEEDS."

And there she was, walking towards him.

She was lovely, dressed in her ankle-length dress, her wide and ready bosom accented by the material. Her face glowed with simple good health and an abundance of cheer. Her hair was done up in a bun atop her head - he couldn't help thinking this was appropriate for her station as a married woman and his wife - but he saw two strands had come loose and framed her face. A light sheen of sweat reflected the morning sun. The autumn had brought a final heat to the Valley, and it soaked her dress in places that awakened his body in kind.

Her dress was simple homespun cotton, a blue to match her lovely eyes. A sprinkle of freckles lightly dusted her face. They were earned beauty marks from her time spent in the sun with the children. They were mostly congregated across the bridge of her elfin, upturned nose. She was a lovely, lovely woman.

He hated her passionately.

He hated everything about her. He hated the way she moved, the way she spoke, and the way she dressed. He hated her clean, good, pure smell, and he hated her strong arms, her soft skin. He hated her taste, and hated the way her face gleamed seductively of sweat and effort.

She set the large can of water she'd been carrying down beside her, and placing her hands lightly on his shoulders; she stood tip-toe, and kissed him on the mouth. Her tongue darted gently against his; once, twice, three times.

"Good morrow, my husband," she said in her lightly accented voice, eyes aflame with hate and frustrated rage. If it were possible she hated him more than he hated her.

"Good morrow, my wife," he replied in a similar-sounding voice. Her kiss was a tender, loving, moist thing. Despite everything, despite the many times he had fantasized about her slow, lingering death, her kiss - still! - aroused him like nothing else. He couldn't help himself, couldn't help the way her touch enflamed him. It was as The Outside wanted it, and The Outside always got what it wanted.

He accepted the clean but chipped porcelain cup she proffered and filled it from the can. He had a long, slow drink.

The water, deliciously cold, tasted of the hollow places in the earth from which it sprang. It ran from an artesian well located in the back of the barn.

He hated the water too.

He drank his fill, and filling the cup yet again, rinsed it out for his wife. Because he had no choice, he thanked her, and then watered the donkey he'd been plowing the fields with. He lifted his hat off his head and armed the sweat from his brow, giving the donkey time to drink.

The donkey he did not hate. They had an understanding. The donkey knew what it meant to have no control, no choice, no ability to change its own destiny in the slightest. The donkey accepted the lot it was given, and did as it was bidden. He appreciated that mentality, and envied it. Gladly would he trade places with this beast of burden!

"How is the plowing today, John Book, my husband?" she asked, eyes flashing. Her body was posed with one hip holding the watering can, her bosom thrust aggressively toward him.

He wanted to slap her. He had no choice either, why should she be the one who was angry?

"The plowing today goes apace, Lora, my wife," he said, his face shaping itself into a smile that felt like a rictus.

"Willst be done by sunset?" she asked him with a smile of her own. That smile never touched the blue rocks that were her lovely eyes.

He laughed, a sickly sounding thing, and slapped 'Betsy' on the rump lightly. "That belongs to Betsy, my love. I am simply the harsh taskmaster. She does all the work."

'Betsy', a prodigiously male donkey, looked up at the mention of his name. He noisily returned to drinking water after a moment, straight from the can. This was just another demonstration of The Outside's control of every aspect of their lives. John Book could see that 'Betsy' was a male; both he and Lora knew the donkey was male. 'Betsy' would occasionally mount other donkeys! Yet The Outside had decreed that 'Betsy' should forever after be 'Betsy', a female donkey. And so 'Betsy' was. Discussing anything about 'Betsy' while The Outside was feeding was strictly forbidden, and so 'Betsy' was never discussed.

John wanted to grab his wife by the shoulders and scream "'Betsy is a male!'" in her face at the top of his lungs. The Outside would never allow this; never allow the acceptance of a male donkey. It defied all reason, for where did "Betsy" come from if not with the help of a male donkey?

He replaced his hat instead of trying to defy The Outside. As much as he hated it, fighting it was an exercise in futility.

"What will ye speak of tonight, my husband?" She smiled that brittle, false, chipped smile as she asked.

"The Beatitudes, I think, my love. Or perhaps our Lord's Sermon 'pon the Mount, entire. What think ye?"

He hated the deferential tone, the solicitation he could hear in his own voice.

She struggled against what came next. He could almost see her rising bile, and yet she had no choice. She set down the watering can, and smiling hugely, she wrapped her arms around him and leaned into his arms. She looked directly in his eyes, and he could see the hate she had for herself and for him clearly there. A trapped animal lurked behind her eyes, snarling to get out.

"Whatsoever ye speak of, I'm sure all will listen." She kissed him then, long and slow. She tasted of mint, madness and bile, and he hated her the more for it.

He broke their embrace, and smiling as he had to, gently disentangled himself with a rising sense of relief. That one was over, anyway.

"We'll see, my love, my Lora. But the day passes, and I get no work done. I will see thee at dinner." She retrieved her can, and he watched her struggle with the desire to turn and run, weeping, or to toss her head and retch. She did neither. She blew him a kiss, and walked slowly back to the house.

He had a brief respite here. He could not move from his appointed place, but could speak as he desired. The Outside's attention was elsewhere at this time, and he spoke aloud as he felt, directing his ire out into that bright light.

"Do you enjoy this? Huh? You sicko perv! This bullshit you've got us running here? HUH? I fucking hate you! I hate everything about you! Why don't you come down here, trade places with me for a while? Oooohhhh, no! You won't do that, will you? You'll stay waaay the fuck up there and watch us like ants under a fucking magnifying glass! Well, watch this, you sick, fucking monkey!"

He was shouting by now, and threw his fist into the air, before turning around and pulling his pants down.

"Lick my asshole!"

He had no idea whom he was addressing. He found he didn't care. A bolt from the blue, striking him dead, would be preferable to this miserable, hell-spawned existence. Even a return to the sleep of nothing would be better than this!

His respite over, The Outside's attention returned and he knew what came next. He knew it like the feel of the sun on his head. It wasn't enough for The Outside to watch, The Outside had to feel as well. The Outside had to know what he was like on the inside, so that its pleasure would be full, so that its feeding would be complete. After all, there is no texture, no poignancy to pain and sadness, if there isn't also a wealth of good cheer to balance it against. He would have given anything to change it. Anything at all . . . but nothing and no-one answered.

So he sang. He sang of Rivers in the Valley and of Lilies growing on Mountains. His voice was high, and clear, and though he tried to force a discordant note into it, all the songs rolled forth perfectly clear, and perfectly right.

They were songs of thanksgiving and worship, and he wanted to die.

~~~~~~

Dinner was miserable. It wasn't bad enough that Lora was unbelievably beautiful; she was also an excellent cook. He sat at his table, surrounded by his eleven children (small clones of him in a chronological stepladder), eating a home-cooked meal. Fried chicken with lemon, pepper, and garlic in the batter, fresh green beans, and cool, cold iced tea. The biscuits were light and flaky, and everything was served hot and quickly. Everything tasted wonderful, and he hated every mouthful.

He looked at these people who were his "family". Strangers all, he knew everything The Outside wanted him to know about them. And though his face was beaming, he radiated and reflected the hate he felt. The room rang with the clatter of a happy family's time at dinner: cutlery clashing, chewing, noises of approbation, laughing, and small bits of conversation radiated out around the table, enveloping them all. Yet, there were invisible wires of high-tension malice passing between them.

Just another Book family dinner. More beans, anyone?

~~~~~~~

He did speak of the Beatitudes that night. He stood at the homemade pulpit, carved from a single tree stump, and ringingly proclaimed the love of the Lord. He spoke about the War being good and just and right. He spoke of how proud he was of his eldest son (a person he could not recall ever laying eyes on), having volunteered to fight. He looked out at the faces of his congregation, hard-working men and women, all. Farmers, their wives and children, all resolutely looking back. From here, he could almost pretend that he enjoyed this, were it not for their eyes. It was always the same, though they acted, said, and did exactly as demanded by The Outside, their eyes still gave their true feelings away. At best they were wolves gnawing on a trapped limb, at worst . . . it was best not to dwell on that. That way lay madness.

~~~~~~~

He lay next to his "wife" later that night, the windows open, an autumn breeze bringing cool night air in. He thought, *"This breeze brings love with it."*

It wasn't a thought of his making, but a demand of The Outside's. He lay there, dreading what was to come, even fighting it with all of his ability, yet he may as well have been trying to catch the sea in a sieve.

Lora reached for him, and they did as lovers, as husband and wife do.

"THEY MADE LOVE LIKE THE WORLD WAS BURNING. IT WAS SLOW AND FUELED WITH THE PASSION OF TRUTH. A THING OF SWEAT, OF UNION. HER DOMINATING, AND THEN HE."

The Outside was never more fascinated then when they made love. Here, there was exquisite, almost painful attention to detail. Never mind that it was unrealistic, never mind that he himself had no desire to notice things, nor did his "wife", The Outside craved it otherwise.

He "TASTED HER BODY'S SALT, AND WATCHED HER EYES GLAZE, HEAVY-LIDDED AS HE JOINED WITH HER, A VICE IN VELVET, DRENCHED IN THE SWEET, MUSKY HONEY OF HER BODY. THEY RODE THE CRASHING WAVES OF DESIRE GENERATED; THEIR BODIES MOVING IN THAT TIMELESS CREST OF WAVE AND REMIT."

He watched as he was forced to, touched where he was forced to touch, and tasted that he was forced to taste. It was not a thing of love - how could it be? It was more a bestial, animalistic thing. They were two people acting on imperatives they had no control over. He could no more stop it then she. His only pleasure was knowing she hated it as much as he, and yet she was powerless to stop the raging orgasms he generated. Again, and again, and again, her moaning his name, until he was spent, and she lay exhausted in his arms.

He hated it, and hated himself. He hated the way The Outside paid such close attention to what was supposed to be a sacred act. He asked himself, in the deep recesses of his soul, what kind of a sick voyeur needed this?

~~~~~~~

The next morning came as it always did. There was no transition into sleep, no gentle dreams, no respite. He lay there thinking the thoughts he had to, with the perfume of their lovemaking slowly sinking into his skin, and then he was working in the fields. It was as The Outside desired it to be. There was no time for niceties, no time for "real".

He plowed, and he sang, and his wife brought him water, her "FACE NOW GLOWING WITH A HIDDEN SECRET THAT ONLY WOMEN KNOW."

He wondered dully at that, wondered how she felt to be treated as little more that a broodmare. He almost he felt compassion for her then, but it was a brief, fleeting thing.

~~~~~~~

It happened, as it always did. But this time was a little different. When Lora came running out to him, the false tears that never truly touched her eyes running dramatically down her cheeks, he saw it. There was a change in the light as she told him of their oldest being killed in the War. He did as he had to, but all of his attention focused on that steadily dimming light. She wept, telling him of receiving the news from the post that morning. He watched her eyes, and saw that she saw it too. The light was dimming! Things lost their edges, their definition. The sun was going out, and the mist was returning. He felt that grey muzziness descend, and was about to lose all of himself, when everything snapped back into full focus, full blaze. The colors leapt back into high-definition, and the light returned to its steady, burning gaze.

Yet, even as he watched, it began again, to dim. It was a relief. He didn't want to see the body of his eldest son, its stomach torn and bloated. He didn't want to receive the regrets of his neighbors, and he didn't want to live through another night of sad lovemaking with this woman he called "wife", yet knew not at all.

The muzziness descended then, and the lights went completely out. Before returning to the nothing, his last thought was, "Bastard must've fallen asleep after reading the juicy spot."

Life with Milton

The blood-curdling screams - those hair-raising, bone-chilling, knuckle-biting, adrenaline-pumping screams! Such utter horror, pain and woe - started up, for the first time tonight.

I rolled over and blearily opened one eye.

Three-thirty in the morning. Right on schedule.

"Shut UP, Milton!" I yelled, hoping he'd listen for once.

Milton gave a few more peremptory yells, more a "You're not the boss of me!" thing than any real attempt at true horror, shook a few pots down in the kitchen, and then, blessedly, did shut up.

I went back to sleep while I still could. I knew Milton would only give me a few minutes.

I'm not entirely sure it's a 'he', of course, and the name's merely a convenience, my way of getting back at him . . . .

I'm rambling. Let me start over.

My name's not really all that important. I'm just a secondary character. If this were a horror movie of some kind, I'd be the guy with the flashlight, wandering around in the dark while ominous music swelled and played in the background. At some point, I'd hear a noise and stupidly go investigate.

"Hello? Is there anybodGWARRGGLUGGHAGHHHH!"

Cue 'messy, painful, bloody death', and then we'd cut scene to the cute chick in cut-off shorts looking worried. "He's been gone for a long time!" (Head tilted coquettishly, hair arranged so that her ample cleavage is displayed to best advantage.)

You'll notice that my part is never played by the Johnny Depps and Brad Pitts of the world, though. No, us 'Killed Guy #4's are usually played by second-rate comics and porn stars looking to migrate across into bigger and better. And that's all you really need to know about my looks and whatnot isn't it?

So let's skip all the boring exposition: what I look like, what I do for a living, whether I consider The Beatles to be a superior rock group to The Troggs. None of that is important.

No, what's important is the fact that I live in a haunted house with Milton, my personal poltergeist. With me so far? No problem. It gets easier once the walls quit bleeding.

I needed to be up and about in a few hours, and if today was anything at all like usual, ol' Miltie was just getting started.

I closed my eyes for what felt like ten minutes when I heard the screeching, whistling hiss of a steam locomotive outside my bedroom.

I sighed. Rolled over and tried to go back to sleep.

Milton wasn't having *any* of that. The steam-locomotive sounds grew louder. The whistle began to blow, as if the train were barreling down the tracks, with me tied to the rails.

I sighed again, got out of bed and walked to the bedroom door. A light, the size of the full moon, shone directly in my eyes and a ghostly train came directly at me, smoke and all.

"Eek!" I said, sarcasm dripping from every syllable. "I'm so scared! Won't somebody save me?" I rolled my eyes and waved my hands irritably.

The train lights and noises quit with a sulky, deflated little honk.

I snorted and went back to bed. We're not the best of roommates.

I did some research back in my "This is so scary!" days. It seems my house was once owned by an eccentric film director at the turn of the century by the name of Count Horace Miltonian, the Third. (And he insisted on all caps, too.)

Count Horace owned a silent film company that made quite a tidy little bundle of money. He bought this house, or built it, depending on who you ask, and then proceeded to go seriously weird.

He went through this whole 'death' phase. He was into watching bodies decompose and started this club of 'deadheads': these freaks were a group of sick, rich bastards who were into digging up corpses and filming them in gruesome parodies of life. Think 'Necrophilia on Ice' and you've got the right idea.

Evidently he managed to piss somebody off, 'cause him and his sicko buddies were found 'grotesquely mutilated' after one of their parties. The faded, yellow clipping I'd found was steeped in Victorian language, so it was hard to figure out exactly what happened, but it suggested 'a dead feast interrupted by vengeful relatives'. The clipping didn't say so exactly, but I kinda got the suggestion that my good buddy Milton choked to death after being forcibly fed his own entrails.

Not a happy way to die.

Milton gets kind of pouty around this time of year, I think. Something to do with ghosts and Halloween, or something - like it's their day to meet some sort of astral quota. 'Scare so many mortals within this allotted frame, 'fore Hallo'een strikes midnight, or thou must parketh out by the dumpster-eth."

I haven't quite figured it out, and I've lived here for like, six years, or so. Milton doesn't answer any questions, but every year it's the same thing. Screeching, train, and all the rest, usually while I'm trying to sleep.

When I first moved in, Milton had a great time. He'd terrorize the cat, draw devilish hieroglyphics on the ceiling in oozing green phosphorescence, replay gruesome murder scenes (one of his favorites was a mad potter feeding his wife to a kiln to get a very particular glaze. Milton took great delight in close-ups of her burning face being a silent rictus of terror just before she exploded all over the inside of the kiln. I was sick for nearly a month after watching that.) and generally being as frightening as he could be.

I had two things going for me, however. One was my hard-headed practicality. I'm a film student. I'm trying to learn how to direct. I don't know if you've ever *been* to a film campus, but there are a whole slew of reasons why I didn't want to live on campus. One of them is the fact that I make less than a hundred dollars a week, working for a Professor as a secretary. The rent on this place is twenty-five a week and the landlord *rarely* comes by to collect.

Do the math. Staying here is a no-brainer!

The second is that, as I've already mentioned, I'm a film student. I've seen it all. I'm hard. Jaded, even. On a dare, I once took fifteen hits of acid and watched every Sergio Leone movie ever made. In Italian. I still go to therapy, three times a week, for that.

What I mean is, the first few times I watched these horrific scenes, I was pretty scared. Anybody would be. But watching Lee Van Cleef and Henry Fonda's faces run, melt, bleed and morph into some horrible Ronald McDonaldesque thing with pointy, beautifully-glaring eyes and spit-shiny, glitteringly-mad teeth . . . .

Plus, I recognized what ol' Miltie was doing, but more on that later.

So I persevered. I learned to live with Milton, as someone else, in another place and time, would learn to live with toothpaste boogers in the sink. This, of course, sent Milton into fits, and he tried even harder.

I got full-sound, 3-D panoramic views of the inside of Hell.

I experienced the pleasure and delight of being eaten alive and digested by some horrible slobbering thing that just should not be. (Sorry. I get Lovecraftian when Miltie's been keeping me awake.)

The walls bled.

The carpets grew maggots.

The furniture regularly liquesced.

The rooms shrunk, grew, changed dimensions and even occupied spaces outside the flow of space-time.

I took some Dramamine and math classes and learned about Mandelbrot sets. Milton really got cranky when I'd yell - fear choking my voice into a high-pitched squeak - that his shrinking room was off by three degrees of perspective along one axis.

Eventually he settled into a pattern. He seemed to be doing it to sulk. Shrieks at three-thirty, train effects some fifteen minutes later, followed by a chorus line of decomposing bodies.

I'm usually dead - if you'll forgive the pun - asleep by the swirling-blood pool-in-the-closet effect. I try not to snore. That makes Milton pout and I have to deal with stink worms in my shampoo for a week afterwards.

I started watching the ghostly effects that surrounded me with a more critical eye. I learned about this stuff at school every day, and soon enough I started having very serious suspicions about Milton.

He set up this whole "swallowed by the screaming maw of eternal death" thing, and instead of freaking out at the screams and colors, I looked around at the "set".

Sure enough, Milton was blocking me! Stage-managing me! He placed me in the exact spot that'd ensure I showed up to best effect on camera, the bastard! But worst of all, I was a secondary character!

In bad light!

Well, I wasn't going to stand for that. I've taken classes. I've studied the masters. I decided to fight back.

In an effect where he expected to flail and gibber after being torn into several different pieces by hands that slimed their way across my bedroom floor, I swallowed my rising panic, tried not to smell my freshly spilled fear-urine, and said, "Did you light that properly? I don't think I got the full effect there. Seems like there was an absence of positive reflection."

You could've dropped an invisible pin.

He tried again, ten minutes later. This time it was midgets, or goblins or maybe dead hobbits, in blood-soaked shrouds, crawling down the walls, their faces on backwards and frozen into an immobile rictus of unspeakable horror. I swallowed, suddenly grateful my bladder was already empty, licked dry lips, and said, "I've seen that movie! Good use of negative space there, Milton! Way to perpetuate the 'little people myth'!"

He left me alone for a week after that. I'm pretty sure he was moping.

By then, of course, it was too late. Milton was revealed for the cliche-ridden hack he was, and I was left - mostly - to my own devices. My face still dissolves in the mirror when I'm shaving or brushing my teeth, and I get the 'horrific dead guy screaming at me silently' thing in every shadowed, reflective surface, but then, I'm a college student, and I don't shave or brush my teeth all that often anyway.

He still tries, but he's stuck in his uneducated, mostly Victorian-era horror rut. I mean, psychological horror is all well and good, but it can't hold up to the blaringly 'juicy' candle of a good Freddie film.

Once you've been sprayed with blood from a fiercely wielded gardening tool, well . . . shrinking rooms and dead babies eating their own feet don't quite have the same effect.

Yeah, things have settled down between us, for the most part. Milton leaves me alone, and I don't point out his screeching ineptitudes in blocking. I'm even going to try and help Miltie out with his nebulous, ill-defined quota. I have plans to run a haunted house for this year's campus-wide Halloween party, charge fifteen bucks a head.

I just hope Milton doesn't make a scene.

A Palate Cleansing Foray into the Absurd

I know you're out there.

I can feel you. I can feel your anticipation and your wet-palm need. You make me so mad!

I can see you.

No, not, *really* see you - in my mind's eye, dummy. I'm not like, stalking you, and I don't see things all that often. While I *am* mad, I'm not nuts; despite any evidence to the contrary you might think you have.

I can see you, sitting on the edge of your seat, holding your breath and waiting with wide eyes full of anticipation.

Hell, I can hear you breathing.

Inhale, exhale.

Inhale, exhale.

Inhale, exhale.

That's you, alright. Usin' up all the available oxygen an' spittin' out gallons of microbe-infested carbon dioxide. You're a regular fountain, you are. I swear, it's enough to make a man lose his mind!

Don't look hurt and sad! You *know* I'm telling the truth! Yeah! Right there! Look at you! You just took *another* breath! What are you trying to do? I mean, gee, just go ahead and *flaunt* your gas-consuming nature at me, why don't ya'!

Oh. I *know* what you want. You're all perched forward, leaning toward the page, eager and ready. You got that 'What's he gonna write about today?' look on your face.

"Entertain us, Nescher!" you say, eyes all wide and dilated. I can smell the sweat on your palms, for crying in the mud!

"Write us something pithy, something edificational! Make us think and feel and dream! We want to sweat and clench our fists and worry about those wonderful characters you create! We want to breathe in seventy percent nitrogen and thirty percent oxygen! We want to digest our breakfasts! Or lunches! Or dinners - depending on what time it was when we read this! 'Cause we're a bunch of food-eating neee-erds!"

You're all like, breathing at me, making the air move in and out, and flavoring it with your lungs, and saying, "We want to be propelled out of our humdrum existences for a while, and feel the closing of deep waters across our faces!

"Make us *sing*, Nescher!"

Every day, it's the same thing; this psychic pressure beats against the fragile, stressed walls of my mind, making me pulse and sweat and worry. This little voice ticks like the second-hand of a clock in the back of my head. Before I know it, I can hear what the voice is saying – 'Gotta *write* gotta *write* gotta **write** gotta **write** gotta **write** gotta <u>*write*</u>' - like a drumbeat, set at ten-million-miles-a-second. And you know what?

It's all *your* fault!

That's right! *You*! You, the one with the face! With the lips and eyelids on it! And the hair! That . . . that . . . hair, all just like, growing out from your head!

How gross and weird is that, Face-hair-head? Whyntchu just join a carnival? You could like, sit in a chair, smoking a cigarette, and let people pay a nickle to come see you and your freaking face-hair-head! The little kids would stare, and be like, 'He's a face-hair-head! Mommy! Save us from Face-hair-head!'

You freak!

Here's a chicken! Whynchtu fry it up and *serve it*? **WITH SOME BEANS AND CORNBREAD?**

HUH?

Yeah! You! You, you cornbread-fried-chicken-eating dork!

FREAK!

This is you: 'Oh. I think I'll-' Yeaaaaaaaaah. You don't like it when I imitate you, with your high-pitched, nine-year-old-girl-French-ballerina voice, do you? That's too bad, ain't it? 'Cause that's what you sound like! 'Oh,' you say, just like that, 'Oh. I think I'll set my alarm so I can get some good rest, and have nice dreams, and then wake up at a reasonable hour and take a shower and get dre-essed.'

You job-having, sleeping-in-a-bed, clothes-wearing, pants-having nutjob!

And then I'll say, just like this, I'll say, 'That's right! 'Cause you're a dweeby-freak-job! And you use - ' Yeah. That's right. I *do* sound like a Russian Drill Sergeant. You wanna make something of it, Mr. 'Lookit me! I wear shoes!'?

I'll write your name!

In cursive!

And then I'll say, 'You use soap! Soap and hot water when you take a shower, 'cause you're trying to be hygienic!'

You tool. You Philips-Head-Screwdriver-Face-hair-head.

Well, it ends today. I got news for you: Ain't gonna do it. That's right. I'm gonna sit here, my hands clasped in my lap, and I'm not writing anything tonight.

Not one dang word.

There are blisters on the ends of my fingers, blisters on my mind! My hands hurt! My wrists hurt! I'm developing a wicked awful case of tarpal cunnel.

Yeah, yeah. I know there are legitimate sufferers, of 'I got weak wrist tendons,' but if they want to complain, they can write their *own* chapter! This whine-fest is about *me*! It's *ALLLLLLLLLL* about me! Can we focus on *me* and on *my* problems, please? I can't change the world, and I want to whine.

Oh.

I see.

Now that I've decided to stand up for myself, you're not gonna read it.

I see how you are.

"He's not writing to entertain us? Well, crap! I'm not reading this bilge! If he's not gonna entertain me, I'm not gonna give him any of my time! He's just a stupid jerk! With funny shoes! And his voice is all goofy! His head has an odd shape and he smells like polyester!"

Oh yeah! Well . . . same to you! But worse! And . . . and . . . your mama!

Yeah!

That's right!

How you like me now?

Bruised

The alarm goes off, and the world, maybe even the universe, gives noisy, labored birth to him once again.

Morning. But that's not quite right, is it? And that's probably part of the problem.

He's lying there, on his face, listening to the shrill mechanical buzz while the fragments of dream evaporate around him. He doesn't want to be awake. Being awake means a return to pain. He reaches for those ethereal wisps, trying to pull them back into a warm comforting cocoon of unconsciousness that he can then burrow into and lose himself in, but the alarm is drilling on.

He sighs, half awake, half asleep.

He has strange ideas sometimes. One of his favorites - and most enduring - is surprisingly existential.

"I don't exist unless I'm awake."

It's a seductive, compelling thought - one that allows him to be a perfect bastard. He plays with it quite a bit and holds it close and dear. The assorted lovers he's shared it with - the most recent lies next to him in a sleeping, naked, fetal huddle - have assured him that based on the raspy, guttural qualities of his bed-shaking snores, that this is, in fact, not true. It is a rather contrived conceit, to be sure, but he clings to it. After all, if the world's only his waking dreams . . . ?

He opens one bleary eye to look out upon that accusing, demanding, unforgiving world through the open window next to his bed. Tepid sunlight swims through grey, dismal skies like hot blood through cold gravy. He groans and turns away.

He looks at the alarm clock. It glares back with a malevolent, red-eyed fury.

'It's five thirty! You need to get up! How dare you lie in bed wasting the day away?!'

The lady sleeping next to him fills his line of sight. He winces, as if in pain, and utters an expletive it isn't necessary to repeat here.

She's an attractive woman. A bit on the mature side. Forty, forty-five, maybe fifty. It's not immediately obvious. She goes to great lengths to conceal her age. It's more a general impression, heaviness in the eyes, or a dignified carriage around the shoulders.

"I'm smarter than you on your very best day, junior."

Yeah.

Her hair is long and luxuriant, blonde as a sunflower and thick as a grassy hillside. It smells of expensive conditioners and treatments, and the way it's styled begs to have your fingers run through it.

Her body displays the clear evidence of being a gym-worshipper: tight, toned and tanned.

Her face is just beginning to display evidence of age: the smile lines around her eyes and mouth are a bit pronounced, there's sagging under the chin. *She* sees it, but we'd need to know what to look for. She spends an awful lot of time, money and effort ensuring we can't see it. There is a sense that she'd be mortified were we to suggest that we could see anything at all.

Vanity lingers in the air around her like a soft, cottony haze.

He sighs - a thick, clotted sound - and mechanically punches at the alarm until he manages to hit the snooze button. Within seconds he's fallen back asleep, leaving the question of his existence, or lack thereof, in the air for the next nine minutes.

The room is a large one, with fifteen-foot ceilings. A sliding-glass door leads out to a grassed, fenced-in lawn we can just see through the Venetian blinds. The room smells like musk and marijuana, perfume and cigarette smoke, sweat, spilled beer and curdled, spoiled dreams.

The room's centerpiece, the bed, is a king, a monster of a thing, big enough to land a plane on. It stands some four and a half feet off the floor, almost like a throne. A harem of seven would be perfectly comfortable operating out of this bed. It's neatly centered on the wall directly across from the bedroom door, and it dominates the room like a stage in a theatre.

The headboard and footboard are done in a cannonball style, with a newel post effect at the four corners. A large, round, wooden sphere sits atop each of these four posts, easily the size of a human head. The spheres are perfectly smooth and the smell of furniture polish clings to them like perfume. The headboard is every bit of eight feet tall and made of a dark, red, hardwood, giving everything the impression of sullen warmth. The nightstands - one to a side - the large, mirrored dresser and the enormous armoire, all match the bed quite neatly.

The bedclothes - sheets, blanket, and pillowcases - are a muted pink color, and have the cooling, rippled, slippery quality of watered silk.

A painting in a gilded frame - of a flower that could only grow in a nymphomaniac's most fevered dreams - is strategically placed over the bed. It's been done with a Georgia O'Keefe attention to botanical detail. The flower's petals spread across the canvas in hot reds and blushing pinks. The blossom itself is just beginning to open. The very center of the blossom is a deep, labial pink. Looking, we almost feel we could warm our hands over it. The overall effect is vaginal; enormously, sweat-inducingly erotic.

Accent lights give the room an intimate closeness that hides and flatters. An aquarium gurgles quietly to itself in one corner, the fish swimming in perfect aquatic comfort. Music softly plays from concealed speakers in the room's corners.

He doesn't resemble his furniture. Hard planes and angles with just the right amount of the unfinished tapioca of youth. He hasn't stopped boiling into his adult form, hasn't quite pupated, so to speak.

He's young, no more than twenty-five, but twenty-two, twenty-three may be closer to the mark.

His skin has a dusky appearance to it, like a tan. It gives him an exotic look, like he's from someplace hot and sultry. He capitalizes on this occasionally by faking a Spanish accent.

His head is shaved. He shaves the hair right down to the skin of his scalp every day. He likes to think it gives him a romantic, gothic appearance, like a raver, or a vampire.

Several hoop earrings line both ears. A large silver post pierces his left brow. His face is thin, narrow, and suspicious-looking, even in sleep. We have the impression that he tries to appear smarter than he actually is, wiser, more adult. There's an insistent idea that this young man gives off a vibe of "knowing the unknowable", like some sort of Gen-Xian Faust, or latter day Bacon.

"Here is a young man," we say to each other with knowing, wise looks, "who walks through cemeteries pretending to listen to ghosts."

A certain muscularity to his body suggests he works at whatever it is he does. His limbs and chest are hard and well formed, and covered in bulging, work-a-day muscle. We almost feel, standing over him and his lady, that upon meeting him, we'd have an impression of an invisible, nearly gelatinous obstinacy of spirit, a slow thickness.

"We're not getting all of him," we'd say, "we're getting a sort of amiable, peeled-off clone that's been cleaned up and taught some manners."

Talking to him would necessitate wading through this invisible force field, and one has to wonder if that would be worth the trouble.

Sleeping, naked but for a pair of boxers, limbs splayed every which way, this impression of thickness isn't bettered any.

When he wakes, he'll wake grumpy. There's no way of knowing this, but we do all the same.

From where we stand, we can see his tattoos. Very proud of his skin art, he likes to believe that his tattoos make him look hard, tough.

"Look out! That kid's tattooed!"

The vanity of youth, maybe, or just a simple character flaw? We're not sure, but they're very noticeable.

One is of a large green snake with blue diamond scales - its face somehow both carnivorous and horribly evil - climbing his left shoulder. It has the look of "one-too-many-beers", and "an-inability-to-communicate-to-the-tattooist-exactly-what-was-wanted". It seems to be a bit gouty. The face of this snake gives one the impression of very slow, nearly glacial mental processes fueled by a desire to hurt everything in its path.

The other is, improbably, of a sad-eyed clown with large, pink bunny ears, placed just above his navel.

It may be best not to speculate as to its nature. Some things are best left unsaid.

But there, the alarm has gone off again.

His eyes snap open, and then close in irritation. He opens them again and rolls over on his back to consider the ceiling for a moment.

We have time to see that his eyes are a surprising shade of green: the soft, gentle eyes of a very specific sort of predator. An entire generation of mothers warned their daughters about these eyes. They've been labeled everything from "bedroom eyes" to "gigolo sunglasses".

He doesn't realize it, but he's searching for faces in the plaster covering the ceiling. It's a totally unconscious desire on his part to impose order on his surroundings, to give his life some sort of rule and order. It's something he's done since childhood and he's largely unaware of it. He'd laugh if we pointed it out to him.

"Finding faces? Guess I better talk to a shrink, huh?"

He spots one, and a thin, warm satisfaction climbs through him. He peers sleepily at it, and tries to concoct a story to go with it.

If he were at all aware of doing this, he'd probably be alarmed at the number of faces he's found over the years. He'd be downright scared by the number of faces he's given "damned souls suffering in hell" stories to.

The woman makes an irritated, sleepy noise. He reaches over and brushes her hair with a hand, smoothing it over her head. It is a completely unconscious gesture, one he is utterly unaware of. The lady, for her part, subsides back into sleep.

A small calico cat makes an appearance then and treads delicately across the bed to the man, meowing just once.

"Good morning, cat."

The cat is a cat: tail, whiskers, feline nobility, and a sense of "if you were just a bit smaller, you'd be a squeaky, crunchy snack."

It was an unplanned surprise, a part of his life over which he has little control. It simply showed up one morning and meowed piteously until he opened the door.

"What do you want?" he'd asked, his face and voice irritated, after listening to those desperate cries for a while. It had looked up into his eyes, and that'd been it. He recognized something shining out from the cat, something only the desperately lonely recognized.

He'd sighed and opened the door wider. "Come on in, then."

The cat walked in without a further noise and helped itself to his dinner.

Cats are quietly evil when it comes to appetite.

Its name is "Cat". He initially wanted the name to be a joke about "why bother to name something that never comes when it's called?" The truth is he felt silly giving a noble creature like a cat a human name. That joke's already been done to death anyway. Besides, our hero is relatively sure the cat can't say any name he might give it. Much better to keep things on a sort of speciesist basis. He knows his name, and the cat, if it bothers, knows the name it has for itself. Why make waves with your roommate?

It also neatly curtails any discussion about the cat's sex.

"Oh! What a beautiful cat! Is it a boy or a girl?"

"I have no idea. I don't know how to tell the difference, and it's not something you ask when you don't know, is it?"

An awkward situation, at best. Besides, he really feels that one's sexuality is one's own business and the sort of thing that should be kept to oneself. Again, why make waves with your roommate?

The cat, for its part, has declined to comment one way or the other about any of these things. This only leads our hero to believe he's right to think the way he does.

The cat meows again, its back arched in greeting and its golden eyes wide and supplicating.

The man smiles wider and says, "Yeah. Me too. Let me pull my head together, and we'll see what I can rustle up."

The cat tilts its head fetchingly to one side. Our hero entertains himself by giving the cat a voice. It is a high, clear contralto, sort of a feline Opera Diva's speaking voice. In the quiet playing hall of his head, the cat says, "You know, humans are a dime a dozen. You can *be* replaced."

He grins and says, "Yeah, but before breakfast?"

It looks at him for a long moment, probably casting vile cat-magic for not immediately leaping to its beck and call, and then saunters off, as only a cat can.

He snorts - a noise that could almost be laughter. He gropes around on the nightstand, his fingers treading almost delicately across the scattered flotsam and jetsam covering its top. After a moment's long exercise, he manages to find a battered box of Kools, a lighter, and an ashtray with "Cuyahoga Falls!" written on it in cheery letters.

He places the ashtray on his belly, winces as it comes in contact with a bruise shaped exactly like a woman's mouth, and digs free a cigarette with one square-tipped finger. He puts it to his lips and lights it with an unconscious flourish.

"Can I get one of those?" a sleepy, husky, feminine voice asks.

He looks over to see the woman looking back from a thick blonde curtain of hair. He realizes, unsurprisingly, that he hasn't the slightest idea what her name is.

He wordlessly hands her a cigarette, and just as wordlessly lights it for her. She takes a thick, deep drag, and looks at him through bleary, hung-over eyes.

They smoke in contented silence for a moment, marred only by the idiot voice of the alarm.

"Aren't you going to shut that off?" she says, her voice heavy and dragging.

"I never do. I don't even know why I set it, to be perfectly honest. It's not like I've got to get up and go to work."

She laughs. Her voice has a breathy, smoky quality to it. It's surprisingly sexy. He likes to hear her talk.

"I think I just I like to let it buzz, let it feel like it's doing a good job and should be rewarded. I mean, think about it for a minute: you're an alarm clock, okay? The only thing you have to look forward to all day long is to go off. You sit there, on a bedside table, or a dresser, or whatever, waiting for that one time of day when your services are needed, necessary and valuable," he says, still smiling.

Gesturing in an expansive way, he throws his arms out as if he were tossing gold coins from a chariot.

"I mean, I'm all about the healthy self-esteem. 'Let the alarm clock blare!' say I!"

She laughs. She's lying on her belly, propped up on her elbows, holding her cigarette at an elegant angle. It's a body position that displays her womanly charms and she knows it.

He wonders at that, at the blatantly stripped vanity of it. It's such an incongruous gesture. She's lying in bed, naked, with a stranger, the evidence of their night of torrid sex all around them, and she holds her cigarette as though she were at a tea, or a fancy-dress party of some kind. Her body almost thrusts itself at him, and a small voice in his head says, "Would you like a scone, dear?"

It makes him smile even wider.

He smokes the entire cigarette, his alarm blaring and buzzing all the while. He thinks evil thoughts at it, and eventually it gives up with a sullen, mechanical, "Whatever, dude."

That makes him laugh, too.

She looks over and he shakes his head.

"Nothing," he says. "The alarm clock got irritated with me."

She lifts an amused eyebrow and he grins.

"Do you play?" she asks, pointing at a black acoustical guitar, with red accents, leaning (so as to be noticed) in a corner.

He places the cigarette in a corner of his mouth in response. He climbs from the bed, fetches the guitar, and returns to the bed. He leans against the headboard, affecting a careless "cigarette-smoking-Elvis-Costello-playing-for-the-ladies-in-bed" sort of vibe.

He spends a moment plucking aimlessly, and then plays an arrangement of Ravel's *Bolero* he's particularly proud of. He plays a few bars and then transitions into the opening licks of Journey's *Wheel In The Sky*.

He plays a few more songs - pieces he's memorized specifically for this reason. He moves between them with a practiced fluidity. She smiles, smoking her cigarette.

As we watch, we get the sense he's playing the only things he knows how to play. There is a very specific limit to his musical repertoire, and we're reaching it. He never tries to learn new music, never plays the guitar out of love for the music. He plays it to be noticed and admired.

He finishes with an unplugged version of Steelheart's one and only hit. She lifts the lighter and slowly waves it in grinning appreciation.

She claps, languidly, giggling. He places the guitar back, bows to his audience, and climbs back into bed. He stubs the remains of his cigarette out, lights another, and offers the woman the pack.

She accepts with a smile, and they smoke in silence for a time.

"Now, don't take this the wrong way," she begins, but is interrupted by our hero's laughter; a surprising sound, full of good cheer and humor, almost musical. It transforms him somehow into being something quite likeable. That sound is all the more surprising for coming from that narrow, suspicious mouth. The young lady looks at him, one eyebrow raised in a quizzical sleepiness.

"Nothing you could say at this point would be the 'right way', I don't think. Look at it. 'Now, don't take this the wrong way, but are you a serial killer?'"

His voice is light, carefully toned to a very specific harmonic that he's found works well with women: deep, but not threatening, rounded, without being obvious about it. He calls it his "Henry the Eighth Voice".

She grins back, and says, "Do you have a collection of pickled heads in your basement?"

He takes a deep drag off his cigarette, pulling the smoke down inside him with a contentment he knows he won't match with anything else during the day.

She smokes hers as well. They lie in bed, each thinking their own thoughts.

He stubs his cigarette out neatly in his jaunty ashtray and rolls on his side to regard the woman. She looks back. He can see the skittish nervousness dancing in her eyes. She's thinking about mistakes and consequences.

He pillows his head on his arm and reaches out to stroke the side of her face. He gives her a warm, lingering kiss.

Her tongue flitters against his, like a playful butterfly. She leans against him, almost eagerly, tasting his mouth. Her mouth tastes like her cigarette; like the sweat of her body.

He gives her what she wants as a kiss and then looks into her eyes.

"I'm not a serial killer; I'm not a rapist; I don't collect pickled heads. I'm afraid I don't know your name, or where we met, or whether or not we like each other, but I make it a point not to make any enduring judgments about people before breakfast, anyway."

She smiles; a warm, genuine smile and he is pleased to see it.

He extends his right hand, and says his name. Her smile widens, and she extends hers and says her own name. They shake.

"Pleased to meet you," he says, kissing her on the forehead in accompaniment to her giggles.

He rolls over and goes back to contemplating the ceiling. He sees the face he spotted earlier, and writes another story in the background of his head. He's just about decided that this one is a Cape Cod fisherman, when she rises out of bed with a groan.

"Leaving?" he asks.

"Yeah," she replies. Her movements are slow and stiff as she gathers her clothes from the floor. Her dressing takes much longer than it should as she's in a great deal of pleased, sore pain. She's favoring those muscles that don't ache and it's making her awkward.

"I can answer one of your questions for you," she says after a long moment of frustrated dressing.

"Oh?" he asks, his voice politely interested, but not really caring. He's already dismissed her and planning the rest of his day.

"Yeah. If the way I feel now is any indication, then we liked each other a whole lot," she says, with a rueful grin.

He laughs for a very long time.

She grins, liking the sound of his laughter, and finishes dressing. She reaches for a handbag, and on an impulse she doesn't understand, writes her name and number down on a cocktail napkin she finds inside.

"Look. I gotta run. I've got to get to work early in the morning tomorrow, and I'm gonna need a couple hours to recuperate, and . . . ."

He gently smiles.

"There's no need for this," he says, his voice oddly quiet and accepting, eyes soft and warm.

She stops talking and lays the napkin neatly on his dresser, reaches in the handbag again and lays several hundred dollar bills on top of it.

She leaves with a smile.

He hears the cat meow at her quizzically.

"'Bye, cat," she says, and he waits until the door shuts and locks itself back. After a few minutes, he hears the distant sound of a car starting.

"That answers that," he thinks, glad he doesn't have to take her home.

Homes can be awkward, what with husbands, lesbian lovers, and boyfriends. He learned that early on after being chased from a front door by a weeping husband flailing a rusty machete.

Getting out of bed himself, he imagines a sucking sound, a Velcro-ripping sound, as he pulls himself out of bed. It makes him smile again.

He doesn't really know it, but he fills his mind with these light distractions and quick little fantasies. They are a learned defense mechanism. They keep him from dwelling on the larger issues, from his sense of perfect self-loathing.

The kiss she left him with still burns on his lips and he can still smell the musk of her body on his. He is tired, sore, and injured, as if he'd spent all night wrestling with a large cat.

Counting the money she left, he thinks about kisses. With a shrug, he puts her money away.

"Kisses are like soft-core porn," he says, looking at Cat. "They're all a question of angles."

The napkin is crumpled without looking at it. If she's interested, she knows where to find him.

Carefully, with measured steps, he walks to his bathroom and looks himself in the eye in the mirror. He sees a wounded, bruised soul staring back.

"Gigolo," he says to his reflection.

The word has such a poetic, lyrical fall. It sounds like something rewarding and noble, something that anyone would be proud to aspire to. It sounds like a poem dripping from his lips. The way he says it makes it sound like the very pinnacle of human existence and achievement. He's an artist, a craftsman! Not a whore.

His neck has several love bites. There are scratches on his back, his shoulders and his chest. Bruises, in the shape of small, slender fingers, have begun to form.

He's very careful not to leave marks, himself, unless he's specifically asked to. Women who ask usually want to make a lover in their own lives jealous. He complies. Money is money.

Some women can be very sensitive about hickeys and such. Visible evidence of a night of heavy sex makes many women - especially the older, professional women who make up much of his clientele - very uncomfortable. They seem to think it's like a large, embroidered "A", pinned to the bodice.

Others ask him to leave scratches and even bruises. They want him to hurt them. It's not something he understands himself. Domination, pain, it's all a very gray, confused area to him.

Some women feel the need to be castigated during sex. They often break down, weeping, and become angry when he tries to comfort them. He's never understood it.

Some women just like to be hurt and commanded, to be treated like dirt during sex. Making money off of them from their pain doesn't bother him a bit. Money is money.

"It's all money."

If he were a philosophical sort, this'd be his mantra.

He washes the scratches clean with hot water and soap. He washes them again with alcohol; wouldn't do to get an infection. Scars, especially sex-scars, are fine. Scars are sexy, and some women like to see this stark evidence of ability and virility.

"This boy gonna give me my money's worth!"

It always surprises him that they aren't bothered by the idea that he's slept with so many different women, that they are, in fact, impressed. He's not sure if this is indicative of how all women feel, or just the select few that make up his client base.

Yes, scars are fine, but an infection would mean he'd be out of work for a week or two, something he tries to avoid.

He brushes his teeth. He flosses. He washes his face. He shaves. His eyes never leave his reflection's eyes in the mirror.

He wants to pull answers from his reflection, to have incriminatory judgments about his chosen lifestyle shouted at him. He wants to be railed at, to be shouted down, to be weighed in a set of spiritual scales and judged.

He wants to be condemned and punished.

His reflection stares back, making no judgments, giving no answers. He smiles at it and his reflection smiles back.

"Hey, good looking!"

His reflection says nothing.

"Yeah, well, screw you too," he says, and turns to the toilet. The calico cat appears and rubs its jaw against the doorframe, meowing plaintively.

"Okay, okay. Just give me a minute here!"

He's always made a concerted effort to never think beyond the necessary, the required moment. Some people focus on infinity and go slowly mad. Our young lothario never allows himself to look beyond the next fifteen minutes. Any sort of self-examination leads him to the edge of personal disaster. He finds himself at the bottomless pit of self-loathing that makes up his center, his core, and he asks himself why he doesn't jump.

No, much better to move from minute to minute. Let the larger issues lie.

He showers, puts on a blue silk robe, feeds the cat.

He opens a can of "Vet Balanced!" cat food that costs five dollars and puts it on a plate. He muses about the fact the writing of "Vet Balanced!" on a can raises the price by four dollars and seventy-five cents.

"I'm in the wrong line of work, Cat," he says, while putting the plate on the floor.

The cat pounces on it eagerly.

"Is Our Majesty pleased?"

The cat purrs.

He smiles and goes into the kitchen to feed himself.

Food is not something he enjoys. Eating is the fueling up of a machine. He eats because he has to. He consults a chart on his refrigerator, counting calories and carbohydrates. He selects fresh fruit - an apple - some vegetables and a lean steak. He eats the apple. He eats the vegetables raw as he doesn't want to leach out the vitamins and minerals. He eats the steak medium rare because he likes it that way.

Every carefully balanced and counted bite is eaten without really enjoying any of the textures or tastes.

The dishes are washed and put away.

A CD is selected from his collection, he rolls himself a joint, and sits down in his living room, with the lights off as the music plays. He smokes the joint, follows it with a cigarette, and tries, desperately, not to think of anything.

He sits through the entire CD, eyes closed. We can almost believe he's gone to sleep.

The CD ends, and he opens his eyes. He stands and goes into his bathroom, to the medicine cabinet.

"Time for drugs!" he says, to his reflection.

Luck has been with him thus far: a couple of urinary tract infections, a cold sore or two, a gonorrhea scare about three years ago. He took the course of antibiotics necessary and actually got a nine-to-five job for six months. It was a bad time, and his mind slides away from thinking about it. The real biggies - HIV, hepatitis - have never crossed his path, and he takes all the measures he can to continue to keep them away. Being ever so slightly suicidal doesn't mean he has a death wish.

The women who can afford his services are, by-and-large, free of the problems of body lice, genital warts, scabies and other hygiene issues. He's quite careful, of course. He uses a condom every time and makes it a point to walk away if at all leery. A vasectomy early on has largely eliminated the worry of pregnancy.

He takes down several little, brown, unlabeled bottles and lines them up on his sink.

He has a tidy arrangement with a young, female doctor. She's aware of what he does for a living, and makes no judgments. She has skeletons in her closet as well. She has a serious heroin problem. In very typical "I'm a doctor! Don't tell me anything!" fashion, she is not dealing with her addiction.

This young doctor writes him scripts for whatever he asks. In return, he acts as a third party delivery boy, ensuring she has a steady supply of her teeny baggies of white death. She's even come over a time or two. She's one of his "Worship me, little man!" clients.

He's pretty sure she's violated every last one of her professional ethics, and it's only a matter of time before her love affair with the horse gets out of hand. But it *is* nice to have one's very own private doctor on call.

He muses about women while setting up his daily doses. Many aren't really interested in penetration. They are perfectly content to have a clitoral orgasm, and since it's not about his needs, he doesn't even need to take his pants off. They are more turned on by the image of a man on his knees before them than anything he can do to them physically. Those women like to be seduced; wined and dined; kissed; plenty of foreplay. He can make quite a lot of money by worshipping them orally, and then telling them how wonderful they are.

Other women think *only* of penetration. They want to be "ridden", "violated", whatever word makes you happy. These women don't want it nice and slow. They want it hard, fast and ugly.

It makes little difference to him. All he needs is an erection, and he's in business. Male enhancement drugs make his life infinitely easier.

He rarely has an orgasm anymore. He'd read once that something like less than ten percent of rapists have orgasms when in the process of a rape. He assumes most of those can probably be categorized as the flaming nut-jobs. It makes him uncomfortable to think that he could be placed in that category himself. His mind skitters away from it, like a bag of spilling marbles.

He walks out of the bathroom to his liquor cabinet. Pours himself three fingers of very expensive gin in a tumbler and carries it back into the bathroom.

He picks up the first bottle: large white pills for possible infections. A cold, a sore throat, a minor case of the sniffles, any one of those are a turn-off. It's hard to reel in a customer when you keep blowing your nose.

He takes two, swallows them along with the gin.

"All of life's inconvenient little pains, gripes and miseries, chased off by the magic in little brown bottles. I don't need to think, I don't need to feel. Just give me my little brown bottles," he says, quoting someone he can't remember, and grinning to his reflection.

The next bottle holds small blue pills: powerful antidepressants. These give him that distance he so desperately craves in his everyday. One of these will keep him from feeling anything other than a very mild euphoria for hours. One of these will let him stay away from his higher consciousness, kiting along on the very surface of his brain for the better part of the day. He's often likened the feeling to driving down a steep hill with no brakes.

He takes three, swallows them with the gin.

The next bottle holds his vitamins, a concoction he's devised himself after long study: massive doses of the B group and the C group, along with some general minerals, vitamins, and some of the trendier herbs.

He's still a growing boy, after all, and he's gotta keep his strength up.

The last bottle holds red capsules. These are his "horse tranquilizers", as powerful a trank as he can get his hands on. His young doctor has assured him that these are as powerful a trank as is made, anywhere.

"One of these would put you out for the better part of three days. Don't take 'em unless you plan to sleep for a while. Okay? And don't *ever* take more than one. You'll never wake up. Okay?"

He holds the bottle in his hand as he does every day. He looks at the pills, as he does every day, and thinks it over.

"Two or three would do it," he thinks. "Just open the bottle, pop two or three in your mouth, and you'd never have to wake up. Think about it: what, exactly, are you holding on for? I mean, it's not like you've got anything to lose or to even live for. Just open the bottle."

He looks himself in the eye in the mirror. He finishes the last of the gin in the glass.

"Gin," he says to his reflection. "Today it's gin."

He puts the tranquilizers back in the medicine cabinet, along with the rest of the small brown bottles. He closes the medicine cabinet with a firm hand.

"Guess today's not the day," he says. His reflection is again silent.

He walks into his living room and checks his messages. Three are from women. He writes down their names and numbers, making notes as to the salient details they leave, clues in their tone of voice.

One is the thin, mad voice of his mother, calling from the home. Her voice is drugged, heavy with the medications to keep her calm.

"Hello? Can you tell them to bring me a cup of water? There's stitches in my head, and I'm sorry for damning that nurse in the ER. She embarrassed me. The nurses say I can go home later today. The doctor hit me in the face with an axe. It wasn't me. It was Nancy Reagan . . . I love you. Good bye."

He sits and stares at the answering machine for a long time. He doesn't seem to realize he's weeping.

~~~~~~

He dresses. He can feel the "falling away" sensation of the drugs beginning to take hold. It feels like a wind is blowing through the wide-open caverns of his body. It's as if someone has poured ice water into his veins. His doctor told him that this is known as a "vasodilation effect".

"Your blood vessels have expanded. Your blood pressure has plummeted, and your heart has sped up. Your body believes it's going into hypovolemic shock - shock where you're bleeding to death. It can be quite dangerous, so don't overdo it," she warned,.after his last check-up.

He could see a fresh bruise on the side of her neck, just where the top of her doctor smock's collar lay. She pressed her breast into his arm as she leaned over to take a blood pressure reading. Her eyes were yellow and dead.

"Doing anything later?" she asked, smiling in what she probably thought was invitation. He could see her skull through the skin covering her face.

"I don't know. *Am* I?" he asked with a soft, smoldering grin.

"You are now," she replied, with a smug smile.

She tasted like dust.

He walks out to his mailbox and retrieves his mail. He walks back in and tosses it, unopened, on his dining room table: solicitations from various charities, reminders from his doctor and a bill or two. It's all very bland.

He steps outside. A breeze is blowing, carrying with it the music of dogs barking and children at play. He can smell summer honeysuckle. He lifts his face into that breeze, closes his eyes and smiles.

"Summer honeysuckle. Summer honeysuckle *and* gin," he whispers.

His apartment has a nicely grassed area behind it. It's fenced in, but the fence isn't very tall. It's perfectly sized so anyone who might look toward his apartment can see him. This has come in handy more than once. There are several lonely housewives in his immediate neighborhood with easy access to an ATM machine.

His days are rarely slow.

He's dressed in his sweat pants and muscle shirt - cut to display his body to good advantage - and, taking his boken with him, he moves through the series of kata he's learned so far.

There is no joy, no transcendental spiritual exploration, no declaration from a body grateful to be exercised in his movements. It's really quite simple. Chicks dig martial artists. He moves through the routines, not understanding or appreciating them as anything other than a means to an end.

He works up a good sweat, and he knows he's giving quite a show to anyone who might be watching. He never checks, of course. That'd be telling.

He spars with himself for several hours, running through each of the kata he's learned several times. His muscles begin to complain a bit. They feel well oiled and stretched. He lowers his boken to the grass.

"You make lots noise last night," a thin voice says from beyond the fence.

He looks up. His landlord, a stout, middle-aged Asian gentleman, is standing there, glowering in stern disapproval.

His landlord doesn't like him. His landlord suspects that his wife and daughters would be interested in learning just how he manages to inspire the young women he brings to his apartment to make all that noise.

He needn't worry, his landlord's women can't afford his services, and he never does anything gratis.

He smiles from his place on the grass.

"Lovely day we're having," he says to that stern face, while licking his lips suggestively, his eyes as hot as he can make them.

He's found that men are sometimes interested in his services as well. He's not as enthusiastic about that, but he's found that many of the things he's picked up to lure a man in can make the homophobic run.

His landlord sniffs mightily and moves away at a brisk trot.

He smiles to himself, wondering what he would've done if the landlord had asked about prices.

He shrugs.

"I'd've told him," he says out loud. Money is money. No matter where it comes from, it all spends.

He stands and goes back inside to shower again.

He washes his body with the same sort of meticulous attention to detail a knight would apply to his armor before entering battle. The selection of cologne and deodorant is carefully considered to provide maximum - yet subtle - effect.

His clothes are tight in all the right places, loose in others. Some women like to sit and talk, others like to dance, still others like to see a bohunk displayed like a sausage in its case.

He puts on pants, shirt and jacket, paying careful attention to colors and fabrics. He smiles, puts on his jewelry and walks out his door.

His car - a 1978 Corvette, the kind of cherry ride that only the very rich with lots of free time can really appreciate - done up in the same exact shade as his eyes, is part and parcel of his "stalk, hunt, kill" routine.

He slides behind the seat and starts the engine. It comes to life with a basso-profundo roar. He grins.

His one concession to modification, a custom sound system, starts delivering a throbbing bass note through the top-of-the-line speakers.

Chicks dig quality electronics, too.

He nods in approval.

Time to go to work.

Time to find someone else to bruise him.

Time to start bruising himself all over again.

He puts the car in gear and pulls away.

Button

"Sixty-five to base. Ten-sixty-one, perimeter."

"Ten-four, sixty-five. Base clear at zero-two-three-oh."

I zipped up my jacket - a few light ounces of cheap polystyrene, or something like it - grabbed my ever-present plastic bag, half-full of cans, and walked out the Fifth Street lobby door.

I don't have to do much as a security guard: a couple of perimeter tours, checking doors and making sure the coffee pots are all turned off. I don't get a lot of exercise, and as a consequence, I look forward to this time of night, the perimeter tour. I walk around the building and make sure no-one was starting fires or urinating in the bushes.

Ms. Mulcaney was standing there, pacing in front of the doors, smoking a cigarette.

"Are they behaving today?" I asked, referring to the drunken monkeys cavorting down on the "Fourth Street Live!" entertainment complex a block west.

Ms. Mulcaney, all six feet, two hundred glowering pounds of her, made a non-committal, non-verbal answer. I didn't expect one, it was merely my acknowledgement of her existence; modern time's version of holding up your sword hand and saying "I see you."

Third shifters don't talk much, anyway. You don't agree to work from midnight to eight in the morning if you're a dynamic people person who thrives on social interaction. You do it because you either hate people or can't find work anywhere else. Either way, you're generally going to be kind of grumpy.

She's a character, is Ms. Mulcaney. Sixty-five, seventy, she's the only person I know who drives a car uglier than any I've ever owned. She works upstairs as a paralegal, is a devout liberal democrat, and as grumpy as the rest of us. She moved from California, God alone knows why, to come to Kentucky to be a paralegal. She'll talk your ear off about how life is so much better in California, and she has no idea why she stays.

"So go back," I once said, grinning in my non-threatening way.

"I can't afford it. They don't pay me enough."

She's watching the drunken antics of the college students reveling in nickel beer night, her cigarette jutting from two fingers held close to her mouth. The powerful halogen lights shine harshly on her iron-colored hair.

I shined my flashlight in the garbage can outside the front door.

"What are you looking for?"

I almost never know how to answer that question. I look a little bit like a cop in my security-dude uniform, and when people see me shining my flashlight into the garbage can, rooting around inside it, I guess I make them a bit nervous. Whatever. I'm not paid enough to do the job I do. It's either collect cans or sell drugs.

I tried my usual: a sheepish grin, a carefully contrived blush.

I held up my bag of cans.

"Aluminum cans."

"Oh. I thought you were looking for a bomb."

"Well, yeah, that too. But you know . . . . "

And I trail off as third-shifters can when they talk to each other, moving off into the night.

"I've got some cans upstairs in my office. Do you want them?"

I stop. Look over my shoulder at her. I don't know why, but I've never really been comfortable accepting something from someone else. It's not self-reliance or anything beneficent like that, it's a streak inside me that assumes everyone's in it for his or her own self-interest. It's deeply cynical and badly damaged, but part of me always assumes nobody's in it for the love; they just want to take me for whatever I've got.

"If you don't watch your back, somebody'll put a knife in it," a thin voice whispers in my ear.

But that pressure, that constant, unending pressure on my poor wallet . . .

"Yeah! I mean, if you don't mind carrying them down."

Ms. Mulcaney makes another non-committal gesture and a vague grunt.

"Thanks! I appreciate that!"

I move off into the night.

~~~~~~~

At the intersection of Fifth and Jefferson is another trashcan. I shine my light into it.

No joy there.

I move along, shining my light hopefully at the mushed debris on the street. Sometimes you find cans in the gutter; sometimes you find cans smooshed in the middle of the road. I look everywhere within my jurisdiction, using half my brain to do the job they pay me for.

There isn't a lot of traffic in downtown Louisville on a Thursday night, at two-thirty in the AM, but you still need to keep an eye out for people. I've been clipped a couple of times, moving out into the road to pick up some cans somebody dumped out of their car. Nothing serious, as of yet. Some bruises, a couple of scrapes, but getting bumped by a car is no fun, regardless of the amount of actual damage the car does.

They never stop, either. They just keep rolling into the night; drunk, high or too self-absorbed to notice me standing there, wide-eyed and clutching my plastic bag of cans.

I check the Main Office entrance on the Jefferson Street side: locked. As it should be.

I watch traffic for a moment. A car full of bass-thumping teenagers goes rolling slowly by. One, a white guy with his head bouncing like it's on a yo-yo, gives me a hard glare while smoking a cigarette. I grin, feeling the male chest-thumping response rise, unbidden, inside of me.

"You want some of this, punk? I'll cut you open like a fish, boy! Send you home to yo' Momma cryin'! They be pickin' up what's left of you, puttin' the pieces in a paper sack! Best recognize!"

I crack me up.

~~~~~~~

I move further down Jefferson Street and check the Allergy Clinic at that corner. The clinic is locked. Still looking for cans, I cast an eye at the parked cars outside, looking for anything out of place, and that's when I see the button.

It's the size of a pencil's eraser, no bigger than the end of my littlest finger. It almost looks like a small coin of some kind. There are lines drawn on it that with a stretch, a squint, and a fevered imagination, could pass for something Conan would recognize.

There is a light side and a dark side to the button. It is made of some base metal: tin, a cheap alloy of some kind.

Magpie-like, I put it in my pocket. It nestles against the "diamonds" I already have there - shattered fragments of windshield safety glass, shaped by the forces that acted on them into long, vertical strands like spaghetti noodles.

I have a half-formed idea of presenting them to my girl with a smile.

"What's this?"

"It's a diamond."

And she'll smile; lay a warm, wet kiss on my cheek . . . 'cause I'm just adorable like that.

I cradle the button between two fingers as I walk around the corner of the building, feeling the impressed surface, so like hieroglyphics to my fevered, two-o'clock-in-the-morning mind.

That's all it takes, that light pressure. Just like that, my mind takes off.

"It's a long-lost amulet! Belonging to the priest-king of far, fallen Acheron! He was here for an allergy shot, and he lost it when he came out!"

I move from the allergy clinic to the garbage can just outside the garage. A can! I moosh it underfoot, and put it in my plastic bag with the others.

"No! It's a library-card for the library in Alexandria-. No, Neil Gaiman did that one, and you've been trying to steal it ever since."

I move to the small park at the Sixth Street corner. No cans in any of the cans.

Bummer.

The usual assortment of homeless guys are out there, though, sleeping, drinking and generally minding their own business in an area that's somewhat safe. I tend not to bother them unless they're naked or look like they're dying.

None of the guys looks at me, and I shine my flashlight on the ground to keep from waking them up. I'm not really paying all that much attention to them. My mind's still working the button.

I hear my brother-in-law Jerry's voice.

"Out in the back counting fairies again, aren't you, Nescher?"

He's a skeptic. One I tend to think of as my personal skeptic. I believe in the possibility of damn near anything, and Jerry likes to try and keep my feet from floating too far off the ground.

Hey, it happens when you work third shift. You drink too much coffee, you eat too much vending machine food, and you don't get anywhere near enough sun. Your mind pickles a little and you get weird flights of fancy that become really important; important enough to write about at length.

Like with this button.

Yes. Okay. I know, intellectually, it is a button; a small, pointless, meaningless button that no doubt fell from someone's shirt. However, pretending, if only to myself, that this button has more significance than a means of holding someone's clothing shut makes me happy.

I smile, answering his voice in my head with a crude gesture, lovingly given.

I walk through the Jefferson Square Park to the Sixth Street lobby entrance. It's the long way, but all I've got to look forward to after this perimeter tour is six hours behind a desk, fighting caffeine poisoning and my own fatigue toxins.

Walking back through Jefferson Square Park, I think about the many meanings of a button, the possible translations of a button; of all buttons! Looking for cans, and avoiding the reality of the situation.

It does not escape me that I am a thirty-year-old security dude, largely getting by on a certain native, shameless charm, and a ceaseless search for aluminum cans. It does not evade my mental grasp that I am, in fact, in nearly complete denial of the reality surrounding me, and I should consider coming back to the real world every once in a while. Any life a person may live where a tiny button can have the kind of significance that would allow a person to write several hundred words about it is a life with gaping, whistling holes in it.

I know that.

But it's also my life, and it makes me pretty doggone happy, all things considered.

And if I spend my time in the back yard, counting fairies, or cradling ancient buttons, or picking up broken-glass diamonds for one fleeting smile from my girl, well, those things are important. Fairies and personal magic are always important, however you make them come to be, and I don't want to live in a world without them.

Calliope

Her name is Calliope.

You'd think, given her nature, she'd come up with something a little more original, but she insists it still fits. One name: Calliope. When she says it, her lips tend to mold over every syllable. It looks like she's eating a jawbreaker when she says her name.

I don't ever remember meeting her; she's just always been there. For as far back as memory extends, Calliope has been around.

She's as contrary as she can be. And I mean in a way that any other woman would look at and admire. She disagrees with all of my opinions, believes almost directly the opposite of what I do in any given argument, and has a value system dichotomously opposed to mine. If we're going to be honest, I'd have to admit to hating her guts and fantasizing about her grisly death.

We drift apart from time to time. All couples do. But we eventually find each other again, and it's back on, hot and heavy.

At some point she grew up. I never have, but somewhere along the line Calliope decided to be an adult, and that's when the problems started.

Our current "on again" phase started just after my last divorce. My ex-wife's lawyer was a helluva lot better than mine and they took everything: the money, the house, the cars, my self-respect and the ice cube trays. I had an alimony payment that was more than I made in three months and I was still responsible for half the mortgage. Last I checked, she was living in Florida with three guys, spending my money like it was on fire. I lived in the run-down section of town, holding down three different jobs and scraping by. Money wasn't just tight, money didn't exist. I couldn't afford to pay my rent or buy groceries, three weeks out of four. If there hadn't been various plasma and blood banks, pawn shops and soup kitchens within easy walking distance of my front door, I'd've probably starved.

It was after one such visit to a plasma bank that Calliope came back into my life. I was sitting in front of the TV the apartment came with, anxiously waiting for Maury to get on with revealing whether or not James was the father of Trenece's baby. (I watched a lot of daytime TV back then. I knew it was bad for you, but it's like the stuffing in certain cookies. It probably causes cancer, sterility and lip warts; you know they make it out of hooves, horns and nasal gristle; they actually use it as an insulating material on the space shuttle, but can anybody really resist them?)

Somebody knocked on the door in a way that suggested they knew I was home and they weren't going anywhere until I answered. I sighed, set down the faux cheeseburger - bread, mustard, chopped up hot dogs and margarine - I was eating and peeked through the spy hole in my door. The woman standing on the other side of the door actually made me lurch back in shock.

I slowly opened he door, wondering what the hell a woman like this could possibly want with me, and half hoping most of it would be obscene. That's when I saw the car and it made me forget the woman for just a minute.

Say it with me: Lamborghini. Diiiiiiiiablo!

Dark malignant beauty, curves and horsepower. It was Italian sex, ready, willing and able. From my humble hidey-hole I could smell this beautiful, beautiful car. Speed and money; leather, chrome and Armor All. Oh, baby, this car made me sweat.

The woman matched the car perfectly. Black as night and sweet as sin, she smiled at me from a flawlessly sculpted face with perfectly formed even teeth. Somebody once called it a "money-shot smile". Yeah. It kinda made you think along those lines. Her eyes were the color of the sky at sunrise as seen from the top of the lighthouse at Cabra. I've never seen eyes that color, real or fake. They were bewitching and powerful, the eyes of a snake watching a fat gerbil.

Long hair invited the pull of fingers. There were the rich, dark, iridescent tones of a raven's wing lighting it, and it fell around her face and back from her head in a sculpted fall that had to be natural. That fall . . . too perfect for anyone to accomplish with scissors and comb.

I don't know from clothes. Never have. I'm a t-shirt and jeans kind of guy myself. But my mysterious visitor chose to call on me in what looked like a tailored brown jacket. It fit her body like somebody glued it on. Underneath she wore a softly pink blouse that sat against her skin like strawberry ice cream in coffee. A short skirt, ending in mid thigh, displayed her shapely legs to good advantage.

A thin-linked gold chain hung from her neck with a pendant of the Greek figure "theta". A gold anklet peeped out at me from above tiny, bare perfect feet.

That male part of me that never shuts up or goes away, leered and said "125 pounds, 5'6", 38-40D, 28-36." Every man between the ages of eleven and a hundred and thirty-six has got a leerer in him somewhere.

I stood there, dressed in my boxer-briefs and a stained t-shirt, smelling vaguely of sweaty tube socks, my mouth hanging open and a bit of margarine drooling from my bottom lip.

The woman stood up on tip toe and kissed it away. I was lucky that time. Calliope's kissed me full-power before, and it's not something I ever want to experience again. This was a low-watt kiss of greeting and still the single sexiest kiss I've ever had: full, lower lip, tongue and the sweetest nip of teeth. Her kiss tasted of frankincense, rosemary and thyme.

"Wubba-ba-duh . . . ," I said, staring in shock and sudden urgent desire.

"Hello, daddy. Miss me?" the woman said, smiling at me with those snake-bird eyes.

She was easily the most attractive woman I had ever laid eyes on, living or dead. Classical verse began to spread its way through my memory, and I stood there, in my undies, completely in her thrall. She laughed, delightedly, and I was reminded of water crossing stones. That's when it hit me. I'd had this sort of experience before. Pretty girl, money in her pocket, poetry and story boiling its way across my brain . . .

"Calliope?"

"Hello, handsome."

"Awwwwwww, hell! I don't need this now!"

She drew close to me and lifted a manicured finger to my lips. "Shhhh. It's okay. I'm here now, and everything's going to be alright."

I don't need to tell you that her finger felt like a lover's nipple against my lips, and smelled like summer wine, do I? My hands started to shake and my head started to pound. Exactly like the very first time she touched me.

"Be-guh, guh . . . " I responded, somewhat sagely, I felt.

"Can I come in or are we gonna do this right here on the front porch? Nod once for yes, twice for no," she said, still smiling.

I nodded. I could no more refuse her than I could stop the way my heart hammered in my chest when she touched me. It was a powerless moment.

"Good! Hey, I've missed you! Let's go inside and . . . talk."

She sashayed inside, brushing against me with entirely too much skin-to-skin contact.

I shuddered.

Let me explain. Yes, Calliope is breathtaking. Yes, she's sex incarnate as far as I'm concerned. But the problem with Calliope is . . .

Well, just listen.

She came inside, still smiling, and looked around my "Joe Sixpack" -themed bachelor hole.

"Love what you've done here. Great energy to this place, great vibe. Listen . . . "

Just then her cell phone rang. (Its ringtones were the theme to 'Rowen and Martin's Laugh-in.') She held up one perfectly manicured hand, rolled her eyes and sighed.

"Sorry, sweetie. I've got to answer this," and flipped open the teeniest, sexist cell phone you've ever seen. I took her distraction as an excuse to look her over.

Hey. I'm a guy, I'm not dead, and I like to look at pretty things! Even if they make life hard for me.

I notice smaller details. I always have. Calliope's hands, for instance, looked soft and unmarred by either work or time. It struck me that I had no frame of reference for her age. She could've been anywhere from sixteen to thirty, with huge variance on either side. She had a timeless quality that defied any label. She looked at me in a distracted way, put down a clipboard I hadn't noticed until then and sat down in my one and only chair, turning Maury off mid "You ARE-."

"Hey, hey! Wassup, baby? Yeah. I've got him right here . . . Yeah? Oh, hey! That's awesome! I could kiss you! Ooooohhh, yeah!" This last said in a growly way that sent a small wave of lust through me.

I shook myself a bit and went into my bedroom. I threw on a pair of dirty jeans and my blue flannel. I'm normally a modest guy. I generally don't entertain guests in my undies. I sat on my bed and took a minute to pull myself together. Yes, she was a stunningly beautiful woman, but I wasn't some schlub that went all to pieces over a hot gal! Besides, I hated Calliope! She never brought me anything but trouble! I took a few deep breaths and mentally exorcised all the nervousness I could. After a moment or so I began to feel better, so I moved back out into my kitchen. She was laughing and making growling noises on the phone, and I felt just a hint of envy towards the person on the other end. I made myself a cup of instant coffee in order to have a cup to hide behind and to cover the shaking of my hands.

"Hey, listen, I gotta go. What? No, I haven't told him yet. Hey! You behave! Why, you dirty tramp!"

Laughing, she hung up and smiled at me yet again. "Hey! Coffee, yeah! Can a sista get a cup?"

"I don't have anything to put it in, I'm afraid," I replied, waving a hand at my empty cupboards.

"That's alright, baby. I like it black as sin," she said, either deliberately misunderstanding me, or ignoring what I was *really* saying - "No. You can't have any coffee!"

She stood with one of those practiced movements really sexy women somehow have. She took my coffee from nerveless fingers and drained it like it was a shot of Absinthe.

"Wow, baby. That's some heavy stuff right there." Holding up her cell phone, she said, "Sorry about that. It was one of my sisters."

That opened a pathway for conversation that I could see was strewn with all sorts of landmines, so I let it lie.

I made another cup of instant, strong, and sipped from it with hands that still shook a little too hard.

She pointed at the mug. "Hey! 1914 State Fair! That was a good one!" Taking my coffee from me, and sipping delicately, she went on. "Okay. Look, daddy. I know we haven't always gotten along-"

"Haven't gotten along? You bitch!"

She looked at me with shocked and hurt eyes.

"Moi? Bitch? No, no, no. Wrong paradigm entirely, sweetie. I'm a-"

"I know what you are, slut."

She pouted at me with a sexy little moue that made me want to hit her. "Oooooh. Rough stuff, huh? Okay, I can work with that, too."

"Wait a minute," I interrupted, holding my left hand in the air. I noticed I had "faux cheeseburger bits" on it, and quickly lowered it. She was always able to fry my wires. Blushing, I tried to regain control of the conversation somehow.

"Listen, you. I don't need you around, don't want you around, and I really wish you'd just get out of my house!"

She sighed, muttered something that sounded like " . . . mortals . . . " and looked at me evenly. She set my cup down on an empty pizza carton and stared at me for a long moment. She seemed to reach a decision and then she began.

"Do you honestly believe that? Really? You want me to go from your life?"

"Absolutely!" I said, marching rubber-legged toward the door, and pointing a trembling finger at it. "Out!"

She sighed again, rolled her head a bit on her shoulders, and said, "Okay. I'll leave. But before I do . . . "

And suddenly the rancid air of my apartment filled with the fragrant smell of peach blossoms. Light, steady even and clean, poured in from every crack in the walls, every hole in the ceiling, every window, every rathole. The apartment filled with a soft, warm light.

I tried to close my eyes, but it did no good. I could no more look away then I could stop the sweat from pouring down my back and my hands from shaking. Calliope stood there, emanating and reflecting a billion different subtle hues and tones of light. She looked like a mobile black diamond and the sight took my breath away.

She moved toward me, step by measured, tigerish step. I could sense building energies, like the shaking in the ground before a volcanic eruption. I backed away and my butt hit the wall. She pinned me in the corner formed by my refrigerator and my stove. Lying one hand on my shoulder, she stroked my face with the other. I struggled to maintain control of my bladder while the air around us boiled. Her fingers felt like melting flower petals and lit off sun-burst explosions in my mind. My knees gave way and blood poured from my nose.

I babbled something incoherent while she looked me in the eyes, pulled my face to hers and kissed me, long, hard and slow.

Never mind the physical effects of that kiss. Apply the usual descriptions - "a slow thing of long desire. Silky meeting of lips against lips and the gentlest possible pulse of her tongue against mine; her teeth toying ever so coyly with my bottom lip; honey and cloves," - and you've got the right idea. What is really important is the way the full-powered kiss collapsed what remained of my brain.

"It usually takes a minute," I heard her say. It took me longer than that to realize I was licking and tasting my lips like an infant on caffeine. I opened my eyes to see her smiling and licking her own lips.

"Wow. You really put up some big walls in there, honey. This is gonna rock your world," she said, backing away.

I stood, shivering like a fawn and hoping that maybe this time-

It was like being hit in the head with a truck full of marshmallows from out of the dark. My mind blew out of my ears with the force of ten-thousand supernovas, driving me to the floor, and leaving me gasping for breath and retching all over myself.

One long piece, coming at me from everywhere, all at once, with no filters.

A FIRST PERSON, CHARACTER ACCOUNT OF THE LIFE AND TIMES OF THE LIBRARIAN AT ALEXANDRIA SET AGAINST A BACKDROP OF ATLANTIS AT WAR WITH EGYPT! IT'D BE A TIMELESS STORY OF LOVE AND BETRAYAL OF THE VERY HIGHEST ORDER! WE'D GET JOHN MALKOVICH TO PLAY PHAROAH, DANIEL DAY LEWIS TO PLAY THE LIBRARIAN, AND A TANNED MERYL STREEP TO PLAY THE CONFUSED, OLDER WOMAN WHO IS TORN-BETWEEN-TWO-LOVERS AND BEING THE QUEEN OF THE LAND SHE LOVES! IT'LL START AS A CRITIC'S DARLING, BUILD MOMENTUM, AND THEN WASH OUT AMERICAN MOVIEGOER'S HEARTS AND MINDS WITH A TREMENDOUS PULSE OF . . .

And then it stopped. I went from picking out directors and knowing, in an intuitive way how it'd sell to the foreign market, to having a last, lingering gasp of what it was trailing out of my psyche.

Calliope leaned cat-like against the counter, cleaning her nails in an unconcerned manner.

"Did you say something, baby-boy?" she asked, without looking at me.

I curled into a fetal ball and belched. Yeah. That was it. One kiss and I was hooked worse than any meth addict ever had been. It was no good. I belonged to her now and there was nothing I could do about it. I wiped my face with a hand shaking too hard to do much good.

Calliope knelt and wiped my face with her hand. She licked her fingers.

"I love the taste of your fear, sweetie. We're not going to have any more nonsense, are we?"

I shook my head in the negative, shivering and moaning.

"Okay. Well, to business, then." She picked up her clipboard and began riffling through the papers on it.

"Oooh, my. Not so much as a word since we were kids, huh? Okay. Well, you tell me. You want to be rich or important?"

I looked up at her from my place on the floor. My confusion must've been evident.

"Rich," she said, staring into my eyes like a frustrated teacher, "is nice. Your words aren't taken all that seriously but people will buy your books because you're you. Important is nice because everything you say is sifted down to the smallest grain. You'll never sell much, but they'll be reading your stuff in egg-head classes a thousand years from now."

"Like Kurt Vonnegut?" I croaked, picking an author I admire at random.

"Well, yeah, we could do that. If you're willing to undergo the same ritual transformation he did. It used to be a lot harder, but with the advent of cheap, electrical powertool-'

I had been shaking my head for a good ten seconds. At mention of the last a thin dribble of vomit forced its way out.

"Okay, boobie, okay. Just calm down. It's going to be okay. I'm going to take care of you, okay?" Calliope said, rubbing my back and wiping my face with her other hand.

I rolled over onto my front and pushed myself to hands and knees. "Can I think about this for a while?"

She gave me a pitying, small smile, and said, "Sure. You take your time, whiteboy. I'm not going anywhere."

~ ~ ~ ~ ~ ~ ~

The next day was a bad one. I couldn't sleep. Calliope kept crawling into bed with me and licking my chest. She insisted on taking off all her clothes. If her body hadn't been enough as a normal, sexy woman, combined with that she had all the unfettered powers of a muse run amuck. When I shoved her off, it seemed to make things worse.

Every time she touched me a new poem or story idea would blast its way through my mind like a bomb. I wrote movies and children's stories, limericks and novels all night long. Calliope moaned and giggled, twitched and shuddered.

"Will you please stop that and let me get some sleep!" I cried, at roughly four in the morning.

"Time enough to sleep when you're dead, sexy. Come party with me!"

And she'd rub up against me while the idea for a vampire story broke my mind open like an egg. She only stopped when I started sobbing. By that time the bleeding from my nose and ears was making me light-headed.

I was up before the sun, pen in hand. Calliope sat next to me, touching me idly here and there while I shivered and shook like a junkie going through withdrawal.

I couldn't stop writing. That was the thing. I wrote until my fingers bled, and then I wrote some more, smearing blood across the white nakedness of the page. My hands cramped and twitched. I got blisters from holding the pen. I sweated and bled and still, I couldn't stop.

Still shivering and sweating, I looked over at my tormentor. She wore nothing at all and seemed to be perfectly comfortable.

"Aren't you cold?" I asked.

She cupped her perfect breasts and lifted them to my gaze.

"Cold? No. Turned on? Yeeeeeeaaah. Write for me, daddy."

I groaned and a shudder of revulsion worked its way through me. I hated her guts for a wide variety of reasons and she couldn't seem to get enough of me. But most of all, I think, I hated her complete disregard of my hate. She fed off it, and used it to torment me.

She laughed. I turned my eyes away from her and wrote my fourth poem of the day:

musings at graveside
there is a noise when they pump the water from
the bottom of the hole
they have to remove it so the dead
won't float through the ground like an ingrown
toenail; bursting through the skin,
followed by corruption
it sounds like a straw at
the bottom of a glass.
it sounds like a forever goodbye

I know. It wasn't very good. But it was better than some of the others:

You love me like a terminal disease.
I can't get any kind of release
I need you, I want you, I crave you so badly
How come I hate it when you call me "Daddy?"

"What are you doing, lover?" she asked, reaching a perfect hand over and idly stroking immaculately manicured fingernails through the short bristles on my scalp.

I knocked her hand away with an irritated grunt. Rereading what I had written, I realized it was awful. I was out of practice and whether I wanted to admit it or not, I probably needed her help to some degree.

She laughed.

"You're writing aren't you?"

I said nothing, burning holes into the paper with my mind.

"I can always tell, you know. It's like bells going off in my mind. Whenever you start to write," pausing she gave a liquid stretch that displayed her body to perfection, "it makes me shiver!"

She shuddered deliciously, as if in demonstration.

I threw my coffee at her in disgust.

It dripped off her naked body in slow, disturbingly erotic fashion.

"Wanna play rough again, huh? Okay!"

She jumped on top of me, knocking my chair to the floor. Straddling me, she grabbed my head in her hands and forced her tongue down my throat.

It. . . hurt.

She raped my body as she raped my mind, and the pain was enough to make me scream.

It hurt so much I can't really talk about it, even now. I had dreams that I didn't understand while stories boiled into existence in the air around us and poured from me like sweat. I actually kept writing while the worst pain I've ever had melted my bones and liquefied my muscles. Here's one that I managed to save:

~~~~~~

She wanted to believe she was a patient person.

Open-minded, well-adjusted, well-rounded: these described Taritha perfectly.

She was not - and it was important to emphasize this, as the clench of her jaw and the spasmodic way her fists were opening and closing are giving this the lie - *not* the sort of person to lash out and lay bloody stripes on those who offended her.

But this orc . . .

This wasn't the sort of thing that bothered her normally. Orcs couldn't help being rude, crude and crusty, but this one seemed to be making it his personal goal in life to persecute her.

He'd been on the bus, sitting next to her, since she'd first boarded. There were empty seats available, but the orc hadn't moved from her side. Taritha, being the witchy equivalent of Glenda - short, small and gently petite - had at first thought it would be rude to move and possibly offend the orc, who, after all, couldn't really help being an orc. And the smell wasn't his . . . hers . . . its fault, either. Orcs were a product of their environment. Everyone knew that!

Being a patient and genuinely kind person, Taritha decided to stay where she was and grimly persevere through the rest of the ride. It couldn't be all that far!

Nineteen stops later, her opinions about orcs had changed shape with every elbow jab and shoulder bash from the disgusting bruiser sitting next to her. And the smell, she was sure, was slowly dissolving the skin in her nose. The orc sitting next to her - she decided in a moment of fury-born passion - smelled like post-digested garbage that had been fed to a horny Flurgianimal, digested again and left in the sun to dry. And if that weren't bad enough, the thing was a profoundly enthusiastic mouth breather. Taritha saw a coating of hot spit on the seat back directly in front of the orc.

Just then, for what had to be the hundredth time, the orc jabbed Taritha viciously in the side with his elbow and Taritha's patience blew into tiny fragments. Through clenched teeth, she turned toward the orc and spoke very slowly and softly.

"Orc."

The hulking, evil-smelling monstrosity sitting next to her turned his yellow eyes her way and leered.

That answers that, anyway. Taritha thought, recognizing the leer.

"Gwuh?" he said, in an unusually articulate fashion for an orc.

"If you so much as touch me, even once more, I'll pull your bottom lip over your head and knock that diseased thing you call a face so far down into your torso you'll have to spread your butt cheeks to brush your teeth."

Taritha turned back to face the front, confident that the orc would leave her unsullied for the rest of the ride. She over-estimated the orc's cognitive abilities, however - not a hard thing to do for anyone, really. Even though Taritha spoke slowly and clearly, enunciating every syllable, it took the orc a few minutes to work his way through what Taritha had said. It took a few minutes more for it to realize it had just been threatened.

Orcs are never very fast, even the smart ones who can understand English.

Taritha, meanwhile, enjoyed the thoughtful silence of the orc and the relief of unassaulted ribs.

She hated taking the bus, avoided it as much as possible, but she hadn't made any real money since moving to New York from her coven in Nebraska. The small pile they had given her as a going away present was dripping through her fingers like water. It had seemed like an impossible fortune back home. More than she could ever spend. But a hot dog was nine dollars, and that didn't include the ketchup. She hadn't found a coven she felt comfortable in, either.

Off to make it in the lights of the big city! It was so different here! Back home, you knew where you stood in a sacred circle, and the stars all had names that made sense. A witch could move from Initiate, to Warlock to Elder in a smooth, unbroken line in no time at all. Here, there were three sorcerers and two spell slingers for every resident. Most people had two jobs. Some had as many as four! The employment situation was so tight that even the Orcish Remove-Yer-Trash-What-You-Don't-Want-No-More Services, or RYTWYDWNMS, (known colloquially as 'Orc's Breakfast') had all of their available positions filled. The idea that there were people willing to wait, for months, to join a squad of barely simian trashmen blew Taritha's mind.

She had just come from a job interview for Rodent Removal, which she'd turned down. Sure, the experience would have proven to have been valuable, even if nothing more came of it then some time on the streets of New York, but she was an experienced Warlock! Her talents would be better suited for something other than rat-killing, surely! She turned the job down as beneath her, but she was having second thoughts. How tough could it be? A temp job. That's all it was. And killing rats? Easy money.

She'd seen a rat when she first came to New York. It was the size of a small gorilla, and glowing in three different shades of blue. She'd been told about the city's rats, but assumed the natives were exaggerating. This one must've been feeding on spell components and potion leftovers for months. Killing it would've taken a team of ninjas, a flamethrower, and a very deep, steep-sided hole.

Maybe not so much *easy* money, then, but money, anyway.

She sighed. There just weren't any good, full-time, paying jobs to be had anywhere, and she was almost at the point of despair. Her thoughts were moving toward the glum fantasy of having to move back home in wretched failure, when a begrimed hand - one that smelled as though it had recently been used as toilet paper - grabbed her chin.

Taritha was so shocked by this contact she just stared at Gork, speechless.

The orc, having wandered his stumbling way through the labyrinthine convolutions of polysyllabic conversation, realized he'd been insulted and threatened. Furthermore, the insultee and threaten-ee, was sitting in easy disemboweling distance.

He'd missed breakfast. This was his lucky day!

In his thick, guttural accent; with his twisted and scarred fingers gripping Taritha's face, the orc said, "Littul ladee ain't so tuff. Ain't so big, nee-thur. Gork gonna pull yur fase off. Then Gork gonna eat yur fase. *Then* Gork gonna pop yer eyes out an' fluggle yur skull."

Taritha was a small town girl. She'd never been so accosted; never exchanged more than two words with an orc in one sitting in her entire life. She'd certainly never had one tell her it was going to fluggle her faceless skull!

And did he ever stink!

And everybody knew that if you pulled something's face off, its eyes went with the skin!

And who did this orc think he was talking to, anyway? Some little school girl?!

And what the hell was *fluggle*, anyway?!

The fury that boiled through Taritha's tiny frame was so far beyond incandescent as to be ultra-violet. The anger expressed itself as tiny dancing flames in her eyes.

Witches are trained from birth to be martial artists of the first caliber. Being a "wise one" meant being "wise" about everything. Everyone in the entire world - except this soon-to-be-dead orc, evidently - knew this.

Taritha hadn't been beaten in hand-to-hand combat by any of the thirty-nine witches in her home coven since becoming an Initiate. Every witch in the state of Nebraska feared being paired with her during Trials. She had a tattoo on the knuckles of her left hand in nicely gothic script that read "BAD". A matching tattoo on her right hand read "ASS".

Without noticeable effort and almost too fast to see, Taritha reached up to the wrist of the hand gripping her face with her right. She placed her thumb between the bones of Gork's hand and twisted viciously downward with a strength that was hard to believe from such a small frame.

Several bright, brittle snapping noises came from Gork's hand and wrist.

Gork howled and sprayed Taritha with the spittle-flecked remains of his last meal. It left oily snail trails on Taritha's face. Losing himself entirely, Gork started gibbering at her in Orkin. Taritha could only follow one word in three, as the orc was sobbing and globbering all over himself. His threats and imprecations were almost comical.

"OWWWW! Gork gonna peel yur boobs off an' make glue! Gork gonna eat yur boobs with eye-jelly sauce! Gork gonna smoke yur toes with yur toenails! OOOWWWWW-OOO!"

And so on, and so forth.

Taritha was tired. All at once, she was exhausted. She was tired of this city. She was tired of Human Resources Personnel taking one look at her wholesome, home-spun Sister's dress and dismissing her as a hick. She was tired of being unappreciated. She was tired of applying for the most menial of jobs, riding the bus, and being harassed on all sides, but most of all, she was tired of this orc!

The light surrounding the two of them dimmed as she opened her trephinae and called forth her power. She used the slow opening. It was a pointless little trick that was nevertheless quite effective. For morts, norms and stupid orcs, watching that azure eye in the center of her forehead slowly open was something a little like watching the moon swallow the sun. They taught you all kinds of neat tricks to intimidate and impress when you made Warlock.

Taritha opened her trephinae as slowly as she could and pushed as much light through it as she could bear. The power danced in all three of her eyes and across her fingertips in a flashing, electric display of perfect cerulean lightning.

The widening of Gork's eyes in fearful shock was enormously gratifying. Gork, being a bit smarter than the average orc, had an 'Awwww, hell!' moment. He felt something warm and soft filling his pants and realized it was probably his breakfast. Cradling his broken arm to his chest, he mewed pathetically.

Taritha glowered at him, the power straining toward the orc. In perfect Orkin, Taritha addressed the cowering figure.

"Now. I'm only going to say this once, so I want you to listen to me very carefully. If you touch me again, even accidentally, I will feed what's left of your smoking remains to my cat. His name is Buster and he's quite fond of burnt orc. Do you understand me?"

Gork didn't understand the multi-syllabic words, or the badly translated ones - "cat" in Orkin was "noisy-scratchy-snack" - but he understood the gist of the threat, and everything that lived on earth knew a witch when they saw one. He nodded, frantically, his mouth open in pain and fear.

"Gork sorry, ladee. Gork not know ladee a Sister," Gork gabbered in Orkin. "Gork clean ladee's boots. Gork eat Bus-tur's poop. Gork sorry, sorry, sorr-"

"That's fine, Gork," Taritha interrupted. She felt sick, dominating the poor thing like that. It was just an orc, after all. Sure, if she was an unpowered and helpless female there *might* be some threat from the three-hundred pound, seven-foot-tall, be-fanged, be-horned monster next to her, but orcs just aren't smart enough to be a threat to a savvy person of will.

Taritha had seen a group of four of them attempting to mug a mailbox when she first got here.

"Just . . . just leave me alone, alright?"

Gork nodded in frantic acquiescence.

Taritha stood and moved to an empty seat. She let the power fade with the usual reluctance. Her third eye closed and she returned fully into herself.

She halfheartedly acknowledged the applause of the badly beleaguered New Yorkers around her.

Finally coming into her stop, Taritha grabbed her precious spellbook and stepped off the bus. The encounter with Gork had left her sad. Being an Orc, he'd be fine in two or three days, but being who she was, as nice and as kind as she was, she still hated to hurt the poor things. It wasn't their fault they were so aggressive. She'd heard that orcs were a direct result of NYC's IAC (Institute of Alchemy and Science) attempting to crossbreed an efficient rat killer from a hyena and a vulture. Whatever their progenesis, it had made them crude, rude and crusty.

It had also made them unusually susceptible to taking on vices of all kinds, which did nothing to improve their social skills. Taritha had heard stories of orcs having drinking contests that lasted until the brain damage made moving the drink from table to mouth too much of struggle. The stories said that the winner of one of these contests - evidently harder brained than his fellows - lit a victory cigarette. Three minutes letter his head exploded from the mixture of hot gases from the cigarette and the fumes from the methane-like liquor orcs prefer. It was called "Dunstan's Boogers" on the street, in apparent loving memory of this poor grease stain. It was cheap, it was readily available, and Taritha found it worked great as a paint remover and wood stripper for the wands she made in her tiny apartment.

Evidently, Gork was too stupid to recognize the dress of a Sister. Stupidity was a common malady among orcs.

"The Sisters of Covenant Mercy" was their official name, but everyone knew them merely as "Sisters".

Sisters were the lucky few gifted from birth with the strange ability to open their trephinae and cast spells from memory. A Sister need only look at a spell cast once, and she could cast it ever after from her memory. Sisters cast their spells by tapping into the latent power of their third eye, otherwise known as their trephinae. Doing this greatly enhanced their physical strength, stamina, and speed. They were, quite literally, superhuman.

The order had been founded during the fifteen hundreds, shortly after the Renaissance began, when it was realized that magic was slowly bleeding back into the world. Mechanical devices were breaking down at an alarming rate, Science was failing. It got so bad that the Laws of Nature were waggishly nicknamed Occasional Occurrences.

Magic cropped up everywhere, uncontrolled and unstoppable. Even the Fae had returned and established Kingdoms throughout the world. There was no logical explanation, and as it seemed to be inexorable, instead of fighting it, the church decided to control it. The Sisters of Covenant Mercy was founded at the same time as the Order of the Knights Resplendent. An order for men, and an order for women. Their charters were simple. "Do no harm. Protect the innocent. Do good while it is yet day." A simple credo that nonetheless allowed untold abuses of power.

Taritha mentally prepared for her thirteenth interview of the day as she walked down the crowded sidewalk. She desperately wanted to get on with a Spellweaving company. Maybe Warlocks Inc, or even Dark Forces Unlimited. Thus far, her hopes had been dashed, as she had been unwilling to accept the Magus tattoo from any of her prospective employers. She thought it an ignorant and silly device, akin to allowing one's self to be used as a billboard. She certainly didn't want anyone who looked at her to know that she was a Sister who worked for say, Fizzy Cola. A tattoo was cool, but one on her face that shifted and changed shape with her emotions wasn't to be borne by one of her station.

Moving with resigned step toward her date with destiny, she heard a shout behind her.

"Ladee Sister! Hey, Ladee Sister!"

Recognizing the moronic slur of Gork's voice, Taritha turned back around, half- expecting the orc to attack. Instead, it stood three or four feet away with a baffled smile on its face.

A sudden suspicion filled her mind and coated her face with fear sweat.

"Oh, no. Ohhhhh, no, no, no, no, no, no! I'm not-"

"Ladee Sister broke Gork's arm. Ladee Sister likes Gork. Gork liiiiiiiiiiiiiiiiiiikes Ladee Sister. We get mar . . . marr . . . merr . . . We get hit-ched now?"

Visibly wincing, Taritha tried, without success, to remember exactly what she was supposed to do in this scenario. Inwardly slapping herself for forgetting that orkin mating rituals included violent, sometimes vicious and bloody assault, she wracked her brains. Meanwhile, Gork stood three or four feet away, puckering his thickly mawed face up. It took Taritha a moment of desperate thought to realize that Gork was looking for the orkin equivalent of a tender lover's kiss. Namely, a boot heel to the mouth.

"Look, Gork, you've got the wrong idea here, dude. I wasn't trying to hit on you; I just wanted you to go away."

"Gork got hit. Ladee Sister hit Gork like a Flurginaminal in heat! Gork can't wait to fluggle Ladee Sister!"

It was too much. People were staring. A Sister was having an orc come on to her in the middle of the street. An idea occurred to her that may or may not work, Taritha slammed open her trephinae and wove desperately. She'd never cast a spell this fast and she was sure she was missing important details, but she just didn't care.

A large black and purple-rimmed gate began to form behind Gork. It took the shape of a mouth in the open air and began to inhale. It wasn't until Taritha felt her feet begin to slip that she realized she was too close to the apex herself! She wailed bitterly as she and Gork were sucked through the obscenely smacking lips of the teleportation spell.

Landing hard, and with a dull thud, Taritha groaned.

A rookie mistake. One she should have outgrown three hundred years ago. But noooooooo! She had to go and teleport herself, along with her current tormentor, to God-alone-knows-where!

Sighing, she stood up and dusted herself off while quickly taking stock of her surroundings as she had been taught. She wasn't roasting or freezing as she had the first few times she had attempted to teleport. The very *first* time she'd been allowed to teleport by herself, she made an ill-advised attempt to find the Dark Side of the Moon. (She was young, and she had more confidence in her skill than sense.) She'd landed on the backside of a billboard in Alaska with a moon on the front. During a record snowstorm. She'd tried again, daring herself. This time she wanted to see what the interior of the Sun looked like. She'd landed inside a lead foundry and had to teleport home naked and smoking gently.

Her lungs hadn't collapsed either. (A *very* long story.)

She appeared to be in a ruin of some kind. There were large buildings all around in various stages of decay and the sun was either rising or setting. She hadn't had time enough to get oriented.

From some distance away she heard, "Lady Sister liiiiiiikes Gork! Gork ain't been smoo-ched so good in a *long* time!"

Sighing yet again, Taritha dusted her spellbook off and mounted a nearby wall with a leap that took her some fifteen feet off the ground. The sight that greeted her literally took her breath away.

"Gork," she called down to her orkin boyfriend, "I don't think we're in Kansas anymore."

~~~~~~~

There was more, but it bled away as the next story pushed itself through my fingers. That was all I got. That was all of the story I was able to save. Another started on the heels of that one, bleeding into existence almost at once:

~~~~~~~

The two of them sat on grass as green as emeralds in a woman's eyes. They picked idly at the grass and tossed stones at the whirling birds.

The one, with oddly mutable eyes, and silver horns just above his brows, reached into the tattered remnants of a denim jacket and removed a pack of smokes.

He shook one free and lit it with an easy, practiced gesture.

He offered the pack to the other man – this one dressed in hides of animals, and nursing a broad series of injuries.

The animal-hide man took the pack and lit a cigarette himself. They smoked in contented silence for a moment.

"So. Know any good jokes?" the horned asked.

"No. I'm afraid not. I wasn't really built with jokes in mind," animal-hide replied.

"Yeah, I think that's my job in this one. What'd you get instead?" the horned-one said.

"I'm full of purpose. I mean, loaded with it. I've been frozen to a glacier, I've had four of my fingers removed, I've been whipped and battered and bruised, and I'm still going," replied animal-hide.

"Wow, dude. Sounds almost like a religious ceremony of some kind," replied horns. He waggled his eyebrows hungrily at a slow moving bird, which flew off with an alarmed squawk.

"Did I mention my son is dead and the only way to get him back is to deliver a kiss to his corpse from the lips of a hybrid bird-woman-egg-laying-demigod thing?" animal-hide said.

"Yeah, I was there for most of that, but you don't really think about it as you're watching it happen, do you?" horny replied.

"What about you? What's your story?" animal-hide asked. He flicked the butt of his cigarette away. It hit the ground and immediately grew into a tree. The fruit looked oddly like unfiltered menthols.

"Ahhh, the usual. Supposedly I'm the bastard grandson of Cain, and I learned magic at like, the feet of this great magus who like, somehow got caught up in Cain's retributive-something-or-other. First time I saw it, I was like, 'Yeah. She's really scraping bottom with this guy. Either that or he's just writing filler.' Lazy hooker, if you ask me," horns said.

"Oh, man, don't I know it! I must've been stuck on that glacier forever! And did she care? Noooooo. It was all, 'I have to find a mind I can work with.' Whore." animal-hide said, with a disgusted blowing of his lips.

"Yeah, well, look at it this way. You know your story's gonna end sooner or later, right? I mean, you sound like you're part of some sort of an epic cycle. You have to end. Me, I gotta like, linger around the edges of a thousand different stories in one form or another. I'm a central character. I figure, 'Hey, she's not using me for anything. I'll nip on down to the pub and have a few. Get into an argument or something.' Soon's I hit the doors, there she is, calling me for some sort of ignorant piece about like, I don't know, friggin' fairies on the side of the hill or some junk. I'm an Id-ulized personification, central to the human experience. I never get to sleep!" horns said, waving the cigarette at a sky so blue it reflected itself.

"Who is she working with now?" animal-hide asked.

"Get this: a poet. We're sitting out here in the middle of unrealized actuality, and she's working with a poet. Can you believe it?"

"Is he any good?"

"What do you think?"

"Well, not yet anyway, right?"

"Yeah. I guess you're right."

"Have you ever met her?"

"Woof! Meet her? Dude! I spent like, a weekend recovering after this one date! Listen . . . "

~~~~~~~

And it ends. Just like that. I watched them as their lips moved, but Calliope's tongue was working in my mouth, and her hips were writhing and grinding against me, tormenting me. It hurt me in ways-

I can't talk about it. Another story:

I don't often get down time like this. I mean, it's been a couple of months.

I've been sitting here, cleaning my pistol, for I don't know how long. The rain's been falling since I got here, and there's nothing on the TV.

I keep thinking maybe I'll call one of those escort services, see if I can find a girl who's willing to sacrifice her dignity for a night with me.

So I'll pick up the phone, and just like that, I'll lose interest.

It's not the human contact, you understand. People are insignificant bugs. It's not even the sex. Sex comes and goes in my line of work. Sometimes it's good, sometimes it's okay, and sometimes it's bloody awful. You learn to pretend and use it as another bullet in the gun.

No, what stops me is the expense. Any call girl I end up with's gonna want more to service a female, even if most of 'em are as gay as can be.

Whatever.

Another night of bad TV won't hurt me any. 'Sides, it's not like the marks are going anywhere, right?

~~~~~~

Eventually it stopped. Calliope sat up and wiped her face. I could see blood running down her chin onto her throat and her naked breasts.

"Give up?" she purred, moving off my aching, prone form.

" . . . yes . ..." I said, whispering it in pain and fear.

"Good. Now. Sit up and do it some more. You listen to your momma now."

It took four tries, and she had to help me in the end, but eventually I managed to fall into my vacated chair.

"Write for me, baby," Calliope said, with a perfect grin on her face.

I sighed. I couldn't remember how long it had been since she'd showed up. One day? Two? Three? A week? A month? I couldn't tell! I couldn't tell! The table I sat at was covered in reams of paper covered in indecipherable writing. I reached over and pulled another piece of paper toward me, my fingers already writing the words.

Calliope said nothing in reply. She sat on the floor, pulled her legs into the circle of her arms, and stared up at me with hungry eyes.

~~~~~~

Time passed. I still don't know how much I lost at Calliope's hands. It might've been a single day; it might've been several years. I ate when Calliope fed me, I went to the bathroom when I needed to, and more often than not, I fell asleep overtop a pile of half-scribbled writings. And the whole time Calliope fawned over me, giggling and moaning like every orgy at once.

At some point in every hostage situation, there is a moment of flip-over, where the hostage begins to display a certain readiness to the hostage taker's mindset. They call it Stockholm Syndrome.

It hit me like a load of bricks. Calliope was playing with the back of my neck with her fingernails, stroking, stroking, stroking.

I looked over at her and started to write about her. Maybe it was some kind of self-defense. Maybe it was part of me telling me how to beat her. I don't know. I just kept writing about her:

~~~~~~

It's her skin, I think, that first tells you, 'Here is a beautiful woman.' It's the color of smoked honey, or a black coffee with enough cream and sugar to make it interesting and dangerous. It's flawless, her skin. Perfect. She has no wrinkles, no scars, no blemishes of any kind. The skin tone is perfectly even, save for a touch of pink on her cheeks that indicate to me a robust good health.

Eyes the size and shape of perfect almonds; grown somewhere hot and lush and warm. They are a single shade of green; the color of growing things, with no variance. They look like two painted diamonds; two luscious smears of color in that amazing face.

They are perfectly eternal, those eyes. You look into her eyes, and you can see from one end of the universe to the other, and you hear whispered snippets of every story in between.

~ ~ ~ ~ ~ ~

Her fingers stopped. "What are you doing? Don't write that! Write about the time you saw a ghost and you chased it off with a Zippo!"

I ignored her some more. It wasn't worship. It was something else, entirely. Hate worked around to the other side, I think, but stopped before it could completely transmutate. I kept looking at her and writing, and trying not to think about beating her, freeing myself from her.

It was so hard!

~ ~ ~ ~ ~ ~

Her hair is sometimes the tawny color of hair that spends a long time in the sun, sometimes as black and dark as the inside of a grave. There is no suggestion of relaxers, or dyes, or perming agents. It flows from the top of her head to the middle of her back, frames her face, and gives a glorious definition to the dignified column of her neck. Given her skin color, you make certain assumptions about the way her hair *should* look, and you make certain assumptions about what's probably lurking in her bathroom cabinets.

I find it's easier to think of it as being *her* hair, hair color and all.

Against my will, I reach out fingers to touch it.

~ ~ ~ ~ ~ ~

And to my surprise, I found my fingers in her hair, working idly through them.

Calliope had a worried expression on her face.

"Don't. Stop. Write about the secret language of music spoken by certain wise animals under the light of the moon. Write about the splitting of the first atom by Chinese scientists before the first millennium. Write about the first moon-landing by Native Americans searching for the Buffalo god. Write me a poem about the noose under your kitchen sink."

I couldn't stop. I couldn't stop. I couldn't stop! Suddenly, *I* was the one holding *her* hostage. Suddenly I held the whip hand!

And, by God, I was going to give it to her!

~ ~ ~ ~ ~ ~

She has no age. She can't. Age is a mortal thing, a time-bound thing. Age says 'At one point I was given birth to,' and that rule does not apply to her. She was not born, she was . . . she was . . . inspired. There is no other word for it. You look at her and you say 'There's no way two minutes of sweaty sex ever made that!'

From the first moment man had dreams, Calliope was. From the first idea that was something more than how to catch the bellowy thing with tusks, Calliope breathed. From the first imagining, the first inspiration, the first attempt at creatures to touch the stars, Calliope sang and danced and made love to poor fools who let her in.

And yet, her eyes have such a worldly-wise sadness to them. Her eyes speak. They say, 'Listen. I've *seen* things. Do you understand? I have seen things that would make your head fall off.'

And you nod and you agree, because you know it's true.

Her lips are full, round. They have a sweetly curving fullness to them that begs for a kiss, a nip, a nibble. They glisten, as if covered in a thin sheen of moisturizer, and smell vaguely of

208

crushed berries. They are a pink so deep it almost looks like pale blood. You want to kiss her so bad you feel like you're dying. Every time I've kissed her my brain imploded.

When she smiles she reveals perfectly even, dazzlingly white, strong, sure teeth. They fit in her mouth like little white doves.

Her smiles are a riddle. Not just enigmatic and indecipherable, no. You see one of her smiles and you start to worry about things. You worry about where she's taking you, where you'll end up when she's done with you. Her smiles scare me.

Her tongue is a cunning thing that dances in her mouth like frenzied gypsies in front of a spring bonfire.

Her voice sounds the way the wind must when it blows between those fallen trees no one's ever seen. She never mispronounces a word, never spits consonants or lisps a sibilant. She has no accent, no drawl, no truncation.

Her body is perfect, long, and lean, and sheathed with elegant muscle. She is strong, but well-defined. She moves with an athlete's elegance, a dancer's confidence, and the striking speed of a martial artist, all combined into one beautiful package.

She's much smaller than me - six feet, five-eleven; something like that, anyway. I have to crane my neck downward when she stands too close, and I think she does that just to annoy me.

The shape of her body doesn't fit any single description. 'A delight both callimastian and callipygian' comes fairly close, I think. High, firm breasts fit under square, sure shoulders, fit over a narrow, flaring waist, fits over the profile of a dancer. Her legs are a mile long and end just below her neck. She has swelling calves and narrow ankles, and there isn't a bone marring this perfection anywhere.

It's not enough to suggest she has perfect symmetry. She *redefines* symmetry. Menelaus caused the whole world to war over Helen, but Paris would've never made it beyond her boudoir if he had seen the lady I speak of. He'd've fallen at her feet and stayed there, in a dazed stupor.

~~~~~~~

And you read this and you think "Well. You want to have sex with this chick pretty bad, don't you?"

It seems that way, I'm sure. But as I stared at Calliope and described her in such vivid detail, she shrank back from me, crawling into herself like a snail. I was taking power from her, and she was finally retreating from me.

No.

No I don't want to have sex with her. And I'll tell you why.

I hate her guts. Seriously. She takes up entirely too much space in my head, goes away for long periods of time, and comes back, trailing long, sharp fingernails down the skin of my chest until I get up and do exactly what she wants me to.

She is my Calliope, and I wish she'd go away.

~~~~~~~

"Name the devil to make it run," somebody once said.

It worked. With a scream that dopplered into silence after far too long, Calliope exploded into bright, harmless motes of dazzling light, taking her poems, her stories, her novels and movies with her. I watched, dazed and open-mouthed as one by one, everything I worked on puffed into silent flame.

An entire novel about donut-eating dinosaurs: poof.

Three reams of poems, set in perfect rictameter, about the lies men tell women about sex: poof.

A doxology of children's books about a cat and her best friend, a dog: poof.

I panicked and grabbed what I could, slapping frantically at the flames. This is all I managed to rescue from my ordeal. It is both not nearly enough to represent how much I suffered, and far, far, far too much.

I haven't heard from her since. It's been three years since I've written anything more complicated than a shopping list.

I can't begin to tell you how much I miss her.

Late One Night at the Casa Nova

The air is hot, stale, laden with moisture.

My fingers click and clack, hunt and peck their way across the faded hieroglyphs of the keyboard. I feel like I'm hunting for words that haven't been invented yet, phrases that haven't been tuned, cleaned of dust and dirt, and polished for popular consumption.

The blood drying on my scalp has run into my ears, down the back of my neck, and it itches.

A mass of sores - no doubt caused by stress and various nutritional deficiencies - coats the inside of my mouth. Every contact of tongue to lip, tongue to palate, tongue to tooth, blares a grinding siren-song of pain.

What the hell, right? Must be time for a smoke.

Sting sings about murdering crows on the hippie station she keeps it tuned to while I shake one free and light up.

It's not working. I know that. It's beginning to look like 'their eyes meet, impossibly, across the crowded room'.

Every time I see that, I want to throw something at the screen. I wrote a scene like it once:

She wore velvet. Her eyes were violet and she drew toward me with a mystified smile on her face like her feet were on casters. She smelled like a vanilla milkshake's dream of coffee and chocolate cake.

"Excuse me," she said, her smile warming, and those violet eyes sparkling.

I sighed.

"Nope. Won't work," I said, shaking my head.

"I'm sorry?" Her voice sounded like oiled honey pouring from a jar, infused with hurt and all too offended.

"You heard me, cupcake. It won't work. You're clearly doing every 'Sleepless-In-Seattle cum Kirsten-Dunst-blushing-at-Orlando-Bloom' scene you've ever managed to digest, and you're expecting me to play along. It won't work. You're not for real and neither is the special effects package you've got stuffed down the bodice of that cocktail dress."

The publishers hated it.

Whatever. You draw from what you actually know and you get buried back in the stacks somewhere, underneath the vampire eroticism, or ignored altogether.

I stand and pace, smoking my cigarette. I walk to the cracked and stained mirror hanging on her wall and examine the results of her latest temper tantrum.

It was a simple misunderstanding. I was down at the Jupiter, having a beer, minding my own business. Candy walks in, sees me sitting by myself, and joins me.

Candy's a simple girl. She likes what she likes and she's not inhibited about going after it. She likes handsome men, likes being paid attention to, and she likes to party - with all the innuendos and permutations that get tacked on to that kind of description. Blonde hair, blue eyes that sparkle with an-all-too-perfectly feigned innocent naivety, and a body that requires power tools.

I can give her two out of three, and while I do have the rakish reputation, I'm also married.

Dim, though. She's one of these chicks who spend more money on hairspray in a week than I spend on gas in a month.

In short, she's your typical varsity-squad-bar-wench.

But I wasn't doing anything! I mean, I was just having a beer, enjoying the company of an attractive young woman who didn't have anybody better to be doing at the moment.

Sure, she had her hand on my knee, but it wasn't like I was pulling her top off, going to town on her nipples or anything. I *could've*. Being married hasn't sapped my juice *that* much.

Yes, I could've bent Candy over the bar and taken her right then and there, but in all honesty, I was behaving myself.

No! Really! It was two friends, having a drink. I swear!

Now, I'll be the first to admit that no-one will ever mistake Candy for a nun. She's one of these chicks that were put on earth to fill a pair of jeans and a sweater, and not much else: boobs, a butt, and a welcoming "How we gonna get in trouble today?" kind of smile.

And does she ever love the dudes. And I'm *the* dude. The dude of dudes. The dudiest of dudes. If Candy loves men, I'm the man she's been in love with her whole life long without even realizing it. Hell, I'm the dude every chick has been in love with their whole lives long.

But it's cool. I was behaving myself. We're having a good time, laughing and talking about nothing much, when my old lady walks in.

I tried. I really did.

"Dear, I'd like you to meet a friend of mine. This is Candy-"

But the old lady, she wasn't hearing any of that. She took one look, walked up to Candy, and cold-cocked her dead in the jaw. Then she threw me a look that could cure leather, and stalked out.

I sighed, paid for our drinks, and left, ignoring the groaning near-corpse of Candy.

The old lady met me at the door with a screech and an airborne lamp.

So here I am, several hours later, nursing an ever-so-slightly-broken head, listening to the light of my life snore while peering at my reflection in the clouded glass of our bathroom mirror. Under the dried blood and clotted hair, I can just make out what looks like a finger-sized hole in my scalp, still gently oozing blood.

I look over at her on the bed. The mirror no doubt reflects the feral hate that dances across my features for just a moment, but I don't see it. I know it's there, I can feel the muscles of my face wrenching into a grimace.

Her face is flaccid, relaxed in sleep - far different from the teeth-clenching harpy who broke her bedside lamp over my head.

I watch her breathe for a moment while blood slowly pools across the surface of my scalp.

And . . . and . . . what the hell am I still doing here?

Why am I tied to this hammer-fisted slummerdudgeon who expresses herself best with flying spit and right hooks? Am I insane? Oh, sure. I can justify it to myself; I'm famous for my acts of self-justification. I've gotten more warm, willing legs spread that way than even the most enthusiastic stories about me imply. I could tell myself lies about love and loyalty, but let's be honest. A lamp over the head is pretty much a wake-up call for anybody.

Us, though . . . .

And it hurts, man. I can feel teeny-tiny bits of glass moving around under the skin of my scalp, burrowing deeper every time I manage to find one of the larger pieces. It feels like something's trying to dig away at my skull with itty-bitty shovels.

What do you do with a woman whose idea of relationship-problem-solving is to smash heavy glass objects over your head?

Well, she's asleep, and I'm sitting here, smoking a cigarette, trying to pick tiny, broken fragments of glass out of my scalp with a minimum of noise and mess – mustn't awaken her, after all – hating her, hating myself, hating life.

The things we do for love, huh?

I have to admit it: I love her, but I think I'm more in love with some kind of idealized dream of her than I am with the actuality of the person in question. (Not bad phrasing for a guy with a head injury, huh?) It's like . . . she's everything I'm not. You know? She's crude, ill-mannered rough, abrasive, and she knows three different ways to milk a goat. She can outwrestle a butter-milked pig, and I've seen cows topple after a blow from one of her fists.

"See, hon," she likes to tell me in her rough pig-killer patois, "ya' hit 'em between th' eyes, they drop like a bag full of sand."

I can have any woman I want. Any. Woman. Any woman anywhere, at any time, however, whenever and wherever I want. I mean, I'm . . . well, not to put too fine a point on it . . . I'm famous.

Wherever a guy tries to get his groove on with a likely lady, you'll probably hear my name being invoked in some way. I've romanced and bedded women all over the world. I can walk into palaces and be having sex within a few minutes of meeting a queen.

It's a gift.

So I have to ask myself: what the *hell* am I doing, exactly, living in this . . . this . . . hovel . . . with what amounts to a potato farmer's daughter, when I could be anywhere? Men and women alike have fallen prey to my charm. Rome, Paris, Mumbai, Cathay, Morocco, I've bedded warm willing flesh around the world and back again, and always been ready for more. Palaces, gutters, churches; rich, richer, famous and noble: I've bedded them all, and resisted offers of love and marriage since I was thirteen.

And I find love; real, pure, honest love, in the face of this pig-wife.

If I believed in such things, I'd suggest I'd been bewitched somehow.

She's . . . she's amazing. She's wonderful in ways I can't explain. She laughs like a stevedore, curses like a Marine, and she can out drink any three men you'd care to name. The word doesn't apply, but somehow . . . somehow, she's beautiful.

Like now. There's something about the way the light falls across her face. It's a play of dynamics: light, shadow, depth and facets. I could be trite and say something ignorant about gemstones, but let's not go there, my head hurts enough as it is.

I don't know what it is about her. She's nuts in all the wrong ways, the dangerous ways, and I could be ten-thousand miles away, being serviced by a platoon of willing, nubile, island maidens, while sipping from a coconut half. And yet, I stay. I put up with her tantrums, I put up with her jealousy, I put up with her blend of crazy. I come home every night, and wrap my arms around her and ask her how I got so lucky.

No, she's not pretty. She is basically a peasant, bred of peasants, and descended from a thousand years of more peasants. Wide and squat, she walks with a swayback gait. Her eyes are dull, muddy things, and her hair sits on her head like a lank wig retrieved from a cess pit.

If I absolutely had to, I'd tell you that she challenges me; that she flatly refuses to put up with any of my world-class bullshit. She is the long-searched-for, perfect entree discovered by the glutton at the buffet. Yes, she's that plate of deep-fried pickled-pig's-feet, the ones you can't stop eating after you've tried everything else the buffet has on order. In a world of trite, cliched, overdone responses to every sexual overture and suggested rendezvous, she is the refreshing slap across the jaw, the hard knuckles to the side of the head, the broken lamp flying at mach-three toward the unprotected face.

Sighing, I pull more glass out of my scalp. Do any of the other guys have to put up with this kind of thing? I mean, you never hear about Romeo or Paris getting a lamp broken over their heads.

Must just be my karma, huh?

Hamen Ibn Saladine, Holy Man of God, and Karees, Daughter of None

A story for the wise and for those willing to listen.

As all men know, the Almighty loves His works with a fierce and powerful love beyond the understanding of mere men. For reasons of His own – beyond our feeble comprehension – the Almighty allows us to be refined and tested. This is to teach us not to eat the poisoned apples that lead to death and there is much that is not what it seems.

Hear then, oh princes and queens of men, the story of Hamen ibn Saladine, Holy Man of God.

In the beginning, before the sons of Adam were fully corrupted by sin, before the birth of Ibrahim, before God sent the waters of the flood, before even the Sons of God looked upon the daughters of man, there lived a man in the city of Ur-burshank named Hamen, son of Saladine.

Hamen was the first born son of Saladine, who was a son of Asshur, who was one of the sons of Jubal – he who was the father of those who played the flute and drum. As such, among the sons of men at that time, Hamen was a prince, the son of a prince, and many there were who would call him a king.

But this was not so for Hamen. For Hamen was a Holy Man of God, giving sin no place in his life either to the left hand or the right. His words were true and noble, and his acts of generosity and grace shone like gold in the eyes of all men. His eyes were cast in true humility before God and God richly blessed everything Hamen put his hand to; all things save one. Hamen had no children, as he had no wife.

Though he was a prince and well regarded by all, he took no wife. His great and noble heart broke within him at the thought of dying alone, but he took no wife. Many were the kings of men who sent their daughters, desirous of a connection to Hamen. And though the princesses lied and pretended to love Hamen, he always saw through their subterfuge, and denied them, one and all.

For though Hamen was richly blessed and given much by the Hand of Almighty God, he was bent and twisted, having fallen into the fire as an infant. The fall left him unable to move as other men do and scarred his face. No daughter of man had yet been able to see past the humped and twisted form of Hamen's body to the spirit of the man that lived inside.

Hamen then declared in the Name of Almighty God that he would never lay with a woman until such time as one desired him for himself alone.

Hamen was a light in that place and that time; a light that burned like a fire on a hill. The Nephilim came to him with their questions and quarrels, for he ever judged rightly, giving no hand to the left or the right. The sons of men came to him for judgments and the rulers and princes of the land listened to all he had to say.

It was said in the Souk that the Eight Winds and the Four Waters themselves sat at Hamen's feet for counsel.

For those who could see, Hamen burned with the light of righteousness. He was like unto a star come to earth in his personal justice. One of those who saw this burning was the Devil.

For the twisted and burned eyes of the Devil, looking upon Hamen was like looking at the sun. His righteousness was a lancing pain on the Devil's skin. It flashed over the Devil's eyes and drew thick lines of pain on his body.

There was no escape. Wherever the Devil roamed in that place, there was the burning light of Hamen's righteousness, thwarting his every purpose. For as all men know, where one righteous man stands firm, many are saved.

For this reason, and many others, the Devil swore that he would destroy Hamen. And so he set out to do.

There was in that place, at that time a tribe known as the Burshanki. They were set apart from the sons and daughters of men and lived in a separate place outside the walls of Ur-burshank.

Now as all men know, the Burshanki were a wise and beautiful people, set apart from the rest of man by the touch of Almighty God. In His wisdom, He had seen fit to bless them with sight. The Burshanki could look into the far reaches of the future and see what would be – describing wonders no man could bear to hear. They could also look into the past and see things as they truly were.

But perhaps the power that men feared most of the Burshanki – with their strange eyes of radiant, unblinking silver – was the way they saw everything as it truly was. There was no way to lie or deceive one of the Burshanki, for they saw through all illusion and subterfuge to the heart of the matter.

In that time they were the judges of men, dispensing true justice with unblinking, noble eyes. They were honest and true in their judgments, seeing always the true heart of the matter, and utterly incorruptible. The sons and daughters of men – as was the case then, and will be the case forever after – feared and hated the Burshanki. Many there were who swore they would seek out vengeance at any price.

The Burshanki lived lives of utter purity, but as all wise men know, such lives are cruelly snuffed out by those who regard them with contempt.

No man knows the reason, for it was not the time of storms, but there was at that time a fierce plague of locusts unlike any seen ever before. They were fully as wide as the palm of a strong man, and the color of freshly-spilled blood. They were utterly insatiable and consumed everything in their path.

This plague of locusts was blown in with sudden ferocity from the far lands to the east. It consumed all of the crops of the Burshanki, and then the Burshanki themselves. The locusts ate the wood, the leather, the metal and the bones of the Burshanki, leaving nothing whatsoever behind them, save only a single survivor – a beautiful young girl named Karees - who hid in a deep hole in the rock for three days while the buzzing of the locusts and the tormented screams of her family threatened to drive her mad.

She stumbled in from the desert, her clothes torn, her body wounded. It would have been bad for her indeed if she had not fallen on the very door step of Hamen ibn Saladine.

Karees was the young and cherished daughter of the tribe's chieftain – a lovely, noble soul; generous to a fault, and as pure as sand driven by wind from the north.

It was whispered in the Souk that some enemy had worked a foul magic in revenge for a loss suffered at the hands of the Burshanki. As is true of all such rumors, no-one could say who they were or what the loss had been.

The end result of all this was that Karees – strange and beautiful daughter of the Burshanki - was left alone in the world. Many were the sons of men who would have wreaked their petty vengeances on her flesh had not Hamen taken her into his home as a noble and respected guest.

Karees, raised as a Burshanki, knew that she would not sit idle in her new home. She would do whatever she could to increase the dignity and respect of her host, working with her own hands to clean and cook – though there were servants aplenty to do this for her – and provide for the well-being of her host and his home.

Hamen was unfailingly kind to her and unfailingly correct. He did not force himself upon her, as could be expected, nor did he require service of any kind from her because of her youth, her beauty, her sex or her race.

They ate dinner together every night, and every night their conversation was filled with such things as two people who were polite and correct friends might speak of, instead of landlord and resident.

And, as such things happen, Karees looked upon the humped and twisted form of poor, scarred Hamen, and saw all that was truly there.

Time passed, as it does, and the days and the seasons went by in peace and harmony in the home of Hamen Ibn Saladine.

While outside, in the cold dark, the Devil gnashed his teeth and plotted grim evils.

~ ~ ~ ~ ~ ~

The night was a cold one and the stars shone down from a sharp and bitter heaven. Karees, sitting alone in her part of the tent, shivered. She could feel something moving upon the wind and her heart beat faster with the fear of it.

Something was coming. Something that bore ill will in its breast and fire in its lungs.

Hamen sat within his part of the tent alone, murmuring his prayers to Heaven. He lay upon his face, his head in his hands. He did this to show the King of Heaven the respect He deserved. It was as he was praying that Hamen heard a soft scratching at the entrance to the tent.

Karees also heard the scratching, though she sat many rooms away. She jumped from her pallet, clad only in her sleeping robes, and ran on quick feet to the entrance.

Thinking that some traveler had become stranded in the night, Hamen respectfully finished his prayers and then stood to greet his guest. He limped painfully to the tent's entrance, his body twisted, his movements slow. When he got there, it was to see Karees standing just in front of the entrance, shivering and trembling. The smoking brazier gave light to her form and shadow to her robes. Hamen, seeing her clad thus, respectfully lowered his eyes.

"What are you doing, my daughter?" he asked, in the perfectly correct greeting of host to a younger woman living in one's house, his voice warm as it always was.

Karees turned to see Hamen standing there, his eyes lowered.

"My lord," she said, in her voice of sweet harmony, "I heard a scratching without and I feared . . . "

"Feared for what, my daughter?"

But Karees, not understanding her own fears, only shook her head. Hamen, not wanting to be rude, but under many obligations as a prince, limped painfully to his room and returned with his own sleeping robe. He covered Karees with it and gently led her by the hand back to her own room.

"Many are the megrims brought on by the silent dark of night, my daughter. But we must not allow them to cause us to sin or fail in our obligations. Return to your sleeping mat, and I will see who scratches at the door."

He smiled at her - something he rarely did, for it twisted the scars on his face horribly – but Karees never failed to return his smile with one of her own. She did so now, though her heart yammered and thundered in fear.

Hamen limped painfully back to the entrance and threw wide the flap in ritual greeting. Karees stood just inside her room, the darkness cloaking her, but not her shining, unblinking eyes.

"Be welcome in this place, whoever you are," Hamen said. Or tried to. For when he opened the tent, he was shocked and amazed to see a hu'r there! She was dressed in tears, the smeared remnants of heavily kohled eyes, a cunningly worked, thin silver chain, and nothing else.

Hamen, in sudden shocked reaction, immediately and unthinkingly - as the righteous sometimes do in great stress - invoked the protection of Almighty God.

The Devil winced horribly at the sound of The Name and cried out, in the hu'r's voice, in pain and fear.

Hamen, not understanding, immediately rushed to the hu'r's aid, touching her shoulders kindly with his hands, before jerking them back in shock at his lack of manners.

"Karees! My daughter! Please, bring me something I can offer our guest as clothing!"

The Devil, thinking quickly as always, choked out a grateful-sounding noise. Speaking in as alluring a voice as he could manage, like the breezes through the palms, the Devil told Hamen, "Oh please, my lord. I am but a poor slave girl - a dancer - and I have fled from my cruel master who would use me in ways he should not."

Karees, Burshanki maiden, saw not the hu'r, but the twisted, leering, serpentine form of the devil himself! And she knew the reason for her fear. Hamen, a holy man of God, would invite the Devil in as the laws of hospitality and obligation demanded!

But she was not the ruler here. She was a guest. She gave Hamen a robe to cover the Devil in and retreated inside, watching always with her unblinking eyes.

Hamen, blessed as he was by the Hand of Almighty God, was still just a man. He could only see the hu'r. And though she was naked, and someone else's slave besides, he immediately threw wide his arms, and bowed his guest within - but only after she had covered herself.

The Devil, smiling evilly, walked in under this invitation. For in this time, and in this place, the sons and daughters of men still understood the powerful protection of hospitality, and what it meant to be a host. The Devil was now safe from any righteous spirit hovering about protecting Hamen, for the Devil had been invited within. And as every wise man knows, the Devil has no power without invitation.

Hamen prepared tea with his own hands, though it pained him horribly, and brought his finest robe out to further cover the hu'r's nakedness. Karees, longing to be within the room with Hamen, could only sit in her room and pray for Hamen's protection. It would not be proper for her to burst into the room declaiming an invited guest to be the Devil. She would not allow his evil to cause her to sin.

The hu'r's disguise was one of the Devil's best. In various skin colors and body shapes, she swims through the dreams of the sons of Adam for all of recorded history. She is sex made flesh and desire made real.

Her hair was as dark as an evil night and as long as a spirited stallion's mane. Her eyes were like deep oasis pools after a long day at the end of the caravan; a cool and invigorating green. Her skin was the color of finest lambskin and soft as The Baby's Breath – the wind that blew in from the sea in the early morning. Her breasts were like ripe melons, hanging delicately upon the vine, with soft and inviting nipples, sized perfectly for the warm kiss of a man's mouth.

Hamen was aware of her, of course. He was no eunuch and his blood flowed in the usual way. But Hamen was a righteous man, and he took great care to treat her with the same respect he would treat his own beloved daughter. He spoke softly and kindly to the supposed hu'r and covered her with the robe. He set the tea before her, averting his eyes to keep himself from sin.

Though the Devil burned and fumed, he could take no further action without invitation. So he sat and sipped the tea Hamen had made and waited for his opportunity.

Hamen, speaking in a low, soft voice, said, "I am Hamen ibn Saladine, humble servant of Almighty God, King of Heaven. You are welcome within my home, and have my protection for so long as you may wish it."

The Devil, still playing the hu'r's role, humbly bowed his head, while The Name burned his skin with lancing pain he strove mightily to hide. He could not force the required words of thanks from his lips, try though he might.

Hamen, taking no offense at his guest's incredible rudeness at closing the tea ceremony as she ought, excused himself to finish his prayers.

The Devil, shaking his head in disbelief, held up a hand, and said, "But my lord, don't you want to know the gratitude of a young woman?"

And at this, the Devil shrugged from beneath his robes, and spreading wide his arms, exposed the gloriously naked body of the hu'r to Hamen. The light of enthusiastic invitation and desire shone from his eyes.

The hu'r's body was cunningly and wondrously made. A smell – like the smell that drives the great cats that live among the rocks into frenzied rut – rose off her body in waves. It was the smell of lust and desire made flesh. Sweat and musk, perfume and skin, and things much older, deeper and primeval; the smell of sex as it was before man learned the rules of law and civilized behavior.

The hu'r's body would have been temptation enough, but the Devil never uses a single layer of temptation. Though his tricks are old, they are subtle, and he has been the master of lies since before the fall of Adam.

With slow and painstaking patience and exquisite attention to detail, the Devil fashioned the hu'r's face into Karees'; adopting the shape of her face – well beloved by Hamen in a pure and untainted way – into the hu'r's. When he was done, he hit Hamen with all of this temptation, all at once.

Karees heard all of this, but saw nothing of the illusions being worked with such malice on her lord and master. She prayed desperately for him to be strong.

Hamen knowing nothing of the ways of men with women - except in the purest, intellectual sense - or of women with men, looked upon the hu'r and was sorely tempted. The smell was caressing strange parts of his body and brain, for he was only a man, and men are easily manipulated by the beautiful as all the wise know. But though the temptation of the hu'r was a strong one, Hamen would not be so easily defeated. And as all men know, temptation is not sin.

He remembered who he was underneath the clouds of lust attempting to cling to his skin, and Whom he served. He looked the Devil in the eye, and in a voice of cold steel narrowly avoiding rudeness, he said, "Are we married, then, for you to so brazenly expose yourself to me?"

The Devil stared open-mouthed in shock. Never before had the hu'r'i illusion failed! Many were the sons of men who writhed in torment after one night spent in her arms! The floors of hell were littered with her victims! But this twisted, humped, scarred little man; this ugly, dwarfish humpback who had never known the touch of a woman's hand, had defied her in her full glory and power.

The Devil looked upon Hamen and knew the desire of Hamen's heart. It showed in the bead of sweat running down his cheek and the way his hands visibly shook. Though the Devil knew that Hamen had never lain with a woman, and a woman far more desirable than any who had ever lived was holding her arms out to him in invitation, Hamen still held himself, irreproachably above the Devil's offer. He looked upon the bent and twisted form of this small, ugly man with new respect. Shaking his head in amazement, he clothed himself in darkest night and left Hamen's tent, forsaking any protection he may have had.

Then Hamen knew that he had entertained an evil spirit that night, and he gave thanks to the King of Heaven for His protection. He went to his mat, said his prayers, and slept the sleep of a righteous man, almost forgetting the events of the night by the next morning.

Karees, seeing the Devil flee, made her own heartfelt prayers of thanksgiving to the King Of Heaven.

When the morning came, Hamen ate breakfast with Karees in the usual way, but he seemed to treat her with wariness. Karees did not know what to think, but believed that something had awakened within Hamen's heart that had not been there before. She looked upon her host and longed to take him into her arms and soothe him the way her own mother had, but this would not be proper behavior for a guest, and a great sin besides.

"My lord," she began, trying to heal the rift between them, but at that moment Hamen stood from the table – something he had never done before and a great rudeness besides.

"Forgive me, my daughter, but I must leave you. I have urgent business to attend to this day."

"Of course, my lord. But perhaps-"

But Hamen had already limped from the room after giving her only the very briefest of nods.

The next night Hamen was again saying his prayers. Karees, sleeping in her room was awakened by a great and awful shout.

"Hamen! Misbegotten whore-son! Stand before your better!"

Hamen respectfully finished his prayers and limped painfully to the tent's entrance. Karees was already standing there, trembling in the light of the brazier, her youthful body innocently displayed by the glow through her thin sleeping robes.

Hamen lowered his head; though his cheeks burned with desire to bask in her beauty.

"My lord . . . please. It is your death that waits outside. Please, my lord! Please do not go outside!"

Hamen, his face still lowered as was proper, shook his head.

"My daughter, though it were the blood-drinking hordes of Gwittal without, I must needs fulfill my obligations. We cannot allow our fears to cause us to sin."

For a moment Karees considered throwing herself upon Hamen to protect him from the evil that she knew awaited him outside. But this would also be a sin, and Hamen would not thank her. She trembled all the more and forced herself to ask the question haunting her.

"And if you die, my lord?"

Hamen looked up at her and smiled a sad smile.

"Life is only well lived when it is lived nobly and without sin, my daughter. To die is the price one pays to live."

With that, he opened the flap of the tent and stepped outside.

The night sky was lit with all the battle fires of the host of heaven. Ten-thousand legions of angels stood in serried ranks, filling the whole earth from horizon to horizon. The earth was filled with the thunder of their marching and the ringing clash of their steel as they marched in ranks toward Hamen.

In pride of place, in front of all, sitting atop a flaming steed, was the mightiest angel of all; bigger than the moon and far mightier, the Commander of the host, Michael the Archangel. His battle regalia was shining only slightly dimmer than the sun itself and his noble visage was stern, carved as if from some strange substance harder than even obsidian. He shone with all the righteousness of heaven and glittered strangely under the night sky. His eyes were merciless and fixed; his sword of molten steel gleaming with the swift sure knowledge of victory, and was pointing directly at small, twisted, ugly little Hamen.

Karees, looking on from inside the tent, saw only the Devil, sitting on a mangy dog, pointing a dried up old stick at Hamen. The scene was so ridiculous she found herself, despite the peril her master was in, trying not to giggle.

Hamen bowed respectfully to this awful apparition. He was afraid, of course, but knew in his heart that he was a righteous man. And as all the wise know, the righteous never have cause to fear. With a voice only slightly trembling, Hamen looked the Devil in the eye and said, "I bid you good evening, great lord. To what do I owe the pleasure of this visit?"

The Devil shook his head at Hamen's unflinching bravery. He took a deep breath, pulling Hamen several feet forward with the force of that breath, and said, "It is your death, Hamen! You filthy son of a camel's groin fleas! I have come to harvest your soul! You have sinned against the throne of the Almighty!"

Hamen, swallowing his fear, bowed again. He knew that his soul was clean, and he knew that the Almighty would not send the host to collect one soul. He believed, though he had no way of knowing for sure, that here was the same evil spirit that had so tempted him the night before. For as all the wise know, evil rarely stops after only one visit.

"As the great lord wishes, so shall it be. Would you come in and refresh yourself first?"

From behind him he heard the unmistakable sound of a single girlish giggle.

The Devil shook his head and laid his stick level with Hamen's chest.

"No! I will not take tea with you, Hamen, you son of a thousand men and one gutter-dwelling woman! I will take your life! On your knees before me and repent!"

Hamen knew he had nothing for which to repent. His soul was clean and he would not repent to anyone save Almighty God alone.

He had had just about enough. He did not fear the Devil or any man or spirit, save God Almighty alone, but he was tired of playing this game. He drew himself up to his fullest height and in a voice perfectly clear and strong, said, "If you will take my life, then take it. But know this, spirit: I will not kneel before you. I will not kneel to man, spirit, god or demon. I kneel to Almighty God and Him alone!"

The flames of hell danced in the Devil's eyes then. His voice was dangerous and low when he spoke again.

"And if I were to tell you that I would spare you, leave you your head and your soul, and not destroy all you hold dear, if you were to kneel before me and repent of your crimes?"

Still looking the Devil in the eye, Hamen said, "Not even then. I will die on my feet, my integrity intact."

Once again, the Devil stood in open-mouthed shock. He felt sure that he had frightened Hamen, but Hamen was defying him once again. For although the Devil is well versed in illusion and trickery, all of his tricks are the same and he has not learned any new ones since even this early time. And when a man can resist the tricks, lies and temptations of the Devil, the Devil is always surprised. Clothing himself in deepest, darkest night, the Devil withdrew himself from Hamen's sight and fled.

A dog, mangy and dirty, now stood before Hamen, shivering with the cold. Though a dog is the uncleanest of animals, Hamen brought it food from his own table. He did not touch the animal, fearing its fearfully displayed teeth, but he said a prayer for the poor abused soul. It is ever the way of the righteous to display kindness to the weak; even the weak that are unclean.

The dog ate the food and loped off into the night without a sound or a backward glance.

Karees, looking on, saw something she had long suspected. And it burned within her heart like a flame. She crept to her bed and spent a long, thoughtful night in prayer.

Hamen watched the illusion around him slowly fade into the nothing from which it had come. It took as long as it takes smoke to disperse on the wind. When nothing was left but the good, clean smell of desert and the twinkling of the innocent stars, Hamen turned back to his tent and limped inside.

But not before turning his face back to the night a final time. With his face held high and his eyes stern, he said in a clear noble voice, "Good riddance!"

That night he slept the undisturbed sleep of a righteous man.

The next morning he ate breakfast with Karees in the usual way, but she seemed to hold herself aloof from him; something she had never done before. There was a strange light in her eyes and a certain set to her shoulders.

"Is everything well, my daughter?"

She looked at him with such determination that Hamen felt himself taken aback. He had never seen such a look in her eyes before.

"Perfectly well, my lord," she said, staring directly into his eyes and smiling an unsettling smile.

The next night, there was a respectful tapping at Hamen's tent entrance at the usual time. Hamen finished his prayers and limped to the tent entrance.

Karees, having been awake waiting for this, sat up and listened carefully.

Standing outside, in his actual form of the twisted man-serpent, was the Devil. This did not surprise Hamen. He'd been expecting something of this nature for some time.

"Good evening to you, oh Devil," Hamen said respectfully, for holiness demands courtesy, even to one such as the Devil. And Hamen was a holy man.

The Devil threw himself down on the ground before Hamen and said, "I wish to make peace with you and your house, Hamen ibn Saladine, Holy Man of God. Know that you have beaten me, and I do bow before you."

Hamen, humble man that he was, knelt in the dirt next to the Devil and tried to pull him up off the ground. "I am but a man, oh Devil. It is not meet that any bow before me, but only to Almighty God. Even one such as you."

The Devil stood, and dusting himself off, looked at Hamen with narrowed eyes. The sin of pride usually worked on the humble, but not even that had gotten through to Hamen. Truly this was a Holy Man of God! He had but one last trick to play and if it did not work, then he was truly beaten, and he would leave Hamen in peace. But if it did, he would have Hamen's skin to hang upon his wall as a trophy for all time. His eyes burned in evil delight at the thought.

Hamen invited the Devil in, as it is the very deepest sin to leave a polite guest standing at the entrance in the night, even if that guest is the Devil.

He made tea with his own hands, though it pained him mightily, and served the tea with his own hands as well. He did not know if it was a sin to withhold the protection of his house from the Devil, but he felt he was justified in so doing. They sat and sipped, and spoke of things such as men do.

Then the Devil spoke and said, "Hamen, I wish to give you something that I feel you want. I wish to give you a wife."

Hamen only sipped his tea and waited. He was ever wary of unasked, unearned gifts, but he was also a Holy Man of God and a polite host as Holiness demands.

The Devil withdrew a box from the nether surrounding him. The box was of human bone worked into shape over long millennia of agony. It smelled of the sulfurous fires of hell and a thick wailing noise seemed to be coming from it, as if the noise came from somewhere impossibly far away – yet as close as the next missed breath.

The Devil laid the box down on the silver tea platter before Hamen. Opening it before his eyes, Hamen saw that the box was full of gems. Each a different color, and worked in different shapes.

"Pick six gems, Hamen. Any six will do."

Karees, listening from the other room, began to pray for mercy.

Hamen looked the Devil in the eye and said, "Swear to me, on the tea ceremony, that you mean me no harm with this."

Hamen knew that the Devil would lie, and he would not blaspheme the Name of Almighty God by asking such a one as the Devil to swear by it.

The Devil meant Hamen no harm with only the gems, and so he did swear.

"Hamen ibn Saladine, Holy Man of God, I do swear to you by the tea we have shared that I mean you no harm with this."

Hamen nodded and withdrew six of the gems. They were cold and yet hot – as if mined from the walls and floors of hell itself - and they smelled of fire, blood and death. He handed the Devil his six gems.

The Devil laid the gems out in a line on the silver tea platter and reaching from left to right, picked up the very first gem and showed its face to Hamen while he looked through the back of it. At the touch of the Devil's hand, the gem began to glow with a poisoned, bleak light, like a diseased heart. Inside the gem was a woman sitting upon a throne, her body covered in the most expensive silks, a crown upon her head.

"Cleopatra, Queen of Egypt that is to come. She will shake the world, Hamen. A fitting queen for one such as you!"

Hamen looked upon the woman's face and saw the pain in her eyes. Hamen was a wise man and while he had never known the burning touch of a desirous woman, he perhaps understood them better than men who had. He saw longing in this women's face and knew that though the Devil could make a marriage possible, he could never give him this woman's heart. That belonged already to another. He shook his head.

The Devil shrugged and lifted the next gem in his left hand and showed it to Hamen. The gem depicted a woman of unearthly beauty. Surely this was the most beautiful woman in the world! Her hair hung in long, glorious coils from her shoulders. It just barely covered her stunning nakedness where she lay upon a bed of gold.

"Vashti, Queen of the Medes and the Persians of the great empire that will be. Her body would make a statue sweat, Hamen. She is fit for an Emperor's bed. Surely this is the one for you!"

But Hamen had looked into her eyes, and he saw a pride there that could stop the tides. This one belonged to no one but herself. He shook his head.

The Devil lifted the third gem in his left hand, carefully avoiding thinking of the Holy Trinity as he did, and raised it to Hamen's regard. The card depicted a woman who resembled a toad! A pipe was clenched between her steel teeth and she rode in a flying mortar with a pestle (such as the wise men used), before an evil moon of blood. Where her shadow fell, there strong men died of fright!

"Aieee! Devil, you swore me you meant me no harm! What then is this creature!"

The Devil laughed and said, "I did not draw the gems, oh Hamen. You did. This is Baba Yaga. A sorceress without peer and a queen in her own right. While she is repulsive to look upon, think of the gains a man married to a woman who could pluck the moon from the sky would be granted! Power such as you have never known could be yours for the asking!"

But Hamen, Holy Man of God who served God Almighty and Him alone, had no use for such power. He only shook his head.

The Devil picked up the fourth gem and raised it to Hamen's eyes. The gem depicted a most beautiful woman; but stern and strong of visage. Her hair hung in long, straight braids in a golden color that Hamen had never seen. Her skin was as white as the milk of a goat. Her body resembled a young dancer's that had never lain with a man, and she wore a strange coat of interlocked chains, and bore a sword!

The Devil laughed, recognizing the full potential of the chaos this gem represented.

"Guineviere. Queen of Camelot that will be. Never more will there be born a mightier woman with sword, shield, axe or bow. With her as your wife, you need never fear for anything save her anger!"

But Hamen saw that this one too belonged to another. He then remembered something his father Saladine had once told him.

He looked the Devil in the eye and said, "My father always taught me that 'A wise man never grasps a lion by its tail.'"

He took the gem from the Devil and laid it down and shook his head.

The Devil picked up the fifth gem, and holding it up to Hamen's eyes, recoiled in horror. He had not expected this, and he was suddenly afraid. The gem depicted a naked woman standing with her hands on her hips. Her eyes were cold and hard, though startlingly beautiful. Hamen felt that he knew her from somewhere, and wondered why he recognized the way her hair fell around her shoulders.

"Lilith, oh Hamen. Eve-who-may-have-been-first. Banished from Eden for demanding an equality with Adam. She is beyond my power to give you, and I would if I could!"

The last was said through clenched teeth.

Hamen, knowing fear himself, only shook his head.

The Devil lifted the very last gem and smiled evilly at what it represented. Hamen saw a blank, faceless figure. It looked like a female body, but only because it had the suggestion of breasts. There were no features on its blank face, no color to its pale skin. It looked like the belly of a fish that had dwelt in dark places all its life.

"Ahhhhh," whispered the Devil in his voice of fire and smoke. "The Goylim. Yes. This would be perfect for one such as you, Hamen."

Hamen looked upon the gem and his curiosity arose. "Why, Devil? And ware, tell me true!"

The Devil smiled his smile of broken glass and waved a hand. The Goylim appeared next to him with no warning. Hamen shouted aloud, fearfully calling on the protection of Almighty God.

The Devil winced, and shrank back, crying out in fear and pain.

"There is no harm here, Hamen!" he shouted aloud.

Hamen looked doubtfully at the Goylim; its blank face and pale, unmarked skin reflected the flickering light of the oil lamp in an ominous way.

"What is it, Devil?"

"The Goylim represents potential, Hamen. Would you have a wife? Would you have a perfect wife? Would you have a perfect wife that catered to your every desire, your every smallest whim?"

His voice lowered into a small, seductive whisper that sounded like a snake crawling through grass. Eve would have recognized that voice instantly.

"Would you have a totally loyal, utterly loving, completely devoted slave, Hamen? A slave that lived only to serve you, and to give birth to your children until such time as you were too old to make them?"

Hamen, Holy Man of God, looked at the Devil, his eyes revealing nothing, but his heart hammering within his chest. Could it be true? Could this creature be the wife that Hamen had always desired? A woman who saw him for himself? Hamen looked the Devil in the eye and saw the dancing glee there. Hamen's heart fell within him.

No. It was merely another trick, another temptation.

The Devil found he could no longer read the desires of Hamen's heart, but that hardly bothered him.

"How does it work, Devil?" Hamen asked in a low whisper of his own.

Karees, listening in her room, choked back a sob.

"Simply tell it what you desire Hamen, it will comply. Tell it what you want it to look like, how you want it to act, whatever you find in your heart, so it shall be. Would you have the Burshanki maiden, willing, able and ready to do exactly when and how you command? Tell it to be so, Hamen, and so shall it be."

Karees drew in a breath and waited. Tears were falling unchecked down her cheeks. She could hear every word and she was afraid.

Hamen looked long upon the Goylim. Then he stood before it and laid his hands upon its shoulders. Its skin was warm, despite its cold, fish-belly appearance, and Hamen could feel fluid like blood flowing beneath its skin. He lowered his forehead to its forehead, and began the communion.

"I do not want a slave," he whispered. "I never have. No man truly does! While your creation is of no fault of your own, I know by whom you are wrought. So I do not ask this of you. Instead, I wish to share my desire with you, oh Goylim. I have never shared it with another, and perhaps I can ease both our pains in the sharing.

"I want only that which every man truly does - a woman who would look upon me with favor despite her feelings of the moment. I want someone to love me for me and because of me.

"If you were to ask me how I want my wife to appear I'd tell you 'However she appears would be perfect to me, for she is my wife, one half of my soul.'

"I only desire the reality of true love not the false representation thereof.

"My wife's skin would feel the way cool sheets do on a hot summer night. Not because her skin is in any way magical or special, but because it is my wife's skin.

"My wife's hair would be like the flow of The River across the stones the people put there to create the music of flowing water. Not because her hair is in any way special, or uncommon to the wives of man, but because it is my wife's hair!

"My wife's smell would be like the morning dew on honeysuckle. Not because she does anything to make herself smell different but because her smell would be that sweetest of smells to me, her husband.

"My wife's kiss would taste like the sweet wine of first fruits, taken directly from the jug, cold from the well. Not because her lips or tongue were covered in the sweet fruit of grapes, but because to me, her husband, how could anything ever taste better?

"If only she loved me then she would be all those things a man most desires, and nothing else would matter. She would be perfect in all ways in my eyes for if she were my wife, I'd love her and she'd love me. That is what I most desire, oh Goylim. Can you give that to me?"

Then Hamen lifted his eyes sadly, knowing what he would see. The Devil had gasped in dismay, for the Goylim, his perfect creation of deception, had faded away into smoke as all illusions of the Devil do when exposed to the overwhelming light of Truth.

The Devil stared at Hamen utterly dumbfounded, and he could not speak. Hamen, his heart heavy within him, and tears racing down his face, bent painfully and retrieved his tea platter. He knocked the gems away carelessly and returned it to its place. Then he limped back out to where the Devil was.

In a loud, clear and strong voice, burdened only slightly by the weight of his personal grief, Hamen looked the Devil in the eye and said, "I abjure you, in the Name of Almighty God, King of Heaven and Earth, leave me be, and take your lies with you!"

The Devil screamed aloud, his protection gone, and fled as fast as he was able.

Hamen took to his mat, and though he wept long and hard into the night for his broken heart, he eventually slept the sleep of a righteous man.

~~~~~~

Then God Almighty looked down from His throne, and saw that His servant Hamen had done well. And He remembered His servant Hamen, and gave unto him that which he most desired. That which, save for his propriety and awkwardness, he could've had from the beginning.

Karees had heard every word that Hamen had whispered to the Goylim. She knew then that everything she had seen in Hamen was as it should be. Her sight had shown her what had always been there.

Late in the night, Karees made her decision. She said a prayer for strength, and then she took herself from her mat and lay boldly down at the feet of Hamen's pallet.

Hamen, feeling her moving about, woke.

"What is it, my daughter? Is something amiss?"

"Call me not 'daughter', my lord. Cover me with your robe, for I am alone in the world and in need of your protection."

"But . . . but, my daughter-"

Karees put a gentle hand across Hamen's lips.

"As I said, call me not 'daughter', my lord. For such is not proper among husband and wife."

And Hamen, holy man of God, was speechless in the face of that perfect love. His eyes filled with tears of joy, and he covered Karees with the hem of his robe.

The next morning the Burshanki maiden, last of her kind, married Hamen ibn Saladine. Their marriage was not perfect, and they were not always happy. This is the truth of men and women below heaven. But Karees was all that Hamen had spoken of to the Goylim, and Hamen – unique among the sons of Adam - was all that he appeared to be in Karees' sight.

And Hamen ibn Saladine lived to be a ripe old age, his wife both a constant joy and an occasional sorrow, and they had many sons and daughters. It is said that kings and the sons of kings were born from their line – wise and unflinching rulers who saw things clearly and without malice.

But such is a tale for another time.

Here ends the tale of Hamen ibn Saladine, Holy man Of God, and Karees, daughter of none.

Flowers of Battle

He sat in his camp chair next to his breakfast table, enjoying the fragrant breeze blowing down from the woods to the north. It carried the scent of iron - cold, wet and somehow green - with it. The breeze felt like it had made a brief stop in the frigid lands far to the north. He breathed it in deeply and thought of his ancestors; fur-wearing meat-eating, blood-drinking savages. He wondered what, really, separated the noble creature he represented from a spear wielding troglodyte.

There had been a battle recently and he was afraid there would be one today. The tribes hereabouts refused to accept the Empire's rule, and he had been sent by his Emperor to quell them, "with such force as was necessary."

This meant bloody slaughter, rape and general destruction. Such was a soldier's life under the flag of the Empire, and he did well not to forget it.

Reaching down between his legs, he pulled a flower up from the grass. It was beautiful, vibrant lavender. The scent was heady and carried a hint of magic. The petals were soft, like the velvety pads of a new born kitten. It was a delicate little piece of botanical glory, no bigger than the base of his thumb. He knew without consulting his notes that he held an undiscovered species of wildflower; something no-one had ever before catalogued - something no-one before had ever even noticed.

Hearing the clatter and clang of a horseman riding up, he sighed and tucked the little flower away in a fold of his robe. It would be one of his Legion's outriders, come to report on the battle to the north.

He closed his eyes and basked in the sun for a moment. It would take a bit for the rider to make himself presentable. One didn't rush up and scatter dirt all over a Vice-Regent, no matter how important the message. It was best to take these opportunities when one could.

"Hail, Scipio!"

He opened his eyes to see the expected soldier standing there, right hand extended in salute. Nodding briefly in acknowledgement, he indicated the camp chair to his left. With his own hands he poured wine from the dew-bedecked pitcher on the table. He handed it to the soldier, who took it with thanks.

"Your report?" he asked after the soldier had quenched his thirst.

"The men fight well, milord. We have conquered most of the rebelling tribes hereabouts, and look to experience only token resistance from this point forward. From the Woods of Mara to the river, the land lies fully under the Empire's control."

Scipio nodded and leaned back in his chair as if he had expected no less. Closing his eyes, he tilted his head toward the sun, unconsciously mimicking a flower he loved dearly: he called it The Sun Flower.

"What of the field, soldier?" he asked in a lazy tone.

The soldier had heard the stories about Scipio. His idiosyncrasies were, by this time, legendary. It was said he'd once halted a march of five regiments, and forced them to travel three miles around a certain field, in order to protect a certain species of moth that was currently nesting there. Some whispered he was half tree god, half river demon. If the way he often put the welfare of natural surroundings above the welfare of his own men was any indication, the soldier believed these rumors could well be true.

"The field, milord?"

"Yes, soldier. The field. What of the field of battle?" Scipio's voice was still lazy, and his eyes were still closed under the sun, but a note of warning was vibrating against the soldier's ears.

"Milord . . . I . . . I don't know what you mean."

Scipio opened his eyes and looked at the soldier. They were grey, cold, full of longing and regret, those eyes. "The field the battle was fought in, man. What of it?"

"Milord . . . there were many slain. The ground was trampled and covered in blood. There are scavengers about - both animal and human - and they feast on what they can. We try to keep the looters away . . . ."

In a whisper, his eyes still boring into the luckless soldier, Scipio said, "What of the flowers?"

The luckless soldier gaped at his tormentor. Men were dying, and he asked after flowers?

"Flowers, milord?"

"Yes. The flowers that grew there. Fragrant things I've seen nowhere else in the Empire. Bright, sunshine-covered petals, soft as a lover's kiss, and smelling like Solomon's Harem. What of them?"

"Milord . . . I . . . I . . . I saw no flowers, milord. Surely they were all trampled underfoot."

Scipio nodded and closed his eyes again, lying his head back upon the chair.

"How many dead, soldier?"

This was firmer ground, and the soldier could answer with authority. "Our tallies are three-thousand dead, twenty-five-hundred wounded - grievously or otherwise, and nine-hundred captured. We estimate the enemy's losses at nearly five times that."

Scipio stared at the inside of his eyelids, unconsciously doing the math a commander was most familiar with. Estimates and numbers flashed across his mind. He stared at them disinterestedly for a moment, knowing it didn't matter. His master would send more troops, should that be necessary.

Scipio opened his eyes and watched the clouds for a moment. He spoke without looking at his guest.

"And you saw not one flower, soldier?"

"Not one, milord."

"Then that is the greater tragedy."

Scipio pulled another flower from the ground. He rolled it gently between his fingers for a moment, enjoying the texture and the fragrance. He smiled sadly and held the flower to the soldier's nose.

"Smell this, soldier. Feel the texture of the petals. Drink in the magnificence of its creation. Experience it fully, for after the battle we will fight here today you will not see its like ever again . . . "

Conversation with the Devil

He lay on his back, gasping among the stones and the brittle desert plants. The sun above his head had long since dried the cold from the sand, and it was becoming blisteringly hot. He had water; the oasis he lay at would keep him from being thirsty at any rate, but it was merely a small pond that collected in a shady place against a cliff. There were no trees here. No plants anywhere, nothing but the desert, the sun, and the dry, sandy wind. Food had become an increasingly distracting preoccupation. He thought of fruit, of bread, of vegetables - fish grilling quietly over an open flame . . . .

With a tremendous effort, he banished those thoughts and gathered himself for another day. His body reeked of sweat and weeks of old dirt and his clothes were torn and filthy. Bathing was out of the question. A small amount of water had been provided and he would not waste it on a simple comfort like basic hygiene. The smell that arose from his body nauseated him. But he started his morning with a prayer of thanksgiving and a quiet hymn of praise.

That's when it showed up. He knew what was coming. His Heavenly Father had warned him. He knew what this was about: "Fire refines steel."

In a distracted, desperate sort of way, he remembered watching his father, Joseph, explain nails to him. Taking one up from a pile in his calloused, work-scarred hands, he quickly and easily bent it into a semi-circle.

"See, son? This one wasn't left in the fire long enough. It's mostly impurities, and does no-one any good. It's worthless for our work or for anyone else's for that matter. Remember. "Fire refines steel. Fire purifies.""

This fast, this desert, and now this confrontation were his "fire-refining." But he was so tired! So weak!

The light of the sun grew dim, as if partially eclipsed. The wind stopped blowing, and a smell, like rotten meat, filled the air. A quiet tatter of semi-solid air coalesced into a vaguely man-like shape that was as black as sin; the arms and legs gently tapered into fragmented wisps of nothing. A burning, feral, grinning smile was the only indication of where the face should be; blood red, sharpened teeth blazed like a galaxy of poisoned suns. It was hungry, that smile - hungry like a roaring lion's seeking whom it may devour.

It moved slowly closer, and then stopped as if pained to get too close.

"So you're Him, huh? You sure don't look like much." That burning hell's gate of a smile never moved.

Jesus didn't respond. He painfully dragged himself to his feet. It took all his remaining strength, but he did it, and then he stood, swaying slightly, and looked at the devil.

The devil continued in a nicely conversational tone.

"In fact, you look awful. You look just like a *man* who's spent forty wasted days and forty miserable nights, fasting in the desert to achieve some mindless goal. You're trying to serve a God that doesn't even exist! You think you're the Messiah, huh? Well, it doesn't look like it to me. "King of the Universe?" Ha! You look like a scraggly carpenter's kid who's starving to death to me. And for what? To prove something about "fire refining?" Please. Stop lying to yourself."

Reaching down, it pulled a stone from the ground with a wisp of what could've been a hand, and turned it into a warm, flaky, fish sandwich. The devil held the sandwich to where a face would be on a human being, roughly correspondent with those glittering teeth and that awful smile.

"Mmm. Sure smells good!"

Jesus could smell it. His stomach growled urgently. He'd never smelled anything better in his entire life.

The devil waved his sandwich closer to Jesus' face.

"Tell you what: Prove me wrong. If you are *really* the Son of God - and hell certainly doesn't believe you are - prove it to me. Prove it to *yourself*, boy. Tap into that supposed power your non-existent Daddy supposedly gave you, and turn these stones into bread."

Almost without thinking about it, his eyes dropped to the ground. Just at the merest reach of his fingertips was a *huge* stone. He could easily imagine it turning into the world's biggest fish sandwich. He could almost smell the flaky skin coming off in warm gobbets, and the fresh crunch of newly made bread. He *could* do it. He could reach down, pick up that stone, and turn it into the freshest, hottest, most mouth-watering piece of bread **ever** . . .

. . . but he didn't.

Instead, he took a deep breath, stepped away from the rock, and looked up at the shadow in front of him.

"It is written, "Man does not live by bread alone.'"

That smile faltered just a bit. The shadow wavered, as if wincing from a blow. It wasn't done yet, though.

"Okay. Well, maybe you aren't all *that* hungry. I can hear something around here gurgling and growling – and I'm pretty sure it isn't *me*, but whatever. Come here. I've got something to show you."

It reached out with the thin wisp of hand, and pulled what it wanted to them.

Jesus stood upon the edge of a cliff and saw laid out before him all the kingdoms of the World.

"Look. Okay. Let's talk brass tacks here. We know how this is going to end. Do you have any idea what crucifixion is really like? First, they're going to beat you nearly to death *before* they hang you on that tree. This is a guarantee, kid, as hell is going to ensure that they do. This is personal. Deeply, profoundly personal. Killing you in agony is part of the job, but beating you to pieces beforehand will be the fun part. It's going to happen two or three times, and then they're going to drive foot-long spikes into your arms and legs. You're going to take almost an entire day to die, and when you do, it'll be because you've drowned in your own blood and rubbed your internal organs into ground hamburger, trying to lift yourself up enough to breathe. It will be so horrifically agonizing that the people who come specifically to see you die - and they're going to come in *droves*. The very same people you loved, and healed; all those lepers and blind men and whores; all those people you did all those wonderful miracles for; the ones who only a few days earlier will be calling out "Hosannas!" and all that other crap. *They're* the ones who will howl loudest for your blood - will turn their heads away in horror and disgust. All this *will* happen – you know it, I know it, and Daddy dearest knows it - but not before everyone you love deserts you and betrays you. And then when you're dead, you're going to be claimed by hell, just like all the rest of them.

"So here's my offer. You can have all this," the Devil said, with a wide sweeping gesture taking in the entire world.

"No need to go through the blinding agony of the cross and all that entails. Hell will release its claim on the entire world, as it's been given into my hands, and hell can give it to whoever it wants. You can have your little "religion", and your little flock of fanatics, and save all the people you want *without* dying on the cross.

"Look, kid. I know from pain. You don't want any of that. And I promise you, if you reject this offer, I'm gonna remember, and I'm gonna take it personally. So all you have to do to avoid all that – the sweating blood, and bits of your intestines falling out of you from the gaping holes in your back in twisted, torn gobbets - all you have to do is bow down and worship me."

Jesus saw the cross. He saw it daily. He knew the agony of it, and he knew that it would be horrific. He knew all of his friends would break his heart before he died, and he would die utterly, utterly alone. This was almost too much to bear; he would be separated from all of creation, separated from his Heavenly Father; lifted up between heaven and hell and made a bloody sacrifice for all.

But the very worst part was that he didn't *have* to do it! No-one could hold him to account if he decided he'd changed his mind. Not even his Heavenly Father would tell him he had to die. He could return to Heaven and condemn the entire world to hell. After all, they had *earned it*!

But there was no atonement without the shedding of blood, and love's demands were stronger than his needs. If he loved, and if he wanted to teach love – *true love*, that love of his Father – then he would have to *demonstrate* that love.

"It is written, "Worship the Lord your God and serve Him only.""

That smile rippled like a stone hitting water. It had never encountered a will like this! It knew that this was the Son of God, but he was supposed to only be a man! This wasn't fair!

It railed in its head, "Look at him! He's so weak, he's weaving and bobbling, but he's still standing, and he's looking me dead in my eyes!"

"Okay. One last offer then." It reached and pulled again, and Jesus saw they were on the very highest point of the Temple in Jerusalem.

"Look here. Those people down there are held under the thumb of their laws and traditions. They won't accept you. You're going to die, and so are all of your followers, and they still won't accept you. All that bloodshed, all that heartache, and for what? Nothing. Things'll continue the way they've been for thousands of years. Hell will get them all in the end. But why allow that? If you are *really* the Son of God, declare yourself! Throw yourself down from here in a mighty display of your power! Get the Angels to back you up and take over! Knock those silly Pharisees and Sadducees for a running loop and declare your kingship! You're the Son of God, right? Well, *prove* it! Make *them* know! Doesn't Daddy's precious word say, "He will command his angels concerning you to guard you carefully; they will lift you up in their hands, so that you will not strike your foot against a stone,"? I mean, look at them!"

The devil pulled reality aside for just a moment and Jesus saw the amassed armies of Heaven, brilliant arms shining in the radiant light of God. They were, indeed, ready to do as Jesus asked, whatever he asked.

Wincing and cowering back in pain from all that light and holiness, the devil said through gritted teeth, "You could call down ten-thousand angels to wipe the Earth clean. There is no need to die!"

There was Michael, sword and bow in hand. He looked at Jesus expectantly.

Only lifting his hands would cause ten-thousand Flights of Angels to enforce his will. He could step down from here and start his kingdom now. There was no need to do this the hard way. But . . . love's demands were tied in with obedience to the will of his Heavenly Father. He would do as his Father had asked.

"It says: "Do not put the Lord your God to the test.""

The shadow wailed as it was resisted a final time. Unable to stay, it fled. The sun grew bright again, the wind blew, and fresh breezes blew the sweat of effort from his face.

Jesus sat and said a simple prayer of thanksgiving as angels, bright as stars, began to step down from heaven to minister to Him.

Cry from the Dark

One of the few advantages of being a third shift security guard for a downtown Louisville, Kentucky skyscraper was having keys to the observation deck just below the roof of said skyscraper.

Nine-hundred-some-odd feet to ground level, and you feel like you're sitting on a cloud.

I liked to sneak up here as often as I could and stand on the edge, watching the airport traffic, the slow vehicle traffic, and the lights from the buildings around us flicker on and off.

It's not difficult. You take a radio, so the console can reach you if they need to, and then you pretend you're working while you're basking in the magic of night.

It was peaceful up here. Granted, a landing 747 coming into the UPS hub could make your teeth rattle, but I figured it was the price you paid for feeling like Icarus for twenty minutes.

My favorite time of year to come up here is spring. Kentucky springs are generally pretty mild, once you get past the blows and storms of March. The air is warm and ever so slightly wet, and the nights sparkle with the promise of ten million stars.

I was standing at my favorite spot, as close to the edge as I dared to get, enjoying the balmy warmth of the evening when I saw her. She was a lighter, moving blotch against the night sky on the roof of the building opposite ours. I couldn't make out much due to the distance and the dark, but I had a sinking feeling in my belly as I watched her.

She held a large cardboard box, big enough to visibly strain her arms and bow her back. She stepped to the very edge of her building and tipped the box up. Papers separated, and began falling like snowflakes, carried on the stiff breeze.

As I've already mentioned, we were some nine-hundred feet above the ground at this point. A dry, clinical, observing part of me felt that those papers would get great ground-coverage from the wind.

She stood at the edge of her roof, just watching the papers fall. That sinking feeling began to increase, and I started shouting at her and waving my arms - maniacally jumping up and down, even; anything I could to get her attention.

"HEY! HEEEEYYYYYY!"

She looked up at me, and for just a moment our eyes met. There was so much pain in her eyes, so much spiritual agony. I felt mine fill with sudden tears. A sad loneliness - more profound than anything I'd ever felt - jumped across the gap from her to me. It was like a silent, sobbing scream that echoed within the walls of my soul. My knees nearly buckled from the force of it and I felt a thick sob building in my throat. She stood there, looking at me for a long moment. I felt utterly helpless to change anything, but I increased my efforts.

"DON'T! PLEASE, *PLEASE* DON'T!"

She watched me for a moment longer - not responding to my shouts or anything else - communicating that hopeless loneliness to my spirit.

Then she put one foot in front of the other, stepped out into the endless gulf of springtime night, and disappeared.

~~~~~~~

Most people don't think of us as being trained and efficient personnel, but Security Guards with access to downtown Louisville, Kentucky skyscraper roofs do get quite a bit of schooling. We're constantly being drilled, briefed and oriented on how to deal with various crises.

Believe it or not, How To Deal With The Suicidal is one of the classes we get to sit through. I passed with an A minus.

I did what I had been trained to do. I called it in on the radio, telling my console officer we needed to call the police and an ambulance. I made note of the time while racing downstairs to where I judged she'd land.

Technically speaking, this wasn't really my problem, as she hadn't jumped off our roof. But simple human decency has a way of overriding the "Not my job" mentality, sometimes.

I raced out our lobby doors, hoping she'd have somehow miraculously survived.

She'd landed on a car, caving the roof in and breaking the springs. The car was still settling gently, rocking back and forth. I rushed across the street, half-believing I could help to save her live. When I saw what remained I put all of that on full stop and hardened my heart.

They teach you what the usual result is of a tall fall on the human body, but nothing can really prepare you for seeing it. I was finding out that if anything, those facts had been under-reported.

The human body is mostly liquid, and it tends to break and splash like a water balloon after an impact from a long fall. She'd been mostly liquefied and the impact had spread her across the top of the car. There was so much blood . . . .

I called the console again and told them exactly where I was. I then began to try and control the scene as best I could, more to stop my own sickening sense of utter failure than through any sense of professionalism.

Luckily for me, perhaps, there wasn't a lot to do. Nobody else was on the street at the moment; the bars were still going strong, it being just after three in the morning on a Saturday night. From a half a block away I could hear techno battling it out with country on expensive, amplified speakers. A small knot of homeless people were the only observers to aftermath of this human disaster. There were hushed, murmuring whispers all around us.

I could smell the thin, high, tinny smell of gasoline and crushed metal, as well as the thick, iron smell of freshly spilled blood.

One of the papers she'd dropped flitted against my boot. Knowing I was committing a crime, I reached down without looking at it and put it in my pocket. The papers were flitting down in thick drifts, covering the ground all around us. From what I could see in a quick, casual glance, they looked like identical copies.

~~~~~~

As the only "official" witness to her suicide, I had to answer several questions from the police. I covered myself in a thick mantle of officialdom and didn't allow myself to feel anything.

I tried to put it from my mind as best I could. I couldn't shake that loneliness though; that silent, pleading cry I'd heard just before she jumped. I finished answering all of the detective's questions just as best as I was able, went through the motions for the rest of my shift, and then drove home.

It wasn't until I removed my uniform that I remembered the sheet of paper. I took it from my pocket and smoothed it reverently.

A picture of the girl was stapled to the sheet of paper. She was breath-taking. I look back on this now, and I wonder if perhaps I hadn't fallen in love with her a bit. Like, maybe my witnessing her final moments had brought us together in such a way as to transcend intimacy. I try very hard not to dwell on this.

Her cheeks had a high, rosy glow to them, like she'd just had sex, or had just finished running a race. There was a shine on her face that had nothing to do with makeup. Her hair was long, curly, and a multi-dimensional brown with sun-lights glinting in it. She wore it loose, and it fell in such a way as to perfectly frame her face.

She leaned casually against a picnic table at what looked like a park of some kind. Her ankles were crossed and her small feet were bare. There was a large smile on her face, making her almond-shaped eyes mere green slits.

Her skin was a light, tanned bronze, displayed to good advantage with her wardrobe of v-neck summer shirt, and shorts. I felt a hot, stinging wash of envy for the lucky bastard who got to take this picture.

The note was a letter, and it read like a final goodbye. There was a very light, fresh, clean scent coming from the paper, like "just-in-from-the-line" laundry; the sweet, clean smell of her skin. There were small - somehow, hot - splashes all over the paper. It looked as though she'd been weeping over the original when she'd made these copies.

Reading her final words to the world hurt me more than I believed possible:

Nothing makes any sense anymore.

I did everything I knew to do. I loved him, I cared for him, I held him when he cried, and I shared in all of his joys and triumphs. I believed in him,

and carried him when he was weak.

And none of that stopped him from leaving me. It was my fault somehow, but I still haven't figured it out. Never will now, I guess.

I could deal with it if I weren't so damn lonely.

It just hurts so much. I dream about being with someone and when I wake up, all I really want to do is to go back to sleep so I can dream some more. Real life holds no more appeal for me.

I'm so utterly alone.

I've made some bad decisions because of it, been with some people that didn't do anything at all about the loneliness, didn't do anything to help me heal my wounded heart.

They just took what I had to give, and left. And that's my fault too, I guess.

I'm not blaming them; it was me that opened my heart and my legs. I just wish at least one of them would've tried, would've made some kind of an effort.

So what's wrong with me?

Am I ugly?

Am I stupid?

Am I somehow repugnant, repulsive?

What is it about me that keeps me from meeting someone nice? Someone good? Someone fucking noble? Do guys like that still exist somewhere? Fuck, how about chicks? Are there noble chicks out there anywhere?

Don't I deserve to be loved?

I give up.

I'm sorry.

I guess this is selfish, but I've got nothing left to give and life doesn't make sense anymore.

~~~~~~

It wasn't signed.

I sat on my couch, trying not to weep for a woman I'd never met, and would never know. I sat there for a very long time, staring at the wall.

The news got her story and dubbed her "A Fallen Angel." For once, I felt they had it just exactly right.

Dad's Fiftieth Birthday

I was driving through the dark, listening to my CD player and thinking about the past.

The fog, the night, the music--it all matched my mood perfectly. I was in a contemplative frame of mind. I get that way a lot, but today was special, a life mark. My father's fiftieth birthday had me pensive, withdrawn, and thoughtful, all at once. Our far-flung family was all coming together and while I intended to enjoy myself, I couldn't help but think about the things that had brought us to this point.

The idea was we'd have the party at my sister's new house this year. She and her husband live in the sticks, atop a high ridge overlooking the Ohio River. It's the kind of place that causes ominous banjo music to play in the back of your head.

About a quarter of a mile down the road from their house is a graveyard, a final resting place for many of Kentucky's Civil War dead. The cemetery always scares me when I drive by, regardless of the time of day. The dead there are restless and angry, and things move behind the stones, just out of sight.

The nearest *lived-in* house to my sister's place was seven miles away. There wasn't much between my sister and civilization save that graveyard and a lot of empty, yet eerily watchful, homesteads.

The party was scheduled to start at eight thirty. I'm not sure why my sister decided to start so late, but it was her house so we played by her rules. I had been asked to take care of the cake, and I was running late, but only fashionably so.

A serious river fog had rolled in, bringing with it a miserly rain that cut visibility down to about fifteen feet. My headlights were cutting a swath through the gauzy swirl, and I felt that I could be anywhere, any place, any time. I wouldn't have been at all surprised to turn a bend in the road and see a party of elves drinking and singing the night away, a minotaur fixing a flat tire, or even Phylegyas poling by in a swirl of dank and corruption. I was halfway hoping for it, to be honest. It was that kind of night.

I had a Clapton CD in and was enjoying the overall atmosphere of dark, amorphous blue. The music was turned up just loud enough to be audible, making the drive a sad, almost dirge-y experience. I was loving every minute of it.

There's something about certain music that is almost holy. It has something to say and it resonates within the human soul. Popular radio stations know they have no business playing important, relevant music and instead offer pre-packaged filler, saccharined and sanitized for mass consumption. You'll never hear Joe Satriani, Leo Kottke, or Paco Fonta on any popular radio station. No, radio stations know they have no right to worship at the altar of higher human endeavor, so they give us Ricki Martin instead. Whores . . .

The Clapton CD ended and I put in my bootlegged Robert Johnson CD. The sound quality stunk, but I didn't care. The way he seemed to weep when he sang "Cross Road Blues," the song reputed to be written after he sold his soul to the devil, was profound and bewitching.

The music wove its spell, my thoughts wandered, and I began again to think about my father. He's a hard man to define. He's amazingly well-educated, but it's all self-taught. He can quote the Bible and explain Jewish mysticism in ways that would have a Rebbe standing open-mouthed, yet he can't spell. He hasn't a prejudiced bone in his body although he's suffered the sting of anti-Semitism all his life. My father would give the shirt off his back to a stranger, yet his own family has suffered. He's not a drinker now, but had loved Southern Comfort in his younger days. He's a devout Messianic Jew, yet somehow a Socialist.

My father wasn't very good at his job when I was a child. Somewhere along the way he started to hit and that became the primary means of expression between the two of us.

You can give me all the popular psychology you want. You can give me explanations about stress and his childhood and all the other things that go along with the abusive mentality; I don't buy any of it. He hit me. It hurt, and that was life for years.

I grew up a little and I hated him. I wanted him to die, not out of some selfish need to control my own life, but just so he'd stop hitting me. I'd dismissed my father as a horrible, abusive man. We didn't talk, we didn't communicate, and we didn't have anything to say to each other. I bruised and bled, limped and slumped and he was never happy.

But the truest thing you can say about life is that it keeps going and people change. Dad got help. He went to therapy, he worked his way through his issues, whatever they may have been, and he looked me in the eyes and said, "I'm sorry."

Then it was my turn to learn how to forgive. It was a slow process. I'm still plagued by memories of my father's anger. I can still feel the blows, the kicks, the verbal abuse. I can remember being sore for days, covered in bruises because of his unreasoning anger. During Desert Storm, I begged God to send my father to Iraq so he'd quit beating and screaming at us. I hated him with a fury I've never equaled for anyone before or since.

It was me that needed to forgive, of course. Now I was the one holding on to the anger and the pain, and t took me a long time to realize that.

Eventually it was remembering that my father hadn't always expressed himself though anger that made me realize I needed to let go. I remember taking long rides with my father in our van- -a monstrous, fifteen-seater Dodge Ram - his lone concession to the desire for a VW bus, I think. We'd all pile in and go looking for hitchhikers to give rides to, seeing the sights and waving at strangers.

We'd stop at a gas station; buy a soda and just talk. Dad took us for long hikes in the woods and taught us each to love every living thing - trees, weeds, bugs - it was all part of God's creation, and should be valued equally. He instilled a tremendous love for God and all of His works in each of us, and I have always cherished those memories.

Perhaps more than anything else, I was able to love my father because of his stories. He had so many and he infected me with a love for stores at a young age.

My favorites are his hitchhiking adventures. He started hitchhiking around the country at the age of thirteen or so, and has a storehouse of tales as a result. He was arrested for hitchhiking to Woodstock when he was nine. A year later, he was back on the road, hitchhiking across the country, sleeping under overpasses and eating out of garbage cans.

I once asked him why he did this, why he put himself through the rigors of homelessness. I had always suspected he was running away from something - an abusive home life, a crime - something dramatic.

He looked at me, surprised and somehow mournful, and said, "I did it for the adventure, son."

I pressed the issue, "Then why run away, Dad? Why leave home?"

"It was for the adventure, Nescher. You ever read the book by that guy, the book about that kid and the black guy on the river?"

"Tom Sawyer?"

"Yeah. Same stinkin' thing."

And that was it. My father put himself through hell when he was half my age so he could experience the great American adventure. How do you hate that? How do you smother that kind of spirit in resentment and grudge?

I had some adventures of my own as a kid, largely inspired by Dad's stories, but my adventures were always such pale, common things in comparison.

One of my favorite stories of Dad's: he had been hitchhiking and couldn't get a ride, so he found a bridge overpass and sacked out for the night. When he woke up, he was some hundred miles closer to his destination. He always explained it as "angels carrying me in my sleep."

I once badgered him for more details, but he simply repeated the same story. My father is either a master storyteller, or it really did happen. I've never cared. I just cherish the mystery in a way that borders on need. I hope he never changes the stories or provides explanation. A little part of me would die if he did.

I had to forgive him. I had to learn to grow up and let go of my cherished victim-hood. I did after years and years of struggle, but I still fought to understand my father, to understand what made him so angry.

What happened to my father? Where had the anger come from? What had happened to poison his spirit?

Things were better now between us, but only after years of counseling, tears, and shoving and shouting matches. We even hang out together occasionally, father and son, laughing and giving waitresses a hard time.

I drove on into the dark, letting these and other thoughts wash through me with little effort. The Robert Johnson CD ended, and I let the CD player start it again. It was working for me in the mood I was in.

I've often felt that music is magic. It weaves a transcendent harmony between possibility and reality, blurring the line between the two into invisibility. So I don't know if it was the combination of the music and my desire, or if it was simply an answer. I was singing along, moving my head in time with the sorcery pouring from my speakers, when I came around a bend. There in a swirl of fog, I saw the hitchhiker.

Standing at the side of the road, thumb lifted, a look of apprehension and surging hope on his face. He was only in my lights for a moment, but the way he stood, forlorn yet defiantly continuing to hope, struck me so powerfully that I immediately pulled over and opened the passenger door.

He was clearly illuminated by my brake lights as he ran to the car, and I got a good look at him in my rearview. My heart started to pound and my hands began to sweat. He stopped next to the door, smiled at me, and glanced quickly inside the car.

He couldn't have been much older than fifteen or sixteen. The rain had plastered his long, brown hair to the sides of his head, and his curls obscured the parts of his face the dirt hadn't covered. He was wearing a sort of caftan, in a dirty ivory color, which looked to be made of linen. He wore a pair of stained and well-worn bell-bottoms, and as near as I could tell, he was barefoot. Hanging on a leather thong around his neck was a turquoise necklace in the shape of a cross. His face shone with a clear, innocent light, and the smile he gave me was genuine. He didn't have anything with him, though I had expected to see a backpack of some kind.

Scientists tell us that a baby penguin can find its mother in a teeming crowd of millions of other penguins through a combination of smell and involuntary subliminal cues. I don't know how true that is, but I knew who this hitchhiker was. My mind had subliminally recognized him before my consciousness did. It was a combination of the way he moved, the way he smiled, and his overall presence.

It was my father.

Add forty years and seventy pounds, some gray and a semi-permanent scowl, and this smiling and smelly young man was my dad.

I was hit with sudden and perfect understanding. It came upon me in the same way these things do in dreams. Yes, it was my father, but I knew I couldn't tell him that. My role in this drama was simply to drive him to his next destination. I had that much time, and no more.

Apparently satisfied that I wasn't a serial killer or something worse, he got into the car and closed the door. I composed my features carefully, fearful that the whole experience would pop like a fragile soap-bubble if I made the slightest wrong move.

With muscles tensed, I put the car in gear and pulled onto the road.

"Oh, wow, man! Thanks for the lift, dude! I've been walking forever!" His voice had a strange lilt and fall, along with an accent that took me a minute or two to place. He talked with the same undiluted "Don'tcha-know?" Wisconsin/Michigan twang my grandmother did.

There is a very specific etiquette followed by hitchhikers and those who pick them up. The hitchhiker's responsibility is to be gracious and courteous to a fault. He is, after all, mooching a ride. Etiquette dictates that you agree with all of your host's opinions (or at least disagree very respectfully), make conversation as much as possible, and if you have any drugs, offer to share.

I realized my father was following this code and that a response was expected of me.

My voice high and tight, I asked, "So where you headed?"

He laughed in a carefree way that I'd rarely seen in his older self and said, "Wherever you're goin' is fine with me, brother. I'm looking for God, and I hope to find him somewhere soon!"

I laughed painfully and said, "Well, there's a truck stop about ten miles down the road. I can drop you off there if you like. You can catch a ride to anywhere you want from there."

"Hey man, that'd be great! Thanks a lot!" He stuck his hand out and said, "My name's Dale."

I took his hand, found his grip to be strong and sure, and choking back a small cry of delight, I said, "Nescher."

"Nescher. Wow, man. That's a name, right there! Does it mean anything? Are your parents, like, hippies or something?"

It was hard. I was smiling and trying not to cry, all at the same time.

"Yeah. They're really fun people. It's Hebrew, supposedly, for Eagle."

"Oh wow, man! Like that Bible verse! "They that wait upon the Lord shall renew their strength!" That's really far out, man! Your parents are groovy!"

I laughed, a short snort. "I'll pass that along the next time I see them, Dale."

He nodded his head at me and settled into the seat.

"Oh, wow! I almost forgot!"

Reaching into his shirt, he pulled out a small bottle. He unscrewed the cap and the pungent aroma of Southern Comfort filled the car.

He wiped the mouth off and said, "Want a snort, Nesch?"

My father doesn't drink. I've never shared a beer with him, never passed a bottle of anything back and forth. When I got married, where other fathers would have a shot of bourbon or a beer with you, he showed up and slept in the car until it was time for the ceremony to start.

He has his reasons for not drinking, and I respect them, but a beer between father and his eldest son would go a long way toward healing the rifts of experience, I sometimes think.

Normally, I hate being called "Nesch" by anyone, but my father has never called me anything but Nescher, son, or a name of some kind. I bit off a very small snort, knowing my father - or "Dale", rather - didn't have the money to buy more.

Dale took the bottle back and drank a bit himself. He placed the bottle back in his shirt and settled back into the seat.

The radio continued to pour out its enchantment, and I realized there was just enough time left on the CD to see us to the truck stop. Only so many songs and a lifetime of questions to ask.

Dale looked over at me and said, "Oh wow! What radio station is that, man? Robert Johnson! Far out!"

I smiled at his childish enthusiasm and asked, "Are you a fan, then, Dale?"

"Yeah, man! Him and the Moody Blues are just totally groovy!"

We listened to the music for a bit, Dale and me, losing ourselves in the misty harmonics and the devilish wail of the guitar.

There was so much I wanted to say and ask, and I couldn't!

What would I say? "I'm your eldest son from thirty years in the future?"

No, I wanted him relaxed and at ease. There was something here I needed to see, something beyond my own wants.

I took a deep breath, composed myself and said, "Hey Dale, it's a long drive out to this truck stop. Why don't you tell me about yourself? What are you doing out here other than looking for God? Tell me all about Dale."

He smiled in a free and open way and said, "Wow. Okay, well, I just need to find God. You know? I mean, I've been going to church my whole life, right? But I don't know about God, and I want to, 'cause I feel like He's got some kind of purpose for my life, you know? And I've just been going around the country to all these groovy churches, and talking to all these preachers, you know?"

I recognized the start of a fire that still burned within him. If I had any lingering doubts as to his identity before, that last statement, however rambling, singed them all away. This was my father, in his first fumbling steps on his lifelong quest to find God.

We talked then, not as father and son, but man to man. We talked about his girlfriend (not my mother, incidentally):

"She's like this totally groovy, absolutely beautiful blonde, and she's got like, the best-tasting kiss."

About getting drunk versus getting high:

"Yeah, I've been stoned on weed, and hash and stuff, but I still prefer my booze."

About his various sexual adventures:

"Okay. It was like, me, and these three other chicks."

He told me about his family, how he felt about his parents and his brother and sisters. He told me things I never knew or would even have suspected, like how to stay on the road with no money:

"Okay? So the first thing you do is make sure there's no store dick, and then you go looking for stuff you can stick in your pockets."

He told me about eating out of garbage cans and getting sick from it; bathing in creeks; sleeping in fields of wildflowers under summer stars; getting beat up by the police; and meeting people from all walks of life. He told me about his hopes and dreams, and his desires.

I told Dale about my ex-wife and the reasons we really broke up (not the sanitized version I usually shared with family and everyone else). I told him about my hopes and dreams for the future. I shared some of my own adventures:

"Yeah, I've been loaded on some pretty heavy stuff, myself, Dale. Ever hear of Xanax? You take enough of 'em and it's like eating mercury."

When he talked about God, his eyes lit up and his face shone with a pure righteousness. There was no profanity in him. Here he sat, Southern Comfort on his breath, talking to a stranger about God, and it was exactly like being at church.

He told me of his desire to be a perfect servant of God Almighty, and was totally unselfconscious about it, seeing no hypocrisy in liberally toasting this declaration with another snort off his bottle. This wasn't hypocrisy to him - he was still too innocent to know what hypocrisy was.

In short, we had the sort of conversation I could never have with my father today. It was totally open and utterly candid. Dale figured I was a stranger he'd never see again and didn't want anything from me except a ride. He'd leave me with some good conversation and the warm glow of whiskey in my belly.

I had become so engrossed in our talk that I completely forgot we didn't have much time. I saw the sign for the truck stop ahead and I began to panic. He couldn't leave now! There was still so much to say and ask.

He looked over at me and said, "Oh wow. That's the stop, isn't it? Man, time has really flown, hasn't it?"

I wiped a tear away surreptitiously and said, "Yeah, Dale. It sure has. Listen, I could take you a little farther if you want . . . . "

He looked at me seriously and said, "Nescher, that's okay, man. I saw the cake in the back seat, and I figure you've already taken me out of your way. I didn't want to say anything until we got here, but I can't let you take me farther, man. I don't want to mooch off you any more than this right here."

I shook my head, smiled, and tried not to weep. That was my Dad, alright, polite to his own detriment. Somehow I knew it wouldn't be allowed, that he'd be taken from me if we tried to travel farther together. The magic was all used up. Whatever needed to be said had been said; whatever I needed to know had been revealed.

He reached into his shirt and pulled out the bottle. He bit off a quick snort and placed the bottle on the passenger seat.

"There ya' go, man. I ain't got no money, but I can leave you some good booze, anyway." He smiled at me again in that clear, beautiful way and I again fought the urge to weep. I shook his hand a final time, trying to impart through the casual gesture the depth of my emotion, fighting a need to hug him with everything within me. He got out, smiled at me, and walked into the dark, drizzly mist.

"Wait!"

He stopped then, and turned back toward me, a questioning look in his eyes.

I reached into the back seat and grabbed the cake box.

"Here, Dale. You take this."

"Awww, Nesch! I can't do that, man! That's for somebody-"

I set my face into a scowl I had seen far too many times as a child.

"Don't argue with me, boy. I think God wants you to have this. You take it, now, or you're gonna end up pissing us both off."

He smiled and took the cake box from me.

"Thanks, man. God bless!"

The music ended then, and I watched him until he faded from sight and then I drove away.

I realized then who my father is, what he had come from.

He isn't a horrible sinner, an abusive ogre, or a loud-mouthed bully. He's just a scared, dirty and innocent kid still trying to make his way through the world as best he can. He's a flawed vessel, just like the rest of us. He'd made some wrong turns and gotten lost a time or two, and he's managed to make a wreck of his life.

But thinking back on my conversation with Dale, I discovered something profound: we were the same. Oh, I haven't got any kids, but I've made some of the very same lapses in judgment my father has, and I have the benefit of knowing his mistakes! Who am I to judge him?

~~~~~~~

I drove on towards my sister's house, pulling off briefly for a good cry. I cried for who my father was, and I cried for who he had become. I cried for all the pain and the wasted years, and for the opportunities I missed because of my own anger and pride.

I wiped my face on my shirt and put the bottle in a crumpled, paper sack I found on the back seat. It took me fifteen more minutes to get to my sister's house, and everyone was worried about me when I got there. Ignoring them all, I went to my father, and surprised him with a hug.

I handed him the paper sack and whispered, "I love you, Dad. Happy birthday."

Dark Night at the Boh Da Thone

In the same sense that "nowhere" is not, and never can be, a place, the Boh Da Thone is not a place. Not really. Not in the strict, three-dimensional way so necessary for humans to wrap their little meat-sack brains around.

That's an important distinction. "Place" is a noun. It assumes all the hard-edged, glinty, concrete aspects of reality. It has width, depth, length, and an awareness, however vague, of existing in, or at least *participating* in, the passage of time. Our quasi-semi-place does none of the above, but it could if given enough of a running start.

It is (was, could be, etc) more the "*embodiment of pre-existent metaphysical potential taking on a tenuous half-reality for the purposes of demonstration,*" than any kind of a "place".

The sidereal place in question, as it were, exists beyond the boundaries of "Maybe" and "Could be", and dwells firmly in the grey haze of the land of "What if?" or, more specifically, its capital, "Wouldn't it be really cool, if . . . ?"

As with any other destination of myth, magic and mystery, there are no maps or street-signs to guide us to our destination. No helpful characters looming out of the fog-shrouded darkness to provide directions; no third star to fly by. You either know the way or you don't. It's just that (un)kind of a (non)place.

If it *were* a place, it might look a bit like a badly lit, dingy bar with innocuous "American Bar Furniture Fixings" slathered over the top of shoddy construction. The over-stuffed red leather booths, the dusty neon, and the fake wall-paneling laid carelessly over the top of basic, square-sided, cinder-block construction might *look* real, but looks, as already discussed, can be deceiving.

The air would probably smell like several generations of badly fried food, perfume bought from the back of trucks, spilled beer, sour sweat and used dishwater. There might be an ever-present haze of cigarette smoke added to our funky miasma for continuity and depth. There'd *definitely* be a tinny country song playing in the background from the ancient juke-box in the corner. Probably Hank Williams or Merle Haggard at his morose best. I

Its lights are long gone, and its glass face plate is punctured by a fist-sized hole.

The juke box is a standard fixture. Good music played badly on deteriorating equipment is *de rigueur.*

Having established the non-existence of our un-place, we move on.

Our other "fixture of note" would be our host. Assuming the potential possibility of the proto-place in question, you *have* to concede the host. These sorts of things have very complicated rules. They are woven into their basic structure like math and physics in the foundation of the Universe.

One of the *main* rules:

"*Any bar-like structure has an owner/host/barkeep.*"

The barkeep doesn't have to fit any *specific* stereotype, but things get a bit woobly – always a problem out here on the fringe - if there isn't at least a suggestion of one. Since there are so many archetypical barkeeps to choose from, this is rarely a problem, more an item of interest.

Our place has a host. He takes up quite a bit of psychic space, being the same size and general shape as a Volkswagen. At the moment we're looking at him, he is lurking trollishly, in every appearance of a foul temper, behind his massive, fake wood bar. He - for our barkeep is quite aggressively "he" - is a squat, toad-like creature in a dirty, button-down, two-sizes-too-small shirt, a filthy, no-color apron, and a glaringly red bow tie. The tie manages, somehow, to peep out from beneath his chins like a chick emerging from beneath the world's ugliest hen.

He is perfectly bald, like a toadstool, and his skin is a very distinct grey color.

Our host doesn't have facial features so much as distinct flaps and grooves in the yards of skin draping his enormous skull that would correspond, roughly, with eyes, nose and mouth in a thinner man. His eyes are deeply set and one wonders if he has trouble seeing from beneath his heavy, lowered "skin-brows". There is good evidence that his neck is trying, valiantly, to throttle his face.

As the mind's eye roves – or recoils; however you like - the barkeep is sullenly wiping badly-damaged glasses in a rote appearance of cleaning them. He isn't accomplishing anything more than moving the grease around on the glasses, but we'll note the effort and move on.

The glower (one *assumes* it's a glower. That suet bag of a face probably isn't capable of much mobility) on the barkeep's face doesn't seem to be directed at anything specific so much as at everything in general. It is the suffering moue of the toothache; the dyspeptic stomach; the foul odor in the elevator – with accompanying sheepish grin - that insinuates itself like burning plastic onto the surface of tongue and nasal membrane.

It's quite the glare, is our barkeep's.

Evidence suggests that there should be some sort of soup-like atmosphere surrounding our barkeep; an odor of epic proportions. Instead, there is merely the vaguest hint of pickled onion.

The hand-carved sign hanging over the barkeep's head declares to all and sundry that this, our not-place, was/is/could be (etc.) the "Boh Da Thone".

Of course, all this is pure conjecture, and we'd do best to remember that, despite the twists and turns of "story".

Looking on, as we are, we are shaken from these reveries by the cascading sound of trumpets, the battle call of the Almighty from "outside". Glancing toward the grease-covered windows, a glaring, dying blood-red sky lights the "horizon".

Having given us an "inside", we now provide parameters for an "outside".

But we'll just stay in here, where we're less likely to encounter anything that would cause us too much psychic damage. The ambience isn't much in here, but all that screaming and bloody bubbling noises are very firmly out *there*.

We can see that only one other figure sits in our bar. The lighting is bad, as it always is in places like this, and we can't quite get a fix on what he looks like. If we hold our heads one way, he looks a bit like a nervous, stoop-shouldered, just-approaching-middle-age businessman. His tie is askew around his neck and his hat is propped carelessly on the back of his head. His face is lined and his eyes are tired and maybe a bit scared. His hair - dishwater yellow; cut far too close - has thinned noticeably from a high, clear, unlined brow. His eyes are a faded blue and have the unfocussed appearance of drunken befuddlement.

But if we move our heads a bit to the right, we might just look at our nervous drunk and see a gargantuan ball of flaming hot gases and immense, controlled, nuclear reactions.

Old woman or young woman; vase or two people trying to decide whether or not to kiss. It really is a matter of personal perspective.

There is a chipped, dirty glass full of the Boh Da Thone's "finest" sitting in front of our lonely customer. The glass is slowly dissolving and melting into the bar from around the liquor. Interestingly, the drink is stubbornly maintaining the shape of the glass.

Henasamef – the name of our barkeep; as it hasn't yet been mentioned, and being quite rude, we haven't asked – calls these drinks "Claw-Your-Own-Eyes-Out-With-The-Bloody-Remains-Of-Your-Fingers" or "Screaming Brain Eaters", in loving memory of the first victim to try one.

They haven't taken off as yet, but Henasamef has high hopes to market them to fraternal organizations. Perhaps as birth control *cum* "Spring Break Euthanizer".

Our singular customer is compulsively breaking open the fossilized peanuts provided by the barkeep and very carefully ignoring the drink – his fourth of the evening – in front of him.

The rolling trumpet call crashes from the "sky" again and a smashing tide of thunder beats against the walls of the bar. The thunder is followed by a tortured, fear-lashed scream that fills the entire world. It sounds as if the planet itself is crying out in fear and pain. Our customer shudders once, convulsively.

Henasamef – our primal Ur-throwback barkeep from beyond the beginning of time – looks disgustedly at him and grunts in an uninterested sort of way.

The leather-padded, swinging door that is the bar's only entrance opens, and a woman enters. We can see a hard rain, blood-colored like the sky, and apparently full of glass and molten metal, falling.

The woman brushes herself off while still standing at the entrance. There is a meticulous thoroughness to her movements, almost as if she were trying not to offend the proprieties of any watchers. Like our nervous, multi-perspectived businessman, the woman's appearance is hard to nail down. From where we're standing right now she appears to be what would be called, in an earlier time and place a "mature" woman; a "matron" in certain polite settings, "a high-steppin' biddy" in others.

There is a motherly roundness to her that suggests the successful raising of a brood of happy, healthy children, and an absolute mastery of all things home-related. You look at her and something says "house-wife." But you don't want to say "house-wife"; you want to say "Domestic Engineer, Ninja Assassin Level." (And if you knew what was good for you, you'd capitalize every word as you said it, too.)

There is something about her that says she's mere seconds away from licking her thumb and briskly wiping a smudge of something unidentifiable from your face.

From where we stand, her hair is a nut-colored brown, and smells vaguely of freshly-baked bread. It's pulled back from her face in a convenient ponytail and shines with a radiant good health.

Her face has all the lines and wrinkles associated with a lifetime's worth of giggling, smiling, and laughing out loud at every opportunity. Her face suggests that if you looked as though you needed a hug, she'd be the one to give it to you. And it would be warm and tight and all-encompassing; everything a good hug *should* be.

Her eyes are merry and dancing, despite the way her garments now seem to be covered in blood and liquid glass from her knees downward, and one gets the idea that her eyes, at least, would suggest that World War Three was simply a bit of "unpleasantness"; a passing bit of "yuck" that'll clear up in no time.

She is dressed simply, in flowing robes that look as though they would comfortably fit a Hellenic statue, although she's quite soaked.

But again, if we moved our heads just a bit to the right, we might see a loosely collected group of flaming hot balls of plasmic chaos, separated by more billions of miles than it would be convenient to discuss, nevertheless, with imaginary, invisible lines drawn between them.

Perspective, perspective, perspective.

The woman sees our hero sitting by himself, and walks up to the bar with brisk, efficient steps that still look a bit too much like dancing not to be.

She puts a friendly hand on his shoulder, and in the matronly, comforting, voice we were expecting, says, "Wow, Shamus! He's really doing it, huh?"

"Shamus" nods once, crushing another peanut beneath his fist.

"I've asked you not to call me "Shamus", Cassie. It's not really how you pronoun-"

"Yes, yes," Cassie interrupts, gently, the way a doting mother or elderly sister might. "Shamus, Sol, Lunos, you've got too many names, boy! I can never keep them all straight!"

"Actually, "Lunos" is the moon, Cassie."

But "Cassie" seems not to have heard.

Shamus grins in spite of himself and crushes another peanut beneath his fist as Cassie climbs up onto the barstool next to his and scootches into a comfortable sitting position. Not an easy proposition in long, flowing, classical robes, but Cassie pulls it off with style and grace.

Henasamef trundles over to Cassie, and grunts something that may, after the appropriate language registers have burned out, be translated as "Woddawant?"

Cassie smiles brightly, as though she weren't addressing a genetic nightmare on legs, and says, "A Harvey Wallbanger, please. With a straw and an umbrella."

Henasamef grunts non-committedly and waddles away.

Cassie says "I've always wanted to try one of those!"

She gives a little giggle. Shamus smiles himself and turns a bit on his stool so he's facing Cassie. There's a certain relief in his eyes now. It's as if he's feeling, "Oh good. *She's* here." There is a tension in our man Shamus that suggests he's addressing someone he respects.

"I saw Mike today, Cassie."

Cassie looks over at Shamus, her hand still on his shoulder. She pats his back in a comforting sort of way and gives a contented sigh. She looks clearly out of place there, with her ramrod straight back and her gently dignified bearing, but she smiles brightly at everything. Her eyes beam, despite the way her hands stick to the greasy bar top. She itches abstractedly as something that fell on her in a dusty shower from the ceiling. A closer observation would reveal that the dust in question is largely cockroach droppings, but even this wouldn't be enough to throw our girl Cassie.

"Did you?" she asks, her voice still carrying tones of warmth and comfort. "Did you say anything to him?"

Shamus shakes his head, turning back to face the bar.

"Naw. You know how it is, Cassie. There's all kinds of stuff going on. Scrolls and seals and what not. Stars crashing down and running riv-"

Shamus is interrupted by another tortured, bellowing scream of agony from outside. It ends on a cracking note that sounds like a stack of dishes – ten million miles high - being neatly torn in half, magnified ten billion times. Shamus closes his eyes and slumps a bit more in his chair.

"Goodness! What was that?" Cassie asks, her eyes wide, but still somehow beaming."

"Australia. Or maybe south-east Asia. I can never keep all of the continents straight. Which one has the jumping rats with the alligator tails and those naked black guys who wander around dreaming all the time and chalking on that big rock of theirs?"

"Beats me, Shamus. I never get close enough to see all *those* kinds of details."

There is a quietly judgmental tone in Cassie's voice; a gentle rebuke for *someone's* apolitically incorrect insensitivity.

Henasamef, waddling along at speed, plunks something evilly viscous down in front of Cassie. It's in a long, thin glass with an umbrella desultorily sitting in it. The umbrella is covered in the remains of several generations of cobweb.

The fluid inside the glass slops over the barkeep's hand with a glutinous "blorp". It is *exactly* the same color and consistency of cold beef gravy.

Cassie smiles her enthusiastic smile and takes a single sip before either man can say or do anything. She smacks her lips and nods, still-smiling, at Henasamef.

Henasamef looks back at her with wide eyes – or his general approximation thereof, anyway. He stares at her for a long moment, as if wondering whether she'll fall out of her chair, and then grunts at her. There is an admiring tone to it.

"Well, I wouldn't worry too much, Shamus. It's like puberty, isn't it? There's some excitement; what, with hormones and what not, but eventually everything settles down. It's just a bit of something that needs to happen so we can move on to the next phase of our growth," Cassie says, the muscles in her forearm flexing as she tries to stir her drink.

The front door "clunks" and a blood-covered body in military fatigues falls inside on the floor. It is still clutching the twisted, molten remains of what appears to have once been a rifle of some kind. It twitches, just once, and then quite audibly expires.

Shamus and Cassie both look around at the "clunk" and then turn back as Henasamef waddles to the door. There is a practiced efficiency to the way he bags the body and drags it behind the bar and on into the back. He moves with grunts and mutters, as if he's doing a chore he's done many, many times before.

The pungent odor of blood, roasted meat, and melted metal briefly overpowers the bar's resident smells.

Shamus, delayed by the disposal of tortured remains, belatedly replies, "Yeah. I guess."

"Come on, now! Let me see a smile!" Cassie says, her own face beaming brightly, while reaching again for her Harvey Gravy-Banger.

"This is really good! Would you like a sip?"

She proffers the glass to Shamus' face, holding the straw perfectly still in an unconscious, perfected, "mother movement".

Shamus takes a small sip.

Cassie, wiping briskly at a bit of schmut on Shamus' face, says, "Besides, this is happening *elsewhere,* isn't it? What's it got to do with you, dearie? Sure, it's sad to see those apes you're so fond of die, but everything does eventually. It's not as if He's mad at *you!*"

She takes another sip, her face giving every indication of total enjoyment. A small bit of her Gravy-Banger actually climbs up the side of the glass and makes a spirited bid for freedom.

"Yeah, I guess," Shamus replies, slumping a bit more in his chair. "There is that whole thing about "heaven *and* earth", though. Do you think that applies to us, too?"

Cassie, enthusiastically trying to suck up the sticky remnants on the bottom of her glass, chokes and coughs, spitting grey-flecked bits on the bar.

She places the drink carefully down, fastidiously wiping her lips. She takes a long moment to regain her composure and Shamus looks over his shoulder at her, his face registering a thin alarm.

"Did you know," Cassie says, very slowly and carefully, "I hadn't considered that?"

Henasamef grunts. Is there just a hint of laughter in it?

Shamus slumps back down on his stool with a sigh, and he and Cassiopeia wait, silently, as "outside" Armageddon continues apace.

David and GOLIATH

They's some funny dam' things go on in th' woods.

Seems like a mighty cavalier thing ta' say, don't it? True, though. You stop for just a minute, an' you think 'bout that. They's places, deep in th' woods, where ain't nobody ever stepped. Them places is th' lair of old things; elderly green. You know? I mean, we say 'Ain't no more dinosaurs. They's all extinct.' But we say it from behind th' safety of our cinder-block houses with all th' lights on. We don't know nothin' 'bout th' silent tread of huge paws in th' deep, dark woods.

We don't really *know* nothin' about nothin', if'n you stop an' think 'bout it. We think we're such a big deal, us humans. With our computers, an' our internet, an' our cable TV, we got all this information comin' at us, all at once, an' none of it means anythin' t'all. We don't know nothin' 'bout things that been livin' an' breedin' and havin' lives fer ten-thousand years, back deep in th' woods where nobody ever goes.

You think 'bout that *real* hard, next time you're dead sure 'bout th' woods. 'Cause th' woods, they'll surprise ya' every time.

I got me a story I wanna tell ya'. It's a whopper, an' ya' might reckon I'm tellin' a long, tall one. But I swear to ya', on my Daddy's grave, it's as true as me sittin' here. I got proof.

This here story's 'bout this one time I forgot that simple lesson; rememberin' th' woods is bigger'n I thought. I thought I was smarter an' mightier than th' woods.

I was wrong.

Wellsir, th' woods don't cotton ta' brave, cocky little man-things trompin' around in it, thinkin' they're at th' top of the food chain. No sir. Makes the woods all grumpy and tetchy.

It's a little spare on detail, my story. I don't give you *all* th' accountin', as I ain't *got* all th' accountin'. Lots of stuff happened when I wasn't quite awake an' aware, if ya' know what I mean. This here story I'm 'bout ta' tell ya' is more in th' way of an outline than a 'true accountin' of events'.

I was too busy tryin' ta' stay alive to remember all th' small bits an' pieces. I 'magine you can put those together easy enough, if you've a mind to.

It went a little somethin' like this. Listen:

I went in to th' fact'ry, half-expectin' it. They'd been rumors boilin' around 'bout lay-offs and restructurin'. I don't pay much mind myself. Long as I can get a paycheck from *somebody*, I'm all right. Don't make no nevermind ta' me who gives me th' paycheck, s'long as I get one. 'Course, it's just *me* countin' on that paycheck. I might feel a touch different, I had a passle of young'un's at home lookin' ta' be fed.

Wellsir, I clocked in, put my overalls on, an' walked out to my post by th' metal-dyeing section. My section leader's standin' there, waitin' on me.

"Davey," he says, his face all sad, but determined. Like he's thinkin' 'I don't like it any more than you do, hoss, but I got a job ta' do, an' I'm gonna do it. Don't blame me, okay?'

He's standin' there, lookin' like he's got th' belly-gripes or some such, an' he says, "Davey, you go on home. We're shuttin' down for th' better part of a week. Ain't got enough work for ever'body, an' yer low on th' totem pole."

He goes on to explain that it's not a firin' or a 'you're laid off' deal, it's just a 'we don't have enough work for you this week. Take a few days off an' come back,' kind of a deal.

Way I understand it, some of th' other guys got real bent out of shape over it, complainin' 'bout missin' car payments an' rent, or some such. Me, I smiled like a jack-o-lantern, shrugged, an' walked out. I went home, fixed myself up a mess'a flapjacks, an 'bout a pound of bacon, an' decided I'd tromp on into th' woods for a few days.

I like ta' think of them woods as bein' *my* woods. After all, you open my front door, walk a hundred yards south, and there they are: loomin', all dark an' invitin'. Them woods has character. Leastways, I *used* ta' think so. Ain't been in 'em since these here events I'm relatin' happened.

'Scuse my scratchin'. It's been a while, but I still itch like fire, I got ta' say. Doctor says it'll itch for a while, which is interestin' as ain't nothin' there *to* itch.

Anyway. Them woods, they's old as Davy Crockett's rifle an' twice as ugly. An' to a feller like me, twice as invitin'.

Now I've been hikin', by myself, since I was knee-high to a can of biscuits. I've got no fear of any woods, anywhere. I can handle just 'bout anything th' woods throw at me: weather? No problem. Find me an over-turned root ball, or maybe an overhangin' rock-face, an' wait it out.

Large predators? Well, this is th' twenty-first century, and there ain't many left. Th' predators that *are* left have an over-healthy fear a' man. Basically, you don't bother them, they don't bother you.

Lost? Get serious. You walk in one direction long enough, 'ventually you'll find somethin' that'll lead ya' to civ'lization. Most folks get lost in th' woods these days, they lose their heads an' just kinda wander around in circles, cryin' an' makin' things worse for theyselves. You pay just a *little* bit of attention ta' where yer goin', an' some of th' landmarks around you, you'll be all right.

I ain't never been 'lost', I just been 'temporarily displaced'.

No. I ain't never had no kinda trouble with hikin' in th' woods. It's been a part of my life forever. For some reason, though, I ain't never been in th' woods just outside my front door. I ain't sure why.

I know *now*, but that's for later.

I think back on that, an' I think that maybe somethin' was tellin' me - like, on an unconscious sort of level - 'Davey, you stay out of here, boy. They's things in here you can't handle, an' you'll be sorry if you try.'

I'm not sayin' that's so for a fact, now, I'm just suggestin' th' possibility exists.

So I stayed out, not knowin' why, exactly, despite seein' some mighty interestin' tracks just outside my front door. Some of those tracks were th' marks a'bigger cats an' bears, even. You look at those mighty footprints, pressed deep into th' mud or th' gravel, an' somethin' inside you starts hammerin' away, wantin' ta' face-off against 'em.

I've kinda half-hoped, for th' better part of my adult life, that I'd run into somethin' that *wanted* a piece a'me; somethin' big and full a'slaverin' teeth, so I could prove myself over it. In all th' years I been trompin' through woods large and small, th' biggest, meanest thing I' ever run into was a grumpy possum. He tried ta' take a bite out my boot when I accidentally stepped on his tail. We growled at each other for a few minutes, an' then he lumbered off into th' woods, hissin' an' spittin' at me in Possum.

It's a bit disheartenin' sometimes.

I know it doesn't make a whole lot of sense, me wantin' ta' see a big ol' mouth fulla teeth, but there you are. I kinda tack it up ta' 'frustrated modern male' syndrome, an' leave it at that. Not a whole lot a'room for self-examination in my life, to be perfectly honest.

I packed my kit bag with enough food and water for three days, packed a lightweight, weatherproof poncho, grabbed my Daddy's bowie an' my rifle, an' headed out. I didn't call nobody, didn't leave a note, or nothin'. Just grabbed up my haversack, made sure th' oven was off, an' set out.

Didn't even bring a compass.

I never have used a compass. Not even was I was just a wee shaver. I just point myself in one direction an' go. Way I figure it, if a bird no brighter than a dim-watt bulb can fly hisself down from the Arctic Circle an' back without a compass, I can too. An' don't give me no guff 'bout metal in their brains or other electro-magnetical effects. They just *know* what direction they's s'posed ta' fly in.

Wadn't nothin' fancy 'bout any of my equipment. My rifle's just a lever action .30-30 Winchester. It doedn't have any fancy accessories: no laser sights, night vision, or any of that crap ya' find in them upscale huntin' stores these days. Nosir, it's just 'bout 150 grains of good, reliable stopping power. You can put pretty much anything smaller than a grizzly down with it, if you pay attention to where you're aimin'. It was my Daddy's, an' he was right happy with it. Took down a few deer in his time an' passed it on ta' me when he was through with it. It's a good, reliable gun, an' I'm right happy with it, too.

My knife's nothin' special, either. Just a bowie I wear on my hip. It's a good, solid campin' tool: 'bout a foot long, and two or three inches thick. It's dam'near an axe, it is. Just a plain wood handle, an' sharp as a woman's tongue.

My poncho's pretty sweet, though. It's a good ten feet square, water-proofed inside an' out, an' th' inside's got a good ol' goose-down lining underneath a layer of water-proofed polypropylene. I get underneath that poncho, it gets nice an' toasty in there

I tromped off into th' woods, bein' as quiet as I know how to be - which is considerable. You want ta' make that effort in a large woods - bein' quiet, that is. You don't know what makes its home there, an' you'd rather not surprise it, if you have a choice. There's 'I'd like to face off against a large predator an' prove what I'm made of', an' then there's 'Hey! Hungry timber wolf! Here I am! I'm covered in cheese! Come get me!'

There ain't a whole lot ta' see in th' woods, if you don't know how ta' look. Some folks, they hikes on into th' woods an' see a buncha trees. They reckon, you seen one dam'fool tree, you've seen 'em all. Now any fool with two bits of sense ta' rub together can tell you that ain't so. Sure, some woods is all one kind of tree, but each tree is an individual, with its own story to tell.

Sounds kinda silly, don't it? But it's true. Listen: maybe this here enormous oak's been around for a couple hundred years, and it's seen Indians an' all kinds of other folk walk through. Maybe this here pine's been struck by lightning and had a bear sharpen its claws on its trunk. Maybe this willow's got a nest from a few seasons back in its branches, still got bits of feather in it.

Yessir, you make a little bit of an effort; take yourself a bit a'time, an' a tree can tell you all kinds a'stories. An' that's one of th' reasons I'm out here, middle of February, trompin' around.

Day one went by without no kind of trouble. I made maybe fifteen miles, just pickin' 'em up an' puttin' 'em down. Th' weather held pretty fair. Sure, it was gusty, an' a mite cold, but I'm used ta' that. I bundled up in all kinds of good, warm, weather proof clothing 'fore I left th' house, so

I wasn't sufferin' any. My boots is good, stout leather; heavily waterproofed, an' I was ready for anything short of th' next ice age.

Or so I thought.

I found me some interestin' rocks, a maple bleedin' syrup - somebody'd been out here harvestin' recently - an' a creek with fish in it. I made a sort of mental note of th' creek, thinkin' I could use it as a point of reference later. I'm not really sure why I wasn't payin' more attention at th' time. Guess I was off in my own dam'fool little world.

Anyway, like I say, day one of my lil' adventure passed by without any trouble. Th' sun starts ta' look like it's reckonin' on settin', an' I get ta' lookin' for a place ta' set up a bivouac.

I'm confident in my woodsmart, havin' been trained by th' best (my Daddy, nat'rally), but I ain't stupid. Only a dam' fool goes blunderin' around in th' woods at night. Way I reckon it, you go hikin' around at night, you deserve whatever you get. Even if you got a spotlight with you, which I ain't, you can't see nothin' in th' woods late at night. Th' trees loom, an' walk, an' throw thick shadows, that're as disorientin' as can be. There ain't no sense in tryin' ta' walk through a tree.

Some woods, they get so dark, you can't see your hand in front of your face. Just askin' for a broke leg, you go off all half-cocked like that. An' you'd deserve it, too.

Now, in looking for a campsite, I'm not lookin' for anything too fancy. I'd just like a spot - mostly out of th' wind - where I can tie down three corners of my poncho. I'm not expectin' luxury accommodations, just someplace flat an' dry. .

Th' sun was maybe an hour from settin' when I found th' rock face. It was everything I could ask for, with a convenient overhang an' a complete lack of runnin' water. (I learned that lesson th' hard way. 'Never set up camp under a rock face with drippin' water. You're likely to wake up wet.') It faced north, an' there were enough screening trees ta' make things downright cozy.

Far as accommodations was concerned, this here rockface was th' Hilton. An' not th' one down to th' airport, neither.

I set up my poncho, an' went lookin' for some fallen branches. I figured I could set myself a small fire an' be right comfortable all night long. I took my rifle with me. Just in case, you understand. I hadn't seen anything bigger than some brown bear tracks, but you never know.

I'd found me a dead fall with some good, dry branches on th' lee side of a massive oak tree, maybe fifty yards from my little campsite. I made myself a nice bundle of th' good, weathered oak, imaginin' th' nice cracklin' flames I'd soon have going', an' I was headin' back, my rifle slung over my shoulder. Th' sun had set, an' th' light was fallin' fast, but I knew where I was goin', an' I could see my brightly colored poncho ahead a'me.

That's when I first heard th' scream. I don't know why I knew it was a cat. Th' knowledge came ta' me, sudden-like.

"That there is a big dam' cat."

It was high, an' it was loud, an' it made th' shivers run up an' down my spine. It fair came to shakin' th' bones in my head, it did.

Now, I've heard th' screams of all th' large huntin' cats likely to be found in this area: bobcat, cougar, feral house cat, you name it. If it lives in this area, I've heard it. Never faced off against one, but I've heard 'em.

This didn't sound nothin' like th' screams of any cat I'm familiar with. It wasn't like nothin' I've ever heard in my entire life. It sounded like a woman, some twenty feet tall, givin' birth overtop a pile of broken glass. I swear, that thing screamed, an' th' hairs on th' back a'my head stood up an' migrated south.

I looked around, thinkin' ta spot it, an' it screamed again. It took me a minute, but when th' realization hit me, it started with shivers. My mama'd tell ya' I ain't th' sharpest axe in th' shed. Sometimes it takes me a minute'r two ta' get things. Wellsir, it did, but I got 'er eventually. See, that there cat was huntin', an' I was th' prey.

I got no good reason for why I was convinced it was a cat huntin' me. I just *knew*. Same as I always know what direction I'm goin' in, same as I know these woods was tryin' ta warn me ta stay out. I just knew it, same as I know my own name.

It was a big cat. It was smart enough to let me know it was comin' without lettin' me see it, an' it was comin' for me at its leisure.

That kinda thing worries me, as it's not the nat'ral inclination of a predator. A predator hunts when it's hungry. When it starts huntin' just for th' pleasure a'huntin', that's when you need ta start worryin'.

Now you got to understand the way a big cat - an' for that matter, most *any* predator - thinks. A big cat, they like ta come upwind a'prey, take 'em down 'fore th' prey even knows they're there. Secret an' deep, are big cats. Silent stalkin' death. This one, it was screamin' fit ta' make my head bust, an' it didn't give a dam' one way or t'other if I knew it was there.

All that led me to believe that this was one mighty cat, an' not somethin' I wanted to face in th' open.

That put a little bit of a pep in my step as I went back ta' my little hidey-hole, as I'm sure you can imagine.

I built up th' fire quicker'n you can say Jack Robinson, an' I was soon feedin' it up big an' strong an' tall. I put th' fire in between me an' th' rock face, crawled up under my poncho, an' sat there, cradlin' my rifle, tryin' ta' see anything.

I was strainin', listenin', an' ' lookin', tryin' ta' see anything movin' out there in th' tricky half-light, out beyond my flames. The night was dark all around me. Night falls fast in th' deep woods an' mornin's usually late in comin'.

I couldn't hear or see a thing. It was like bein' in a cave.

Even th' wind died down ta' almost nothin'. Weren't no bird calls, no sound of branches moving against each other, nothin'. It was just my breathin', th' cracklin' of th' flames, and th' occasional flap of my poncho in th' wind. I start to relax just a little. You know, come back off th' edge of adrenaline. I fed th' fire some more of my branches, an' if you can b'leve it, I'm thinkin' about maybe fixin' myself a little somethin' ta' eat. I start ta' maybe b'leve that th' cat's gone off ta find somethin' else ta do. (I call that the 'eternal optimism of prey-thinkin'.) I go so far as ta' break out my food, an' my makin's, an' start cookin' supper.

I'm halfway through my first cigarette an' my third biscuit, an' sure enough, that dam' cat screams again.

Now th' cat's pissed off. Again. I can't explain why I know this to be so, I just do. I'm sittin' there, a hand-rolled cigarette stuck to my bottom lip, listenin' to th' awful sound of that cat, an' somehow I just know this here cat is *mad* at me.

Well, maybe 'mad' ain't th' right word. 'Offended' more like. It's offended I'm not runnin' an' scrabblin' for my life away from it. It's like it's thinkin' 'Gonna sit there an' have a biscuit an' a smoke, huh? We'll see 'bout *that*!'

273

That scream makes th' dam' fluid in my ears judder. It sounds like metal bein' torn in half; like a shower a'molten rock pourin' into a cold stream. It sounds awful, it sounds mean, an' it sounds *big*.

The screams are comin' from up above an' behind me; from up top th' rock face I'm cowerin' against. I get a shower of mud an' loose rock on my poncho. Nothin' bigger'n' a pebble, but it's enough ta' make th' poncho sag just a bit.

I figure th' height of th' rock face is a good thirty, maybe forty feet. It's literally a cliff face. Kinda like a small mountain, in th' middle of th' woods, like you find all over th' dam' place aroun' here.

I'm down here at th' bottom, huddlin' under my poncho an' feedin' wood to my fire. This cat is up top, tryin' ta' get me ta' run like a scared rabbit. I don't know if it's afraid of th' fire, or if I'm just spoilin' its fun, but this cat is tryin' ta' use psychology on me.

I wadn't actually scared until right then. I mean, okay. It's a big cat, it's hungry, an' it's picked me as a potential meal. I'll sit tight, take my shot when I get th' chance, have myself some tender steak an' one hell of a story.

But now I gotta factor in the fact that this big, mean, scary cat is usin' *psychology*, too?

Yeah. I started ta' sweat a little at that point, and they was parts of my brain started sendin' little 'Run!' messages to my legs.

'Course, th' rest of me, what's smarter than that part of me, knew that runnin' was th' very worst thing I could do. If I did that, I was gonna end up bein' kitty chow.

I figure I got two choices: I can huddle under my poncho all night, hopin' th' cat don't come for me when its got th' best advantage, or I can snake out from under it, an' see if I can't sneak in a few good licks of my own. Who knows? Maybe I'll get lucky. 'Course, it's as dark as th' inside of a bad woman's heart, I can't see nothin', an' th' cat's got home turf advantage, but I ain't gonna let none of th' reasonable facts bother me none.

Wellsir, wadn't really no choice 'tall. My Daddy didn't raise no scared rabbit.

I load th' rifle an' quietly move out from under th' poncho. Remember: I'm as quiet as a whore in a room fulla nuns when I want ta' be, an' right now ain't no diff'rent.

I can hear th' cat movin' an' mutterin' to itself up there on th' rock face. Way I reckon it, if I'm a little careful, an' a *lot* lucky, I can put a wad of hot lead in it that'll convince it ta' go find itself a less well-armed entree, at least.

I huddle under some cover, 'bout twenty yards from my hidey-hole, behind a fallen oak. I line th' rifle up with th' top of th' cliff face, an' I wait for a shot. I was thinkin' I could use the flames of my fire ta' maybe outline th' cat if it broke th' top of th' ridge.

Wellsir, it just wadn't gonna work out that way. 'Bout th' time I get ta' set, th' fire chooses then ta' flare up with a breeze, an' it outlines that dam' cat in stark pinks an' reds. Lord be my witness, it was a sight!

I mean, it was dam' near painted up there, up to that rock face, an' all I could do was stare. I b'leve I completely forgot I was even holdin' a rifle. You'd'a been starin' too. Don't even try an' tell me you wouldn't. That cat was as pretty as a three dollar hooker to a bus fulla Marines.

It was tawny, coppery bronze in th' fire's light, an' big as a Volkswagen bus. It leapt from th' cliff face. In movement it looked like liquid gold bein' poured from a pitcher of th' gods. It was elegance and fluidity defined.

Dam', but that cat was *pretty*!

This cat leapt down and out, from th' top of this small hill, or mountain, or whatever-th'-hell-you want ta' call it, for thirty, maybe forty feet a'vertical free-fall. Same time it was leapin' - or fallin' I reckon - vertical, it was also leapin' horizontal, ta' land *behind* where I was crouchin'.

I know that sounds like a mighty load a'bull, but this here cat cleared an acre a'woods with one jump. Lord be my witness.

Now I know what you're thinkin': 'Davey. What *were* you drinkin' out there?'

May th' good Lord strike me deaf, dumb and blind if I'm lyin'. It's th' truth. That cat took off like a UFO an' covered seventy some-odd feet a'distance with one jump. I swear it on my dear Momma's grave.

That cat leapt, an' 'fore I knew it, it was behind me. It hit th' ground 'bout five yards away from me, an' I felt th' ground shake. It turned toward me, eyes big as truck headlights, an' I felt - not *heard*, mind you, *felt* - this sound comin' from it. It was this low rumblin', like stones way underground, grindin' up against each other. For the life of me, I couldn't figure out what th' noise was for a second or two. .

You're smarter'n I am. You probably already know th' noise I was hearin' was this here great big cat growlin'.

It was too big to look at. I don't know how ta' say it any better than that. As close as it was, it was just too big for me ta see proper. I still hadn't got more'n fleeting impressions of size and color. It was big, an' it was golden, an' it was growlin' at me.

Wellsir, I lifted my rifle, an' I let fire. They musta heard that cat scream in three counties away. Course, I didn't so much as graze th' thing. I mean, less'n twenty feet away, eyes glowin' like hell's own jack-o-lanterns, an' it's screamin' at me, an' I didn't even singe its fur. Big as a barn an' I can't hit it from fifteen feet, I'm so scared.

That cat turned an' ran off into th' woods, an' I turned an' ran off to my hidey-hole. I scampered up under my lil' poncho coverin', put my back up against that cliff, an' I started ta' shiver.

I ain't never been so scared in all my life, an' that's the Good Lord's Own truth.

I been hikin' all my life. Been chased by a swarm of hornets for a third of a mile. Been stuck up on th' side of exposed rock faces durin' a lightnin' storm. Been dam' near swept downstream durin' a spring flood, but I ain't never been as scared as I was right then, not even when that cat was less than fifteen feet away.

I could feel th' cold of th' rock through my jacket. I could feel the sweat beadin' an' runnin' down my face. I could smell th' stink of my own fear comin' out of my pores. An' all I could think of was th' way that cat's eyes glowed like th' lamps of th' damned. I start ta' shiverin' an' shakin' an' I even give out with a few hiccupin' sobs.

I ain't ashamed ta' tell ya', I was scared all th' way down to my roots. There was somethin' evil an' glittery in that cat's eyes. It was like lookin' into a reflection of all th' worst things about yerself, an' seein' that it just kept goin'.

I looked into them eyes, an' I knew - just *knew* - it didn't want ta' *eat* me . . . it just wanted ta' *kill* me.

Th' cat, for its part, was out there in th' woods, yowlin' an' howlin' an' screamin'. I'm tryin' ta' pull myself together, an' this cat is makin' as much noise as a monkey in a microwave. I can't explain it to you. I ain't smart enough, an' despite all evidence to th' con'trary, I ain't got th' words. It was just a *knowin'*, same as I know anything I know. Call it 'psychic', call it 'empathic', call it whatever you want; somehow, I just knew th' cat was out there in th' woods, out beyond th' flickerin' light of my campfire, makin' all that ruckus 'cause it was tryin' ta' reach inside my head, an' steal th' heart from me.

Th' image that came ta' mind was th' way a rabbit freezes when it feels th' eyes of a hawk fall on it. That ain't quite so, but it's close. That cat was tryin' ta' get me ta' freeze up an' come meekly for the crunch of its jaws. Way I figured it, it was tryin' to unnerve me with all that noise it was makin'.

Wellsir, that just proves it wadn't as smart as it thought it was. Once I realized what it was up to, instead of unnervin' me, I got mad. I crawled out from under my poncho, an' I lifted my rifle to my shoulder.

"You want some of this, you mangy so-an'-so?"

What I *really* said ain't fit for polite comp'ny, so I won't repeat it here.

I took aim toward th' noises, an' watched a tree flex as that cat moved against it. Be damned if it weren't th' biggest thing I *ever* saw! I let fly with a couple a'rounds while bellowin' obscenities at th' top of my lungs.

"You ain't nothin' but a whore's so-an'-so!"

BLAM!

"Your Momma didn't know your daddy an' couldn't pick him out of a lineup!"

BLAM!

"The best part of you ran down yer Momma's chin!"

BLAM!

"Your Daddy didn't know his such-an-such from his so-an'-so an' a hole in th' ground!"

BLAM!

An' all kinds a'foolishness like what ya' hear bein' yelled on any playground. I apologize for th' crudity of th' language I used, but ya' got to understand th' stress I was under at th' time. I was mad, an' I was scared. I wadn't thinkin' about what I was sayin', I was just screamin' my defiance into th' night, lettin' that cat know I wadn't gonna go down easy. I'd yell some foul thing at it, an' fire a round into th' dark. Didn't hit nothin' more'n a tree or two - I was shakin' too hard to aim - but it shut th' cat up. I like to think it gave him pause, too. Like maybe he was thinkin' that the rabbit's got teeth all of a sudden.

I grabbed up a bunch more wood and stacked it near ta' hand, while listenin' to that cat move off into th' woods. It wadn't hard ta' hear. It sounded like a 4X4 movin' at top speed. I watched th' trees it knocked against bow an' flex an' even come close ta' fallin' over. It stopped runnin' about a hundred yards away from me, an' gave back with one of them screams of its.

"Yeah? Well, so're you!" I yelled, an' fired another round at it.

I piled them branches high on my fire, 'till it was dam' near unbearable. Then I crawled under my poncho, an' commenced ta' endurin' one of th' longest nights of my entire life.

Every so often, that cat'd try ta' sneak up on me. I'd look out of th' corner of my eye an' see a pair of hate-filled eyes glowerin' at me, close to th' ground, behind all kinds of screenin' bushes an' vegetation, on my left. I'd send a round in that direction, tryin' to steady my hands enough ta' maybe graze it at least. Th' cat would scream an' bound off, almost quicker'n my eyes could follow. Couple of minutes later, I'd see those eyes from my right.

I still hadn't got a good look at it. In between my head-spinnin' from left ta' right, tryin' ta' see everything at once, an' th' flickering shadows cast by my fire an' the settin' sun, I wadn't gettin' but the very briefest glimpses of it. I'd see those eyes, or maybe a muscled flank, bigger'n I am, an'

I'd send a round in that direction. Th' cat'd disappear, an' I wouldn't see or hear anything more for a few minutes.

I'd plunk seven rounds out into th' dark an' then I'd have ta' reload. Th' cat would wait until I was reloadin' ta' start makin' noise an' tryin' ta' sneak up on me. Now, I ain't no kind of gunslinger, or nothin', but I am fast. I can reload my rifle in under a half minute - in good, safe, normal conditions.

These weren't.

I was fumblin' rounds into my rifle, droppin' 'em an' scatterin' 'em ever'where. Came close a time or two to dam' near blowin' my foot off.

Th' cat always came at me from th' front. For the life of me, I couldn't figure out why it didn't just climb th' rock face an' come at me from th' top. Don't get me wrong, I was grateful, but it didn't make no sense.

After about th' fifth try, I looked inta them eyes, an' just like that, I knew. That cat was comin' at me from my front 'cause it wanted me ta' see it comin'. It wanted ta' experience my bowell-loosenin' fear as it pounced on me an' tore my head off. Wellsir, that came as close to unmannin' me as anything yet had. I started thinkin' prey-thought, an' I started ta' get unscrewed.

That cat, it kept comin' back. It wadn't even makin' an effort ta' move silently or invisibly. It'd pop up at my right side, 'bout fifty yards away, an' start slinkin' in on me on its belly. I'd put a round in that direction, an' it'd take off, quick as a comet. I wadn't hittin' nothin'. My hands were shakin' with fear, an' I was too keyed up ta' calm down. Th' cat didn't seem ta' be worried about gettin' hit, an' 'less I got it in th' vitals, I ain't real sure one bullet woulda done too much. It was still a cat, though. Th' roar of my .30-30 was enough to scare it off for a while. But I was gettin' tired an' my thinkin' was loosenin' under th' stress.

I thought things was bad enough at that point. Then I realized what th' cat was doin' with those belly-crawlin' sneak attacks. It was tryin' ta' get me to use up all my ammo. I could put seven rounds in my rifle at any one point, and I had left the house with three boxes of twenty rounds. I had already used up an entire box of ammo, leaving me with just forty rounds. That cat was smart enough ta' know that I only had a finite amount of ammunition with me.

I swear, that dam' cat could *count*.

'Bout that time, I start ta' hear a noise out there in th' dark. It's a low, guttural, rumblin' noise, kinda rhythmic and fast. I tilted my head, tryin' ta' figure out what the noise was. I'd heard th' cat growl, an' I didn't think that was th' same noise.

It took me a long time, but then, I ain't th' sharpest pencil in th' box. I figure you've already guessed what that sound was, despite knowin' that big cats don't make that noise. Wellsir, you're right. That evil thing was sittin' out there in th' dark, purrin' at me.

'It might take me all night, boy, but eventually I'm gonna getya'. You sit right there under your poncho, an' you watch th' fire burn down. Eventually it's just gonna be me an' you an' can't nobody save you. Nobody even knows you're here.'

That's what that purrin' was meant t' indicate, an' it went right past my ears to that part of my brain that's been around since th' cave men days. Things started ta' fall apart pretty quickly after that.

Now, I know some of ya'll are a bit dubious about this story, an' I understand that. After all, it's a bit on th' high, tall side. But I need ya' to stick with me 'till th' end. It's gonna get a mite higher an' taller 'fore we end, but I swear, it's as true as I breathe.

Now things is bad. I'm havin' me a right, royal, 'long, dark night of th' soul'. I'm stuck here, penned down by a murd'rous cat, an' I'm runnin' out of ammo fast. My options is dwindlin', an' I ain't havin' no flashes of insight as to what might be a good way out this predicament. An' if all that wadn't bad enough; as if I weren't havin' a hard enough time already, it picks then ta' start rainin'.

If I had been in a tight spot before, I knew I was in real trouble, then. Th' cat could sneak in on me under the cover of the noise th' rain was makin', an' with th' dark, th' confusin' shadows thrown by th' fire, an' th' falling sheets of water, I'd be lucky ta' see him 'tall 'fore he was on top of me, diggin' big holes in my skull.

Then there was the problem of my fire. I needed th' fire for light. If it kept rainin' like this - an' I had no reason to b'leve it wouldn't - my fire was gonna go out, 'less I dam' near burned th' woods down, tryin' ta' keep it lit. I could maybe keep a small, sheltered fire goin' in that rain, but the bonfire I *needed*, in order ta' keep a good eye on that cat, wadn't practical nor possible.

That cat, its purrin' goes up a notch, like it knows th' very same thing, an' just been waitin' on it. Th' cat was some twenty, forty feet away, an' I could still hear it purrin', like its just as happy as it can be. A little part of my brain was all panic-whisperin', 'Th' dam' cat made it rain! Th' dam cat made it *RAIN!' TH' DAM' CAT MADE IT RAIN!'*

Wellsir, you start thinkin' things like that when you're already under a load a'stress an' you're gonna start havin' all kinds'a strange fancies. I know I sure did.

For th' moment, I swallowed all that down an' got right ta' work. First order of business was to feed th' fire. If I was real lucky, an' just a tetch careful, I could feed that fire enough ta' keep it smolderin'. Ideally, I wanted it to keep burnin' till th' rain quit. But I knew if I fed it enough ta' last through th' squall, it'd get beyond my control. Weren't no sense in feedin' a bonfire ta' keep a cat at bay if I was gonna burn myself up doin' it.

If I was *really* lucky, th' smoke would drive th' cat off. 'Course, there was th' added danger that *I'd* choke, but I thought maybe I could get out over th' top of th' cliff face. Th' cat sure didn't seem ta' want ta' go that way ta get ta' me, an' I was all for gettin' away from it.

Way things was workin' out, though, I didn't anticipate any of that succeedin' 'tall. So I laid me up a store of good dried wood under my poncho, figurin' I could build a smaller fire there from the guttering remains of th' bigger one. I figured th' poncho was far enough from th' ground ta' keep it from meltin', long as I kept th' fire reasonably small. An' if worst came ta' absolute worst, I could make a torch, at least.

The wind picks up, an' it starts ta' rainin' in earnest. I just kep' on feedin' my blaze, hopin' against hope I could keep 'er goin' through th' storm. It wadn't quite cold enough for th' rain ta' turn ta' ice, but it's plenty cold enough for me ta' be mighty uncomfortable. My only real consolation was the fact I was reasonably dry, anyhow. With all th' layers I had on, I s'pect I'd'a been dry through anything short of a minor flood.

My mind's goin' a mile a minute at this point, an' I come to a decision. I could stay *here*, patiently waitin' for death, or I could go out *there* an' bring death to th' cat. I could die like a rabbit under th' claws of th' hawk, or I could choose th' time an' th' place of my death.

Wadn't all that hard of a choice.

Now, I ain't exactly one a'them 'lympic athletes. I ain't big, an' I ain't all that strong. My daddy says he was twice my size when he was my age. He figured I must'a just been born teeny an' stayed that way, though he couldn't recollect me bein' special small when I was born.

I am in good shape, though, with a wiry frame, a strong grip, an' a set of forearms like them bridge cables. I ain't braggin', I'm just tellin' ya' what's what. Workin' down to th' fac'try twelve hours a day, handlin' them seventy-five pound, undyed, metal ingots keeps me lean an' mean. I guess I handle 'bout a hundred of them fifteen by eighteens a day. You add all that up, that's a mighty load of metal, an' I got my hands on every last bit of it. For a little while, anyhow.

I got good endurance, too. I can walk, settin' a steady pace, all day long.

So I'm relatively confident I can give this cat th' fight it seemed to be itchin' for. First off, I need ta' set things in my favor.

I give 'er a bit of thought, an' then I pulled my bowie, an' I set to work. Now, like I say before, my bowie ain't pretty. Ain't nothin' fancy 'bout it 'tall. It ain't one'a them filigreed ones like you find in th' mall. Them thing's got all kinds'a gold wire an' scroll work, an' they ain't worth two farts in a high wind. My bowie's a utility knife. It's a mean, thick, wide, long length of metal, sharp as daylight an' twice as mean. I keep it sharp's I know how, an' I keep it clean. Th' metal's scarred, an' so's the wood on th' handle, but I'm willin' ta' bet my bowie'll be here two, three hundred years from now, still cuttin' an' doin' what it's for. I take it with me whenever I go hikin' or campin'.

My bowie was handed down from my daddy, who got it from his daddy, who got it from *his* daddy. Long tradition of hardy, wood-lovin' men in my family, an' ever' one of 'em was smart enough ta' take a big ol' knife out with 'em.

I sorted out ten lengths of wood from my pile; 'bout two, three inches across, 'bout four feet long. I lopped off all th' little branches 'till I got me a nice, straight, clean length of wood. It took me a little while ta' get th' hang of it, an' I 'bout dam' near cut a finger'er two off. After a couple'a mis-tries, my hands got th' idea, an' I could get me a good spear length of wood after about forty-five minutes of hard work.

I didn't have a lot of good, straight wood like I wanted, so I had ta' chop, an' cut down, an' basically shape what I wanted from what I did have. It was long, hard work, but it kep' my mind off th' idea of gettin' killed by a homicidal wildcat.

Once I had me ten, fifteen lengths like I wanted, I set to sharpenin' th' ends. This wasn't as hard work, but it was a mite tricky. 'Bout like sharpenin' a pencil with a butcher knife. You sharpen too fine, ya' break yer point. You sharpen too shallow, ya' end up with a blunted point. Neither one would'a done me a bit'a good.

This took a lot of practice, an' I shortened my spear lengths down a good foot doin' it. I musta cussed th' air around me blue, what with th' slivers an' th' nicks I was gettin'. When I reckoned th' ends' was as sharp as they was gonna get, I set th' tip of my spear in my fire for a bit.

Now, I don't know nothin' about th' way Indians used to harden arrows. I mean, I know they used green lengths of wood, an' they hardened th' shafts somehow in fire or smoke, but I don't know how they did it. I'm not tryin' ta' make me a perfect spear, though, an' I ain't out here, revitalizin' some long, lost tradition. This here's about basic survival. I'm just lookin' ta' do what I can ta make sure my spear tip ain't gonna splinter inta' ten-thousand slivers against th' cat's hide when I toss it. That wouldn't do me a bit of good, an' it'd make that cat madder'n hell.

I wanted th' spear to penetrate; like one a'them matadors do with them bulls they fight. If I could get enough of my spears in its hide, it slow th' dam' thing down an' get some blood flowin'. Eventually, after enough a'that, we'd be on even-er ground.

After givin' it a bit a'thought, I reckoned leavin' th' spear tip in th' flames just long enough to blacken it just a bit was as good as I was gonna get.

279

Ever' so often, that cat nosed around th' fire's edges, lookin' ta' see what was what. I was canny to its game now, though, an' I let it prowl. I even took ta' mockin' it just a bit.

"Yeaaaaaaahh! You don't *like* it when a feller starts ta' *thinkin'*, do ya', ya' overgrown rug? Starts makin' ya' *nervou*s when a man settles down an' starts usin' his superior intellect, don't it?"

That cat, it'd give one of its screams in response to my voice, an' go back to lyin' down, waitin' for me ta' move.

Me, I hunkered down an' made spears.

I reckon I made spears 'till th' sun come up.

I was tired by that time, an' my fingers was just as sore as they could be. I reckon I busted 'em enough times to qualify for one'a them record books. I got me little nicks all over my hands, my wrists, my forearms, an' I could barely close my hands to make a fist, my hands were so swole.

Only good news was, I reckoned that cat had been awake all night, too. An' it hadn't had th' warm, comfortable night I'd had. It was out there in th' cold an' th' wet, hungry an' irritable, while I was warm an' dry an' reasonably well fed. I reckoned he'd be lookin' ta' take him a quick cat nap here pretty soon.

It'd quit rainin', at least, an' that much was a blessin'.

I cupped me up some water from my canteen, an' I let my hands soak for a few minutes in th' cold. Wouldn't do me a lick a'good ta' not be able ta' close 'em. After that, I started ta' thinkin' on how I'm gonna carry my spears. I must'a had me about thirty of 'em - maybe forty - and I wadn't even gonna try an' carry 'em in my hands like a bundle'a firewood. I give 'er some thought, an' I started ta' havin' some 'do or die' thinkin'. Way I figured it at th' time, I was either gonna die, or I wasn't, so anything that wadn't immediately useful to prevent my dyin' wadn't gonna come with me.

That included my poncho.

Wellsir, it 'bout like ta' break my heart ta' do it, but I went ahead an' cut my poncho down inta strips 'bout two feet wide, an' a couple'a feet long. I took my spears an' wrapped two or three of th' strips around 'em real tight like. I tied th' ends of th' strips together 'til I had me a sort of half quiver. Then I took th' remaining strips, an' tied th' quiver so it set low on my back, off one hip. Th' spears stuck out 'bout two feet in front a'me, an' two feet behind. It wadn't pretty, an wadn't nothin' elegant about it, but it wadn't gonna get in my way, so I was happy about that much, anyway.

Like I say, I wadn't tryin' ta' win no prizes with this. I was tryin' ta' stay alive.

Once I had my spears set, I had me some breakfast. I et all th' food an' drunk all th' water I could hold, and then I et some more. I et so much, I felt like a tick on a buffalo's backside. I was so full I could barely stand up!

Th' cat, it gets to growlin' an' yowlin, mutterin' an' gruntin'. I figure it reckoned I'm 'bout ready ta' make a move.

Me, I just hunkered down an' waited for th' sun to come up proper, feedin' my fire up with what was left of th' wood I'd set by.

It was wet, an' drizzly-cold, tryin' ta decide whether it was gonna snow or not. I wadn't happy 'bout that, but there wadn't much I could do about it, either. I shrugged, an' said, "I'll take 'er as she comes, Lord."

I figured it wadn't much of a prayer, but even a weak one's better than none.

Once th' sun got up proper, I set out. I couldn't see no sign of th' cat. I stepped real careful, away from the rockface, an' I just stood there for a minute, listenin'.

My daddy always said, 'Boy, you go out to th' woods, you spend a minute listenin' ta' what she's got ta' say. Sometimes she'll tell you all you need ta' know, right then an' there.'

Daddy didn't say it, but I kinda picked up what else he meant when he said that - 'Stand still an' use *all* your senses. Let your mind attune itself to th' woods an' pick up on what she's sayin'. It's just like steppin' into a cave. You gotta take a minute an' let yer eyes adjust.'

Wellsir, I stood there for a good five minutes, listenin', an' breathin' through my mouth, tastin' th' air.

I couldn't hear nothin' but rain an' th' dyin' crackle of my fire. I couldn't smell nothin' but smoke, mold, an' normal forest smells.

I had one hand on my spears, an' one hand holdin' my rifle, my finger on th' trigger. It wadn't 'tall safe, an' I was a mite concerned I'd trip an' blow my brains out, but I figured sittin' still was sure suicide - by cat, no less - while holdin' a loaded rifle an' traipsin' off through th' woods was only a 'maybe' sort.

I stood there for a minute.

Then I stood there for another minute.

Then I stood there for yet another minute.

My head's yammerin' at me, an' I'm burnin' daylight, standin' there. I'm lookin' all around, an' this little voice in my head keeps sayin', 'Alrighty, David. Now step away from th' rockface.'

An' I tried. I surely did, but I couldn't do it.

I tried ta' make my feet work, tried ta' get 'im ta' move me away from that rockface, but my feet wouldn't move. They was frozen in place. Not by cold, mind you, they was frozen in place by fear. I was too scared ta' take that all important first step. I kep' imaginin' twelve-hundred pounds of feline death hurtlin' at me from nowhere. I kep' feelin' rippin' claws an' bitin' teeth. I guess I'd still be standin' there, tryin' ta' get my legs ta' work. I was still listenin' ta' what the woods was tryin' ta' tell me with half my mind, but th' other half rose up in some sort of survival instinct, an' reached back through my personal his'try ta' drag up somethin' that'd get me movin'.

For no reason 'tall, I flashed on my daddy. For just a second - while I'm standin' there, tryin' ta' get a sense of what th' woods is tellin' me, an' ta' get my dam' feet movin' - my daddy was there with me.

He was near enough seven feet tall as made no difference, an' as broad across th' shoulders as a barn door. 'Strong as a bull an twice as ugly,' is th' way my Momma put it. She'd grab him by th' back of his head an' kiss im 'till Daddy's knees started ta' wobble.

'Hoo-ooooooooo-WEE! What a man!' she'd say, an' Daddy'd blush every single time.

She cried every day for ten years after he died, an' that's all you need to know 'bout their relationship.

Daddy, he'd take me with him sometimes when he went huntin'. Some of th' huntin' he did wadn't strictly legal, an' Daddy'd be philosophical about that. 'Boy, way I figure it, it's a man's duty to poach every so often. Otherwise them game boys'd be outta work!'

He 'd grin down at me, a wad a'chew bigger'n my face in his jaw, his rifle held causal in both hands an' a mischievous twinkle in his eyes. He'd put his hand on th' back of my neck an' he'd smile that shark-eatin' smile'a his.

"Boy," he'd say, for no particular reason, "you get ta' havin' some mighty fee-low-saw-fuh-cull maunderins when yer facin' an immediate sort'a mortality."

Then he'd raise th' rifle in one continuous movement - like it was as nat'ral as breathin' - an' blow some poor critter ta' hell.

"But fee-low-saw-fuh-cull maunderin' beats bein' dinner any day."

Then he'd drop me a wink an' we'd go get whatever it was he'd just kilt. Daddy'd have no problem with this cat. He'd grab it up by th' scruff of its dam' neck an' shake it 'til all its bones broke.

For that frozen instant, my daddy was so close I could smell the Skoal. My heart clenched like a fist inside me, an' I 'bout dam' near burst into tears. I was scared, now! Scared'a what was gonna happen soon's I took that first step away from th' rockface. But then I felt somethin' like a hand on th' back of my neck, an' a deep, warm voice whispered in my ear.

'Beats bein' dinner, boy.'

I swear he was laughin'. That was all it took. I stepped away from th' rock, an' I kep' goin'. I like ta' think Daddy laughed, leaned over his cloud, an' spit a wad a'chaw in that cat's eyes, blindin' it just long enough for me ta' get started.

One thing ya'll need to know 'bout my woods. They's full of ravines, cliffs, bog-holes an' sink holes. My entire state is built on this loose an' crumbly foundation a'limestone. I heard tell 'bout this geology feller who suggested that if we went plumbin' deep enough, we might just find th' whole state's sittin' on this loose bubble a' limestone. One good earthquick, an' we'd all be breathin' sod.

On account of this here natural phenomenon, you got ta' be careful an' keep an eye on where you're steppin'. You go ta' take a step, you might just step right off into glory. That becomes important later, so make sure you hold on to 'er.

I reckon I made about a mile. I think back on it now, an' I can't tell you what I was thinkin' when I went out into them woods and the cat's territory. I must'a been half-blind, an' deaf in th' bargain.

I'm walkin' along, quiet as a mouse in a cat's boodwar, an' I can't hear nothin' but th' rain. I mean, weren't no bird song, weren't no critters, weren't nothin' 'tall in that woods makin' normal life noises.

'Boy,' my Daddy's voice pipes up in my head, 'that's 'cause that dam' cat a' yourn done et it all.' Wellsir, I don't know if my Daddy's ghost was right or not, but it made for a nervous hike, I can tell you that.

Now, as I'm tryin' ta'; get *out*, I'm lookin' an seein' all kinds of sign that I just plain missed on my way *in*. Over there's a tree been marked by fifteen, twenty seasons of claws. An' them claw marks is seperated . . . wellsir. Lemme explain. See, with a big cat, they'll approach a tree an' stretch their claws, just like a little cat'll do on a couch. Most claw marks like that are - dependin' on th' type a' cat - maybe five, six feet off th' ground. Lemme see if I can explain this better. When you get home, go into your bathroom an' shut th' door. Turn the hot water on, an' let 'er run for a bit. What we want here is for th' bathroom mirror to get good an' fogged. Now. Spread your fingers, wide as you can, an' drag your fingers across th' surface of th' mirror, makin' trails in th' moisture. How far apart is them trails on your mirror? Two inches? Three? If you got some mighty big hands, it might be as much as four inches. For an average cat in these parts, the claw marks is usually pretty close together. You might find one with a spread of three inches, maybe a bit more.

These marks, the ones a good seven, eight feet over my head, an' a good six feet down the trunk of this here tree, is nearly a foot apart. I ain't never been no good at math, but I do some quick figurin'. Way I reckoned it, if these claw marks belonged to th' cat, that cat's eight foot tall. At th' shoulder. Th' biggest tiger ever lived ain't as big as this cat.

282

You ever seen a tiger? They's about nine-hundred pounds, an' maybe five foot tall at th' shoulder, if they's a *big* tiger. This cat's three, four foot taller than *any* Tiger.

You startin' ta' get an idea of how I felt right about then?

I start seein' tufts of hair everywhere. I mean, I don't know how I missed all this comin' in! This cat's been livin' here for a *long* time, these clumps a'hair are any indication. Now that I'm attuned to it, I can smell th' cat's musk, too.

Again, I don't know what I was doin' to have missed all these clues. Th' dam' musk alone should been enough to clue me in. I musta' just been 'bout half asleep. This cat, it don't do nothin' by no half measures, neither. Ain't no little bit of musk. This cat's dam' near tear-gassin' th' whole area. It's makin' tears run from my eyes. I can taste it!.

I'm gonna tell you th' truth. I 'bout lost it right there. I'm standin' there, starin' at these grooves dug into the heartwood of this tree, spittin' my mouth clear of the taste of cat piss, an' I'm realizin' that this here cat shouldn't - *can't!* - exist. I mean, this ain't Africa or India. Ain't no great big lions or tigers out here. Even if I was mistaken, an' these claws belonged to a bear of some kind, that bear'd hafta be the size of Godzilla. That bear'd be the great-grandaddy of every bear ever.

An' if I don't know nothin' else, I *do* know sign. Them's the marks of a cat, an' tryin' ta' pretend they ain't won't do me a lick a'good.

I start to panickin', I start havin' prey-thought. Instead of bein' th' highly armed, reasonin' human bein' I am, I turn into this jittery glob a' human jelly. I start hyperventilatin' an' I whip my rifle up, my shoulders hunched, eyes wide.

I must'a stood there a good five minutes, tryin' to get some kind of a grip on myself, just sweatin', shakin', an' whimperin' gently. It wadn't one of my finer moments, I can tell you that.

Right about then, I hear this ground-shakin' yowl, from back near my camp site. See, in th' midst of all my panickin', I had forgotten somethin' mighty important my Daddy had told me.

'Animals is smarter than we are, boy. They got them Professor Noses. You ever out in th' woods, you remember that.'

With all my sweatin' an' shakin', I had become the incredible human-fear-pheromone-givin'-off-fac'try. I'd just told that cat *exactly* where I was, an' further, that I was 'bout ready ta' piss my pants. Hell. That cat could tell my brand'a toothpaste by now.

Wellsir, 'bout then I just lost it, an' I started runnin'. Didn't have no idea where I was runnin' to, I just ran.. It took that cat 'bout two minutes to cover th' distance 'tween us. I could hear it crashin' in th' woods behind me, yowlin' an' growlin'. It sounded 'bout like a helicopter caught in a threshin' machine. Luckily I had th' presence of mind to loop my rifle over my chest before I took off. I reckon that was Daddy again. It was th' kind of thing he'd do, hangin' his rifle over his chest before he took off.

I'm runnin' for all I'm worth, just pumpin' an' hustlin, and I ain't payin' a bit of attention to where I'm goin'. I'm crashin' through bushes, bouncin' off trees, trippin' an' slidin', runnin' flat-out. Wellsir, be damned if I didn't manage ta' run right off th' edge of a dam' cliff.

I guess I fell 'bout ten feet, screamin' like a banshee, an then my half-quiver a'spears snags on a outcroppin' a'rock, jerkin' me to a stop, an' knockin' th' air out of me. Wellsir, I hung there, hiccupin', sweatin', an' sort of half-sobbin'. I weren't makin' no noise, mind you. It was more of this sort of chest-hitch, on account of I ain't got no air. After a minute of this indignity, I try ta' pull myself together as I'm tryin' ta' get my breath back. Once I got myself breathin' somewhat normal, I look around an' try ta' get a handle on things. I'm danglin' like a worm on a hook, 'bout twenty feet of th' ground. Below me there's a sluggish crik full'a slush, mud an' th' melted remains of last night's semi-sleet-snow storm. I gasp an' pant an' try ta' get 'holt of myself, best I can.

Right about then, I hear this low, grumblin' mutter from above me. Without thinkin' about it, I spin over in my lil' sling. I got adrenaline surgin' through me all of a sudden, an' it ends up bein' mighty easy. My poncho gives me this warning rip, but that's not nearly as worrisome as what I see, now that I'm facin' th' edge of this here ravine.

I'm ten feet down from th' edge, and when I see th' face that comes over the top of it, I suddenly wish I'd fallen th' rest of th' way.

I reckon it's about time for me ta' tell what had been chasin' me all this time. Only problem is, I really can't. I was too busy tryin' ta' stay alive ta' take detailed notes, you understand. I can describe it to you, let you make your own assumptions, but you're just gonna assume I'm a liar. An' that's fine. In this great country of ours, you're entitled ta' b'leve whatever you want. Long as you keep your opinions to yourself, an' don't call me a liar to my face, you can think anything you want to. 'Course, if for some reason, you just feel like startin' a fight . . . .

No?

Well, alright. I reckon I wouldn't do much more than bleed all over ya', anyhow.

Lemme back track a little. Where was I? Oh yeah! So there I am, danglin from th' edge of this here cliff, like a worm on a hook. I ain't strugglin'. I ain't makin' no noise. I ain't so much as breathin' hard.

I got my mouth open, tryin' ta' make as little noise as I can, an' the taste of that cat comes boilin' over th' edge of that cliff. It 'bout like ta' suffocate me, then an' there. It was like I was cleanin' out th' bottom of some circus lion cage, or somethin'. It was awful.

That cat's growlin', low in its chest. I can hear it creepin' up on th' edge, an' I can feel its growlin' in my own chest. I don't reckon I had a thought in my head 'tall. I was plumb froze up with fear, shakin' an' tremblin' in my little poncho hammock, twenty feet above th' ground, ten foot from th' edge.

When it finally come over that edge, it come over like a tsunami, an avalanche; unstoppable an' it just kep' comin'. It started with th' eyes, an' that's where I'm gonna start. That's what I saw first, after all, that dam' cat's glowin', emerald, devil eyes. It come over that edge like a growlin' sunrise, eyes first.

I heard it told enough times when I was a boy, an' I know it to be true: you can tell th' devil by his eyes.

'Boy,' my Daddy'd say, in his voice of fallin' timber, 'you make sure you look a man in his eyes when you talk to him. You can tell th' devil by lookin' in his eyes.'

Wellsir, I'm here ta' tell you, that's the Good Lord's Own truth, sure enough. I know. I done looked th' devil in his eyes an' lived ta' tell about it. I ain't braggin', I'm just sayin' what's what.

They was about a foot apart, them eyes, set in a skull bigger'n a rhino's. Them eyes was th' size of a softball, or maybe a small bowlin'-ball, with a slit pupil in each - a blade'a darkest night - like you see in any cat's eyes. The eyes themselves was th' green of jade, or deep forest green.

Like I say, th' eyes was the size of a small bowlin'-ball. 'Bout eight, nine, maybe, ten inches across. They was a foot across from each other in that cat's skull.

Now, if you was drawin' somethin' ta' scale, you'd take an eye, an' you put it between th' corner of th' eye an' th' ear, if you're viewin' it straight on, like I was. Add up th' diameter of th' eye, an' the distance seperating each eye. Then add up th' diameter of all th' eyes together, an' you get th' diameter across, if my math's at all correct.

Wellsir, I been convalescin' for a while now, an' I had time on my hands ta' do some figurin'. If my math's correct, I got me some fifty-two inches wide, from ear to ear, give or take a whisker. That's four feet *wide*, not long, you understand. That cat's hed was fifty-two some odd inches *wide*.

But that's all after th' fact reckonin'. That's stuff you think about after you done laid up in a hospital bed for three weeks, lettin' 'em stitch ya' back together. Right then, I was too busy seein' th' outer dark beyond infinity in that cat's eyes. I looked into them eyes, an' I swear, I could see beyond forever.

They was hungry, those eyes, mad. But what scared me even more was I could see that cat was lookin' back at me. You know what I mean? I ain't talkin' that th' cat was lookin' at me. That's obvious. What I mean is, that cat was lookin' at me, an it was *seein'* me.

Ahhh, hell. I ain't got th' words. I'm just a poor, dumb redneck. I reckon one a'them poet fellers could tell you right away what I was sayin', but y'all're stuck with this good ol' boy. It's like, th' cat was lookin' down on me, an' it was *thinkin'* at me. You know? Not 'Unngah. Cat eat mouse,' but like, 'Well, boy. You thought you had run away, didn't ya'?'

That cat was lookin' down at me, an' I realized I was lookin' at an equal, mental-wise, if not a superior bein'. An' that's mighty dam' humblin', I can tell you that.

Th' head, like I say, was bigger'n a rhino's head, but flat, like any cat's. It was maybe, four, five feet wide, an' sloped back from th' top of th' cat's head. Th' most remarkable thing about that cat's head wasn't its size, b'leve it or not, but its *teeth*.

Now, like I say, you're probably gonna say I'm a liar, but you keep that to yourself, an' think whatever you want to. I'm just tellin' you how it was.

This cat had two enormous front teeth - almost like them Cavalry sabers th' boys down to the VA break out, an' use in them re-enactments they do every Fourth of July - that curved down below its lower jaw. Th' lower jaw had these two recesses - like, slotted ratchet holders in a tool box - where th' front teeth came down an' fitted. I reckon th' mouth of this cat must've been able to open wide enough to neatly snip my top from my bottom, like poppin' a dandelion poof.

Them awful, saber-like front teeth was about four feet long, and easily a foot an' a half wide. Each. I could smell dead things on its breath. I saw see bits of rotted meat clingin' to them awful teeth an' its lower jaw.

That head just kept comin' over th' edge, long after I thought it was done. By the time th' cat was lookin' down at me, its head fully visible, th' dam' sun was nearly eclipsed!

Wellsir, there we were. Man an' cat, each regardin' each th' other.

Th' cat's lookin' down at me from its place above me. I ain't of a poetical bent, but I reckon th' cat was tryin' to swallow my soul. I *know* it was takin' th' heart from me, just sittin' up there, lickin' its lips an' lookin' down on me.

I ain't ashamed to admit it: I was scared. I was scared I was gonna die, here, pretty quick, an' it was gonna be relatively awful. Nobody honestly wants ta' die, but don't nobody never want ta' get eaten by some psychotic, homicidal devil cat, what shoulda been extinct twelve grillion years ago, neither. I mean, if you're gonna go, there's much nicer ways a'doin' it!

'Course, that's all back-of-my-mind, after-th'-fact, thinkin'. At th' time, all I could think of, all I could even *see*, was that cat's eyes, like th' lanterns a'hell, glowin' down on me.

285

Wellsir, that cat gives with one of its roars. It reared back from th' edge of th' cliff, throws its head at th' sky, an' roars, triumphant-like. Th' noise is awful. It shakes th' small bones in my head, an' sets my teeth to rattlin'. It's almost as if th' cat picked th' exact harmonic frequency necessary ta' make my head come unglued. If th' noise is bad, th' thin layer of cat spit I subsequently got sprayed with is even worse. It was almost as if it was rainin'. It smelled awful, an' it felt like I was gettin' pissed on.

I ain't never seen, nor heard, of any kind of a cat doin' that; roarin' triumphant over prey that ain't dead, an' it spurred me to action. Truth be told, it made me mad's, what it did.

'This cat's roarin' over me, an' I ain't dead yet? No, sir! We can't have nothin' like *that*! If I'm goin' out, I'm gonna make this dam' cat remember me, at least!'

I like to think that's what I thought, but I 'magine I was operatin' more on primal instinct that any sort of intelligent, reasonin' thought.

I reached back with one hand an' pulled my rifle up. Wellsir, I lifted that rifle up an' fire it 'bout th' same time as th' cat's swipin' down at me with a paw th' size of a tree. Good news was, I winged 'em.

Bad news? Th' cat connected too.

'I been shot! I been shot!'

Leastwise, that's what I was thinkin' as I commenced to fallin'. That cat had reached down from th' edge an' swiped at me with its paw. I felt th' enormous impact as its paw connected with my chest, an' before I could do anything about it, I was fallin' again.

I fell for ten-thousand years an' hit that slurry of dirty snowmelt, in the crik beneath me with a splash, half-convinced I was dead.

Th' fall must'a knocked me out for a few seconds, or maybe I was just too discombobulated ta' make much sense of up or down. At any rate, I don't remember a whole lot in-between fallin' that twenty feet an' 'comin' to', a little while later.

Earliest I remember, I was lyin' in some freezin' muck, waitin' for th' afterlife to begin.

My ears is ringin', an' I can't hear a thing over th' Gene Krupa solo goin' on in my head. I lay there, in th' mud, waitin' for angels or devils or whatever, when somethin' strikes me as bein' kinda funny.

'If I'm dead, why's my heart hammerin' so hard?'

I didn't know it at th' time, but here's what I've reconstructed after th' fact. When I lifted my rifle, th' cat was swipin' down with his paw. He connected with my poncho - shearin' through it like it was paper - my rifle, an' my chest, in that order. My shot got him, but his claws got me. Meantime, I'm fallin' down th' cliff, since my poncho is so many tatters, flappin' away in th' breeze.

Wellsir, I sat up, coughin' an' splutterin', an' I stumbled my way over to th' bank of th' crik. I flop onto th' bank like a grounded fish, an' just lay there, on my back, breathin' as deeply as I can an' enjoyin' th' sensation of bein' alive.

After a bit, I took stock. First off, I got a deep, burnin' ache in my chest an' belly. I look down, an' I see my coat's been ripped from th' left side, all the way across my front, to about my belly button. Th' cloth is hangin' off'a me in shreds an' tatters. The cat tore through a layer of leather, my plaid huntin' shirt, my undershirt, my t-shirt, an' a layer of Gore-Tex underwear. It also dug four trenches across th' skin of my chest, each 'bout an inch deep an' two foot long. They ain't all that bad; kinda thing you'd go to th' 'mergency room for, get some stitches an' some antibiotics. Couple'a inches deeper, an' I'd be lookin' at the loops an' whirls of my own guts. It hurt like fire.

They's bleedin' pretty steadily, though, an' I ain't got th' proper means to stop that 'tall.

I rip off a shred of shirt, an' hold it to th' cuts as best I can, while I look around for my rifle.

Wellsir, that's more bad news. That cat hit my rifle so hard, it's done bent th' barrel a good fifteen degrees out of true. It ain't nothin' but so much scrap now.

I look around, tryin' ta' find even so much as *one* spear, but they's all spread ta' hell an' gone.

From above me, I can hear th' muted yowlin' of th' cat. He ain't soundin' so triumphant now. Now he sounds hurt, surprised, and most unfortunate for me, awfully dam' mad. Th' cat's yowlin' an' roarin' up there on its cliff, 'bout twenty-five above me. I'm down here, soaked to th' skin, bleedin', shiverin' an' tryin' ta' pull my scattered thinkin' together.

I'm fast runnin' out of options. I didn't much fancy my chances of tryin' ta' outrun th' cat; not with those holes bleedin' steadily in my gut. Fire was out; I didn't have any, nor did I have th' time ta' get one started. My rifle was no good, 'cept as maybe a club'er somethin'. Diggin' a pit, linin' it with sharpened stakes, or somethin'? Some kind of a trap? I ain't got th' time. My spears was gone.

I started pattin' my pockets, watchin' th' grass an' underbrush thrash at th' top of th' cliff I done just fell off. My hand lights on th' hilt of my Daddy's bowie knife. I draw 'er out, an' give 'er a good look.

Like I say, my Daddy's bowie was a thick, stout, hunk'a metal, sharp as a preacher's comments on Sunday after Saturday night. It's closer ta' bein' a skinny axe then it is a knife, an' I can't tell you how relieved I felt when I finally remembered I had it with me.

I wadn't all that confident about my abilities ta' fight off a two-ton-homicidal-devil-cat, hurt or not, but 'least I wouldn't go out without leavin' a couple'a holes in that cat's hide.

We was kinda even-up at this point: th' cat's hurt, I'm hurt. The cat's got razor-sharp claws as log as my forearm, I got my Daddy's bowie. Only trouble was, that cat could absorb a dam' sight more hurt than I could, an' do it without too much trouble. I just shot th' thing in th' face with a .30-30. You'd think it'd lie down an' die! Nosir. If anything, th' dam' thing's madder'n it was before.

Lucky, lucky me.

Th' cat didn't give me much time ta' think, neither. 'Bout a minute or so after I pull myself from th' crik, th' cat showed its face over th' ledge.

I got 'im, alright. I got 'im good, too. Th' right side of its face was a mass of blood an' gore. Its right eye was completely gone, an' I could see splintered fragments from th' orbit of its eye lyin' on th' fur of its cheek. Near as I can figure now, with th' luxury ta' do so, I got 'im in th' side of th' eye. My round exited th' right side of its right eye, takin' a good chunk of its face with it. That close, there weren't no spallin'. Th' round must'a entered th' center of that cat's right eye, an' just kep' goin'.

A couple'a millimeters closer to th' left, an' I'd'a got it in its brain. It'd'a died, but I 'magine it'd've rolled right off a th' cliff on top of me. I'd'a been deader than my Momma's Sunday night pot roast on Tuesday mornin'.

I ain't gonna lie. I got me a nice, warm, defiant kinda glow, seein' th' blood runnin' from that ruined eye socket. I might'a even smiled.

'Course, that cat didn't want me feelin' good. It didn't want me feelin' no kinda'a positive emotion, an' by this time, I'm half convinced this here psychotic-devil-cat could read my dam' mind.

It threw its head up at th' sky an' roared sprayin' blood an' all kinds'a nastiness everywhere. It almost sounded like it was tryin' ta' clear its throat, an' roar, all at th' same time. I reckoned it was havin' a mite'a trouble with blood runnin' down its airtubes.

Th' roar was loud, mean', an' fierce, but it also sounded just a mite bit crazy. Like I say, I ain't got th' words for describin' things, but I reckoned there was a madness in that roar, now. Th' cat was losin' whatever sense of 'straight-thinkin'' it might've once had, an' it was goin' for th' blood-spray; revertin' ta' type; jazzin' itself up ta' spread me across th' landscape in a thin layer'a David-innards.

Yessir. It was *go* time.

Th' cat, it kinda looked down at me, an' roared an' growled an' muttered. It looked down th' face of th' cliff, an'then it looked down at me. It roared some more, an' shuffled around up there, movin' like it was lookin' for a way down.

I half expected it to pounce on me from way up there, but th' cat surprised me. It sorta trotted its way off th' ledge, into th' crick. Mind you, this was my first good look at how big this thing really was. Th' cliff was twenty, twenty-five feet high, an' it looked for all th' world like th' cat was just walkin' down stairs as it came down that cliff. I swear on my Momma's grave: th' cat's front paws was in th' crik at the same time its hind paws was still on the cliff-ledge.

It kinda poured from th' cliff like God's own pitcher'a sunshine; all tawny-gold and an infinity a'mighty muscles ripplin' like snakes below th' skin. 'Bout took my breath away, th' magnificence of this cat. Wadn't an ounce a' fat on it anywhere.

My next-door neighbor, he owns him one'a them new tractors, with th' air-conditioned high-boy cab, an' all. It's got that GPS feature, what can make th' tractor turn down a row of tobacco with th' precision of a Swiss watch. This cat was just about th' same size as that tractor. Th' tractor's taller than th' cat was, but not by much.

I wadn't really payin' much attention to th' cat's walk at this moment, but if I'd'a stopped an' give 'er some thought, I'd'a realized that it was stumblin', pitchin', an' rollin' in its walk. It looked like it'd gotten into the 'medicinal' still my Daddy kep' in th' basement.

'Course, that information came ta' be important later, an' luckily I managed ta' remember it, but at th' moment, I was too busy scrabblin' backwards an' tryin' ta' learn how ta' fly.

Wellsir, th' cat, he crawled up out that crik an onto my bank, stumblin' an' reelin'. This close to, I could see the cat's fur really well. There was patches of green, yellow, red an' ochre in this cat's fur, an' it looked for all th' world like there was moss growin' on it in places. I look at that cat's fur in my mind's eye now, an' I get this sense of incredible age.

'Course, that weren't no comfort then.

Th' cat was yowlin', an' roarin'; kinda lookin' up at me out th' left side of its head. It was kinda approachin' me from an oblique angle, with this lurchin' forward-an'-back movement; like it was doin' a dance of some kind. I watched that forward-an'-back dance for a bit, tryin' ta' figure out what that cat was up to. It came up close to me, an' it yowled at me in a high-pitched, crazy-like way. I 'bout pissed my pants right there.

It kinda sat up on its haunches an' bats at me, like you see a cat at home do with a string. Didn't touch me, just batted at me with its paw.

'Boy,' my Daddy's ghost said in my head, 'that cat's tryin' ta' bluff you. You stand your ground, now. It's gonna be alright.' Now, it didn't take no kind a'rocket-scientist-thinkin' ta' see that was so. If th' cat was confident of bein' able ta' take me, it woulda done did so already.

So I switched my Daddy's bowie to my dominant hand - my left - and I started lungin' at th' cat, like you do on th' football field: shoulders forward, arms out to grab. I started yellin' for all I was worth right back at th' cat.

"Hey, you dumb so-an'-so! You're nothin' but a walkin' rug! You're ain't nothin but a sumbitch, an' so's your Daddy!"

I apologize for th' crudity of my language, most 'specially to th' lady, but it *was* a life-er-death kinda situation.

Like I say, I'm cussin' at th' cat. An' I reckoned I was makin' him good an' mad. Somebody said th' things to me about my Daddy, I was sayin' to this cat, I'd cut their dam' head off. An' that's a fact.

Wellsir, th' cat, he kinda reared back, when I started shoutin' at it, an' he looked for a minute like he was surprised. I wouldn't put it past 'im. He was a *powerful* smart cat. I could almost see him thinkin', 'Hang on a minute, boy. This here ain't th' way this is s'posed ta' go! Somethin' here ain't right t'all!'

He takes him a minute 'er two to think things over, that surprised look on his face th' whole time. Meanwhile, th' two of us was steadily bleedin'.

That cat, he decided that volume is th' way ta' go here. He jumped up on all fours again, an' he roared fit ta' shake th' leaves from th' trees.

I can't match 'im for volume, so I go th' other route.

'Whinchat shut up, you . . . you . . . big, dumb, grass-ape! You're gettin' on my dam' nerves!'

I admit it. I wadn't exactly scintillatin' in my tauntin'.

Th' cat, he reckoned he's heard just about enough of my voice, I guess, an' that's when he decides he's gonna take a swipe at me.

You ain't never seen nothin' move so fast in your life. I guarantee it. One minute, he's standin' 'bout six foot away, peerin' at me from his one good eye. Next minute, my hair is blowin' back from my face, an' I have me a sudden, perfectly clear 'moment-of-death' vision; with th' light an' th' dead relatives beckonin' me onward, home ta' glory, an' all that. I saw my whole life pass before my eyes while I'm watchin' - like it's in slow motion - this paw th' size of a helicopter blade come at me. I swear, I could see th' air compress in front of that paw.

It's loomin' larger an' larger in my vision, comin' at me inexorably. It gets ta' be about th' size of th' moon, an' that's when I reckoned I didn't really want ta' see this, so I closed my eyes.

I heard this sort of whooshin' noise, and I thought. 'Welp. That's it. Here I come, Daddy.'

I opened my eyes in time ta' see th' cat lookin' confused, its paw swipin down below it, like it ain't quite got control of where it goes. I chance a look down my front.

I'm still bleedin', of course, but there weren't nothin' *new* there, neither.

Near as I could figure it, his paw passed inches away from where I was standin'. If he'd a been just a bit closer, he'd a strung my intestines across three acres of trees, evacuating my abdominal cavity with one swipe.

Wellsir, I reckon I shoulda bought th' farm right then an' there. He shoulda got 'holt of me an' shook me to pieces like a rag doll. But he missed. An' that's when I realized he was probably havin' *serious* trouble with his depth perception. I'd done shot out one of his eyes - it was too much ta' hope I'd plugged 'em in the brain - but a one-eyed cat with screwed-up depth perception wadn't nearly th' threat that same cat would be whole.

He didn't give me much time ta' put this information ta' use, though. I started backin' away, given myself some fightin' room, an' that's when th' cat swiped at me again. This time, he got a piece of me.

I heard this noise when th' cat hit me. It was th' loudest noise I've ever heard in my whole life. It was so loud, it left itself engraved on th' soft tissue of my soul. I can still hear it now. It comes roilin' an' boilin out of th' swamp I carry around in th' underside of my head. You got one too. It's th' swamp where that little monkey inside us lives. It's important, that swamp. Th' sound, it plays itself in my dreams. It's like this giant tore up a great, big pine tree an' then he broke it, slowly, over his knee. I get a shock of pain, all th' way up my shoulder, every single time I hear that sound in my dreams. .

It's th' sound of my right arm breakin' in sixteen places after gettin' hit by a saber-tooth-tiger paw.

Th' cat, he reared up in that impossibly fast way of his, an' he swiped at me again. I had my left hand out, with my Daddy's bowie in it, and my right hand was kind of wardin' th' cat off; like a traffic cop directin' a particularly bad snarl. I guess I wadn't really thinkin' all that much about it, at th' time. It didn't have a knife in it, after all.

Th' cat, he got 'holt of my right arm with this swipe an' it broke.

It broke *bad*.

Wellsir, I screamed. Weren't no other option possible. I just felt my right arm get tore off, I'm gonna spend a minute or two screaming in pain. Simple.

I screamed bloody murder. I screamed like I got all th' devils in hell, pitchforks in hand, pokin' me in the ass. I scream like somebody's cuttin' at me with rusty knives an' entirely too much enthusiasm. I scream like . . .

Well.

You get th' idea, I'm sure.

I ain't never hurt so bad. That cat, it dam' near ripped my arm off at th' elbow with that swipe. I looked down, all panicked-like, an' all I saw was this bloody mass. Everything below my elbow was utterly trashed. There was this bloody wad of skin, muscle an' splintered bone - hangin', like th' world's biggest booger - from th' remains of my arm. Everything below my right elbow looks like ground hamburger.

My brain was sendin' messages to my right arm, tryin' ta' get some response, but my right arm was just screamin' its agony out for th' universe ta' hear.

Th' cat, he kinda roared this triumphant sort of roar. 'See that, boy? That's what you *get* for messin' with me. You took my eye, I took your arm. Now then. Let's settle this once an' for all, so you can get to digestin'.'

Wellsir, I went totally ape-sh . . . crazy.

I tried, later, ta' reconstruct what happened there; to reason out why my mind just snapped like that. Weren't no good. I can't remember much of th' reasons why, or how, or any of that. I tried for a while, then I give it up as a lost cause. The doctors say it was probably one a'them 'survival instinct' type situations.

I remember the flashing of my Daddy's bowie, an' I think differently. Weren't nothin' much ta' do with *me*, I think. Daddy's bowie knife was always a little . . peculiar . . . after Daddy died.

Ain't no easy way to explain that, an' I'm not real sure I want to. Let's just say that I don't think Daddy let go of it proper after he died.

Then again, maybe I just wanted ta' make sure that if I was gonna die, I was gonna have some company with me when I went.

I got mad. I got madder then I had ever been in my whole life, before or since. I reached down deep within myself, an' from somewhere at th' very beginning of time, I pulled up this scream. Weren't no words in it. It was just this . . . this . . . mindless yell. I opened my mouth, an' this thing come boilin' out, ready for blood, thunder an' all th' rest. It was a scream a trapped Mastodon would've recognized an' feared. It was a scream a herd a'buffalo would'a run from, stampedin' th' plains in their haste ta' get away from it. It was th' scream of every small thing that's been pushed too far by th' large things with teeth. It was th' scream of th' scared, desperate, cornered, an' dyin' rat.

I screamed out with everything I had, an' then I leapt up on that cat, landin' on its back, an' just started stabbin', screamin' th' whole time.

Th' cat, it don't know what's goin' on. Here it was, gettin' ready ta' *finally* eat, an' its meal loses its dam' mind an' starts stabbin at it. It kinda makes this yelpin' noise, an' sorta gets confused for just a second.

Me, I just kep' screamin' an' stabbin'.

Th' cat, he came to a realization, I guess. 'This rat's gonna kill me if'n I don't do somethin' quick!'

Meanwhile, I'm *still* stabbin', screamin', cussin' an' bleedin'. Th' cat ain't exactly built right for me ta' stay put, so I ain't holdin' on all that good. Plus, I only got th' one hand, and that's full of knife.

Th' cat, he kinda tosses hisself a little, an' I end up underneath 'im, on my back, starin' up at his great big teeth.

That cat's eye, as big as a truck's tire, is inches from mine. Th' gaping hole where his other eye used ta' be is drippin' blood an' gore on me. I can smell th' dead things on its breath, an' I could count th' hairs along its muzzle. Th' cat lowers his face closer ta' mine.

He kinda snarls down at me, an' I can see 'im openin' his mouth, gettin' ready ta' tear my head in half. You might think my fight was all done at that point, but not quite.

That same somethin', that same defiant survival-whatever-it-was, it took 'holt of me, an' my left hand, th' one still full of my Daddy's blood-slicked-bowie, an' it buried that sucker up to th' hilt in that cat's breastbone. An' then it twisted it a full three-hundred-sixty degrees, screamin' th' whole time.

I won't never forget th' way it felt when that knife went into th' cat. It was like punchin' through drywall. There was a moment a'resistance, and then she just slid on home. Twistin' it wadn't hard 'tall. Like I say, it mighta been some kinda survival instinct thing, but I like to think it was my Daddy holdin' th' knife. He was th' one with th' hunter's muscles.

Wellsir, didn't neither one of us realize what had happened for a second. That bowie knife slid right in and then twisted around like a doorknob.

From where I'm lyin', mere inches away from th' cat's face, I had me a perfect front seat for observin' th' cat's reactions. Th' cat, his eyes, both th' good one, an' th' destroyed one, they got real wide; like he's had a sudden realization. His lone pupil contracted down ta' nothin' more than a pinprick.

The he let loose with this horrible wail. It was an awful sound. It was full a'fear, an' pain, an' denial an' . . . well, I ain't got th' words, but when that cat wailed, you could hear it dyin'.

It backed up off me an' kinda fell on its rear feet. There was blood pourin' from it, where I stuck three feet of knife, an' it's face was twisted into a pain-filled grimace.

'Boy,' my Daddy's ghost says in my head, 'you get up now. That cat's done, but he's gonna take a while ta' realize it. You keep lyin' there, you're gonna die, an' you're gonna die bad.'

To this day, I don't reckon I know whether it was my Daddy talkin' to me from Heaven, or if it was the smarter, wiser part of me, like, *pretendin'* to be my Daddy so I'd listen. I just don't know. All I know was I heard my Daddy's voice, an' he was given' me some mighty good advice.

I scrambled up, as best I was able, an' I put some distance between me an' th' cat.

Th' cat, he sees me gettin' up, and he growled, low in his throat. It was an evil growl. It was like th' cat was sayin', 'Where you think you're goin', boy? We ain't done yet!'

Wellsir, I kinda held my busted arm as close as I could to my chest.

Up to this point, it really wadn't bleedin' all that much, leastways, not as much as you'd expect. There was blood everywhere, but for th' amount of damage done, it wadn't near as bad as it coulda been. Th' doctors say they ain't never seen anything like it. They took all kinds'a pictures an' wrote me up in some yankee medicine journal. I even got ta' meet th' Surgeon General. Nice guy, but he's got a silly uniform.

Anyhow, th' doctors say I shoulda bled ta' death within moments of that cat rippin' my arm off. Instead, th' action of th' breaking somehow served to sort of tourniquet off th' major arteries in my arm.

Myself, I kinda have this mental picture of my Daddy, sittin' up on his cloud with a smug smile on his face, his jaw fulla chaw, an' a acetylene torch in his hand. It's th' kind'a thing Daddy would'a got a kick out of.

I hunkered down like a wrestler, starin' th' cat down, waitin' ta' see what he's gonna do, my busted arm held close to my chest as best I was able.

Th' cat, he lurched to all fours. He had blood comin' out of his mouth now, an' I could see a little poolin' in his right nostril. (His nostrils were as big as my fists, an' he was less than six feet away. I half believe that if that cat had flared his nostrils just right, I could'a seen his dam' brain.)

He put his head down low to th' ground, an' he kinda tried ta' get down low; like he was gettin' ready ta' pounce. He couldn't quite work that angle, though. Th' pain was too much for 'im, or his brain wadn't workin' right, or somethin'. He lurched on down, an' then he gave this yelp, an' lurched right back up.

Wellsir. I was mighty happy ta' see that. If this cat could pounce on me, I was done. Wadn't nothin' I could do ta' stop him from bowlin' me right over. Cat musta weighed close ta' fifteen-hundred pounds. If he'd'a jumped on me, I'd'a looked like somethin' that tried ta' cross I-65, goin' the wrong way.

Th' cat, he kinda circled around, his head close to th' ground, peerin' at me out of his one good eye.

I wish I could describe th' pure look of evil hate in that eye. I wish I had th' words ta' make you understand what I saw there.

It was like . . . it was like th' cat was makin' me a solemn oath; th' kind of thing you ratify with blood. 'I'm'a kill you, or die tryin', boy. That's all. I don't even care about whether I die doin' it. All I care about is that you go first.'

I saw all that in that cat's lone eye, while he's circlin' around me, tryin' ta' find an angle he can get at me from. Meantime, I'm circling right along with 'im, watchin' th' blood trickle from his mouth an' nose.

Th' cat, he gave with this coughin' roar. There was blood in that roar. This great gout of it comes out of his mouth an' coats his jaw. He spent a minute or so lickin' his muzzle, but th' blood don't stop. It continued ta' run freely down his lower jaw.

For th' life of me, I couldn't tell you how he stayed on his feet. My Daddy's bowie was stickin' out of his chest, low down. He was covered in holes that were bleedin' an' musta hurt considerable. Th' right side of his face was a mass of gore. An' he was still comin' at me, murder in his eyes.

We must'a spent ten-years circlin' each other, tryin' ta' break our impasse. Every so often he'd sort'a weakly swat at me. I just kep' right on circlin'.

Th' cat, he can't find an angle where he can see me right, an' I was plannin' ta' wait him out. I was hurt, but he was hurt more at this point, an' he was bleedin' ta' death faster'n I was.

Finally, that cat's eye . . changed. That's th' only way I can describe it. It changed shape. Th' eyelids slit down ta' knife edges, an' his pupil dilated out to th' size of basketballs. He gave this almighty roar - fiercer, louder an' crazier than anything I'd heard yet; like he was puttin' all th' rest of what he had into it -an' launched himself into th' air at me.

I said me a quick, fierce, dirty, little prayer, an' stood my ground.

"Holy Jesus, here he comes . . ."

I ain't got too much more ta' say about this cat. I 'preciate you listenin' to me th' way you have, an' the way you've set still on any rumblin' you might have 'bout th' honesty of this here story. It's a rare person'll listen to somethin' as fanciful as a story 'bout a cat shoulda been extinct twenty qwillion years ago. I want you ta' know, I appreciate that.

I know it's a hard one ta' swaller, an' you're probably thinkin' I'm just goin' on with a long, tall one. But I tell you what: you hang in there just a bit longer, let me finish this up, I've got proof I can show you. Proof what can't be refuted.

Now I reckon I know what you're thinkin'.

'Davey, why'n th' hell, didn't you just dodge out th' way?'

Wellsir, I'm gonna try an' explain it to you. I ain't quite sure I'll get it. Like I say, I ain't got th' words right, ta' describe it. I reckon I could try'n pretend th' cat was movin' too fast for me ta' dodge, but that wadn't so, a' I ain't lied to you yet. I could say I was so scared, I was froze to that spot, and that wouldn't be far off th' truth . . . but it wouldn't be th' *whole* truth. If ya' held me down, an' made me tell ya' why I stood there, I reckon I'd have to admit part of me just didn't *want* to move.

Sounds strange, don't it? Here I am, in a position ta' get out th' way, but I'm too busy starin'.

See, it's like this: watchin' that cat lift hisself off th' ground like he did was like watchin' a sunrise. Big, evil and nasty as he was, he was a beauty. True, he was a billion pounds'a snarlin', psychotic death what wanted ta' rip my throat out, but watchin' 'im move was *still* . . . hypnotic-like.

It's hard to describe. I ain't a poet, an' I ain't th' type ta' say things in a pretty way. It's not my style. I ain't never been one ta' describe things in a pretty way. What's so is so, an' what ain't, ain't. That the way it is.

But this here cat . . .

Wellsir, this here cat . . . he was majestic. Even drippin' blood everywhere, even rippin', an' snarlin', an' causin' all kinds'a fuss, that cat, he was . . . he was beautiful.

I mean that. I surely do. Even after everything that's happened, watchin' that cat move was surely the single most beautiful thing I ever seen in all my days.

Them muscles moved like they was oiled beneath his skin. He was fluid an' he was dynamite, all at th' same time. You watched 'im move, an' it was like watchin' a star explode; watchin' 'im pour metal down to th' plant. He rose up from th' ground at me an' it looked like he was flyin'.

It was effortless, an' it was perfect . . .

'Scuse me for a second. I got somethin' in my eyes . . .

That's better. Them dam' airborne dust mites, they kill ya', don't they? But anyway. If I was gonna be perfectly honest with you, I'd have ta' say I stood there an' watched that cat come at me 'cause he was too beautiful *no*t ta' watch. That's all as it may be, but th' bottom line is, I stood there an' I watched that cat come at me like I was takin' a photograph. He filled th' whole sky, an' all I could see was teeth.

This is of th' topic a little, but I can still feel th' impact of my Daddy's fingers an' hand on th' back of my head every time I think about just standin' there.

But anyway. This cat's comin' at me, an' a small voice - not my Daddy's mind, but somethin' else - in my brain, pipes up an' says, 'Well, Davey. You done had it now.'

An' with them gigantic teeth comin' at me, I didn't have much choice but to agree with that assessment of th' situation.

So here he comes - all teeth an' claws, an' flyin' juices - an' I knew I couldn't stop 'im or even slow 'im down. He was just gonna roll right over me like a truck over a slow, overfed groundhog. I have just enough time ta' close my eyes an' tense up a little when that cat hits.

Now, you have to understand th' way a cat hunts. Most of th' time, when they're comin' at you straight on like this one did, they aim ta' get above ya' an' come down on top of ya'. Most cats, th' bigger ones anyway, can make a vertical leap of ten, twelve feet with no problem. This one was dam' near ten feet tall anyway, an' a vertical leap of thirty, forty feet was well within' th' realm of possibility.

This cat took off like a helicopter, an' he come down on top of me, with th' basic feline idea of bowlin' me under. Wellsir, he got into th' air - musta jumped forty feet, straight up. May th' Good Lord strike me dead if I'm lyin' - an' he come down . . .

'Scuse me for a minute. I got an itch like you wouldn't *believe*!

Ahhhhh.

I know. Looks awful funny, don't it? Don't seem like it'd make much sense, but it *does* help. Th' doctors, they say it's normal, an' they call it 'phantom' . . . 'phantom' . . . aw, hell. I forget. 'Phantom-somethin'-or-other', an' it's perfectly normal, an' even expected.

"It'll go away eventually, Davey," they says. 'Course, they ain't itchin' like fire, neith-

What?

Oh.

Sorry.

Where was I?

Oh! Right!

Yessir, that cat, he come down, but he didn't reckon his landin' space right. His depth perception was messed up good an' proper, an' he was losin' blood by th' bucketful, besides. Instead of landin' on my head an' just smooshin' me down ta' somethin' he could swaller with

294

no effort, he hit me with a full-on body tackle. I reckon it musta' looked like one'a them cage wrasslers, comin' down from th' top rope; or a football tackle, huntin' up some glory.

You remember that time Mississippi was playin' Duke, an' that ol' boy smeared that quarterback across ten yards'a field? Yeah. It was kinda like that. Th' dam' sky fell in, I was knocked right th' hell down, an' we just kep' goin'.

I felt somethin' hard an' round - like a brick fist - hit me square in th' chest. That cat, he let out a scream that made my ears bleed, an' we just kep' rollin'.

That cat, he hit me so hard, I forgot my Momma's name. I swear to ya', it felt like gettin' hit by one'a them New York subway trains like what you see on th' TV. He hit me, an' we tumbled, rollin' end over end, right into th' crik. There's this powerful splash, an' then I don't remember nothin' else for a bit.

'Davey. You got to get up now, boy. You got to get up!'

I reckon I musta lay there for a couple of hours, that gentle voice tryin' ta' get my attention. I didn't know which way was up, an' which way was down. I didn't know day from night, an' I couldn't remember my own name.

All I knew was that I hurt all over, I was wet, an' somethin' was sittin' on top of me, tryin' ta' push me into th' water.

'Davey. You got to get up, now, boy. You got to get up. C'mon, Davey. You get up!'

My eyes were bleary, an' I couldn't figure out why I couldn't see nothin'. I raised a hand to wipe at my eyes, an' this pain, like a hot iron, shot down my side. I think I screamed or groaned. I don't remember which. After that, th' lights went out for a while.

My eyes kept tryin' ta' shut, an' I kept losin' focus. I'd open my eyes and th' sun would be up. Then I'd close 'em - for just a second, mind - and it'd be as dark as th' grave.

I don't know how long I lay there. I'd think to myself 'You got ta' get up, Davey,' an' I'd try, but then I'd wake up a little more, an' realize I was still lyin' there, just as I had been for a while. So I'd try again, an' I'd open my eyes an' th' sun'd gone down again.

An' all th' time, I kep' hearin' this voice; this still, small, gentle voice, almost like a singsong.

'Davey. You got to get up, Davey. You got to get up!'

Th' doctors, they say I musta been havin' one a'them hallucinations. They say I couldn't've survived - with th' blood loss an' all - out in th' wild for as long as I claim I did. They say I was dreamin' when I opened my eyes an' saw that th' sun had gone down. Th' doctors stand around with knowing, smug looks on their faces; all smilin' an' pretendin' I don't know what they're thinkin'. It'd bother me, but I got proof that what I say is true

'Davey,' they say, their faces all serious, 'weren't no way you lay there that long. You'd be dead, boy!'

I don't know nothin' about that. I'm just tellin' th' story like it happened, an' since it happened ta' me, I guess I'd know. Anyhow. This here's how I remember what happened. You'll forgive an old story-teller for any embellishments he might just choose to use, won't you?

I remember comin' to; really an' truly comin' to. It was like I was swimmin' across this great ocean. It was cold, deep, dark, an' all around me, an' I just kep' swimmin', tryin' ta' find some kind of a shore. I didn't know who or what I was, or what I was doin' there. I just kep' swimmin'.

Eventually, th' sun came out, an' I realized I'm lyin' on my back, with this great cat sittin' atop my legs.

I'm lyin' there, in th' crik, with this cat on top of me, an' I had me a brief moment of clarity. I looked up through eyes gone hazy an' blurry, an' dam' near gummed shut with blood.

Standin' over me, on th' bank of th' crik, bigger'n life, is my Daddy. He's squatted down on his haunches, with his rifle 'tween his knees, just like I'd seen him so many times before.

He looked down at me, an' he smiles, real big like.

'Davey. You listen to your Daddy now. You got ta' get up. You got ta'!'

"Daddy," I said, my voice croakin' like somethin' from th' grave, "I can't get up. I'm all broke-up inside, an' I think somethin' awful's happened to my right arm."

'Davey, you got to get up,' Daddy said, 'You got ta' get up right now.'

I blinked my eyes, tryin' ta' get Daddy ta' come into some kind of focus.

'Davey, you got ta' get up, now,' he said.

"Daddy?"

'Davey, you got to get up now.'

I blinked an' blinked until my eyes ran with tears. I blinked some more, an' eventually my vision cleared. Standin' over me, in th' place where my Daddy had been, was th' biggest, ugliest turkey-buzzard I'd ever seen. It kep' clacking its beak an' rustlin' its feathers, lookin' down at me with one beady eye.

It cawed then - a long, odd, drawn-out, high-pitched, sing-song-like sound. A little ghost of memory turned the sound of the caw into my Daddy's voice, somewhere away in th' back of my head.

Th' turkey-buzzard kep' battin' an' slashin' at another turkey-buzzard that was tryin' ta' sidle up close to me. I looked an' saw that there musta been about ten or twenty of 'em, drawn to th' smell of blood, just waitin' for me ta' be a mite less twitchy 'fore they started ta' eat.

Turkey-buzzards ain't all that picky about eatin' somethin' that's still alive, long as most of th' fight's gone out of it.

Wellsir, that threw a pailfull of cold water in my face, an' no mistake!

"Get! You go on! Get!" I yelled hopin' ta' scare them turkey-buzzards away. They rustled an' shuffled, but they stood their ground.

'Boy, we ain't goin' nowhere. This here's where dinner is,' they said, with caws, an' flappin' a'wings.

Now, I reckon you're sittin' there thinkin', 'But Davey, what happened to th' cat?'

I 'magine most've you have figured it out by now. I ain't quite sure this's what happened, but it makes sense. Wadn't nothin' too spectacular about it. Way I reckon it, when th' cat hit me with his flyin' body tackle, the butt of my Daddy's bowie was driven in th' rest of th' way. I reckoned that bowie must've sliced through somethin' vital, an' th' cat was dead 'fore we quit movin'. If I hadn't been standin' right next to th' bank of th' crik, wouldn't none of this have happened. 'Course, I might be dead now, too, but there ya' are.

Wellsir, th' sight of all them turkey-buzzards, just waitin' ta' pull strips off me, set th' rest of th' fog in my brain a'runnin'. I reckoned it was time ta' get up now.

Th' cat was layin' on my legs. He'd pinned me in place by layin' atop me from th' waist on down. He was a heavy, solid mass a'weight that was rapidly stiffening an' startin ta' change colors.

Gettin' out from under that cat was a nightmare I'd rather not repeat. Between th' juices leakin' from th' cat, th' water of th' crik, an' the mud everywhere, I didn't have too hard a time of squirmin' my way free. Nosir, th' problem was th' pain I was in. My right hand kep forgettin' that' it - for all intents an' purposes - wadn't there anymore, an' it kep tryin' ta' help.

I scrabbled, an' dug, an' wept an' clawed, until I stood on th' bank of th' crik again, bobbin' an' weavin'. Th' remains of my right arm had started ta' bleed after all that exertion, an' I took some time ta' tie that off with a strip from my shirt. Doin' so nearly used up th' last of my strength, an' I thought about sittin' down, restin'; for just a minute, mind.

I heard th' sound of dusty wings from behind me, an' decided against it. If I was gonna die, it wadn't gonna be as buzzard bait.

Between you an' me, I think that th' adrenaline that musta got pumped into my body every time my right hand so much as twitched, probably saved my life.

Th' woods were still an' cold. I couldn't hear nothin' but th' wind, an' th' sound of them turkey-buzzards squabblin' 'tween themselves over who got ta' eat first. Wellsir, I didn't stop to congratulate myself. It was cold, an' it was gettin' colder. I looked up for th' sun. I reckoned I had about four hours of daylight left. I was cut, bruised an' all-together maimed, an' I knew I needed help just as fast as I could get it.

My basic problem was that I was fifteen some-odd miles into th' dam' woods. I knew, if I wanted ta' get out of here alive, I needed ta' start hikin' back ta' civilization.

I closed my eyes for just a second, lettin' that internal compass in my head find my way. Then I turned in that direcion, an' started hikin'.

For a mile or so, things went pretty well. I hurt pretty badly, an' I kep' wantin' ta' fall asleep, but I was trudgin' right along.

Then I started ta' see things: little things, at first; little flashes of light, an' things at th' corner of my vision, like you see when you've had too much ta' drink. I ignored them as best I could, an' I kep' walkin'.

Then I started hearin' things: little snatches of music, or conversation. I'd be trudgin' right along, an' I'd hear a burst of noise - like a TV turned on real loud to some car commercial - off to my right. I'd spin 'round in that direction, an' th' sound would disappear just as fast.

I ain't no dummy. I knew what that was an' I knew what that meant. I needed help, an' I needed it *fast*.

I kep' right on pluggin' along, tryin' ta' keep my eyes open, an' my head up.

Then th' cat - that great, enormous, psychotic-homicidal-devil-cat - came runnin' around th' base of a tree an' leapt at me.

I had just enough time ta' close my eyes . . .

'Course, th' cat wadn't there. Th' cat was lyin' dead in a crik, 'bout a mile behind me.

I opened my eyes, and. of course, there weren't no cat. There was a small puddle of blood, down near my shoes, though.

I kep' seein' 'im. He kep' poppin' out from behind trees, an' from above me, his teeth an' claws flashing', his lone good eye open wide with a malicious hate and hunger; mouth open in a silent roar. Every time I saw 'im, I 'bout wet my pants an' my heart started ta' thunder. He was dead, a mile behind me, but that didn't change th' fact that he was still stalkin' me. He'd sworn ta' see me dead, an' now he was tryin' ta' make good on that oath. Every time I saw 'im, I closed my eyes, shook my head, an' kep' hikin'. Somehow, with th' silence of th' woods, th' cat's silence was even worse. It was bad alive, but it was th' devil hisself dead.

I kep' hikin'. Every so often I'd stumble, an' I'd have to spend some time an' effort gettin' back to my feet. My right arm would start screamin' pain at me again, an' I'd see little flashes of light before my eyes. Every time that happened, it was a little harder ta' get back up.

After one of these occurrences, I looked up an' saw that cat sittin' in a branch of a tree. His branch was directly overtop my chosen path. His tail was swingin', an' his face was drippin' gore everywhere. He had my daddy's bowie stickin' out of 'im, an' a spurt of blood gushed out of th' hole with every beat of his heart.

I didn't say anything, I stood there starin' up at that cat, waitin' ta' see what it was gonna do. Wellsir, that cat starts talkin' to me.

'You're gonna die, Davey,' he said, his voice all low an' growly. 'You're gonna die, and they're never gonna find your body.'

Th' cat stood up on th' branch an' started screamin' at me, swishin' his tail back an' forth, back an' forth. flingin' pinecones.

'You're gonna , Davey! You hear me! You're gonna die in pain an' alone! Your body's gonna lie here an' rot; unmourned, unremembered, and unknown! They'll never find you, Davey. You hear me? You're gonna die, you're gonna Die, *You're gonna DIE!'*

He started laughin' this high-pitched, fearful laugh. He stood up an' started high-steppin' on his branch, like he was doin' a dance of some kind. His face sprayed blood an' bone,

'You're gonna *DIE*, Davey!'

An' that's when it came at me, snarlin' an' spittin' an' hissin'. Somethin' shifted - I still don't know what it was; a branch creakin' in th' wind, or a squirrel clabberin' over a branch - but as I watched, th' devil cat kinda . . . bled . . . into a handful of dried, dead leaves. One minute, I'm standin' there, watchin' my death comin' at me at ninety miles an hour; next minute, I'm gettin' hit in th' face with a fistful of dead leaves.

Strangest thing I ever saw in my whole life.

Way I reckon it now, I must'a been 'bout half-sleep walkin', dreamin' an' hikin'.

Wellsir, I blinked a few times, an' wiped at th' tears that was tryin' ta' freeze to my face. I wadn't cryin', understand, wadn't scared a'no devil-cat's ghost. I just got some leaves in my eyes.

Anyhow, I firmed my jaw an' shook my head. I looked around a little, an' then yelled, "That was a dirty trick, you dam' bastard. But I'm still here!"

I was convinced that this cat's ghost was still lookin' for me. You'd think it too, you were in my shoes. Somewhere behind me, I thought I could hear somethin' yowl, but that was most likely th' wind.

Things get pretty hazy at this point. All I remember is walkin' an' walkin' an' walkin' some more. I was cold; I was hurt, an' things kep' fallin' apart on me. My vision was hazy, my head hurt, an' all I could think about was puttin' one foot in front of th' other.

Eventually, a moment came when I don't remember nothin' else.

When I came to, all was dark an' silent.

I was surrounded by a white sheet, hangin' above me. A soft, muted light was shinin' down on me from above. For th' first time in as long as I could remember, I was dry, clean, an' in no pain.

I was purely convinced I was dead an' in Heaven.

I heard a soft peepin' noise. I slowly moved my head to th' right - it felt like it weighed about fifteen-hundred pounds - an' saw one a'them heart machines. I looked up, an' I saw one a'them IV machines what they pump medicines into ya' with. I was all plugged up an' connected to 'bout fifteen miles a' plastic tubin'. My right arm was covered in bandages, three miles thick, an' I was slathered up in all kinds of ointments, goo an' whatall.

I looked to my left, an' there stood Daddy. He had a smile on his face.

"Daddy?"

He nodded at me, still smilin', an' then he turned around an' walked through th' sheet. Left without a word.

My eyes was as heavy as cannonballs, so I closed 'em, reckonin' on closin' 'em for just a few seconds, an' then lookin' for Daddy again.

When I opened 'em again, th' sun had come up, an' everybody I knew was sittin' at my bedside.

"Davey?" my best girl Rhonda asked, "Davey? You awake?"

I ain't never seen nothin' so pretty as her black roots bleedin' through them blonde locks.

Th' doctors, they tell me I wandered out of th' woods, mumblin' incoherently, an' walked right into th' side of a tree a deer hunter had set his stand in. The deer hunter, he had hisself an ATV with an emergency field kit. He fixed me up, best he could, and then he tied me to the cargo deck an' drove me out, fast as he could go.

He had his pick-up nearby, an' he took off, hell-bent for leather, for th' hospital. Got me there in under twenty minutes . . . or so they say.

I ain't met this hunter yet, an' details is mighty sketchy as to who he was, an' what he was *really* doin', deer not bein' in season this time'a year, but he saved my life. Ain't no doubt 'bout that. I ever meet 'im, I'm gonna shake 'is hand, an' buy him a beer.

Even if he *is* a weed farmer.

Th' doctors, they tell me I was in a coma for three months. I'd lost most of my blood, an' I was settin' up for some kind of a dam' siege infection.

"Davey," they said, "we don't know what you got into out there, but th' stuff tryin' ta' grow in you ain't never been seen before. You got ta' tell us what happened."

They had ta' take th' arm. Doctors say I broke it in more places than they was places ta' connect pins to. I reckon it's a fair trade, though: one dead cat, one lost arm.

I ain't told nobody none of this. Not even Rhonda. I figured you had th' right to know first. Th' doctors, they tell me I got to come back every week an' do all kinds of therapy. That's all right, I reckon. It's a small price for bein' alive.

Now.

I want to show you somethin'. Let me get my shirt up here.

Right.

You see them trenches? You see how they curve across my abdomen? Lookit th' way they're separated. You see that too, don't you? Looks like somebody tried to open me up with th' world's biggest rake, don't it?

Now. Reach on over there for that box on th' shelf. Right. That one. Th' one next to th' Elvis plate. Pull that box down an' give 'er here.

Now, 'fore I show this to you, I got one final thing left ta' say.

Once th' doctors said I could go home, I took me a little hike. I followed my own internal compass, an' I went back to that crik. It wadn't hard 'tall. It was like th' woods was tryin' ta' tell me how ta' get there. I wanted ta' see, you understand, ta' know.

Wellsir, I found th' ripped an' torn remains of about forty turkey-buzzards, slung all over th' place. It'd been a while, so there weren't a lot ta' see, but I ain't one ta' miss things I'm actually lookin' for. Th' ground was all chewed up, like somebody had played a game of football there.

I didn't see no sign of that cat, but I did see a long trench, leadin' away from th' site of where th' cat had landed. Th' tracks I followed went right to th' base of th' cliff. I had a hunch, so I looked for a way up that cliff that I could manage. I followed th' crik around, an' found a slope I could climb pretty easy.

Turns out, I was right. Th' tracks continued at this point. Somethin' had drug that cat out of the trench, an' up *over* th' top of th' cliff we fell off.

I saw tracks. Lots an' lots of tracks. *Big*, feline tracks.

Needless ta' say, I didn't follow 'em.

Finally, I found this.

Yeah. Go 'head, take holt of it. You see th' way th' handle is all chewed, an' the metal is twisted? That thing's dam' near six inches thick. You have any idea what kind of force would be necessary ta' twist that thing?

See, this is th' way I reckon it. That cat, mean an' evil as it was, it had family, same as me. They came for that cat, an' took it off for burial, or whatever, an' they left my Daddy's bowie knife. I reckon they're tryin' ta' tell me somethin'. Sort of a 'You got this one, boy, but there's more of us, an' we're bigger an' meaner than this poor cub.'

I don't know that's so, but I reckon it is.

An' I'll tell you this for free:

I ain't been out in them woods since.

Desire

She sat across from me on the mattress, legs crossed beneath her. The thing I admired most, I think, was her innate ability to look graceful and comfortable, no matter the circumstances. Like now, for instance. I could see she wanted to cry, was trying not to, and yet the look of radiant beauty and perfect self-confidence on her face instead suggested she'd just stopped dancing a moment ago.

She had on a loose-fitting, sleeveless summer dress, the kind of thing bare-foot hippie mamas go around in. It had a floral pattern of some kind, but I couldn't spare the concentration to find out, and she wore nothing beneath that dress, as was her way.

Her hair- long, loose, and curly- was pulled over her left shoulder. It looked like a turbulent river, and I fought the desire to run my fingers through it while kissing her lips, her neck, her . . . .

But that was dangerous territory.

I took a long, slow drag off my cigarette, avoiding her eyes.

They were glimmering mirrors, those eyes; an unbelievable shade of gray, and they had never missed the mark yet. So full of life, explanations, reason balanced by desire, and all like that. I knew if I looked her in the eyes I'd be lost, off again on whatever it was she wanted from me, and I was determined to pull myself back from that abyss.

"I don't understand. What do you want?"

Even her voice modulated in such a way as to make my heart tremble. How do we end up like this? Why do we give people so much power over us?

I stubbed the cigarette out and stared at the wall. I found myself wondering why all motel walls are such a universal shade of yellow. Even if the walls are supposed to be like, red or blue, they always eventually morph into a sad, lonely, sin-filled yellow. The dire poet in me wanted to write lines about the "hole from nowhere, leaking sulfurous fires of hell leak through like blood from a stubborn wound". My dire poet's a pompous git.

She leaned towards me then, and I the scent. Sweat and sweet perfume, the kind you find in those dollar places that have off-label names. Perfume that only certain women can get away with wearing. She smelled of musk, heat, life; our kiss and our past together, and . . . Woman. Her scent reached back to the beginning of time, and mimicked her mother Eve. That must've been the scent Adam was bombed with the first time her saw her, with the feel of God's fingers lingering on her arms and legs. I felt myself reaching for her to bury myself anew within her grave.

I stopped. Lit a cigarette, hands a-tremble. I surveyed the walls again, trying to find answers under peeling yellow paint.

"What do I want?" My voice was husky, rough.

"I want a garden. Some place where I can plunge my hands into moist Mother Earth, and feel the draw and pull of the energies there.

"I want a fenced-in yard, someplace where a dog could romp, and play, and crap and bark its silly head off to its heart's content.

"I want to live in the boonies, out where even the coyotes get lost, where I can get drunk, scream obscenities at the stars and urinate off the front porch, naked.

"I want to wake up around noon after going to bed at midnight. I want to sleep without fear, eat without pain, and see without knowing everything all at once. I want to reach over next to me and feel the warm, sleeping body of my *wife*, not a transient lover.

"I want children, small replicas of me, made in the image of me and my wife, through the tender loving hands of God's mysteries in the womb.

"I want to feel my wife's heart race when I touch her.

"I want to see the eyes of my son glimmer in joy when he tells me about his new girlfriend.

"I want to be alive, and to feel, and to hurt, and to breathe."

She'd drawn back from the force of my desires and looked at me strangely for a moment. Then she stood - a fluid, graceful movement - and put her shoes back on. She reclaimed her bag and walked out, all without saying a word or even looking in my direction.

I watched her leave, and then smoked cigarettes and stared at the walls until the sun came up.

Falls of the Ohio

My father once told me that everything in life is a test. Everything we do, everything we are, it all stems from that one truth. Everything in life is a test. I was never more fully aware of that than when I was visiting The Falls of The Ohio.

These sorts of places are everywhere. Call them what you will: "High or Holy ground", "Thin places", "Rent Lands", what have you - it all means the same thing. People recognize that this is someplace special.

Our ancestors drew on the walls of caves and erected towering stone animals to memorialize a "special place" for the coming generations. In the Bible, the People of Israel would erect a large altar or a pile of stones. Other people have done other things, but it all amounts to the same thing. It's a gigantic, unmistakable sign.

"Hey. Pay attention! This place is important!"

The Pyramids in Egypt. Stonehenge. Easter Island. It's all a piece. Humanity finds a place that needs a marker, and somebody will put some kind of a memorial - even if it's a simple as a pile of rocks or as complex as an obelisk - over it like a navigational beacon.

Here in modern life, we're less in tune with those universal harmonics, I think, but we still make our obeisance. We just name things, ignorant of the fact that naming something forces it into a shape, gives it form and places rule upon it.

We are uninformed, fumbling sorcerers, and we are not paying any attention to the scars we leave behind us.

As for myself, I've stumbled across a few of these places and I've always had cause to regret it.

If reality - our reality - is a sheet of skin, then a thin place would be like a slowly scabbing hole, a bruise, a break in the fabric.

People who are sensitive to such things will understand that it is a gathering place, a focal point of power; a place where things can and do happen. It's a hind-brain experience, and I'd be surprised to hear that more than one person out of a thousand has felt anything like it.

I'd wanted to see this particular place for a long time. I'd lived in the area for nigh on twenty years, and I'd never made much of an effort to see the "sights".

This one, The Falls of The Ohio, was less than a fifteen minute drive from where I worked. I found myself, one bright Sunday morning, with no place to be and no place to go after work let out, so I drove on down.

The Falls of The Ohio bills itself as one of the largest collections of fossils in the tri-state area. It is situated on the Indiana bank of the Ohio River and it's an important site for scientists from all over.

I walked around, surrounded by the petrified remnants of vast, forgotten seas; trilobites and their cousins lay locked in stone all around me.

I stood there on a large shelf of rock, seeing the millions of tiny fossils beneath me and I felt the gathering of some kind of force.

It started as a pressure under my shoes and worked its way up my spine to the center of my head; a squeezing, gently probing, throbbing sensation that was not at all pleasant.

I sighed. I'd really just come to look at the fossils!

Looking around me, I soon spotted the evidence I needed to confirm my suspicions. There were cryptic drawings all over the sand here. They looked like complex mathematical arrangements drawn in Esperanto.

Yes, you could dismiss them as being the random circumlocutions of a nine-year-old with a branch, but humanity doesn't draw in the sand at random, even if it thinks it does.

It was as I stood there, kicking myself, that I first noticed him.

I'd seen the canvas chair at the riverside and the tepee-like-construction of driftwood that accompanied it when I first pulled up. That hind-brain part of myself noticed it before the higher-thinking part could even get started. They seemed almost to be companion pieces in some sort of "Ohio River Abstract Tableau." I hadn't paid it much mind, probably dismissing it as the well-established, favored fishing hole of a local. I guess I should've known better.

When first I noticed the chair, it was empty. I would swear to that. I drove up, parked my car, noticed the chair and its tepee, and the chair was empty.

Feeling that force boiling its way through my nervous system, I looked at the chair again. Sure enough, it was occupied. He sat there like he'd been sitting there for a thousand years.

The force coalesced and I sighed as that mescaline-like clarity of thought that accompanies the Opening of a Way fell over me. The little water bugs, locked in their matrices of stone beneath my feet seemed to chitter and dance in greeting.

Some things you learn. Some things are taught to you. Some things you only absorb after long, cold experience and pain responses.

And then there are the things you just know, know it in the way you know the inside of your eyeballs. You know it in the good way you know the smell of your lover's skin; you know it in the bad way you know the fear-pulse behind your ears. It's as much a part of you as anything is.

I knew - knew like I knew the feel of my own skin on my skeleton - what he was, and what he wanted. Strangely, though, I didn't know *who* he was. Looking back now, I think that was a case of my existence being mostly land-locked. I never really lived very close to either an ocean or a river.

Granted, I lived quite close to any number of creeks and brooks. And creeks and brooks have their own gods sometimes - in the C.S. Lewis sense of the word, of course - but usually they're just big ditches with water running through them.

"One more reason it sucks to be me," I mumbled.

I walked over to where he sat. He looked me up and down and said nothing.

Being raised right, I nodded deferentially in his direction and said, "Good morning, Grandfather."

I put my hands in my pockets and touched my pocketknife. It's just good manners to let them know you're carrying or wearing steel. Most of the Old Ones don't care about steel too much, and wouldn't be too bothered about it if you were, but it's good manners.

He sat there for a moment letting me regard him while he regarded me in turn. The air around us held tension and a general tightness. It was like the slow closing of some mighty fist. Something was building its way to happening.

The man before me was elderly, bowed beneath a heavy mantle of years. His skin was the color of river mud after a long period of heavy rain. His hair was slate grey. His eyes were black dots in a heavily lined face. There was a hungry, angry light in them that made them seem to swim in a stew of their own making.

A strange photo-luminescence - much like the rainbow stain of petroleum bleeding into water - crossed one eye and flitted into the other.

The smell coming off him was of a heavy rain, dark, deep mud, drowned things, and the murky insanity of the bottom of a well.

He wore a long, sleeveless shirt - like a dress for a small girl - that looked as though it had been sewn together from whatever he could find here at the river's edge. It was his only covering.

There were bits and pieces of assorted garbage clinging to his long beard and his long hair. That hair fell across his shoulders and onto his breast where it blended seamlessly with his beard. I couldn't tell where it ended and his beard began.

His hands were clenched on the canvas chair and he remained silent, looking at me with those disconcerting eyes while the tension in the air swelled to a bursting point.

When he did speak, it was quiet, leaden. His voice sounded like stones moving in still, deep pools of cold, clear, deep water.

"Aye. 'Grandfather' I am, though not truly yours. Mother, perhaps?"

He continued to look at me for a long moment, and then said, "Nigh. Not even Mother. Your true Mother lies across the firmament boy, as does your Father. Still, you were born in *this* land, and I can call you my own should I so wish. And I see the marks upon your heart that the Fair Blue Maiden has left. You are mine if any is, so I do think."

Sighing heavily, he sat back in his chair. He seemed to relax just a little, or maybe it was just a loosening of tension somewhere.

The air around expanded as well, like the deflating of a large balloon.

He looked out across the water and directed his words at the far-bank.

"Hail, Dowser. I bid you Good-Morning. We are well met?"

I'd heard this term before, too. I've never understood it, really, and never really had the nerve to ask. There are some glimmerings of understanding back in quiet places in my head, but it's never been clear. Every time I meet an Old One, they address me as 'Dowser.' One of these days, I'll ask why.

His greeting was part of a very formal ritual that was older than humanity in some ways. The back of my brain understood that, even if the rest of it didn't. My response was almost automatic.

"As well met as any, Grandfather."

The smile that crossed his face was as quick as a mirage.

"Aye. 'Grandfather'. Grandfather, Father and Mother, too. But how many of your kind remember, boy? How many of your kind look to the water and see?"

It was getting deep here, thicker than I could deal with. And it was happening much faster than I would like. I shook my head in dismay. I've long since resigned myself to these sorts of experiences, but that doesn't make them any easier and I'm often left fumbling around, trying to make sense of things nobody can explain.

Sometimes it's best just to keep your mouth shut.

At that moment, a UPS plane flew overhead, taking off from the Louisville hub across the river. My work was much closer to the hub, and I'd often remarked that those planes couldn't be flying more than a couple hundred feet above us when they took off and landed. You could feel the rumble of their engines in the walls of our building.

From where we stood, the engines shook the sky. The fossils beneath us chittered and danced, shaking as if they were in fear.

The old man shook his fist at the plane and muttered something unintelligible at it. It took several minutes for the noise to die away. The fossils beneath us squirmed for long afterwards.

The old man turned to me when all was once again still.

"Loud. So loud! Everything in this time and place is loud, Dowser. Sometimes I wonder why man has not driven himself mad with his need to deafen all around him."

I nodded dumbly.

He sighed. It was a tired, weak sound. Shifting irritably in his little chair, the old man looked back out to the water's edge.

"What do you here, Dowser? And why do you come to me in the costume of law?"

That took me by surprise. I had no idea what he was talking about, at first. I gaped at him. He waved a hand irritably at my security guard uniform.

"Law, Dowser! Law! You upold the laws, do you not!"

"Oh! I mean . . . I'm sorry, Grandfather. I didn't understand you. No, I am not an upholder of law. I'm just a security guard. This is just a uniform."

"Ahh. So you serve the forces of chaos, then?"

Yeah. I was way in over my head here, paddling in waters so dark and deep I was drowning without even knowing it.

"No. I mean, I don't know, Grandfather. It's really just a job."

"Think you so, Dowser? And so may it be. So may it be. But I think me you are responding to the truth of your nature. Upholder of laws you are, whether you will it or no."

I shrugged, non-commitedly.

He sighed again. We were silent for a long while, listening to the river flow. When he spoke again, his voice was almost an inaudible whisper.

"They take from me, you know. They take what they will, when they will and leave their filth behind. And you? Would you forget? Would you come to this golgotha to plunder my bones, my secrets?"

A tricky question. I *had* come to see. And while there are signs posted everywhere telling visitors they couldn't remove the fossils from their resting places, there didn't seem to be any kind of prohibition against the normal flotsam and jetsam of a river bank. If I found something cool there, something rock-like and beautiful; river-glass or even just an interestingly-weathered bit of wood, couldn't I take that?

Legally maybe, but what would the old man in front of me say if I asked? Nine-tenths of the time, discretion is the better part of valor.

"Not I, Grandfather. I come only in respect."

He slouched in his chair and it creaked alarmingly. He sat with hooded eyes, staring out across the water. His voice was even heavier when he spoke again, loaded with bitter resignation.

"I was a god, once. I was worshipped on these very shores. I took what sacrifice I felt was due me and in return I gave of my bounty. Now look!"

He spread his arms to indicate the river in front of us. There was a set of dams and locks downstream from where we sat. A barge trundled busily inside the lock, and I could hear the groaning of machinery in operation.

The Ohio River is a major commercial thoroughfare. I had never given this much thought, but the free never really think of the slaves, do they?

"They fetter me, Dowser! They strain my body, dump poison into my blood, and taint me in such a way as not to be borne!"

310

His voice rose on a shout at that last and he strained himself into a sitting fist, clenching his hands and arms tightly and drawing his legs up into a near-fetal position. I watched as a swelling surge of water, nearly twenty feet high, raced to the locks and slammed against it with titanic force, washing over the barge and filling the newly emptied lock with water.

Water rushed over our feet, soaking my legs to the knee. There were concerned shouts from the locks. The voices, clear at first from where we were, faded, as though the locks were receding into the distance. Or perhaps we were moving and the locks stayed still. I'm not sure either way.

After long moments there was nothing but the silence of the river-side. Gone was the noise of planes flying overhead, the interstate a few minutes away, the commercial traffic up and down the river. Gone was the smoke, fogs and fumes of the major metropolitan area not a stone's throw from where I stood.

Several million people lived within forty-five minutes of where I stood. Within a few seconds they were all gone.

The river itself was empty save for me, the strange man next to me and the creatures who lived and died in the primal water. For the first time in my life, I could hear the sound of a mighty river flowing unimpeded. It was awe-inspiring.

He relaxed then and sighed. "But I'm so tired. And the river flows. Every day the river flows."

When he turned to look at me again his eyes were indescribably sad.

"The Fey have left my waters, Dowser. Man has so fouled me that the Fey can no longer dance in even my stillest, deepest pools. It pains me. It pains me in ways man cannot understand. It is lonely, not hearing their voices in my silent halls, not feeling the tickle of their dancing steps in my echoing solitude."

A sense of his desperation washed over me then and my knees nearly buckled. I thought I had some experience with loneliness, living through the nuclear winter of my recent divorce, but what are my experiences when compared to an immortal's?

"I was a god once," he weakly whispered again.

Sometimes it's best just to keep your mouth shut. And sometimes, in order to keep being who you are, you just have to speak up. He'd said it earlier and I hadn't said anything in response. This time my mouth sprang open and words leapt to my tongue.

I composed myself. He might be an immortal, but here was a soul in pain. I decided to address his conceit. Maybe I could work my way around it and salve his wounds somewhat. Besides, good Christians have to speak up when certain things are said.

And everything in life is a test.

I took a deep breath and drew deep within myself.

"Never that, Grandfather."

"Oh? Why?" He responded whip-quick, his mood altering in the turbulent way that so clearly defined my growing realization of who he was, who he had to be.

"There is only one God, Grandfather. Only one. Should you insist on equal status with Him, I will deny you."

He looked at me incredulously, like I was some new bug that had crawled out of his river and demanded he recognize me as an equal.

"You would deny the evidence of your own eyes?"

311

He swept both hands to indicate the empty river in front of us. Something surfaced twenty feet from where I stood. A thick dorsal fin split the water and a mouth heavy with sharp teeth grinned at me for a moment before whatever-it-was dove back under the water.

That mouth looked as if it could bite the front-end off a mini-van.

But sometimes you just have to be who and what you are; you have to stick even in the face of sharp, sharp teeth. Backing down now would be a denial of myself, and the immortal never reward cowardice.

Everything is a test.

"I would deny it to my last breath, Grandfather. There is only one God. One Master, one Ruler, one Creator, one God, one King. Only one."

He shook his head at that and seemed disappointed in me, as if I was badly belaboring something quite obvious.

"I know this, Dowser. I know well there is only one God. Would the pot not recognize the potter, when it is His hands that formed it? I know well my God, Dowser. But to deny what you see because it contradicts your philosophy, well, that makes you a fool, Dowser."

The realization was slow, and I have to say, I felt like a dolt when it hit full-force. But I can admit to being a little hesitant on the draw, a little lazy on the uptake. He was testing me. The old snake was testing me! I could feel it! He was arguing with me as a test!

I choked a smile down. This was serious stuff, here. Whatever my examiner was, he controlled things here. I needed to be respectful. Still, I couldn't help but be amused at the absurdity of it.

"Perhaps, Grandfather. Perhaps that does make me a fool. But if that is true, then I am my own fool."

He looked at me for a long moment, his face still. And then he threw his head back and laughed, long and loud.

"Aye! So be it then!"

He laughed for a long time, his shoulders shaking in mirth.

"Ahhh, Dowser. Dowser in truth you are!"

Finally, he turned to look at me, and in a different, subdued sort of voice, said, "Name me. Name me if you can, Dowser."

I've said it before. Names are powerful. Names force a shape on you. They make you conform to the parameters of the name itself. If you don't know your name, you don't know your shape. But if you've forgotten your name, if you somehow lose your name . . . you lose yourself.

Again, it was just knowing. It blew out the dams of conscious, rational thought, and jumped out on my tongue. I opened my mouth and there it was.

"You are Old Man River, Grandfather. In this place, and in this time, your only name is River. Where I come from, you are known as the Ohio River."

He sighed, but this time it was a rich, happy sound. It was the noise you make when your wife, armed with strong, healthy fingernails, finally gets at that place just below your shoulder-blades that'd been itching all day.

When he spoke again, there was still the suggestion of mirth in his voice, but rich satisfaction covered every syllable, too.

"Did you know, I had forgotten?"

Tears stood in his eyes. I looked out to the water to preserve his dignity. It wouldn't do for me to see him crying, after all.

He reached a strong, wiry hand out to the stone beneath us and plucked a beautiful fossil of a trilobite forth from the stone matrix it lay in. He used no more force then you or I would use to pick a penny up off the ground. Still, there was a cracking noise that I felt more than heard and the sound of stone protesting vibrated in the bones in my head.

He handed me the fossil. It was as lifelike as the day it was formed, and stained a beautiful bronze color from the touch of his hand. It lay warm in my hand, like a well-earned boon.

"It is beautiful, Grandfather."

He nodded in a dismissive sort of way.

"These things have rules, Dowser."

The sound of the locks began to fade back, as though we were somehow traveling towards them. Old Man River sighed. The sound was half-exhalation of breath, half sob.

"I'm so very tired," he breathed out, nearly sub-vocally. "The powers I once commanded come only hard to me, now."

Reality was bleeding back into things, and the noises that were absent were slowly coming back. We were traveling back to my present. I had named him for who and what he was, and he had given me something of himself in return.

I had a question I wanted answered, though and I think it was okay to ask; it was almost expected of me.

"Grandfather?" I tried to keep the nervousness from my voice.

He looked at me with a sudden turn of his head, his face closed. He said nothing. Reality continued to bleed into this place we were.

"Grandfather, I would know. What does 'Dowser' mean? What does it mean when an Old One calls me that?"

He threw his head back and laughed long, loud and sincerely at that. It was a strangely hypnotic and enormously cheery sound, like water rolling happily across stones in a brook high in the mountains.

"You don't know, boy? You've forgotten? The Dowser doesn't know the meaning of his name?"

"Not 'forgotten', Grandfather," I said, a bit peevishly. "I've never known."

His face suddenly grew serious and he looked back out to the water. A barge, loaded to the brim with coal, floated slowly past.

"Time was I would've required a gift from you for such an answer. But that time has passed, I see, and perhaps I've sinned by ever requiring it."

He shook his head and looked down into his lap before continuing, "Dowser" you are, boy. Both a blessing and a curse. It means "The One Who Can Find". In your case, I think it means "The One Who Never Stops Looking."

"That doesn't sound like any kind of a curse to me, Grandfather."

He smiled a hard, bleak smile at me.

"Oh, no? Perhaps not. But I should think it would be a heavy curse to be one who never stops looking for the truth of a matter. Would any reasonable person argue with a river as to whether it should think of itself as a god or not? Would any reasonable person lecture a river on the nature of godhood? A curse, Dowser. A heavy one, at that."

A hard cold hand of despair clenched my heart. I knew what that meant. Everything is a test, after all, and truth can only be tested so much before it turns into an untruth. There is no gray. There are no shades of half-white or dingy-black. There is only truth and untruth.

"You are not allowed lies, Dowser. Not the ones told you, and not the ones you tell yourself. Your eyes are ever open, though sometimes you cannot see."

I closed my eyes then - I think mostly to spite the Universe - and sat down on the cold, wet stone. When I opened them, he was gone and the noises of the locks had fully returned. The men who worked there were busily swarming everywhere like ants in a kicked-over hill.

The chair was empty and the three logs that had made up the tepee were slowly drifting downstream. I opened my hand and looked at the trilobite. It lay there, tickling in my hand for a moment. It warmed further, and seemed to almost wake itself.

Its antennae moved slowly across my palm and then it crawled from my hand and made its way to the water. It stopped, felt the water, and splashed into the river.

I stood up, brushed my hands and the seat of my pants, and hiked back to my car. When I looked back I couldn't tell where we had been sitting. I sketched a final, respectful salute to the river, said a quick prayer for the trilobite, and drove away.

Bullshwa

A pizzle is a dried and preserved bull's penis.

Isn't that a fabulous way to start a story? Here you were, ready to be inspired and edified by something deep and meaningful, and instead you get dismemberment and taxidermy.

I would like to state, from the outset, that this is not really my fault. I am writing this story in a mercenary fashion. I am writing it in the in hopes of actually winning a bull's pizzle mounted on the head of a cane. The only catch is, I have to write a story about a bull's pizzle.

I've seen pictures. It's an awfully nice cane.

However, there isn't much I can think of I'd rather write a story about *less*. So I've gone around the rules, and done some research about bulls, their pizzles and other things bull-related. There's some awfully interesting tidbits, that I'd like to share with you after spending a lot of time wandering down unexpected avenues of thought - one of them bring the interconnectedness of all things.

You've heard of Six Degrees of Separation from Kevin Bacon. I like to think of this as being "Eleven Levels of Bull Penis."

Interconnectedness is everywhere. For instance, I am writing this story, and for a brief time, I drove a Ford Taurus. Taurus is one of many words that means, quite literally, "bull". It was a very nice car, and it suited me. Taurus is also one of the astrological signs. I, myself, am not a Taurus; I am a Gemini. However, I am married to a Taurus. I was still allowed to drive the Taurus, but this may simply be because the powers that regulate astrological signs haven't yet caught on to me. Maybe they figure marrying the Taurus was enough. I'm hoping the penalty will not be too severe when they do, as I'm quite happily attached to my pizzle and I'd hate to see it mounted on a cane, nice or otherwise.

Parts of my Taurus were probably assembled in Mexico. (Ford, along with many other American motor companies, is quite bullish about manufacturing in Mexico. It's cheaper, and this can help keep a company from going bearish - an embarrassing sort of thing. Kinda the way a bull must feel when he thinks of his dried and mounted pizzle.)

Mexico was colonized by the Spanish. (Although a very convincing argument can be made by the very learned that Mexico was colonized by the Olmecs - who were thought to sacrifice bulls regularly. History is silent on the treatment of the pizzle afterwards.) The national sport of both Mexico and Spain is often believed to be bullfighting; machismo at its finest, and a reaching for one's cajones to prove the size of one's pizzle.

Bullfighting has been considered to have originated with the Minoans, about whom not much is known, other than they revered the bull in some very genuine and odd ways.

As far as animals that are revered, the elephant and the moose rank highly in many cultures. Both the male elephant and the male moose are known as 'bulls,' but generally only if they are uncastrated. I don't know what an elephant or a moose's pizzle is called, or if anyone has ever removed one, preserved it and mounted it on a cane.

And can I ask, who has the lucky job of 'bull elephant castrator?' Is this a job a person aspires to? Or is it more of a 'gored by Destiny' sort of thing? Who provides the training? Is it handed down from father to son; perhaps it's passed along genetic lines like a certain part of male anatomy? Whatever the case, I can only assume it's a job that's done very, very carefully.

Speaking of jobs that have to be done carefully, correction officers are sometimes known as 'bulls', while police officers are often referred to - rudely and unwisely, in my opinion - as 'pigs'. This can lead you to wonder what the difference between a 'pig' and a 'bull' is, although the assumption of 'uncastrated, bovine, mammal' may be assumed. I've never had the nerve - even after drinking what back home we call Bull's Piss - to ask either a cop or a correction's officer what they think.

A 'bull' is also an official document issued by the Pope, but only if a 'bulla' is affixed. A 'bulla', in this usage, is an official seal. If the 'bull' does not have the 'bulla' attached it may be confused with a 'bull' of another color: a blister or a vesicle - a fluid filled protuberance of some kind. It can be safely assumed, I think, that the Pope knows nothing whatsoever about vesicles or pizzles. The world would be a much stranger place if it were otherwise, though, wouldn't it?

Does the Pope have a walking stick of some kind? What would it be called? I'm sure it doesn't have a pizzle attached.

Ironically enough, pizzle, especially tiger pizzle, is believed to have very potent aphrodisiac qualities. This begs the question: if it's been sawed off an animal - which was dumb enough to be caught and allow its pizzle to be sawed off, and is clearly no longer using it - what makes you think it'll work for you? It's not doing the poor tiger any good, that's for certain.

I've often been accused of being 'bullskulled'. Thus far I've managed to resist the urge to ask whether or not this means that the accusee believes I am prodigiously equipped with enormous . . . horns. It's only a matter of time before I cave, though.

One of the very first stories humanity ever told itself was about Gilgamesh and Enkidu. These two were friends - or perhaps lovers - who fought a bull that sent by Ishtar -The-Star-Slut in response to Gilgamesh's refusal of the star-slut's advances. Enkidu actually tore the hind end off the bull and threw it in Ishtar's face. I often wonder if that meant she was covered in bullshi-

Nevermind. Some questions perhaps don't need answers all that urgently.

And finally, can a bull, whether four-legged or two, still get 'horny' if his pizzle has been removed? Can an elephant or a moose? How about a cop or a correction's officer?

Am I being bullheaded about all this?

Dear You

"Hey!"

Hello.

"You look great! I mean, you always did, but you really look like you've been taking good care of yourself. Exercising, eating right, that kind of thing."

Flatterer.

"Yeah, well. You know me. Seriously, though. You look beautiful!"

You said that to all of us.

"Doesn't change anything. You all *were* beautiful. Even after-"

All of us?

"All of you! Really! I mean, just because . . . what I mean is . . . well, you know."

Yes.

"Yeah."

. . .

" . . . "

This is a nice place.

"You really think so? You don't think the red-leather-European-pub thing is a little much?"

No. It's very nice. Is this the pub you carry around in your head?

"Yep. This here's my very own Boh Da Thone."

Where does the name come from?

"A Rudyard Kipling poem."

Oh? We didn't know you were poetically inclined! How interesting.

"Yeah. Well."

The barkeep is . . . interesting.

"Yeah. I'm not really sure where he came from. When I visualized the place, he just kinda showed up. His name's Henasamef, and as near as I can figure, he's from Ur."

Urrrrr?

"Close enough. You want anything? He's a grumpy bastich, but he can fix any drink you want. Some munchies, maybe? Hen does a *mean* fried egg sandwich."

No. Thank you.

"Well, I'm gonna have a beer. That okay?"

We never could stop you.

"Yeah. Well. So. Anyway. How're things going?"

You know. A little of this, a little of that. Things are . . . . How are you?

"Yeah. I hear that. Me? Well, you know how it is. My life's pretty much the same as it's always been. You get up, you go to work, you try to forge the conscience of your race in the smithy of your soul, you pay bills . . . "

I see. Wasn't that a New Yorker cartoon recently?

"Yeah, well, you know. It's a little more interesting than what's actually going on in my life. I referred to myself as a "landmark" in conversation recently. In the "things never change" sense of the word."

It's nice to see that you still blush.

"Yeah, okay. So, anyway. I guess you're curious as to why I've called you all here today . . . "

It had passed our minds, yes.

"See, the things is, I've met someone."

Ah.

"Yeah. And she's freaking dynamite. I mean, like, in a bottle. You know? I mean, she has this smile that starts at like, her hairline, and ends down around her navel. It just swallows her freaking face."

Do tell. What does she look like?

"She's gorgeous."

You say that about all of us.

"It doesn't change anything. You *were* all gorgeous. At least, for a little while. Until the crap started to roll downhill."

What does she look like? What color is she?

"She's white, with red hair, green eye-"

Have you discarded your dream of being with a proud, black sister, then?

" . . . "

Nescher?

"I'm not going to answer that. It's a racist and horrible thing to say."

So the truth is now something to be avoided? We were under the impression you liked "all things honest".

"Look. She's white. If she was black, she'd be black. But she's not."

Very well. Tell us more.

"She's just the best. We've been going out for a while now, and I asked her to marry me."

So. She's a stripper, we guess?

"Look. Are we going to have one of those awkward ex-"

Only if you want to, Nescher.

"Not me, kiddo."

Neither do we. Not really. You didn't answer our question, though, and we'd like to clarify things before we go any further. What is the attraction? Does she have a perfect body? Is she some sort of goddess? An adult film star?

"She's a geologist."

Really.

"Yeah, *really*. What, I can't attract a brainy chick? All I go for is bimbos?"

You were the one who said it, not us.

"Yeah, well, whatever. She's *not* a bimbo. She's as far down the scale from "bimbo" as you can freaking get. She watches Star Trek. She collects rocks. She's an utter, total, complete dork, and I'm *crazy* about her. I mean, we spend about eighty percent of our time laughing; *at* each other, *with* each other, whatever. And she's got this absolutely delightful laugh, too. It's like, this giggle that cascades down like, I don't know, glass or ice wind chimes or something."

How poetic.

"Fuck you."

You first.

. . .

" . . . "

. . .

"Look: I didn't call ya'll here to fight. I'm sorry. Okay? For whatever reason, I wasn't up to the task of being your . . . your . . . whatever. But you had your failings, too! You wanted me to live up to some idealized standard you carried around in your head, and when I didn't fit you mold, you got mat at me. You lied, you stole, you cheated on me. I mean, you dug my heart out with a dull freaking spoon!"

Yes.

"I loved you!"

Yes.

"But okay. Water under the bridge, right? Bygones and all that."

What is it you want, Nescher?

"I don't know, dude. Forgiveness? Absolution? Permission?"

. . .

" . . . "

. . .

"You know, I never really was very good at hiding things from you. That's not true at all."

We know.

"Yeah. See, the thing is, I'd like to not have to carry you around in my head anymore. I mean, I'm with this chick, and things are wonderful. She loves me for me, and lets me *be* me, and she doesn't care that I'm a quivering jar full of masculine insecurities. She doesn't care that I'm damaged; used; broken goods. She just kinda looks at me, with this brain-melting smile, and says "I love you." And for once, I believe it."

. . .

"Got nothing to say there, huh?"

I thought you said you didn't want to fight.

" . . . "

. . .

"I'm sorry. Old wounds heal slowest."

Yes.

"Can you help me out? Just a little?"

It's fine to ask, Nescher. You can ask all you like. But it's not so easy to do. *We are part of you. Every scar, every hurt, every good memory, every bad memory. Remember: part of the reason she loves you . . . she does* love you?

"Yeah. Lips lie - as you're well aware - but eyes don't. I think it's pretty safe to say she's as crazy about me as I am about her."

Yes. Well, part of the reason she loves you so much is that we are part of you as you are now. We put you through the wringer; softened you up; taught you a few things. To ask us to leave would be taking away a very important part of who you are.

" . . . "

Does this hurt you?

" . . . "

. . .

"Can I tell you a secret?"

Of course.

323

"I used to pray, like, all the time, that God would erase your names from my head and my heart. I wanted to start each and every relationship anew. And I guess that's what I'm really looking for here. I'd like to start over. I mean, I still dream about you from time to time. I'd like that to stop. I'd like for the only woman in my heart to be her. Can you dig that?"

We can understand it.

"Yeah, well, whatever. Look: I've got something for you."

Presents?

"Something like that. Here."

My. It's certainly heavy and such pretty wrapping.

"Yeah. I can it Eau De Canvas Sack."

What is all this?

"Go on. Open it up"

. . .

" . . . "

Ah. So that's how it is, huh?

"What? No! Look, it's all there. Our first kiss. The first time we had sex outside. The night we spent cuddling. The laughter we shared, the tears, the walks in the rain, all that crap you gave me. It's all there, all your stuff. Go on, look!"

So you want us to have this back?

" . . . yeah. Yeah. I do. I want you to take it all back."

That's . . . cruel.

"Well, that's stupid. You know I'm not smart enough to be cruel. I just want to start over. Start everything over. I don't want you hanging around my neck with your woulda-coulda-shouldas. I mean, I was fourteen! I joined the Army for you! I defied my parents and married you! You were twenty-some-odd-years my senior, and we dated for years! I tattooed you nickname over my heart! I don't want to feel hurt or affection for you anymore. I just want to be able to love this woman the way she deserves to be loved, without seeing reflections of you everywhere."

Would you really? Would you give everything we shared away? Yes. I lied to you, but I told you truths about yourself you were afraid to admit. Yes. I cheated on you, but you weren't blameless. You say I hurt you. How much would you hurt yourself by erasing all the joy I've brought you?

. . .

Ah. So you're going to retreat into silence. That's typical of you. Does your new goddess know how much you sulk?

"I didn't want to fight. I just . . . I just wanted to do it right, you know? Get it all lined up and flying in the correct direction."

That isn't our fault, Nescher. It never was. You were the one who said it took two to tango.

. . .

. . .

" . . . yeah. I know."

Should we leave?

"I don't think you can. I think you're stuck here with me."

As you wish.
"I never meant to be a bastard. I'm sorry."
. . .
. . .
"Hello?"
. . .
"Hello? Are you listening to me?
. . .
"Well, crap. Hen, bring me another beer."